THE CULLING

THE CULLING

Published by Frajil Publishing

Website: www.theancestraltrail.com

Copyright Frank Graves 2000

ISBN 978-1-873133-04-0

The characters and situations in this work are entirely imaginary and bear no relation or any real person or actual happening

Book Kindly Edited by Allan Gauci

THE CULLING

Written by Frank Graves

CHAPTER ONE

"Kick him *again!*" Like a vicious pendulum the heavily black-booted leg swung in a long arc towards Patrick's head. The nanosecond before it made contact, Patrick jerked his swollen face aside in an attempt to ride the incoming full force ferocity, the blow crashed into his collarbone. Rolling over twice he came to a sudden halt with his back firmly against the concrete wall; blood oozing from the gash in his cheekbone felt warm and silky. His eyes strained to identify the two menacing assailants looming large in the dimly lit alleyway.

"The older one, that's my best chance" he muttered quietly to himself

Using the wall as support he pushed himself onto one knee, dislodging a pile of garbage; stretching out an arm, he located a smooth rounded object that rested against the outside of his hand.

"Thank Christ!" His prayer was silent but fervent; stealthily he moved his hand slowly until he had a firm grip of the bottleneck. Any sudden movement would ensure a speedy attack as he knew exactly how they operated and thought; they believed he was trapped and assumed him defenceless. Like vultures preparing to swoop, he allowed them their thoughts by convincing them that he posed no threat; they thought he was powerless. Patrick was being ultra careful not to betray his unseen lifesaver, it allowed him that slightest of edge as he continued levering himself into a standing position. Like a wounded animal with nowhere to run he was

3

dangerous, and his only chance of survival would be to fight them... Kill if necessary.

The bright streetlights allowed him to try and gauge his two aggressors in the gloom; the older man had a face resembling a dried riverbed, his unkempt beard hung halfway down his barrel-chest hiding the opening of his tattered mouldy coat.

"Definitely not Saville Row" Patrick reflected amusingly to himself.

The dried leathery features cracked into a thin cruel smile, rheumy eyes glittered triumphantly, like that of a cat about to take a mouse. His unkempt hair drifted gently on the light night breeze. Patrick steeled himself as the younger man nodded at his elderly companion before moving forward one deliberate pace towards his frightened quarry. Following his example, the shorter and older man made exactly the same move; they were like a pair of wild hunting dogs working in tandem.

"Now" The older man shouted as he lurched forward; Patrick lunged out, but even the bottle smashing against the old man's skull didn't impede his forward momentum; it did swing him to the side and he collided into the younger man, knocking him over like a loose skittle.

Quickly ducking to the right and out of harm's way, Patrick turned to face the young man; the bottle in his hand had broken, and now its jagged edges gleamed menacingly in the faltering light.

"C'mon you bastard" Patrick growled at the young man. "C'mon, kick me would you?" The younger man was desperately trying to untangle himself from around his older companion, who had partially collapsed trapping his colleague's leg on the cold concrete. Patrick could see that his vicious blow had worked; the elderly man was out cold. Only then did the man notice the jagged edges of the bottle and, after sensing the venom in Patrick's voice, he stopped struggling and put up both hands in surrender.

"We meant you no harm guv" he whined.

"Oh no, then why the fuck were you kicking me" Patrick shouted as he grabbed the rancid lapels of his jacket, the broken bottle now thrust menacingly close to the young man's face.

"We wus only trying to find some money for a drink, honest guv"

"Answer my question" hissed Patrick, "why were you kicking me?"

"You woke up and we wus scared you were going to shout for help" jabbered the man, "so we had to put you out again. That's all. We needed a drink real bad, and you seemed to be a soft touch, being new to this manner and all. Be reasonable, guv..."

"Take your mate and piss off before I decide to cut you to pieces" Patrick spat in disgust, shoving the young vagrant away from him with all the force left in his tired body.

He took some slight reassurance from knowing that at least the incident would quickly be reported among other street inhabitants and tramps in the region. With any luck, from now on he would probably be left alone and that's all he wanted at the moment, just to be *left alone*. The older man's hair looked damp and matted; Patrick inwardly hoped that he hadn't killed him. He watched with considerable relief as the younger man helped his groggy companion to his feet, and the pair slowly staggered off along the towpath.

"Shit!" Patrick limped back to the shelter that he had hastily fashioned out of cardboard boxes that he had found himself; shivering uncontrollably, as he again covered himself with his ancient greatcoat and lit a cigarette.

Deserted, as it was at this time of night, camped just off the towpath he looked towards the river; the Thames looked oily and malevolent despite lights bouncing off its ever-moving surface. He wondered what time it was, the normally buzzing liquorice-black streets were empty too. The silence of the bandaged night was disturbed only by two lovers quarrelling as they walked along the river embankment.

"Oh Christ" thought Patrick, "did I really deserve this, and why am I reduced to sleeping under the bridges of London? What the hell happened to me, that I am reduced to being attacked by drunken tramps? Who's out there terrorising me? I suppose, in a funny way, I've become no better than those two drunks."

He put out the cigarette, the cold night breeze made his cardboard shelter flutter but it wasn't the chill that made him shake, it was terror that chilled him to the bone. For the hundredth time that night he peered into the dark for any sign of movement. Would they find him tonight? How much longer could he run? Why had he not taken George's advice and simply walked away? Inevitably, his mind drifted back to the first time he had seen Kim...

"Why ?Why? Why?" There were more questions then answers as he tried to recall how this declining road had all begun.

"Hello. You must be Patrick Rodgers?" Patrick looked up from the computerised sheet in front of him, in the doorway stood the most exotic looking woman that he had ever seen. Her finely honed Oriental features were perfection: high cheekbones, elongated eyes and a lush heavy curtain of black hair. A dark navy-blue tailored-suit flattered a small, but curvaceous body.

"Patrick Rodgers?" she repeated.

"Yes, yes; I'm sorry, forgive me" Patrick replied, rising hastily from his chair; obviously annoyed with himself for being so captivated by her appearance.

"I'm Kim Lee" she said, holding out a small exquisitely manicured hand. Patrick couldn't help reflecting on the strength of her handshake, or that it had lingered a fraction longer than was necessary.

"Ah! So you are the famous Miss Lee? I'm so glad to meet you face to face at last."

"Yes. We have been discussing this project for quite some time now. It's also nice to be able to put a face to a voice at last."

"Please sit down" Patrick indicated towards a leather sofa in the corner of his large office. It afforded visitors to his office an extensive panoramic view across the Thames towards the city.

"Would you like something to drink?"

"Could you let me have some boiling water please?"

"Surely I can offer you something more than that."

"No thanks. I carry my own herbal tea bags with me and never drink anything else."

"I've never met anybody that carries their own tea with them."

"The reason is that very few people have herbal tea to hand; this is my way of making sure that I don't embarrass anyone, as everyone can supply hot water."

"Ah, I see that we have single-minded woman in our midst" he said lightly.

Privately the notion that such a fragile-looking woman could be so uncompromising, even in the choice of tea bag, appealed to him. There was something self-assured, yet mystical, about her that made him want to know more. Certainly he could not believe being suddenly overwhelmed by the sight of anybody at a first meeting.

"What a lovely view of London!"

She stood looking out towards Tower Bridge, fully aware that he was gazing appreciatively at her back. Just then Patrick's assistant came in carrying a tray.

"Your *boiling water* is in that one" she said crisply, pointing.

Kim Lee was the London sales director for Silver Beam International, a South Korean conglomerate that ranked in the world's top fifty companies in size and turnover. Silver Beam's diverse product range included electronics, oil refineries, shipbuilding, chemicals, cloth manufacture, foodstuffs and toys.

South Korean companies were increasingly challenging America and Japan; Silver Beam was by far the largest company in that country.

Kim spoke five languages and had been posted to the company's offices in Singapore before being appointed Director of European Operations in London. She was responsible for all sales in the electronics division; the hub of the group's activities and the largest and fastest growing sector. The chairman had taken personal charge of this division and turned it into Silver Beam's flagship.

Kim had started negotiating with Patrick's firm more than eight months ago, with the view to installing their most state of the art computer hardware in Patrick's offices throughout the world; in order to centralise the outdated and disjointed accounting system they currently used. The installation and changeover to a new computer program had to be carefully monitored and, as chief accountant, it was Patrick's job to look at all the options; because this was a major investment for their group, running into many millions. He had finally narrowed his choice to three companies; an American, Japanese and the South Korean computer system, which he thought were best for their particular application.

Kim's company had tendered its price for a complete package and their offer had been far below the other competitors, this bid left Patrick somewhat sceptical as, from past experience, he didn't trust prices that were so well under the competition. He also felt that they could have made a mistake, or that certain extras would have to be invoiced once installation had begun. After many telephone conversations he eventually invited Kim Lee to his offices to check out their like-for-like comparative offers against the other bids.

"Shall we begin?" he asked, when she finished her tea.

"With pleasure" she answered, as she selected several large folders from her briefcase and placed them on the coffee table in front of her.

Patrick went to his desk and brought three files back to the sofa. Several hours of note comparing took place and, as far as he could ascertain, everything was present and correct because she was able to show him that they had more than matched their oppositions' bid. He was most impressed by her complete understanding of the electronics industry as, on several occasions, she had lost him completely with her detailed knowledge. When thinking that she was trying to shroud something with technical jargon he requested explanations; she immediately expanded her answers to make it easier and simpler to understand.

"Lunch?" she asked.

"Where"

"Let's utilise my expense account on this occasion and push the boat out, anywhere!" she laughed, "you choose the venue and I'll pay."

Patrick had never been invited to lunch by a female before. Times were changing for the straight-laced, old school tie Patrick who, until recently, had been living in a chauvinistic world; so it naturally went against his dignity to accept.

"I tell you what; let's order something to be brought in instead. We'll finish up much quicker that way then, if you agree, let me take you to dinner tonight."

"OK I would like that."

Patrick called his secretary on the intercom and arranged for a light buffet lunch and more boiling water to be brought in.

Most of the afternoon was taken up by finalising details of the anticipated installation, commissioning and final on-line operation. By mid-afternoon they had completed their task.

"Thank you for everything. I will be able to let you know if your company has been successful by late next week."

"Is the final decision yours?"

"No, my proposal will go before the board next week, I'm sure that they will accept my recommendation though."

"Which system will you be recommending?" She was certainly direct by asking the question.

"Ah, now that would be telling wouldn't it, you will just have to wait and see" he teased.

In his own mind he now knew which system he wanted and although the final decision didn't rest with him, he was already thinking how he could best persuade the board to accept his preference.

"Is our date still on for tonight? Asked Kim "or will that be considered bribery?" They both laughed.

"No, I would like to take you to dinner if only to get to know you better. We must not let the business interfere with our private lives, no matter what the eventual outcome may turn out to be."

"Here's my address" she said, scribbling it onto the back of her business card.

"Until tonight then" they shook hands and he watched her as she walked towards the elevator.

"Nice bum" he thought, as he sat down in his chair behind the large desk; his secretary came in and collected the remains of their lunch.

"Any calls?"

"Yes, I'll bring them through in a moment."

"I need to get some e-mails away; bring in your notepad too, because we must start preparing the proposal for next weeks board meeting."

Patrick stared out of the large window. River traffic was busily plying up and down the Thames and it was the summer tourist season, several pleasure launches steadily chugged their way to and from Tower Bridge, he was looking forward to meeting Miss Kim Lee again that evening.

The Culling

CHAPTER TWO

Kim Lee went straight back to her office in Kingston and immediately went through to see Mr. Kang, the managing director.

"What do you think?" he asked.

"I'm not sure but I suspect that we will get the contract, we still have time to work on him before a final decision is made."

"We want this contract and it is up to you to make sure that we get it. Mr. Lee, will not be pleased if we fail."

"I will do all in my power to please you and the Chairman."

Kim knew that to fail now, with all the work that had been put in, would cause her and Mr. Kang to lose face with their Chairman. Though she had risen to the top by a combination of skill and beauty, she realised that this type of contract didn't come along too often. She was determined to make sure that their company's name was on it.

"Mr. Lee is going to be here on Friday, he's giving his annual garden party for senior staff and customers on Saturday. Why don't you invite Mr. Rodgers?" suggested Kang.

"I'll ask him to accompany me, which at least will give me more opportunity to work on him in a friendly environment. There simply was not enough time to do that today" she said, smiling wickedly at her managing director.

Kim left the office and drove to the semi-detached house in Chiswick that had been rented for her by Silver Beam. The white double-storey building overlooked the river, it had a small basement garage but she parked in the street this time, just in case she needed to use her car later.

The Culling

Once inside, she made herself a cup of tea, drew a bath and carefully chose something to wear for her evening out. As she soaked in the bath she read a magazine, since her childhood this had always been her way of quietly relaxing; but this evening she wasn't able to concentrate. Her mind was filled with Patrick Rodgers; she'd always had a penchant for larger men and he was well over six foot tall. How old was he? About thirty, she guessed, and the thing that had attracted her to him was that he was bright to boot. He certainly held a very senior position in a large organisation and what she had seen that day was a strong, quiet self-assured personality. She wondered if he had a girlfriend, or even a wife for that matter, if he didn't then maybe there must be something wrong with him.

Nobody that attractive ever managed to stay away from the opposite sex for very long, maybe he was gay, but no, she was just speculating madly and so decided that Patrick would have many friends and was inwardly a very private person. Normally she wouldn't feel this keyed up at the prospect of going out with any male client, but she had instantly liked the quietly spoken dark-haired man. There was something deep and unfathomable about him, he had an almost feline ability to side step any possibly tricky conversation and to avoid commitment. Coupled with this, he was a man of *really large proportions.* She stopped herself short and decided that tonight she was going to relax because it was going to be a fun evening.

Presently she stood in front of the full-length steamed up mirror towelling herself, the one thing that she constantly regretted was that she had been blessed with a typically Oriental physique, she stood a fraction below five foot tall with narrow boyish hips and tiny breasts. How many times had she wished that her boobs were much larger? With a small sigh she unpinned her long dark hair and shook it free before turning to examine her back view.

"Yep, not much wrong back there" she thought, then, wrapping herself in a large towel, went through to her bedroom and lay down on the double bed for half an hour; letting her body cool to its natural temperature. She began massaging herself with her favourite aromatic oils as her female intuition had now kicked in and she knew that he wouldn't be able to resist her. She was going to make sure that Silver Beam got this contract.

Patrick hadn't wanted to drive home to his large bungalow in Amersham to change; the afternoon traffic would be murder now. On a mad impulse he walked to a little tailor shop two blocks away from his office, deciding to rather purchase a complete change of clothing. At exactly seven o'clock, happy with his new acquisitions, he was driving his BMW on Blackfriars Bridge heading directly towards his ex-wife's place in Battersea.

He had it all, everything had gone exactly to plan; an enviable position within a large company, a bungalow in the country and small flat near London, several beautiful girlfriends, a large circle of friends and enough money to take up flying as a hobby. If there was a small flaw in the gloss of his life, it was his failed marriage to Sue; that had been a bit of a disaster. They had got married straight after he had completed his final exams and the marriage seemed destined for 'happily-ever-after'; but it had soon become apparent that although he and Sue were great friends, they were just terrible lovers.

After Sue had got involved in a torrid affair they decided to split up; one good thing though, reflected Patrick, was that she was now indeed his very best friend. They regularly had dinner together and he often consulted her on matters important to him. He miraculously found a parking space right outside Sue's flat; grabbing all the clothes he had purchased earlier, he galloped up the steps to the apartment.

"Hi" Sue said, putting her arms around his neck and giving him a friendly kiss.

"I'm glad you're home. Can I use your place to have a quick shower and change?"

"Sure, what's this? New clothes, must be someone special; is it business or a new friend you're trying to impress? Come in, I'll pour you a drink."

"Thanks. I won't take up much of your time. I've got a date with this remarkable-looking woman this evening" Patrick stopped to look at the reporter on the television; she was reporting on an unfolding story about a major terrorist attack on innocent bystanders.

"Damned fundamentalists" Sue exclaimed "the world seems to be full of them, why can't anybody do something about it? I know I'm always wary now whenever I'm on a flight to the Middle East or Asia; it could be me next!"

"Naah, who would want to capture or kill my best mate? They would then have *me* to deal with" Patrick joked.

Sue felt a twinge of jealousy because, even though she had been the cause for the marriage break-up, she had always felt strangely possessive about him. She accepted that they could never be partners again, but every time he confided in her about a new girl in his life, she became fearful of losing him. Patrick got ready, Sue checked him over, smacked him on the bottom and told him to get out because she too had a date - she lied.

After he had left, Sue poured herself another drink and sat down in front of the television to watch the rest of the news. For the first time since the divorce, she instinctively felt that this new woman would become important to Patrick. Why else would she have this hollow sensation in the pit of her stomach? She watched the news but took nothing in; this was the first time since their break-up that she began to question her real feelings towards Patrick.

"Silly bitch" she thought, "you tried it and it didn't work; he wasn't exciting enough for you when you were both younger, so what makes you think it's all changed now?"

She leaned back in the chair and started questioning why she should be feeling so miserable about just another unknown beauty; he had had so many since the bust-up.

Patrick eased the car out of the mainstream into a narrow road running alongside the river; he found Kim's house and at exactly eight o'clock pushed the front-door intercom.

"Patrick, come on in!"

Inside, a carpeted stairway led straight up to a first floor landing; the entire floor was taken up with an enormous lounge cum dining room - perfect for entertaining. The blue-grey walls were contrasted with a dark-wine coloured ceiling, on the far wall, above an ornate Victorian fireplace, was a magnificently carved wooden royal Chinese dragon. Patrick knew that the Royal Dragon was genuine, because it had five talons on each foot. Various Chinese scrolled pictures adorned the other walls; the floor was covered by a large blue and white Chinese carpet supporting delicately lacquered black tables contrasted with heavily carved timber chests. Patrick found the room strangely tranquil.

"Please make yourself at home" Kim called out, "the drinks are in the cabinet on your right, I'll be down in a minute."

"Don't rush; we've got plenty of time."

Patrick poured himself a small straight whisky and ambled across to the window and looked down at the slowly moving river. The tide was out and the water level was very low; a lone oarsman sculled along the narrow centre sliver of water.

"Good evening Mr. Rodgers" she said. She was standing in the middle of the room dressed in a full length royal blue one-piece Chinese cheongsam, richly embroidered with a golden dragon and buttoned right up to the stiffened collar. With her dark hair floating loosely, she looked heart stopping.

The Culling

"Miss Lee! I didn't hear you come in" Patrick stuttered. "Please forgive me. I'm...I err... Rather, I was admiring the river view; there's something about water that tends to make my mind float away from its immediate thoughts."

Kim smiled, knowing full well that it was her appearance that had caught him off guard and surprised him enough to render him almost speechless.

"I love the water too, in summer I sit on that window ledge for hours, happily watching life drift by. A colony of otters has their home on that central island and they're so fascinating to watch" she replied, pointing out a reed-covered embankment that split the river.

"I must say, I envy your solitude; and right in the heart of the city. I didn't think that places like this existed in London, you are very lucky."

"I know; it took a long time to find it. The good thing is that when I leave work I like to be away from the bustle of the city; and, other than living in the country, this is a very good second best."

The two stood looking across the river for a few minutes, the lone oarsman had now almost reached the far bend.

"Shall we go? I'm taking you to one of my most favourite restaurants."

Pierre's Restaurant was small and intimate, specialised in excellent seafood; no hovering waiters, while an unobtrusive harpist provided the live music.

"This looks lovely" said Kim, "Patrick, I'm interested in you, tell me something about yourself."

"Not a lot to tell" Patrick replied, "I'm thirty four, unmarried, no children, I live in Buckinghamshire. Very much a middle class survivor I suppose but I do enjoy my hum-drum life."

Kim looked at him quizzically; she knew that beneath his amiable countenance lay an obvious ambition that separated him from most of the people battling on the conveyor belt of life.

"Well, that's precise enough, but how did you become the director of such a large company?"

"Pure luck, I met the managing director of the London office on a flight back from Canada and he told me that he needed an accountant, I needed a job" He shrugged.

"I don't believe that you walked straight into the position of financial director?"

"Right place, right time; but it was a year before I was given a position on the board."

"So, you must have done something right?"

"The company needed fresh ideas, I had been working in Canada where thinking tends to be less staid than in 'Old Europe' and I injected some new ideas that I had seen whilst working in Toronto. They liked some of the concepts and that's how I got promotion, that's all I know."

"Is Monsieur and Mesdames ready to order?" They had been so busy talking that they hadn't noticed Claude coming over to their table.

"What do you recommend, Claude?" asked Patrick.

"I have something very special tonight, Mr. Rodgers" Claude signalled and a waiter drifted into view with an enormous silver tray containing two large crayfish, surrounded by an assortment of crustaceans and molluscs.

"Voila! Plat de Mer." The proud restaurant owner beamed from ear to ear.

"Whoa! What a feast for the eyes, I'll have that if you please, what about you?" Patrick asked Kim.

"You must be a little psychic; this type of food is Chinese heaven."

"To drink Mr. Rodgers, may I recommend something like a nice Chablis; are you happy to leave the choice to me?"

Patrick looked questioningly at Kim, "you said that you only drink herbal tea, can we tempt you?"

"I love a good wine; when I said I only drink herbal tea, I meant while I'm working."

"Fine Claude, we leave it to you."

"*Très bon!*'"

"Now it's your turn; tell me about Miss Kim Lee."

"Like you, there's not much to say; I was educated in a convent in Hong Kong then went to university in Paris. Started work to repay my tuition to my sponsors in South Korea, worked for four years in Singapore and was then transferred to London a few years ago. At first I lived with a girlfriend until she was transferred abroad and I moved into the house in Chiswick. I'm unmarried but don't, for one moment, think I'm about to reveal my age." Patrick laughed; he somehow hadn't expected such a sharp sense of humour.

"All right, I won't push for that."

He already knew that she was one of the toughest negotiators that he had ever encountered, with an obvious will to succeed in what was generally considered a man's world; he believed this was of paramount importance to her. Her attitude was both challenging and somewhat refreshing.

"Now you are the company's European sales director? Like you,

I don't believe you walked straight into that position. You must also have done something to please the powers that be?"

"I was very lucky and managed to secure one of the largest computer installation contracts that the company had ever had, in the Far East. We even beat the Japanese and our chairman looked on this with favour. South Korea is having an industrial war with Japan and this was a great coup in his eyes. He took an unheard of step by deciding to promote a woman to a senior post. Again, like you, I was just lucky and happened to be in the right place at the right time. He couldn't fill a senior post in the East because businessmen are still far too conservative there; so I was moved to London."

"Impressive! What would it do for your career if you landed our contract?"

"No harm at all."

They were still laughing when the food arrived, Claude turned out to be a ringmaster with a touch of culinary artistry. Not only did it look appetising, but he had made sure that everything was creatively arranged.

"Oh wow, this looks more like a fantastic work of art than a delicious meal; it's a pity to even touch it" Kim commented

"Bon appetite" Claude held his hands apart in joyful gesticulation.

"It's hard to find anywhere that can beat this place for atmosphere and food" said Patrick.

"Now I know where to bring my chairman for a meal next week" replied Kim.

"You won't go far wrong as I've never had a bad meal here."

"That reminds me, talking of my chairman, will you be able to come to the company garden party that he's giving on Saturday.

Here's the invitation." Patrick glanced at it. "I will, but only if you partner me."

"Agreed, I may have to disappear from time to time though."

"I accept that, but I'll be glad to come and see more of how your company works and plays."

Kim was very good company; but Patrick was in no doubt that she was single-minded in her quest to secure the computer contract. At every opportunity she steered the conversation back to business; not once did she allow him to see the real woman behind the business facade.

"Would you like to come up for a drink?" She asked when they arrived back at Chiswick slightly after midnight.

"Umm…a cup of coffee would be nice" said Patrick, wondering whether she was even prepared to offer him her bed as an incentive to secure the deal. Secretly he hoped that she was; besides which it was a long drive back to Amersham. He sat in the lounge while she busied herself in the kitchen.

"Really nice bum" he thought again; speculating whether she was wearing any under-garments as she returned with a tray and seated herself opposite him on the floor on the other side of the low coffee table. He knew from her actions that she had no intention of tonight being more than a business dinner.

"Thanks once again for a lovely evening" she said, as he finished his coffee. "Come; let me walk you to the front door."

Patrick held out his hand and she took it, as if to shake it, but then leaned forward and kissed him gently on his cheek.

"Thanks once again" she whispered seductively.

"I'll see you on Saturday at the party."

"Aren't you coming here to collect me first?" she enquired.

"Why yes, that would be good. All right, see you here on Saturday then."

Patrick left then turned his car around in the narrow street. He wondered whether he should check into a hotel for the night, but then decided to drive home. He just hoped that the police weren't around tonight because if they were they would automatically breathalyse him, which would do his future prospects no good whatsoever.

She watched the car disappear around the corner then thoughtfully, gave herself a large pat on the back.

"Let's see what Saturday brings" she thought.

The Culling

CHAPTER THREE

Patrick arrived at midday to collect Kim for the chairman's garden party. When he walked into her lounge she was seated on the couch finishing some notes which she popped into her small handbag.

Today she wore a lightweight simply flared cotton dress with a matching pillbox hat, the slightest hint of makeup being used to help enhance her almond shaped eyes to best effect. She stood up and twirled around. "What do you think?"

"You look fantastic. We should be going to Ascot rather than a stuffy business garden party."

"Thank you, kind sir." She curtsied low in acknowledgement making them both laugh. "Would you like a quick drink?" Patrick moved straight to the cabinet and poured a very small whisky for himself and an orange juice for Kim.

"Let's make a pact? For today, we will not even think about the contract, we'll just enjoy ourselves. Is that agreed?" Kim said.

"OK." Patrick was puzzled because the other night she had had pushed for a decision and now, when she was taking him to a business function, she didn't want them to discuss the contract. He wished he knew whether all this was simply her modus operandi of obtaining business or whether she could possibly be genuinely interested in him.

"It's a deal, no business today." At the outskirts of Kingston she directed him away from the town and when they were some distance into the country she indicated that he should turn into a narrow back road. It opened up as the passed by beautifully manicured paddocks some with sheep others with magnificent horses it took a while before they joined up with a long drive that curved in a long arc to a large overflowing parking area. Vehicles were now parked in rows on the neatly manicured lawn.

"This house cost the company over thirteen million and the only one who uses it, is our chairman and then, only twice a year when he comes to London."

"Why doesn't he simply rent something big?"

"Prestige. He has the same type of properties in seven different locations around the world."

"It must be nice to be so fantastically wealthy," said Patrick clearly unimpressed, flaunting one's wealth had never dazed him because he had seen too many high flyers come to earth with a bump not to realise that a company asset was not the man's personal possession.

They were guided straight through the house to a huge white marquee on the front lawn.

"Mr. Lee. May I present Mr. Patrick Rodgers?"

"Ah! Mr. Rodgers. It is indeed *my* pleasure to welcome you, I have heard much about you and we must speak again but for now, this gentleman will show you and Miss Lee to your table. Once things have settled down, I would like to meet you again, but lets get the formalities done and out of the way."

"I would enjoy that and look forward to it." Patrick was surprised that this quietly spoken South Korean spoke such a crystal clear and flawless English accent.

"Mr. Lee - Is he any relation to you?" Patrick enquired as they sat down, Patrick turned to her seeing Kim giggling.

"Every second person in that country is called Lee." Patrick relaxed. He looked around at the gathered crowd, as far as he could tell the majority of the guests were mainly European and

English while most of the Oriental crows seemed to be acting as their hosts. Once every had arrived and settled in lunch was served, Mr. Lee made a welcoming speech in several languages, later on as the final course was being cleared, a tall man approached Kim and whispered something in her ear. She nodded then turned to Patrick.

"Mr. Lee would now like to speak with you."

"Right now? Are you coming as well?"

"No. He wants a private audience with you."

"Oh, oh! You know what he wants to discuss, don't you?" Under the table she grabbed his hand and gave it a firm squeeze. Again he reflected on the strength generated by one so small.

"Just listen and understand. Don't say anything." Patrick followed the tall man inside the main house. They entered the study lined from top to bottom with gold-bound books. "Mr. Rodgers. I'm so pleased you decided to come to our small gathering today. Can I get you something to drink?" Patrick had been particularly cautious, except for one small drink he had specifically stayed away from alcohol today.

"No thank you Mr. Lee."

"Then please be seated." The two sat on a beige leather sofa facing each other.

"The reason I wanted to meet you was to discuss this contract that your company is about to award. What do we have to do to get this contract?" The man didn't mince his words.

"Mr. Lee, I'm not prepared to discuss the contract here and now because it goes to my board next week and then a final decision will be made."

"I admire your frankness, Mr. Rodgers. Please don't be offended by my question. I simply wanted to see what reaction and loyalty I could provoke."

"What do you mean?" The chairman smiled. "We have had you under observation for some time. Our company requires an exceptional accountant. We have searched the world for the right man. You came to our notice some six months ago when the tender was first announced."

"What!" Patrick couldn't believe his ears.

"We would like you to consider becoming the financial director of our Western Operations, irrespective of whether we win the contract or not. We are not trading this position, we've decided you are our man. You can name your terms." Patrick didn't say anything for some time he simply studied the man's face letting the statement sink in. His only thought was there is a price for everything and by offering him this position, the South Koreans must have been hoping they had found his.

"Mr. Lee, I'm quite happy with what I'm doing at present and I don't want a change course thank you very much."

"I understand your situation this has been thrown at you and. somehow, you must think that we are desperate to win your contract by our proposition?"

"Well…it looks that way, doesn't it?"

"You could not be further from the truth, we are quite prepared to withdraw our bid if it will interfere with your decision to reconsider my offer. I simply ask that you first have a good look at what *we have to offer*?" Patrick's indignation subsided slightly, perhaps the man was bluffing and had no intention of withdrawing. If they did, the extra cost for the Japanese system would increase his own firm's costs by several millions.

"Right. Let's consider what's on offer." For Patrick's own peace of mind he had to know. "Mr. Lee, I could in fact be interested in your proposal but will have to inspect what is on offer first because I never do anything lightly. "

"Very sensible." Lee countered.

"Now, I must tell you something else, there is a very good possibility that we are going to shelve the project next week." Lee's face was inscrutable.

"What will be must be, that is the way of business because you are still the main reason for our discussion, I want you to come over to us on your terms, please think seriously about it, I am here for two weeks. Please call me if you decide you are interested. It will surprise you when shown what sort of overall package we can offer you." Lee rose up, indicating their meeting has come to an end, he shook Patrick's hand warmly.

"We will send around the proposal on Monday, give it your best attention and I look forward to your answer." Back in the marquee he made his way towards Kim, she was animatedly talking to a handsome man who Patrick recognised as being the director of a major airline. It surprised him that for the first time in his life, he felt the slightest twinge of jealousy. Kim turned, saw him making his way the tables, excused herself and made her way to their table.

"So tell me, what happened with Mr. Lee?" Kim asked excitedly, that's when she noticed the perplexed look on his face.

"He ha just offered me a position within the company."

"So?"

"I don't think your chairman and I got off to a very good start."

"Why?"

"I've told him that our project may not go ahead." Kim suddenly looked at him strangely, he knew that look, she had now become visibly alarmed.

"You see his offer as a bribe, don't you?"

"Well frankly. Yes I did."

"Patrick, Patrick... If he wants you to work for us, then it's got nothing to do with the contract, I'm the one that is going to be really be disappointed because between us we've already put so much work into this project, that I would be upset if your company cancelled the project. Naturally the chairman would like me to get our system installed, but, as for offering you a position as a bribe - never!"

"Let's leave it and see what pans out next week." She took his hand and squeezed it again.

"No business today, that was our agreement." Patrick ordered a large whiskey. Now he could enjoy the rest of the afternoon but, despite his misgivings he felt strangely elated.

On their way back, the surrounding weather changed and the heavens had opened, the rain was flooding down it almost horizontal streaks when they arrived at her house after the party. He moved his car as close to the door as he could, but there was still about a ten-yard sprint to the front door.

"Let's wait until it eases off," said Patrick. "Why? In Asia this would be like monsoon weather, come on don't be such a baby Patrick, it's only water!" shouted Kim as she opened her door. "C'mon, we can always dry off inside." She raced towards the front door; Patrick shrugged his shoulders, grabbed his jacket from the back seat, jumped out, locked the car and ran. His new leather shoes had no traction and as he tried to stop he found himself on the concrete pathway skidding half-way through the front door on his back, it was like being on a skating rink.

"Patrick! Are you OK?" He had came down with a mighty solid

bump and now Patrick lay on his back wondering if he had broken anything as he looked up at the ever blackening sky. He new clothes soaked through, but more than all this, he now felt that he had managed to make an absolute fool of himself.

"What a prat?" He tried sitting up as Kim left the open doorway and knelt beside him.

"Let me help you. Can you move?"

"Yes, at least I think so, I don't think that I've broken anything. What an idiot I am." Kim's small but powerful hands grabbed hold of his two hands and pulled helping Patrick to lunge back onto his feet. By now she too was soaked through to the skin. Patrick moved his arms in a long circular movement only to check that everything was still in working order.

"All present and correct," he said sheepishly. She giggled loudly; it was more a nervous reaction of relief than anything else.

"You fool. You are lucky not to broken anything. You could have hurt yourself quite badly."

"I am sooo stupid now let's get inside because, your beautiful dress will get ruined! Don't worry, I'll buy you another." They traipsed into the lounge leaving dampening trail marks on the carpet.

"Now mister, its time for you to get those sopping clothes off, don't worry, I'll bring you a large warm towel," said Kim, heading up the stairs to the first floor.

In the hallway off the lounge, Patrick felt somewhat slightly sheepish as he stripped down to his underpants. Kim returned from the small bathroom, she was now draped in a large bathroom towel, she handed him another and then immediately scooped up his sodden clothes.

"I'll put these in the drier, c'mon hand me those as well." She pointed at his underpants; he wrapped the towel around his middle before removing the wet briefs. Patrick felt cold. He was glad of the brandies she poured for them when she returned. Kim moved to the kitchen and soon returned carrying two glasses

"Here drink this, it will at least warm your insides." He accepted it without argument, the brandy burnt all the way down right into the pit of his stomach.

"Now young man, it's bath time for you, we are going to have a hot bath to warm up before we catch our deaths of cold." He didn't dare argue.

It wasn't long before the whole bathroom was filled with steam; she continued to fuss around him like a mother hen before switching off the hot tap and filled the bath with cold water until happy with the temperature.

"In you go." She picked her clothes off the floor and disappeared, leaving Patrick to gingerly lower himself into the piping hot water. A nasty welting bruise was forming on the underside of his right arm where he had attempted break his fall and now he realised that his back as well was beginning to be very painful.

As he allowed the soothing heat to seep to penetrate into his aching limbs he started to relax, he thought of the tough minded girl in the next room, she had taken his clumsiness all in her stride and never before, had he ever allowed anybody to simply take over as she had just done. At the same time he was feeling a little wimpish because he hadn't been treated like this since his earliest childhood.

"How's it going," she called from the bedroom.

"I think I've done something to my back!" Suddenly she was standing next to the bath. He wasn't sure what to do - lie back or cover himself up?

"Move up." She commanded, dropping her towel and slipping into the bath facing him. "Now, where does it hurt?" All he could do was lift his arm and point.

"My lower back hurts as well." She gently touched the swelling.

"I hope you haven't broken anything, you silly man." Pouring shampoo into the palm of her hand, she began washing her hair, he just could not believe how unselfconscious she was at that moment, when she finished she got out and started drying herself. "Have you warmed up yet?"

"Yes."

"Then get out and let's see to your back." Patrick did as he was told, she stood for a moment studying his naked body as he towelled himself, then went through to the bedroom, when he finished, he again wrapped the towel around his middle and moved through to her bedroom where he found her comfortably seated in her double bed, she had already covered her bare body with a short kimono.

"Get in." She commanded, folding back the duvet, he dropped the towel next to the bed as he climbed under the quilt.

"Roll over." She again commanded, Patrick rolled onto his front allowing her to start gently probing up and down his spine. Patrick winced as she pushed at the tender welt, he watched as she got out of bed and went to her cupboard and took something from one of the shelves. Then, she came to his side of the bed and folded back the duvet. Patrick didn't move as he felt her straddle him, he felt something cold being poured onto his back then her hands moved to his shoulders starting at the top she began massaging the muscles down to the base of his spine. It felt really good as her supple and slender fingers kneaded in the now warm oil into his skin. He could feel himself slowly coming alive as she moved around his back with strong, powerful strokes. Without warning she moved her hands from his lower back moving downwards as she started massaging down the backs of his legs and the insides of his thighs.

Deliberately, she stopped just short of his scrotum an in long slow and deliberate movements, she ran her hands from the soles of his feet up to the twin humps and back down to the feet again. Each time her hands moved upwards, they got ever closer to his sensitive manly parts and each time, he found himself tensing uncontrollably awaiting a moment of ecstasy but, each occasion her hands then lingered on his backside until he relaxed his muscles. Every time, her tantalising fingers moved ever deeper into the slit of his buttocks. She continued until he found himself completely relaxed to let her strong hands take over all control, her tempting fingers brushed softly against his anal passage. She rubbed gently at and around the outer edges, it felt good. Patrick felt a sharp sensation as her long nail scratched the tender inner skin, he sucked in deeply because he hadn't ever known such simultaneous pain and pleasure before.

"Jeez!"

Her relentless onslaught continued to remorselessly move away and downward again, by now his thoughts were located elsewhere because his lying on his front was now becoming uncomfortable and his solid penis was attempting to force itself into his tender stomach.

"Right, roll over," Kim ordered, suddenly giving his bum a hard smack..

"Ouch! That hurt." He obeyed, at least the excruciating pressure of from lying on his swollen penis disappeared.

"My, my. ...What have we here?" She teasingly trickled some oil onto his chest and down his legs, again the strong fingers worked their magic along the length of his body carefully and intentionally avoiding any touch of his now very proud manhood. Slowly and deliberately, she was causing him to lose all control, her tantalising fingers got closer and closer to his vulnerable pole with each pass. Her fingers elastically pulled and pushed every square inch of his body, her gleaming eyes never wavering as she firmly held his gaze. His legs spread apart slowly and willingly to allow free access to his inner thighs, Patrick was loving every second being totally defenceless and exposed to her every whim and at that moment, he couldn't care a jot at what the hell was happening at that moment.

From a different container, she again poured oil into her hands, this time Patrick couldn't ascertain the highly aromatic fragrance and the longer she rubbed, the warmer his body became. The liquid began to exude a far more pungent smell than when it was still at room temperature, this abnormal odour didn't strike him as unpleasant, simply different.

Finally, her warm hand closed tightly around his bursting member.

"Jeez!"

A stinging sensation shot right through his entire soul as an excruciating phenomenon invaded every pore of his body, at that moment he felt that he was almost passing out, it felt as if his entire individuality was suddenly being flogged with a thousand cactuses.

"Jeez!" he screamed more loudly as Kim began working the liquid more vigorously into and around his searing manhood. That acute initial shock was very quickly overtaken by a gentle warming glow seeping from an unfathomable depth within his body. The harder she worked his genitals, the more his instant suffering subsided being replaced by thousands of tiny pin-prick type electric shocks emanating from he knew not where but, seemingly all were being concentrated towards this one region. One of Kim's hands worked at the hardened statue, her other hand moved between his legs to begin playing teasing circles around his back passage.

"Christ! Help me."

Still, her eyes never left his face, the constant rhythm of her attack remaining steady, sounding to him like the lapping of water against some distant shoreline. His body began tensing again as the next incoming wave of pain mingled with pleasure frantically arrived with unidentified force. Patrick felt as if Kim had suddenly driven a tree stump against his swollen testicles, it felt like were bursting open and he was powerless to do anything except scream loudly. Had she ripped his appendages from his body? What was happening? His head swam, he just felt as if he wanted to pass out when a massive trembling started a long way off and built very quickly from deep within. Like an oil gusher there was no stopping it once his pressure seal had broken and started to move.

Suddenly Kim pushed her finger hard into his back passage, like the previous burning rod, this caused an involuntary searing throughout his body.

"Jeez! Jeez! Make it stop!"

That is when his release was almost instantaneous, he had never encountered anything like the unprecedented force with which the white liquid shot out of his charged well. His large organ pumped away uncontrollably, all the time continually releasing the gigantic built up pressure and everything he had felt from within.

"Ahh!" Patrick screamed his relief.

Kim moved so quickly, that Patrick hardly even realised she was now straddling him and that she had placed him inside her and began moving up and down in piston like rhythmic fashion. Her one hand was still firmly grasping him and the other systematically worked between him and herself while maintaining her metrical stroke.

Patrick opened his eyes, she was still holding his gaze, her beat however, becoming more and more urgent, forcing her tiny body down harder and harder onto him.

She screamed loudly as she moved into a tumultuous orgasm for what seemed an endless recurrence to Patrick, her whole frame seemed to vibrate with the repetitive force of a pounding steam hammer, her vigorous vaginal muscle contractions threatening to decapitate his defiant manhood.

"Ahh!" Patrick detonated once again

As quickly as it had appeared, so it was gone, exhausted, Kim slumped forward against him.

"Wow!" what the hell was that? A juggernaut?"

"Shh!" She didn't even try to answer.

He pulled the duvet over her back and they fell asleep like that, him still inside her. Later, when awake, they continued where they had left off, this time revelling in much gentler lovemaking. They remained in bed for the whole weekend, making love between sleeping and eating, she teasingly wouldn't reveal what the substance was that she had used, suffice to say that she promised she would show him different Oriental practices in time. He knew he was hooked, fully understanding that he didn't want, or need to make love to anyone else after this.

Patrick obviously didn't return home during that weekend.

The Culling

CHAPTER FOUR

Patrick called Mr. Lee to make an appointment three days after the party, he had made up his mind to at least have a deeper look at what the Koreans could offer him.

The board meeting to discuss the computer tender was scheduled for nine o'clock, neither Mr. Lee nor Kim knew that the board were meeting to decide on the what tender was going to be successful. Patrick had not volunteered the information either, he wanted to see what would happen and whether Silver Beam were still so keen to acquire his services if they remained in the dark about the contract award.

On Monday evening he took Kim to his house in Amersham, mainly to open his guarded life to her. As they arrived she could see that its brown tiled roof and reddish-brown bricked wall were screened from the road by a long privet hedge stretching the full length of the property.

"This seems so peaceful," Kim said as she idly deadheaded a shrivelled hydrangea.

"You are right, when I am here I always feel somehow secluded from the outside world as soon as I pass those white swing-gates," Patrick replied.

"I'm fascinated, how does a busy man living on his own keep this place so neat and colourful Do you enjoy gardening?"

"Hate it! But then again, can't stand mess, so I have a gardener come in twice a week." They moved inside into a large sitting room overlooking the long manicured backyard. She stood at the lead-light French doors.

"So much space," she reflected. "There must be at least an two or three acres out there?"

"See those, that's what made me acquire this property." Patrick pointed to several ageing trees bordering the back of the property. "They are over three hundred years old and developers were going to destroy them. My feeling was that anything that had lived that long should be taken care of and not killed off."

"This is so peaceful as well as beautiful."

"Mind you, this place would be too much to handle if it weren't for my housekeeper, Mrs. Jones, and the gardener of course. Come and have a nose around and don't be afraid to tell me what you think after you've see everything." He guided her around the rest of the house.

"Patrick, this is like a museum? I'm scared to touch anything. I've never seen such a tidy place. There is not a spot of dust, or anything out of place, your kitchen is so spic-and-span, its like... well like nobody ever lives here. Even the sink has been polished and that's unhealthy."

"It's my fault, Mrs. Jones and I always fight because I cannot stand messy surroundings."

"I can see that," she replied briskly. She was seeing a side to him that she had not expected for with her tidiness was not that it was a bad thing, but this place was more like a shrine, it was unnatural for anybody to be so tidy. Then she thought back to his office, there too nothing had been out of place. She wondered whether this obsession would interfere with her plans, it was something that she hadn't bargained on.

That evening they went out for dinner, throughout the meal, her mind dwelt on his obvious eccentricity for cleanliness. She couldn't help wondering whether his mind was as compartmentalised as his surroundings; she knew that she would have to find out. Returning home, she stood looking down at an elaborate chessboard with its ornately carved chessmen that was carefully placed next to a large leather chair.

"Do you play?"

"Very much so, would you like a game?" He smiled.

"This is my favourite toy. It is attached to an intricate computer housed in the cupboard below. Every time a master plays, or a world championship takes place, an electronic update is sent to me, which I load into the computer. In effect, I have one of the most sophisticated chess programs available; it is almost like playing against the world's best.

"Do you ever win?"

"Most times."

"Do you ever enter any competitions?"

"Oh no. That takes nerve, something I don't have but here, it doesn't really matter to anyone but me. I was never cut out to be a hero; I tend to be more of a lover and not a fighter." She smiled outwardly, but felt a slight twinge of apprehension, because like the house, his mind was so obviously compartmentally ordered and well thought out. She would have to try to interrupt that clearly defined machine by messing it around and get him back into the real world. She declined his offer of a game in preference to making love, so the evening finished up relaxing having fun in Patrick's bed.

Patrick drew his vehicle into the visitors' parking space, he could see that the four-story building was fairly new, large silver lettering highlighted the company's logo in front of him. He was looking forward to the meeting.

"Come in, Mr. Rodgers, it's good to meet you once again, please be seated." Mr. Lee was already seated at the head of a long boardroom table and pointed to the chair on his immediate right.

41

On his left was the tall man that had shown him into the house at the garden party.

"This is Mr. Kang, our London office managing director. I've asked him to join us, so that if you have any questions about our western operations, he can fill in any technical details. I hope you don't mind."

"No." Patrick studied the man more carefully this time, as far as he could make out, Kang was at least six foot four with very gaunt features seemingly looking as if he had recently been on some form of starvation diet, or else, he was suffering from an unseen ill-health problem.

"Pleased to make your acquaintance." Kang said politely, bowing slightly while seated, he then put out his hand. The man's grip was almost effeminate and reminded Patrick of holding a dead fish.

"I'm pleased to see you have considered my offer, Mr. Rodgers. Now, what all do you know about Silver Beam conglomerate?"

"I've seen your literature and I know that you are among the top fifty companies in the world also that your most active division is your electronics sector, as well as your company is challenging the Japanese giants for electronic supremacy."

"You have done your homework well." He nodded towards Mr. Kang. "Not too long ago, South Korea was a backward agricultural country. Our country sits squarely between Japan and China and for some time we had cheap manpower resources and before the sleeping Chinese giant fully awakens, we want to be completely established in our own right, otherwise countries in that area will simply be swallowed up by them. We have one of the world's largest markets on our doorstep now, so when their industry wakes up to its full capacity, we want to be able to stand on our own feet around the world. So, we have diversified and spread this strength throughout Asia, Europe and Americas by opening offices in all main cities."

He lifted a glass of water and took a sip before continuing.

"We are expanding too quickly and although we can train artisans and machinery to carry out the work, we do not have sufficient management skill to cope with this accelerated growth. We, like the Japanese tend to be very protective and don't easily accept westerners as management because it all comes down to our differing cultures. Unlike the Japanese, we now accept that certain roles will have to be played by outsiders within our company and that's where you will fit in." Patrick waited keenly, he was here to see what they had to offer.

"You were born in Japan and have some understanding of the Eastern mind and more especially how it works. Your formative years in that country gave you the type of thinking and logic that we require in this company." Patrick flinched, they had certainly done their searching well.

"After schooling in England, you moved back here and finished your accountancy articles. You then worked in Canada and North America for four years before being headhunted by your present firm. Am I right?"

"Quite right."

"Therefore you think like an oriental, but have the business brain of a Westerner. There aren't that many people like you and with your cultural background in the world today Mr. Rodgers. We need someone we can trust and that's why we want you to work for us." The only thing they had not told him, was that his mother was half Japanese but he expected they already knew that, but hadn't thought it relevant to discuss.

"Well, Mr. Lee, I can see now that you have all my statistics at your fingertips and I applaud you. Where do we go from here?"

"I would like you to take two weeks, sort of an exploratory holiday. You will come to Seoul and be shown everything in the first week. The following week will be spent at our American office and here. Once you have seen everything at our expense of course, then, you name your terms and start working for us."

"It's as simple as that, is it?"

"Nothing is as simple as that Mr. Rodgers, but I need a right-hand man in the west. You are that man, I know you'll do the right thing, once you have seen what we have to offer."

"Let me think about it for a day or so, I'll have to see if I can take leave as well." Kang pushed a large file across the table to Patrick.

"Read this information, it will give you a far more detailed account of our activities and you can always speak to Mr. Kang if I'm not here or you need longer to think about it." The meeting was at an end as all three stood up together; Kang came around the table and shook his hand, then carried on straight out of the office. Patrick automatically realised that Kang had been ordered to do this so that he would be left alone with the chairman.

"Mr. Rodgers. If you decide to join us, I must warn you that others here will not take it too kindly because our culture dictates that we should not trust Europeans and you, by the very nature of the position, will be God. Kang is the only one who knows and he is bitterly opposed to this appointment."

"That would be inevitable and if I join your company, it will be because I know that I can do the work and gain their trust."

"As long as you understand the position, I will back you all the way." The chairman put his hand on Patrick's shoulder as they walked to the door.

"Well, Mr. Lee, I want to thank you for your time and your offer and by the way, you'll be pleased to know that your company has been awarded the installation contract. I'll get Miss Lee to finalise the details with me next week."

"Really?" The man's face suddenly beamed pleasure; this was the first time that he had allowed himself a genuine smile.

"All I ask, is that because she worked so closely with me that I be allowed to break the news to her myself?"

"Of course, I know nothing until I'm told, then, I'll insist that she takes you to have a triumphant lunch, or supper on the company. This is indeed, good news."

"Please, could I impose on you to have your secretary ask her to contact me at my office this afternoon. I'll ask her to come in and tell her myself."

"Certainly, you leave it to me, I won't spoil her surprise." He left the happy chairman standing in the doorway.

"Miss Lee," Patrick's secretary announced.

"Ah, Miss Lee, how nice to see you again, please have a seat." Patrick turned to his secretary. "Could you please bring my usual and a pot of boiling water for Miss Lee?" When the door shut, he took her in his arms and gave her a long kiss.

"Sit down, I've something interesting to tell you."

"I already know." Kim countered. Patrick was crest fallen at her remark.

"You met our chairman today." So much for trust, he thought, the man had promised and then immediately broken it.

"What did he tell you?"

"That our company is head-hunting you and that you are considering their offer."

"Anything else?"

"Yes, that you may visit the head office in Seoul. That's all and that you wanted to discuss something technical, regarding our offer." The door opened, and the secretary brought in a tray and set it down in front of the two and immediately left.

"I have a letter for you." He went to his desk and picked up the letter, she looked around the office, the paper in his hand was the only sign that she was in an office. She immediately thought back to his house and now wondered just where he kept all of his paperwork. This office looked so unworked in.

"Read this." He sat down across the coffee table so that he could watch her reaction. Her frown changed to a smile as she looked at him.

"This is marvellous. I'm so pleased, you don't know how much this piece of paper means to me, thank you so very, very much." Suddenly she burst out laughing

"What?"

"It's such a relief. I really thought that the contract would go to the Japanese."

"Let's go to your restaurant again tonight to celebrate in style and then you stay the night because I feel that I have to repay you somehow."

"There's no need to repay me, if your company had come second, then you wouldn't have got the contract. Yours was the best offer but certainly, I'll be glad to take up your offer and celebrate."

Later he met up with her at her house, they had a bath together and left for the restaurant. Claude was his usual self, the food was every bit as good as on their previous visit. After their meal, while having coffee, she said something that took him by complete surprise.

"We have to make a decision, and there's no better time than now."

"What's that?"

"What do you think of this, either you move into my place or I move into yours?" His mouth dropped open, cold shock and reality struck him with a force of a steam hammer and saw his dismay.

"Don't look so surprised, the first day that I met you, I immediately decided that you and I were going to live together." Just like her chairman, she had known all this time what *she* wanted. It seemed like his future was being mapped out and that he didn't have a choice in the matter. Right at this moment his own views were secondary, it was as if all was cut and dried decisions being made without his knowledge.

"Your place is handier for work." He said rather meekly, still in a mild state of shock, he had simply uttered the first thing that came to mind.

"Fine, it's settled then? You'll move in with me hat are you going to do with your place?"

"Nothing really, I could probably rent it out or something." They arrived back at her house and when they entered the bedroom, she changed completely, no longer the clinical businesswoman, Kim became a soft, moulding creature of love. Patrick realised that he hadn't yet begun to even penetrate her oriental mystery and that he would have to watch his step otherwise these people were going to take over his very soul. Things were moving too fast for his liking but for the moment he would go with the flow to see what came of it in the long run. Patrick had always managed his own life very well, except for that business with Sue and suddenly felt as if all his freedom were being eroded or somehow attacked. He wasn't usually the complaining type but this sudden burst of activity into both his private and business life made him feel very wary and more than a little uneasy.

The Culling

CHAPTER FIVE

Patrick was exhausted when he arrived back into a cold gray London, having spent his last two weeks in Seoul and New York at offices of Silver Beam International, finding out just vast the company because it was so internationally diverse, he had felt that he needed at least another fortnight at the company to even scratch the surface. Now realising that the Asian traditional markets such as and woven cotton sectors among others, had faced a complete market revamp with the alternative growth areas now being switched into electronics and pharmaceuticals. The company was also actively involved in micro-surgery, bionics and human genetics among other allied hi-tech projects, major point that had struck him forcefully during his time with them was that these expanding scientific sectors, were inevitably linked to Stock Markets and high cash-cow growth areas. This huge range of scientific projects worried Patrick, because he felt sooner or later with the speed of development that something would be bound to go wrong and eventually, effect the genetic inheritance of some of the human race species. He knew that this genetic line of treatment was clearly open to abuse by manipulating humans there was a chance that something unspeakable could be passed down to their descendants. The Koreans had an advanced stage of being able to send laser cameras through the human artery system to inspect disease and damage, hopefully able to repair any affected spot in-situ, without having to carve into the body at all. Complicated computer systems were now aiding intricate microsurgery while especially developed electronics, toxins and chemicals prevented any rejection, *this* was all groundbreaking stuff to Patrick. The amount of money raised in their research had staggered him, he had always wrongly presumed that countries like China, Indonesia and Thailand were more third-world countries within basic peasant agricultural environments. What he had seen over the last couple of weeks had changed his mind quite dramatically, for these countries were capable of continuing human experimentation without fear of being countermanded or questioned by the huge army of uneducated human guinea pigs on tap at their disposal. There were definitely certain areas of moral issues to be addressed yet as these blossoming countries were already well ahead of the their western counterparts in some of their long term thinking strategies. Patrick had enquired as to why they were specifically concentrating within these subject areas, the answer by the scientists was invariably that it was for humanity purposes and in order to allow the human population to live longer while becoming free of all known diseases. Somehow and without raising an arguments, he found that this reasoning, coupled with a host of deadly chemicals being manufactured and brought to the Asian markets, was a contradiction in terms. The East, like the rest of the world was slowly being poisoned to by vicious chemicals produced by these uncontrolled multi-national giants. Not only were these vicious chemicals being manufactured for agricultural but, some of the more deadly substances among them could be used in human trials. He couldn't see the sense of the contradiction, the Koreans were now so intent on becoming the largest industrial power in the East, they had even managed to square this among themselves without calling it what it was or even in the name of suicidal financial greed. He also found that they were not selling their expertise in these fields to the outside international community just yet, however, were already exporting vast quantities of finished products to USA and Europe. Certain divisions that excelled, had now drawn level and in some cases were even ahead of the Japanese in the race to become the world leader. Everyday household items like motor vehicles, shipping and chemicals were still a major priority, yet in the field of robotics and pharmaceuticals, they were now far ahead of most systems that the rest of the world had come up with. A few of the things Patrick had been allowed to inspect, scared him, South Korea was not as backward as he had imagined and their technology was so modern and complicated, that he had been taken aback because in the West, the spin was that Korea were still being portrayed as the makers of toys. This he now knew was *not true*, his visit was something like seeing the white light into heaven, he had now seen the reality. On the other hand, it was these self-same accelerated advances that excited him now, making him want to be part of this fantastic growth.

Before leaving Seoul, he had a meeting with Mr. Lee and two Korean directors to set out his package terms, which were surprisingly and readily accepted after him explaining that he would have to work out a three month notice period with his existing company, before he would be able to join them. He made it abundantly clear that he also wanted free access to all financial matters concerning the company throughout Europe, Africa and both South and North America which were also agreed to. He explained that like the money markets, he intended that all activities be channelled via London on a daily basis, any funds and goods coming from the East to the West had to be cleared through the central system in London. Likewise, all transactions from the West to the East would also be relayed straight to the head office in Seoul with twin accounting systems in to be put into operation. His zone would mainly cover west of the sixty degree longitude line, while the Korean's head office control stopped at one hundred and eighty degrees east, by doing it this way, he would be able to monitor all group movement in his region and head office could have a day to day overall picture of the group's growth and movement.

"So, have you decided?" Kim met him at the airport and drove him straight to her house.

"Yes. I'm going to start as soon as I possibly can."

"Where will you be working from?"

"The financial department will take over the complete second floor... It is already agreed."

"What? Kang will be furious. He's not happy that he will have to report to a foreigner but then to lose an entire floor to you is to add insult. You/re going to have to watch your back, he's a vindictive sod and he'll be trying his utmost to get you out of the company."

"Don't worry. I've taken on tougher men than him. Nobody feels comfortable when accountants start checking on them or measuring their performance levels, we're just a necessary evil." He smiled wryly, "It sort of makes them feel... well, vulnerable."

"While you were away, he constantly let me know what a bad decision the chairman was making, for some reason, he seems to think that you are somehow going to bring disgrace to the company."

"I wonder why he hates me so, or, has he just always been paranoid?"

"You're an outsider and never before has Kang had to work with, let alone report to a Gwailo, if he knew of our arrangement he would a heart attack, I'm sure."

Kim laughed loudly as she pulled into a parking bay in front of the house, she lifted her briefcase, leaned over and kissed him lightly before exiting and opening the front door the moved up the stairs to the lounge.

"There's plenty of food. Oh, by the way, welcome home, it's good have you back." He grabbed her around the waist and pulled her to him

"Get away! You'll mess my hair and I must leave straight away." She playfully grabbed him between the legs, he stood back, arms raised in surrender mode. She kissed him on the nose and moved away into the house, he could stood on the stairway just taking in her high pitched giggle disappearing down the hallway.

"God. I'm tired. My body clock hasn't yet caught up."

"Why don't you have a hot bath, then go to bed and catch up on your sleep. I've got to get back to the office but I'll be back at about the usual time."

The Culling

"If I'm still asleep, wake me, otherwise I'll be awake all night and if you think I'll let you sleep then, you've got another thing coming." The front door closed, and suddenly everything was very quiet, this was the first time that he had been left alone in her house, his naturally inquisitive streak was the reason he was such a good accountant. He moved around and opened, touched and examined a range of her private things, he was simply being nosey and since childhood, had always loved rummaging through other people's belongings. In fact, he really wanted to know more about Kim, starting with the large carved box in the lounge, he began to glance through the papers, although many were written in unknown Chinese script, he still examined them carefully. Much later, he did as suggested and when still warm from bath, hauled himself into the double bed and immediately fell into a deep exhaustive sleep.

Kim arrived at six and went straight to the warm bedroom to find him stretched out on his back, the duvet was on the floor revealing Patrick in his glorious nakedness, she sat down on the bed very gently, so as not to waken him. For a time she studied the form of her gently snoring lover, he was at relaxed peace. She moved away from the bed and through to the bathroom to have a quick shower, she returned and went to her dressing table and came back to Patrick's side of the bed with a small bottle cupped in hands. She rubbed the bottle to warm it before emptying a small amount of potion onto her right hand before placing the purple flask on the bedside table and proceeded to rub her hands hard together vigorously until she felt they were warm enough for what she was about to do to the prostrate figure. Slowly but so skilfully, she moved back onto the bed above him before then starting to knead his temples very lightly making sure to rub the solution into exact spots, he did not stir while she moved her fingers in soft circular movements, she reflected that must be pretty exhausted. When she had finished with the head, she carefully turned her body and concentrated on his feet, continuing the light motion within his instep. Again on completion she moved like a cat, off the bed, Patrick did not even stir as she again returned to her bathroom and thoroughly washed her hands for about five minutes before returning to again seat herself on the bed next to him. Her hand went straight to his limp penis, she cupped it and blew gently on the head before licking it softly, it had the desired effect as she felt him responding to her touch. Then, Patrick began to awake.

"What a way to be woken. This is the type of alarm call I should have every day."

"How are you feeling?"

"Fantastic. Normally it takes me two or three days to recover such a long haul, but I feel as if I've just returned from a holiday."

"Well then. If you're in that kind of shape, I suppose you could stand a little lovemaking." He tried to raise himself, "No lie back. Let me do the work today."

"I can't. Somehow I'm a horny as a rabbit it must have been a combination of the sleep and missing your gentle caress. Come here!" He tried to pull her towards him. She smiled knowingly at him as she allowed herself to be taken into his widespread arms.

Patrick had never felt entirely happy with his present company because there was always a situation within the firm that had always made him feel uneasy, he couldn't quite place it but, he never felt that he was fully in charge of the finance department. The reason was that, his fellow directors insisted in retaining a thoroughly rotten accountancy firm in Patrick's view and worse still was that heading the practice, was a nasty little man called Vladisky Ormon. Patrick found the company of Heker Jong & Associates to be, lazy, extortionate and when he had first arrived, he immediately asked for accountants to be changed. For no given reason, his co-directors refused to this request no matter how hard Patrick worked trying to get them replaced, nothing it seemed would budge the board. In the end Patrick sensed that the *old school tie brigade* was preventing him from having them replaced. Heker Jong & Associates just kept interfering with his updated methods and he and the accountants were at continual loggerheads, especially Lividsky, Patrick had never hated anyone before, but, now he did. It seemed as if the man and his firm were out of touch with modern methods, they couldn't seem to appreciate various changes Patrick and his staff were attempting to implement, hence Patrick always complaining that the accountants were useless, but was helpless to prevent their guiding hand and presence being felt with other board members. This was the main reason given to the board for his resignation, that he wasn't allowed to run the financial section properly because of the continual interference from Heker Jong that disallowed him proper control of the company's affairs also, he was completely unable to work with Vladisky Ormon. He made certain that at the resignation meeting with his chairman, he had it documented that Heker Jong & Associates were blatantly overcharging the company by as much as four times the going market rate. For the little advice and work they produced, he found that their methods were clumsy and antiquated but it rather took Patrick aback when he was immediately paid in full in line with his contract terms and asked by the Managing Director to clear out his desk and to leave the premises immediately. Slightly bewildered by the turn of events, Patrick returned to his office to find Vladisky appearing at his doorway within seconds.

"So we're losing you, Patrick?"

"Ormon, what're you doing here?"

"We've been retained to take over the company's affairs until I've found your replacement." Patrick felt sudden bitterness creeping in, he had been a loyal servant to the company and now he was being treated like a criminal, they hadn't even waited for his departure before sending this scavenger in to clean the bones. This insignificant little man with a huge chip on his was here, gloatingly overseeing his departure, making sure that nothing of value was removed. Patrick, under Vladisky's eye packed his personal belongings, he shivered, the little man was like something that crept through sewers on dark nights he thought, the words evil and

55

slimy came to mind. Suddenly without thought and knowing now he was leaving for good decided he should air his opinion.

"Before I leave, I want to tell you that it hasn't been a pleasure working with Heker Jong or you, I have never, in all my years in accounting come across such a crooked firm of accountants, in fact you even make Mafia hit-men look like amateurs. I don't know what pull you have or who you've got in your firm, but if I could have ever have proved it, I would have had you put away a long time ago and had that filthy firm wound up and tossed into a trash can where it belongs."

The little man fumed, all his working life he had bullied people, he just wasn't the sort of person that liked hearing the truth or anything said against himself.

"Patrick. I suggest you leave the premises right now."

"Oh I will, but, first I want to get it off my chest." He felt he was on a roll now. "Heker Jong and you are ripping this company off, you... You little pea brained accountant are the most vile man that it's been my misfortune to meet. Your methods of are so inefficient that you should be struck off and *never allowed* to set up an accountancy practice again."

"Get out!" Patrick could see that man going red and presumed that he had touched on a soft spot. Calmly Patrick picked up his briefcase together with a box of personal items and on his way to the door. He raised his voice slightly.

"By the way, that assistant of yours who I've *had to* keep on as my secretary is no better than you, she too wouldn't know what was going on even it was shown to her in black and white. You didn't think I knew did you?" he said smugly. "Your slime and stupidity have permeated this company to such a degree that I need to bath daily to wash off your stench, I'm sooo pleased I'm leaving."

"Get out!" Both surprise and displeasure struck home at his revelation for Patrick had made sure that both of them could hear him when he had uttered this fact. Turning, he saw that the girl was blushing uncontrollably, walking past her desk he turned to her again, "You're welcome to that bastard."

Leaving the building was like being hit by a breath of fresh air, leaving him wondering why hadn't he noticed it before now, he thought, probably he had simply been too closely connected with this firm in the past suddenly passed through his mind.

"Oh well. That's that another chapter in the window of life completed, I wonder what the next chapter will bring at Silver Beam." He hailed a taxi, the firm had offered him the use of his company car for a further month but, but he had decided to make a clean break rather let his parting fester any longer by using the company's car. He didn't want to ever meet Lividsky again, because he felt he would not be to control himself as he had just done. "Chiswick please."

"What are you doing home so early." She was surprised to find him lounging in the window with a drink in hand.

"Been chucked out. They thought that I may give away the company secrets, so they asked me to leave immediately."

"I hope they've paid you."

"Oh yes, all present and correct sir."

"What are you going to do for three months then?"

"Take a holiday first, then start straight back with Silver Beam."

"Where are you going?"

"You mean we, don't you?" You must be due a few weeks leave, come and join me? Let's go somewhere really exotic like Seychelles.""I don't know but, give me a few days to talk Kang around. I'm overdue a holiday but he's so very strict about his staff rotas. If he is able to bend a little and for me to bring it forward, then let's go." Two days later she announced that she had been able to talk him around. Patrick managed to find two late bookings to Reunion. They left on holiday two days later.

CHAPTER SIX

"Good morning, Mr. Rodgers and a hearty welcome to Silver Beam International."

Kang stood up offering his hand and once again, Patrick shuddered as he took hold of the limp fingered handshake.

"Morning, Mr. Kang."

"Let's go straight down. Your offices and staff are on the second floor."

Kang led the way to the lift, the second floor was laid out in open-plan fashion. Patrick was surprised to see that there were about forty South Koreans all seated in neat rows at their desks and it reminded him that somehow, this was a nation of being born to this assembly-line existence. Against the far wall was his office that adjoined two conference rooms, Kang held up his hand like a schoolteacher bringing order to a class.

"This is Mr. Patrick Rodgers, our Western sector financial director, you will be under his control from now." Patrick understood exactly why he had stressed the word '*Western*'. Nobody moved or even really acknowledged him as his eyes searched the faces for some form of acceptance, but he couldn't find any, they were robotic just like the people he had seen at their work stations in South Korea, simply a mass of automatons except he knew from experience that they were all probably very nice people when away from a working environment, but here, they accepted this practice as the norm.

"This is your office." Kang showed Patrick into a small cubicle that had just about enough space for a small desk.

"Your secretary Miss Han is at that desk." He pointed to the desk nearest the door, Patrick realised that there was no privacy because there was a only a glazed panel in the partitioning.

"I trust this is all to your satisfaction." The time had come for Patrick to stamp his authority on Kang.

"No it certainly is not. Mr. Kang, let's get one thing straight. I am going to be working here *with you*, and not *for you*. Whatever changes I see fit to make, I will make and from now on, you run your sector and I'll look after mine, that way we will become the best of friends."

The man showed no emotion whatsoever except for a slight reddening around the mouth, it was obvious that he was not used to being put in his place.

"I understand, if there is anything I can do to help you, please do not hesitate to ask for my assistance." Without a backward glance he walked straight back to the lift leaving Patrick to start work, Patrick sighed, for looking around at the sterile surrounding outside his window, he shook his head.

"First, we get this place to *look like* an office." He called to Miss Han to come in, Patrick watched as the slightly squat figure left her desk and made her way to his office. He couldn't even guess her age but estimated that she was about thirty, her smile showing yellowing and unlined teeth seemed out of context with her neatly trimmed short black hair and smart white and blue company uniform.

"Get me a partitioning contractor, a lighting contractor and I want a meeting called with the entire staff here one by one starting now."

Within two weeks Patrick had the entire floor transformed dramatically. He felt happy with his decision to make the changes as looked at his handiwork from his enlarged office door; the whole area was still open-planned but now, with free standing screens and masses of green foliage he had created cubicle offices for each individual member of staff. Added to this, the external windows now all had vertical blinds to blend with the new surroundings and the conference rooms had been turned into one large boardroom and one small interview room. His new centralised computer system had also arrived and installation was going well during this turbulent transformation period. Patrick was becoming happier with what he could see because in two weeks, he had managed to change the atmosphere from suspicion to relaxed discussion with each member of his team. Somehow, all now had their own identities and were urged to practice their own individualism without the constant gaze of their surrounding colleagues. Already, he found that constructive ideas were starting to emerge and flow into him, the only black spot was still Kang receiving subtle pressure from his own staff to change as well. They felt that the important upgrade to the second floor meant their accountant companions were now being treated as company superiors and Kang's staff now wanted equality. Kang was not happy with Patrick at that moment.

During the next few months Patrick travelled extensively to all the group's operational centres under his control. They had all received their satellite computer systems and he also travelled around with technical software experts, who job it was to help operators install and implement the new system coordination. Like spokes of a wheel, London now became the main hub while the array of satellites started feeding information in to the focal hub, an overall picture of the group's Western Operation started to emerge. Patrick was coming to realise just how diverse the company was while in London, he began to break up each group activity into individual cost centres, and in this way, he could start monitoring the growth or decline of every individual sector. Each day, London would send the overall information to Seoul and would receive information from them in turn. He was fast becoming like a painter with an electronic paint brush, each time his office created a stroke, a little more of the overall picture came into view but, he knew it would take some time for him to complete his masterpiece and like the proverbial artist, he chopped and changed the structure of the picture, adding a bit here, taking something away there, the whole accounting picture began to take shape. Within six months, he felt confident enough to inform Seoul that the Western sector would be changing all financial controls to his system. The London office was able to switch its attentions from a monitoring role, over to its correct management function.

Patrick had already found that certain sectors were overstocked while others were screaming for the same items. Financial investments were being poured into certain regions, while others were battling. The London centre would now be able to research over-capacity in one field and direct it to another that needed it. He knew that Seoul was happy to receive his daily update in fact, it was the board in Seoul that had continually pushed him to get his operation into gear and take on full management responsibility of their entire Western sector. Patrick didn't want to rush until he knew that all the bugs were out of their new operating system because his London base was going to be responsible for many billions of dollars worth of sales turnover, movement, stock control and investment, he couldn't afford mistakes by rushing. So far, he had movement of goods, sales and stock control organised and was ready to implement full management on them, but there were still many unanswered questions to be resolved in some of the huge investments made by the group. He hadn't been able to account for some of these irregular payments being made... *As yet!*

"Patrick you've been like a magic wand over the last six months, the company in London has changed beyond recognition." Kim was lying on the sofa reading, it was Sunday morning and the two always relaxed in the lounge before heading for the country to have lunch. He had a pile of Sunday newspapers next to him, while Kim only looked at the magazines and comics. She preferred a good book and was an avid reader.

"Why do you say that?"

He looked over the top of his newspaper.

"The entire office now beginning to look like the second floor, the whole place has taken on a completely different character and feel since you arrived, why, even old Kang has had to admit that production output from his staff has at least doubled."

Patrick smiled. She hadn't even looked towards him as she spoke. If only he had been an artist, this would make a lovely picture; she wore a very short red silk gown, which highlighted, yet blended in against the black leather of the couch. It was a study of concentration.

"What has he said to you?"

"I think he's starting to develop a grudging liking for you but, he would never say as much, though every now and then he uses you as an example to his own staff."

"By saying what?"

She looked up from her book.

"Look what this foreigner can do in six months and if he can achieve this much, then why can't we? Those are just two examples."

"Well that's nice to know."

"I hear on the grapevine that Seoul is also very happy with your performance so far."

"You seem to hear a lot. I thought all Eastern people didn't give much away."

"Oh we do talk among ourselves, it's only outsiders who think we are guarded in our ways. I think that most people are wary of someone different."

Patrick smiled at his little imp, understanding that she was not only pretty, but also very perceptive.

"I don't want to teach you your job, and I'm not interfering, but be careful. You are making several people at the top very nervous."

This came out of the blue, he slowly put down the paper.

"What do mean?"

"They didn't realise, by allowing you to set up your system would place certain controls on them in Seoul as well, some are now saying that it's like... well, a creeping death. The system is starting to question their decisions and that, they don't like."

"I don't understand what you're trying to imply."

"Those men have been able to do what they want, pay who they want, hire and fire who they want, without anybody ever questioning them but now your systems are showing up some of the major blunders made by these men. If it ever gets out, they will lose face, it's making them nervous. I'm just warning you to watch your back, that's all. Make sure somebody covers it for you all the time."

"What sort of blunders are you talking about?"

Kim looked slightly surprised.

"There have been rumours of some very bad investments made and if the government thought for one moment that these men were making big mistakes, then all hell would be let loose. As it is, at present they have managed to bury their mistakes but, if you start raking them up to the surface, they would want you out of the way."

"Well, I haven't come across any yet."

"My advice is that if you do, just leave them buried."

"I'll do no such thing!"

"All right, then on your own head be it, I'm only making a suggestion. If you decide to open the can of worms, make sure you have a net to catch them in otherwise, my very dear friend, those same worms will make a feast of your rotting carcass." She turned back to her book. He stood up and went to the window deep in thought. The river was high today and he could see that the lonely oarsman was once again battling his way against the current, just as he had done every day since Patrick's first day here. Kim's comments would explain the massive holes in their investment portfolio that he had found. These amounted to various gigantic sums, some of the numbers being larger than some Third World government budgets. The oarsman was almost at the bend in the river.

"Come on. Let's take a drive to Salisbury. There's a super little place I want to introduce you to." Kim went upstairs to change; they left in the direction of the M3 in Patrick's new Porsche ten minutes later.

"Miss Han. Bring me the investment file."

Kim's words had haunted him all day, knowing that there were several large payments left unaccounted for, yet nobody had supplied satisfactory answers to his questions about these sums. Kim had inadvertently supplied the missing link.

"The files, sir."

He carefully studied the computer records and noted down several large amounts on his pad. After going through the entire sheet he called Miss Han again.

"Please ask Mr. Li to come and see me."

He returned to the computer file, three names seemed to stand out from the rest.

"Miss Han says you want to see me."

In the doorway was a short, square-jawed man. George Li was fast becoming his right-hand man. He was an extremely clever accountant, but more than that, Patrick found that he could think for himself and was an absolute wizard when it came to anything that was computer related.

"Yes, George. Please sit down, I've got a small problem that you could possibly help me with." Patrick liked George Li because the thick set man always seemed to have a jovial air about him, no matter how difficult any task given to him seemed to be. He excelled with anything that had a hint of challenge to it, he had also confided to Patrick that he was unable to visit South Korea because he had been one of the leaders of the student revolt against corruption and now the government would arrest him on his return. Patrick looked at the man and couldn't imagine that such a gentle looking teddy bear could have led a revolt of any sorts. The two men poured over the file for several hours.

"It can't be anywhere else can it?"

George Li tried several times to convince Patrick that the unaccounted holes in their portfolio must just have been directed to different accounts and that they wouldn't stay hidden for long once they had mastered the system. Patrick had searched the computer's memory banks with George and the funds were not accounted for.

"Patrick. Let me work on this a while and see what I can come up with."

"OK. See what you can find out."

A week later George came into the office carrying two files under his arm.

"Found it." His self-confident oriental eyes were almost closed as his smile stretched right across his face.

"Where?" asked Patrick.

"There's a special escrow account in New York and all of these amounts seemed have disappeared into this mysterious black hole. I finally ran a thorough check through every single payment made by us into this account and look here." He pointed to a column on his sheet.

"Jeeesus! That's more than two billion dollars."

"The other thing that I've found out is that this amount has never come back into Silver Beam."

"How did you find that out?"

"I shouldn't tell you this, but I have a method of hacking into the main computer both here and in Seoul and searched it during their off duty periods. No matter where I went, I couldn't find anything."

"Did you manage to find out which account they used to supply these funds from by any chance?"

"It's a special development fund, set up jointly between the government and the company."

"Well, that explains it then. There's some type of development finance being used to fund some secret project."

"Not quite Patrick. I also found the code to check the bank account."

"And?"

"I know I shouldn't have done this, but...I went into the account."

It was like pulling teeth from the man.

"And what did you find, George?"

"Nothing... Nothing at all, that's what. There is not a cent in the account." Patrick suddenly felt the hairs on the back of his neck rise, no wonder Kim had be so persistent that he keep his back covered. Somebody was milking both the company and government.

"You've found a massive computer fraud by the looks of it, listen carefully, only you and I are ever to know about this... What the hell do we do now, we tell Seoul and we risk letting whoever is behind this know we're on to them. Let's be guarded with this knowledge because it is dynamite, we cannot rush in, we must be discreet and nail it down tightly before doing anything. The other question is, how do we find the full and true story before letting head office in on the secret?

"Let's set up a small computer base somewhere away from the office and track these funds, with my computer technology, it's easily done."

Are you prepared to help me?" George nodded his head eagerly.

"But I must warn you, George, that it could be dangerous for us. If, whoever is behind this, knows we're onto them, we could be in real danger, those disappeared amounts will buy a lot of muscle."

"I understand, leave it to me and I'll set up a hidden entry code in the main computer that no one will ever track back to us."

"Remember. Not a word to anyone, not at home or your friends, we can't be too careful, this is massive. People have killed for far less." Again Patrick couldn't help reflecting on Kim's words, but he had to trust someone as he questioned himself to whether George could be leading him into something that he might regret later on. He had scanned the files and found very little comfort about George's background, the man was in his final year at university when the students revolted against the South Korean government by taking to the streets. It had been found that George Li was one of the ringleaders, but had managed to get out of the country before the government caught up with him. Other leaders were not so fortunate and had simply disappeared without trace. From the file, Patrick had seen that there was still a warrant for his arrest and that he had married an English girl to obtain British citizenship. The South Koreans had recently tried to extradite him without any success, the company allowed him to work for them because of his linguistic, accounting and management skills, him knowing that he would never be given a senior role because of his background and the fact that he was a clock watcher, always leaving the premises at exactly five o'clock.   This surprised Patrick, as during the previous week George had spent inordinate amounts of time trying to locate the source of their problem in his own time at home. Patrick felt that the man needed watching, not only as Korea was doing with him by employing him, but now by Patrick too.

"Miss Han. Can I have a cup of coffee please?"

He lifted the receiver and dialled a number; he needed to use someone as a sounding board. Sue would be able to give him clear and unbiased advice but her telephone went unanswered. Perhaps she was on duty and off in some far exotic place, Patrick felt a sense of disappointment tinged with regret. He really wanted, no, that was the wrong word to use, *he needed*, to see her he thought because, things were becoming too complicated, he had to confide, discuss and listen to someone outside his immediate sphere and it had to be with someone he could trust implicitly.

The Culling

CHAPTER SEVEN

Patrick entered the boardroom of the fourth floor. His chairman, Mr. Lee and three co-directors of Silver Beam were already seated at the long table.

"Patrick. Come in and sit down." The chairman visited all main branches offices at least twice a year and when he did, he stayed in the large house and used the main boardroom during these visits to London.

"We are very impressed with your progress, yet you have not placed the investment portfolio into the system. Why is that?"

"There are still some amounts that need to be reconciled, they appear to be very, very large funds and I can't place them anywhere as yet."

"And why not?"

"For a computer system to work efficiently, everything must have a code. There must be a credit for every debit, these particular funds have appeared on New York's office records, but there doesn't seem to be any record where they originated. Stranger still is that the funds are no longer in their account in fact, they've just disappeared."

Mr.. Lee's eyes flashed towards his co-directors.

"Correct me if I'm wrong, but what you're saying is that large sums showed up on their records yet, these same funds are not shown as arriving or leaving. Have I got it right?"

"Absolutely."

"It would seem that by all accounts we have a bug in the New

York computer, a large amount has mysteriously showed up then vanished again on the old system. If it had shown a credit or a debit, well, that would make it a different story, the reason it must be a bug, is that it is nowhere to be found. There must be some sort of financial accountability somewhere, funds go in, funds come out, they do not just become a vacuum, or do they? "

"It would seem so."

"To make sure, I will ask Mr. Chen our security expert to take a look at the matter. However, I don't think there's anything to be concerned about. I will arrange for him to come in as soon as possible and just have a look at this strange phenomenon."

"All right. I'll show him what we've found to date." Like a deflated balloon, Patrick sensed a huge sigh of relief being let out around the room.

"I'm not very happy about the situation. But, if you, the main board of directors, are prepared to issue an office memo saying that you're happy and that I simply delete it, and carry on as normal, then who am I to argue. I've just got to make sure that I do everything correctly. I hope you understand."

"Of course. You will have the memo this morning. We must get the whole system working as quickly as possible. Therefore, I'll instruct Mr. Chen to come and help you delete this information."

"Meanwhile, I will start getting the financial portfolio prepared today."

"Well done. By the way, your influence here is certainly having the desired effect. Our people seem to be much more content with their surroundings." Mr. Lee smiled warmly, as did the rest of the men seated at the table. Patrick knew the meeting was at an end as he mentally patted himself on the back for the way he had handled it. Kim's warning had prepared him for this subterfuge. Silently he thanked her.

The Culling

Within the last two weeks since their discovery, the two men had managed to transfer all the backup information onto a George's rigged up outside computer. Patrick and George had now become the financial detectives, George having set up a several servers inside one of his friend's empty flat and with his computer expertise the whole lot was skilfully connected to a sophisticated connection in the main office.

"George. Who is Mr. Chen?"

"If it's Raymond Chen, then he's trouble." George answered without looking up.

"That's him. He's coming in tomorrow to help us clean away any record of the missing funds."

"Then we are worrying them. Raymond Chen is supposed to be the company's security advisor, but rumour has it that he is connected to a government special task force. If he's involved then you can be sure that we also have his several of his spies in our office and that every move the company makes, is immediately being reported back to him.

"I don't believe what I'm hearing."

"Oh, yes. Every company, every street corner, everywhere in South Korea people are watched and reported on and if they oppose government thinking in any way or4 form, then Raymond Chen sees to it. We must tread very carefully from now on."

"What do you suggest?"

"Right that's that, we have now saved everything. Go ahead and destroy the incriminating information tomorrow and then when he's satisfied and gone, we can place it back into the main system under a secret file name that nobody else will know about. That way we can carry on trying to locate the missing funds."

"Are we safe, or could he get any inkling and find out what we're doing?"

"Don't worry, our tracks are well covered. I have hidden files set up in such a way that not even the best experts would know that we have anything hidden away in the computer's memory. We are safe from that angle, but I suggest from now on, that we don't even think about trying anything while we're at the office. Everything related to these missing funds must always be done from here, there are too many watching eyes at the office."

"Agreed. We talk to nobody, not even your wife or my girlfriend about what we're doing." He specifically didn't mention that his girlfriend happened to be someone who also worked for the company. The other thing of concern was that he had been unable to contact Sue. He tried calling her for the umpteenth time and at last there was success, a woman's voice answered the telephone.

"May I talk to Sue, please."

"I'm sorry, but she's away on a course in America and won't be back until next week. Who's speaking? I'll leave a message for her."

"It's Patrick. I'll call her next week." He replaced the receiver and threw his head backwards wondering why it was that when he needed his friend, she had to be away on some course or other.

"Good morning, Mr. Rodgers. My name's Raymond Chen and I've been asked to have a look at a small problem that you've been having with your computer." The drawn eyelids immediately reminded Patrick of Vladisky Ormon of Heker Jong except, that this man was skinny and lithesome. The tall man spoke softly, trying to lull his victim into a sense of security. He was like a cobra, quietly moving to and fro before delivering a deadly strike.

"Ah, yes. Mr. Chen, I've been expecting you, do come in."

"Please call me Raymond and from what I understand, you've got a computer gremlin invading the works and I've been told to have a look at it before you lose it."

"That's right. I just had to be sure that the company wasn't being defrauded of huge sums, but the directors have also sent me an email instructing us to delete the whole thing from our records." Patrick took the file from his drawer. "You see, these are the amounts unaccounted for." The man studied the file for several minutes then looked at Patrick.

"Nobody could be that stupid. If there really were somebody defrauding us of those huge amounts and these sums did pass through the account, then surely they would've taken these amounts out of the computer so that there was no evidence at all to trace back to them. I don't think we have anything to worry about, nothing checks out here. Go ahead, do what the directors instructed, let's get rid of these unwanted amounts."

Sometimes people did forget thought Patrick, the man was too glib and had passed over the matter too quickly for his liking. Patrick was certain that somebody high up had made a mistake and not erased the evidence and now they were covering their tracks by pretending that there was a bug in the system. For the rest of the day Raymond Chen watched as Patrick and his team got rid of the figures from their respective computer files before they placed the new files into the worldwide system. By late afternoon the international system had been fully updated and now, working without any trace of the missing funds. Patrick, George and Raymond went through the reams of printout files to double check that everything was in position and that they had got rid of the computer bug or virus.

"Well gentleman that's that, you're back on line again. It's amazing just how quickly you can dispose of a glitch such as this, I'll take these old printout files and study them, but I'm sure there's nothing to be concerned about there." Patrick had been made to hand over the only remaining record of the transaction and their computer had now obliterated all existing records once the new programme had been installed into the world-wide system. He was also certain that any computer printouts in New York would have already been destroyed.

"Our side is comfortably covered because the board has given me permission to disregard it, at least we won't have to spend weeks and even months trying to track down a phantom bug to make sure. This new move has helped us to get our proper operation back on course." Raymond's thin-lipped smile told Patrick everything he needed to know, that the snake standing before him was sure that he had overseen any remaining evidence of the ghostly transactions being deleted.

"It's been a pleasure watching a professional at work, we will probably bump into each other from time to time." Raymond collected up the printouts and offered his hand.

"Until next time Patrick." The hair on Patrick rippled in warning ever so slightly.

"Thanks for all your help Raymond. If we find any bugs in the system we know who to call." Both men laughed. No sooner was he out of the office, than George appeared.

"Well, do you think he was happy?"

"I don't know, anyway the system is back on line once again." Patrick wasn't prepared to discuss anything in the office. "I've done a hard days work, and now I'm going for a drink. You look as if you could use one as well, George." They left the building and walked along the road to the local pub.

"So?"

Patrick shrugged his shoulders.

"George. I really don't know, Raymond doesn't give much away but I think that we must be ultra, ultra cautious about what we do, or say, until we know everything. My gut feeling is that Raymond's very dangerous and definitely nobody's fool, if he suspects anything at all we are in trouble, from now on I think we are going to be watched like hawks. Starting now, we forget about those funds while we're at the office and until we are alone and away from there, we must carry on as if nothing's different."

"George, leave any searching alone for a couple of days, simply shut down your computer and don't even try to find anything. Let's wait and see if anything happens, then when everything is normal, we start searching again."

Patrick tried Sue's number.

"Hello." It wasn't Sue's voice, but the women that had told him Sue was on course in America.

"It's Patrick."

"Ah yes. Sue was in and out again, she'll call you when she gets in from her trip to Australia."

"When will that be?"

"I'm not sure, I only work with her and take care of her plants when she's away. I suspect she'll be back later this week."

"Please leave a message for her to contact me urgently just as soon as she returns."

After ten days, George and Patrick again met at the flat.

"OK. Let's see what we can find."

George loaded the computer and tapped away at the keyboard, after a few seconds his system was connected to the computer at their office, he was now simply another keyboard of the larger computer. He tapped away and waited, the main computer connected him to their New York terminal, again he worked at his keyboard.

"There! We are now into the bank's computer." He tapped in a number and waited. The figures that Patrick had been shown by George flashed onto the screen.

"Look. There's been another payment but this time it hasn't left the account yet."

Patrick was amazed at how quickly George had locked into the bank's most secret inner sanctum. George had all this power at his fingertips to transfer millions to his own account if so wished.

"George. Can you try to find out where all the money is being sent, that way we will possibly find out who's behind this scam."

"You can see that those transfers are all dated and coded, we're going to have to match the dates with the amounts before we can find out. There could be millions of names, dates and codes, what we are going to do, is take two of the largest sums and run them through. The other thing that we must watch out for, are special keywords, if we try to override these, it sounds an alarm and we will be found out. This may all take time to find the way through. Why don't you go home, if I find it then we will be able to check the rest of those accounts quite quickly."

Again George tapped away.

"See that marker. That's a security trap, fortunately for us, I have built in a counter system that can identify and highlight most traps. If I didn't have this technical knowledge, I would have passed it without even knowing it was there and they would be onto me in seconds."

On the screen, Patrick saw a word between asterisks flashing on and off.

"First I must find the key to that word, don't look so worried Patrick, how the hell do you think I got it to work this far? It took a week to break some of the more difficult codes. You go home, I'll work on it and don't worry about it, another thing you don't know about me and I've never told anybody is that my hobby all my life has been to hack into major computers world-wide. There are a small group of us that work together, it is our policy to never disturb anything, we go in we search around, we leave a signature and we leave it alone, It's like playing a game of problematical chess and some day, I'll introduce you to some of the interesting places that I've been in to."

"Where do think this one going to lead us George."

"I don't know for sure but believe me, once we find out, I'm ducking out. For sure, there will be people gunning for us if this ever becomes public knowledge, there is too much at stake and my initial gut feel is that it's CIA or Mafia behind this somewhere and I do not think its a straight theft job by the company or Korean government, it's just too calculated and highly developed."

He decided that George was right, there was no sense for him to hang around, he wasn't contributing anything. Everything in the files about George seemed to be turning out to be incorrect, the man was working like a slave and Patrick suspected that it was not just for the love of the company that he was doing all of this work. Yet his intimated words to duck out if the going got tough made Patrick very wary, did George know more than he was letting on, or was it simply a sense of survival at their precarious position that was making him nervous?

"Why are you so late?" Kim was seated on her favourite couch reading her book.

"Went for a drink with George Li, it's been a right bitch of a day."

"Why?"

"We installed the last section into the system today and we had some security man around looking at something that cropped up." She put her book down, he could not help noticing a slight frown.

"That's unusual. Who sent in this security man?"

"The board asked him to look at a problem of unaccounted funds that we found appearing, then disappearing again."

"And the board sent him in?"

"Yes."

"Something smells. The board would never act on their own like that, they would leave it to the person in charge to do what had to be done. Who was the security man?"

"A man called Raymond Chen."

"There you are, he's government, not Silver Beam. I told you on Sunday that your system is ruffling feathers. The information that you send to Seoul can now be checked. Raymond Chen scares people back home, his methods are unorthodox, and people just disappear without trace. Either they suspect one of our people and you've tipped them off or, he wants, no not right he needs to see for himself how the system works first hand."

He looked at her admiringly. Was there nothing that she didn't know about the company and its dealings.

"Well, remember what I told you. Keep your back well covered, the odds are heavily in favour that most of your staff are under his control."

"Have you cooked anything yet?"

"No. I thought it might be nice to go out and pick up something."

"Tell you what, seeing I've completed the system, let's celebrate and eat out."

"Why not?"

CHAPTER EIGHT

"C'mon my beauty, Come to daddy and open your secrets, my lovely."

For five evenings George had been seated in front of his large screen trying to decode a series of extremely complicated security password codes that would allow him access to the more detailed bank records. Each evening Patrick stayed with him for an hour then went home to Kim, he somehow couldn't but help admire George's tenacity and devotion to what was primarily George's hobby, maintaining that he would have given up in frustration a long time ago. Whatever skills George had used, seemed to fail or lead him through a technological maze but, working diligently he would simply go through the complicated procedure again and again. Each time trying and failing seemed to make he more determined and he would make a series of notes on a pad. Each time he jotted codes down Patrick could only stare at them in amazement because to him the notes all simply looked like some form of hieroglyphic scrawl.

"I told you t that this all takes time, each time the bank security defeats me I have to come back to the account to start the correct entry procedure again, I've learned that from long experience. It's like being a mountaineer, you climb, you find your way blocked, it is better to retreat back to an area you know before attempting to find another route. Eventually you conquer the mountain, in my case each time I come away I've managed to find out what the code cannot be."

"What do the complicated charts on that pad mean?"

"Well, you see, each time I try a word or number there are a makeup of letters or figures all strung together. The computer doesn't understand words or numbers as such. It does understand digits and I have a seeker programme in my computer that, in effect, talks to the bank's computer. Each time we try out a different series of digits, their computer takes fractionally shorter or longer time to check its memory. If my first letter or number is correct it will double check itself, then come back and tell my computer it's wrong. What I have in my programme is a sensitive timing mechanism that then lets me know whether we are on the trail, by the length of time for the response. I could end up having a ten or fifty digit word which means I may have to go through the complicated entry process two hundred and sixty times or more. Numeric codes generally tend to be the worst to crack because each part of the code can be up to fifty digits long. So far, I've come through fifteen security locks and I have to follow the same new routine each time. If I don't, then *I am bound to be found out.* It's something like putting a card into those cash machines at your bank, if you put in the wrong identity number then you get your card back but if you keep putting your card in and the wrong identity number, then the card disappears. It's a security check, so, if I make a mistake, I then walk away from the machine before then switching identities and trying a totally different card. That way, I avoid the security traps because at the other side they cannot recognise my new imprint; it's all about what their security perceives me to be." Patrick knew most of this, but was fascinated by the step-by-step checks and counterchecks within the bank's security procedure. One slip and they could be found out and this time it wasn't just some computer game being played, this was for real. There was a difference, he was beginning to understand just how high the stakes were.

"It's fascinating, something like a game of chess where you're both trying to outsmart each other."

"Not quite, but a similar scenario, I'm also trying to enter the other computer operator's head to understand how they are thinking or how technically strong they are or what skills they possess, only then can I start getting to grips with their security checks."

"How far down the line of security checks do you think you've gone so far?"

"I don't know Patrick, so far I understand some of the logic used in building their defences and there could be another hundred codes or this could the last one. I really don't know at this moment because it's like searching the digits, each time you manage an unlock, another series pops up but it does mean that we are one step closer to our goal. Fun ...isn't it?"

"I wouldn't have the patience."

"When you have opened the door once, it becomes like a drug. You've got to do it again and again. During my lifetime of doing this, I could have been rich beyond measure and stolen millions but, I have never taken as much as a cent. It's all about the chase and the buzz living right on the edge, getting in like a thief and the excitement of possibly getting caught that keeps my adrenalin levels high, I just love putting my skill up against an unknown opponent and this is why I do this. Once the hunt has ended and is at an end, we always leave our trademark signature notifying the opposition that we've broken into their system and taken nothing."

"You're joking. You go to all this trouble, purely for the buzz of being able to tell them you've paid them a visit?"

"That's about the sum of it."

"George this is just a big game to you isn't it?

"On the contrary, do you know what my fate would be if we got caught invading some of the sensitive areas or government files we have visited during my life? They wouldn't just lock us up and lose the key, oh no, that would be too risky, they would make sure that we met with an accident or are just disappeared. Your friend, Raymond Chen is expert at that game "

"I know and have been warned about some of his tactics and

that's why we are here, you and I just have to be that extra vigilant. Now, would you like a cup of tea?"

George nodded and continued. Patrick went to the kitchen and started making tea for them both, right then he was feeling very useless because there was nothing he could do until George had completed his task. He knew his time would come but for the moment all he could was sit around and wait until George had finished his computer game. He finished pouring hot water into two mugs and started on his way back but almost dropped them as he entered their computer sanctuary.

"Eureka! Patrick I'm in! Come and have a look." George's happy face at that moment, reminded Patrick of the beautifully drawn pictures of the Cheshire Cat in Alice in Wonderland that he remembered from his childhood days.

"Really?"

"Now we're in real business."

"OK. Let's do it."

George lifted the mug to his lips and noisily slurped at it before starting again. Searching through his papers he found the slip of paper where he had written the two transferred amounts that he had scribbled down. Checking the dates first, he entered the amounts shown. Thousands of rolling numbers flashed by on the screen, coming to stop on the figure he was looking for.

"Well. That's where the money's gone."

Patrick looked at the screen.

"Nothing wrong there I suppose, but why the hell would Silver Beam act as an intermediary for the South Korean Government?"

"I have no idea."

"Surely the government would give them the funds directly?"

"One would automatically presume so."

Patrick felt slightly disappointed, the name on the screen read *'United Nations Fund Number Two for Special Environment Programs'*. George scribbled down the account name and number on the piece of paper. He then left the account and went back to the start again.

"Let's see if the other amounts reveal the same account." Once again he started the laborious task of entering the account file on the selected date.

"Same thing. It's all being channelled into that same account."

"It would seem that the government is simply paying money into an environmental account." Patrick said.

"My question is why, it does not make any sense to me. Why use a company account to shift government funds to an aid fund? "

"Maybe the amounts were sent by mistake to Silver Beam, then sent on to the UN for them." Patrick was now grabbing at straws, inwardly he knew George was right and something wasn't quite right. He wondered where to go from here.

"Patrick, you go home? I'm going to first check all the transfers, then, if they check out and are all the same, we'll need to follow the money trail amounts right into and through the UN account to see what I can find out." Patrick had felt sure they would locate something more sinister when they had started this venture, but now felt somewhat deflated because seemingly the entry of the United Nations behind the transactions gave the whole thing respectability and legitimacy.

"This is becoming a bad habit, Mr. Rodgers. What's your excuse tonight?" Kim was seated on her couch, she smiled when she pointedly asked the question in her pouting manner but he understood that she was half teasing him.

"Oh well, Miss Lee. You see I met this fantastic fat dragon, well he was some kind of a genie really and he offered me so much money from his dollar account that I couldn't refuse going on a trip with him just to see if the money was real."

"Can you introduce your friend to me?"

"Nope! This is my friend. We flew into some of the biggest banks and looked at all the delightful money, then he brought me back to London."

"Did you pick up any free samples on the way?"

"No. All we were doing was looking at it, perhaps if he allows me to enter his domain again, who knows, next time we might collect something, we will have to wait and see." They both giggled loudly, he felt very guilty and desperately wanted to tell her what he was doing and this was his strange way of letting her know that he was on to something big and yet, she worked for the company and he could not afford to drop his guard.

"Really though. I am going to work late for some time."

"Why. What's wrong?"

He had to allay her fears with a plausible excuse.

"Nothing is wrong but until such time as the system is fully on line and all the bugs straightened out, I have to stay on and see that it's working correctly. The main problem is the time difference between America, South Korea and England. We only start transferring data at nine o'clock and that's why I'm late. How did your day go?"

"Don't ask, everything that could go wrong went wrong and don't feel like talking about it right now." Kim shuddered and pulled her lips back over her teeth in a gesture of disgust. "I'm feeling a little unwashed with the day's events why not join me in the shower room, then let's go and have a late meal."

The following morning saw George was waiting for Patrick as he pulled into the company's parking lot. He had waited in his car until he saw the red Porsche arrive and excitedly made his way to the car.

"Morning, Patrick. It's a pity you didn't stay on last night." He called as Patrick got out his car,. Patrick turned around and instantly noticed that George's normally calm appearance seemed somewhat agitated.

"George we agreed not to even discuss it here."

"That's why I waited for you here and not inside, I tried you mobile number on several occasions but either you were not picking up or I don't have a correct number for you." Patrick pulled out his cell phone and looked at it.

"Damn batteries, I need to get a new phone, this one loses charge at a rate of knots. Sorry about that, .well, what's up?"

"I followed the trail of funds into the UN account. I think you should have a look at it as soon as possible because there's some fascinating reading when you get inside there. I definitely think, no, I know that our hunch was correct, we're on to something ...*Really BIG!*"

"Why?"

Patrick could suddenly feel that same tinge of excitement creep in without knowing what it was that made him suspect that there was more to this than had first met the eye. His understanding of accounts and nose for trouble told his brain that there was something not right out there and now George had confirmed his fears.

"I'll show it all to you tonight but I think there's a lot more funny business to this account than we at first thought there was." The two men stopped talking about George's find as they entered the building. Raymond Chen had followed the two men into the building and was now in the lift with them, Patrick was trying hard to act as calmly as possible, with this security man everything had to appear normal as Raymond started talking to them.

"I've been right through all the amounts both here and in America and it seems as if there's nothing to be worried about."

"I'm pleased to hear that, what a relief. So it must have just been some kind of a bug in the system somewhere, I don't really understand how that happens. Computers? We have this sort of love, hate relationship with them because we can't live without them but would love to discard them."

"It would seem so, anyway I've destroyed all the printout files now, so we've got it right out of the system and have nothing to worry about, it will never show it's ugly head on our computers again. By the way, how's that new accounting program working, anyway?"

"Fine. I think we'll be on top of it by the end of the month."

The lift door opened and George led the way out as Raymond carried on his journey to the top floor. The lift doors closed.

"That man scares me. I wonder if he was watching us or heard anything."

"George. Your imagination is running away with you, now shut up and forget about it until later. OK?"

"Right."

Patrick lifted the receiver and called Sue's number, he was becoming a little worried because it was very unlike her not to return his calls, thinking back, he tried to think whether he could have said or done might have possibly upset her somehow. The phone at the other end just buzzed as it had on so many occasions over the last few days, for the first time he found himself wishing that he had not said anything about Kim or his move to her place.

It was a lot later when the two got together in front of George's computer, Patrick could see that George was excited, it was like watching a person taking Speed for the first time and the rush it provoked.

"Just give me a few moments to boot up and get back into the system." Patrick watched George's deft fingers transfer their command to the machine.

"Damn!"

"What's wrong?"

"The UN obviously change their entry code on a daily basis. I'll just have to break this one security check. Patrick watched as George manipulated with the new security code and it didn't take long for him to break through to the main UN account. He came out of the system and then went back into the account again.

"Just had to make certain that we weren't tripped up by any security alarms, there we are. Look at this." Patrick scanned through a list of the names on the screen and what interested him most, were the quantity and amounts transferred to this one special account.

"Have you checked to see how much has passed through that account?"

"No, do you want me to do that first?"

"Yes, it will be very interesting."

George tapped in various instructions, after a few moments the debits and credits appeared on the screen.

"Jesus wept! Look at that."

Patrick had never seen anything like it, the number showing on the screen amounted ran to many billions of dollars more than the most mid-sized country's entire gross annual budget.

"Why would they need that sort of money for an environmental program?" Patrick was talking to himself, more than talking to George.

"Patrick, I don't think you understand what I was getting so excited about when I first entered this account, just have a look at the providers of the funds, it makes for fascinating reading." Patrick started going through the names one by one.

"So? They're just major industrial companies, so what?"

"Tell me something, how many major companies do you know that will give away these sorts of amounts without creating marketing mileage out of it? How many companies would even give this sort of money away to save the ozone layer or whatever? To check back they are all huge and their accounts are a matter of record, guess what?"

What George was inferring was absolutely correct. Patrick shrugged his shoulders as he continued to stare at the screen trying to take in the enormity of the account in front of them.

"Patrick, big business is greedy, they do *nothing for nothing.* The world would know of any kind-hearted contributions, their accounts do not mention or show up these fantastic sums, they have chosen to shut up about such huge sums being donated to the UN, just like Silver Beam has. Something about this whole thing stinks of some kind of an elaborate worldwide conspiracy."

George had already had time to mull it over and think about it but Patrick was too busy trying to understand his companion's profound thoughts. If George was right, which he probably was, then there was something going on here that was going affect the world, Patrick thought.

"How long would it take to print all of these name and the amounts?"

George tapped something into the computer. He was checking to see how many transactions had taken place.

"About half an hour to forty minutes on that new laser printer at the office."

"George we are keeping away from the office. I don't want you to use the office computer at all."

"Don't panic, I'll simply place this information into our secret file now, then I'll drive to the office and do some work and when I can, will quickly print out the names and then, get back here. The whole thing will take an hour."

"OK, make sure that you leave nothing on file that can be traced. If you do and it's reported you could find yourself dealing with Raymond Chen. No, I don't like it, it's far too risky, printers have counters and possibly would leave some kind of footprint for us to be discovered. We must get ourselves a laser printer and set up here.

"Patrick, I have the knowledge, trust me, there will be no trace that that machine was ever used. We use the one at the office today, then never again." George's fingers tapped out the instructions to deposit these details into his hidden computer file in their office.

"Are you going to wait here or do you want to come with me?" Patrick felt that it would probably be better to meet George away from the office.

"Tell you what. Let's meet at eight at that pub on the corner.

I'll buy you a drink."

"OK. See you later, boss." Patrick phoned Kim to tell her we would be home before ten but she wasn't in yet. He tried Sue's number; it too also just rang leaving him to wonder what the hell was going on. This was all becoming too much, now there were shadows forming everywhere, especially in the little dark corners of his mind.

CHAPTER NINE

"Miss Han would you come here please?"

Patrick had used the list after collecting it from George, he made up several notes, writing down the names of all British companies involved. He found to his surprise that one of the names that appeared on the UN list was that of his old company. He had never been aware of any donations given to the UN and now needed to know whether they had admitted having moved large funds into the UN environment fund. To avoid any suspicions from his staff, he had added several names of major public firms to the list.

"Please contact these companies, ask them to send us a copy of their most recent company accounts by return." He handed the hand-written sheet of paper to his secretary.

"Mr. Patrick, somebody called Sue phoned and left a message that she called. She didn't leave a number."

"At last. Thank you Miss Han, that's all" He immediately grabbed for his telephone. Sue's phone just rang and rang.

"Shit!" He slammed down the instrument and settled into the matter in hand.

Patrick had always able to read a balance sheet like a book and if such enormous sums had been moved through any company, then it should be recorded somewhere. He would find it, no matter how cleverly they disguised it and he knew that nobody would even give the matter a second thought that he was requesting their company's figures. He was after all, the financial director of a huge conglomerate his eyes scanned the printout once again thinking that George must have been right, nobody moved funds of this magnitude to the UN without it creating waves or marketing mileage. From previous experience he felt that at least one of the participants would have splattered such important news right across the world but none of them had differences added to their advertising budgets from what he could make out. He opened the UN folder once again hoping to find a lead, after a short while he noted something of interest.

"George must have missed this."

Patrick had picked up on the fact that all of the amounts from the special account had seemingly been sent to only two recipients, Patrick made a mental note to ask George to follow the money. He was now sure that if they stayed with chasing the funds, they would finally find out what was going on. Within three days he had received the accounts from all the firms requested and took them home to study them in depth at the weekend.

"Don't tell me you're bringing work home now."

"It's not really work, I'm just looking at some of the larger public companies and how they produce their figures."

"Patrick, tell me something? Are you seeing someone else?"

"Whatever makes you ask a silly question like that?"

"The other evening I had to finish up something for that fool, Kang then I went to the second floor and there were only two people left. I asked George Li if you were still there and he told me that he thought you had gone home already, you remember that night don't you? You only came in at after ten and told me that you had been working. I've been wondering how to speak to you about it without seemingly checking up on you."

Patrick was trapped, he either had to tell another lie or he had to tell her the truth and he felt himself blushing, anyway the less she knew the better he thought.

"OK. I did you a lie, but I didn't purposely want you to be hurt and you are right, there is another woman that I have been meeting up at least once a week, you have nothing to fear because she's my ex-wife. It's been a standing ritual for the last three years and I've never mentioned it to you because I thought it would seem odd to you that I visit my ex-wife every week."

"I don't find that too strange, the big question is, are you still in love with her?"

"Not at all, we're very good friends but could never be lovers, ever since our break-up we have become best of friends, we have shared our thoughts once a week, she knew about you from the very beginning, in fact she would love to meet you sometime.."

"Tell me about her."

Patrick had managed to put Kim off the trail for the moment and knew that, somehow, he would have to find a decent excuse for the evenings that he was going to be away. He told her all about his marriage to Sue and the disastrous consequences following their wedding when she had her affair. He continued to tell Kim that after a cooling period how they had finally gone out again and decided that could become friends again, mainly because they had so much in common. That solid friendship had continued to mature until he now found a best friend in her.

"That's nice."

He wasn't certain that she completely believed his story but it had given him slight breathing space for the moment.

"As I have already told you, she does know everything about you and one day in the not too distant future we must arrange that you meet up." He kicked himself mentally, for the very first time, it sank home he had been rather stupid not thinking that she may have friends working within his department and they would be able to keep track of his movements if she was inclined to really check up on him.

"There is one other thing that I haven't told you about mainly because I didn't think it would be of interest to you, for several years I've been playing chess with friends. Now because of our chess relationship they are short of a major player for one competition, so can I ask you a big favour?"

"What's that?"

"These guys are really good and have entered a round robin chess competition and asked me to be the fourth member of their team, I don't want to let them down so I'll need to put in a lot of practice time to get back up to my old level."

"So you want time off?"

He pulled his mouth awkwardly.

"Well, yes"

"OK. I don't mind. How long before I get you back full time, if at all?"

"I just need a couple of weeks."

"Right." She turned back to her book, leaving him uncertain whether she was playing the matter down, or whether this was her way of handling the situation she found herself facing. Most girls that he knew would have gone mental if he had put this same proposal to them, so rather than force the issue any further he did a man thing and picked up one of the files that Miss Han had acquired for him. He searched through all the figures and nowhere could he locate anything that even looked remotely like the funds transferred to the UN special account. These large conglomerates were all hiding these funds from the public, the shareholders and the investors for a reason and Patrick was nervous about what they would find.

"I've managed to follow these funds into these two separate accounts and It becomes stranger and stranger the deeper we probe and penetrate."

"Why?"

"I've managed to work out what one of the two account designations could mean, the two accounts are UNSEDP and UNSECP and obviously both belong within the United Nations organisation. I think that UNSEDP stands for United Nations Special Environment Development Program."

"How would you know that?"

"Look here. I've broken into the UN computer via a Berkeley University link that I discovered many years ago in my early days of hacking. Seeing I had the name from the banking account it was easy to gain access to the department. Looking at their files, orders and expenditure tells me that it's a special environmental research division. With more time I should be able to work out exactly what they're researching."

"And UNSECP. What does that stand for?" His Korean companion intrigued Patrick, the man was an absolute genius with technology and Patrick found himself again wondering why George wasted his time working as an accountant.

"That's the strange part. The UN computer can't locate the name. Possibly it's in a hidden or special security file and if it is, then maybe we've reached the end of the road. There is no way I can locate it if it's been hidden if it's anything like my hidden file in the office, I'm the only one that gets to it.

"Why is that, surely you must be able to find a file with your experience?"

"No, you must understand, it's something like a ghost floating within the system, hiding itself behind genuine programmes. If anybody starts looking at what's on record, it hides and can't be found unless it is called up in a very a special way. If it doesn't want to be found, nobody will find it no matter what programs you use."

"What about searching through various UN computer files to see if anything of interest shows up."

"I would be searching for months or years because somewhere, someone knows how to call up the special account but I do have some ideas of my own. Our first place of reference is the bank account number and that's where we start searching. From here on in this little game of ours is where it starts to become fairly risky but, if we're search it out, it's the only way to go." Patrick could understand how hackers became hooked over time, seeking more and more danger but now, they had reached what seemed to almost be George's ultimate game, pitting wits against some of the best computer brains in the world and not knowing if you were found out, because if you slipped up just once, there was a very certain price to paid. More than likely it would be both their lives, Patrick was extremely apprehensive at that moment.

"So how do you do it?"

"Tonight I am going to devise a special sleeper programme and place it in the deposit and withdrawal file at the bank and hope nobody comes across it. It too will be a similar hider virus but they may have a specialist security scanner that hunts through their computer files before they start up using the account. They use programs like this to scan for computer viruses, it acts like a patrol guard checking a property perimeter. Starting at the outer fence, it makes a systematic search of the whole system like the guard checking the buildings and if it finds nothing it reports that all is well and the account is allowed to move on. This way there are no losses to the data on record because specialised computer viruses can cause havoc to any system."

"Like what?"

"Computer viruses can be a nightmare, some wipe out the

information or tie up traffic on a network for hours, turning an innocent machine into a zombie by replicating and sending themselves to other computers. That may not sound a lot but you would have many execute programs loaded into the computer and it keeps using up large blocks of working digits so that you quickly find that there is no space left anywhere. Others will on every Friday the thirteenth simply wipe out all the execute files. Every single programme in the computer is useless and you have to start programming from scratch. On a large computer such as the bank have, the results would be catastrophic."

"Have we guarded ourselves against this at our office?"

"Oh, yes. I made sure that I had an inspector programme installed and that's how I can have a hidden file having instructed the inspector to disregard my ghost file. So each day it comes back with nothing to report."

"Can't you do that to the UN's files then?"

"No! Unfortunately not, it has the ultimate security device. If you even try to break the code, it immediately shuts down the entire system if the first digit offered is not correct and then they will know we are trying to get into the system."

"So what's the risk?"

"Quite high. The only way I can try to beat an inspector is to place a warning on my sleeper. It's something like a thief, so when it hears somebody coming towards it, it quickly moves to another hiding position and when the inspector has passed it returns to its original position but I cannot be sure it won't be discovered because this is the first time I've attempted to use this particular programme, it has to be highly-developed and extremely sophisticated to go up against that lot."

"What will they do if they find it?"

They'll follow it back down the line until they reach the Silver Beam computer and then they'll lose the trail for a while, but if they do spot us, then all this work will have been for nothing. Also, they could seize the Silver Beam computer and with enough time, they will be bound to discover my ghost programme."

"What are the chances of them catching us?"

"Maybe two per cent, but it will still be a risk. Shall we do it?"

"Yes. We have no other alternative." George began working frantically, placing his sleeper into the bank account. After an hour he started checking to see if it was doing it's work.

"Now we sit and wait, let's see if any funds are touched. If they don't discover our sleeper then, it will wait for any instructions to the account. When they are made, somebody will have to call up their ghost file to send the money to, as soon as they do, our sleeper will watching and recording."

"If you manage that, then it should be a simple matter getting into the account?"

"Not necessarily. There could be a system of changing entry codes on a daily basis, there could be a thousand and one other clever devices to stop us."

"Where do we go from here, George?"

"I'll check my sleeper every morning, lunchtime and evening from now on and that way, as soon as a move is made, I'll be able to get in and copy the detail onto the new laser printer so that even if the code changes we will still have full details down on record. If I don't pitch up at the office on any given morning, you are going to have to cover for me. It will mean I'm in and that I'm copying their files, I cannot leave this computer until I've exited from the system properly. It may take an hour to copy, it could take a day, who knows?"

Patrick knew this was going to be a tense time for both of them because if they got caught now, they would have spent all this time for nothing.

"Well, I suppose there's nothing more we can do until somebody activates the file now.?"

George carefully exited through the system and only once he was satisfied that everything was in order, switched off the machine.

"What strikes me as strange, is that the UN must be aware of, or at least knows of that one division, but the other one that receives the majority of funds is kept secret or, the more plausible answer is that only certain UN officials have sanctioned this hidden account. There's something extremely crooked going down. Patrick, you must pray that the sleeper does its work. If it does, then we will have a much clearer idea as to what's going on."

"C'mon lets go and have a beer. You look as if you need one." George offered.

"Not tonight George, there's someone that I must try to contact."

He drove to Battersea, Sue wasn't home, dejectedly he made his way across to Chiswick.

"*Where the hell are you Sue?* I need you like I've never needed you before."

Kim was stretched out on her couch as usual.

"How did the chess practice go?"

"Rotten thanks, I'm so out of touch that I'll never be ready on time."

"So, what can you do about it?"

"The only thing that'll help is more practice, don't worry about it, if you try to contact me at the office and I'm nowhere to be found, then I'll be putting in practicing time, that will be our little secret. OK?"

"Whatever you say. But please Patrick, don't let this become some kind of an obsession and take over your life, if anybody finds out what you're doing you will be risking your entire future." Patrick looked at her, feeling a little uncertain and wondering whether she talking about chess or was she hinting at something wider. This oriental inscrutability could be carried too far sometimes, he thought, feeling he was getting to be like George, becoming suspicious of everything around him.

"How did your day go?"

Terrible thank you, bloody Kang has brought in a management company called Heker Jong and there is an obnoxious little man called Vladisky Ormon, he is driving me crazy."

"Oh hell, not again, What in the world made him do that?"

"Why? Have you heard of them before?"

"Oh yes, the last time Ormon and I crossed paths was the day I left my last place of employment. He is a total misfit; it is beyond me how he manages to crawl his way into the best firms."

"Everything I do or say is not how they do it at Heker Jong but he is so far behind modern day methods it's laughable."

"You told me to watch out, it's you who must be careful, he is spitefully vicious. The man has an obvious chip on his shoulder and tries to prove it by being nasty to everyone."

"I know and there's something unclean about him."

"Luckily Ormon will be in America for a few days, he suddenly had to rush off this evening and he called the office to tell my secretary. No matter what happened, that bit of news has made my day."

"I wonder what he's doing in America."

"I don't know and I don't care, all I know is that he'll be away for the rest of this week and I won't have to put up with his whining. It suits me down to the ground, I could kill Kang for doing this."

Patrick didn't like the detestable man or his company and certainly didn't know that Heker Jong had American offices. Then he suddenly had an idea, somewhere within his papers he thought he had a copy of the financial accounts of his old company. He went upstairs and searched through some of his private papers that he had brought from his house. Near the bottom of the pile he found what he was looking for. At the front of the financial accounts was the name of the auditors and their various addresses world-wide. There it was, Heker Jong *did* have subsidiary offices in New York. Patrick put the papers away carefully again and thoughtfully made his way downstairs to the lounge wondering what bit of slime the man was digging himself into this time.

The Culling

CHAPTER TEN

"Mr. Rodgers, George Li hasn't come into work today."

"Yes, I know Miss Han, he called me to say that he was going to the doctor first, he's got a slight back problem and just wants it looked at."

"He's never complained about anything like that before?"

"Well, now you know by the way would you get hold of Mr. Forrester at the bank on the line for me." Patrick was almost certain by now that Miss Han worked directly for Raymond Chen. She always seemed to be nosing about and asking irrelevant questions, he wasn't certain if she was monitoring his calls but for now, he needed an excuse to leave the office. His phone rang and Miss Han told him that Mr. Forrester was on the other end.

"Hello, Alf."

Patrick spoke to him about certain transfers that needed to made to their head office account and the dates that they had to be. He told the bank manager that he would be by later that day to sign the transfer documents, replacing the receiver, he got up and put on his jacket.

"Miss Han. I'm going out for a short while, if anyone needs me, I'll be at the bank later with Mr. Forrester."

"Do you want the good news or the bad news first?"

George looked terrible, his puffed eyes were almost blood red, he hadn't shaved, and his clothes were a mess, with a large coffee stain etching down the front of his shirt.

"What the hell happened to you? You look as if you've been on a binge for a week."

"After you left last night, I came back here just wanting to check that I had missed nothing, the sleeper had been doing its duty and the bad news is, I think I may have possibly run straight into an inspector programme.

"What does that mean?"

They haven't shut the program down so, what I decided to do was enter into the UNSECP file and start downloading. If we left it until tonight they would be able to lock us out and stop our program getting in altogether by changing their bank codes and then we would not be able to find the UNSECP account again."

"Can they trace you now?"

"I think it's going to take a very long time. What I've done is, to lay several trails for them to follow, sort of snakes and ladders and they will have to check out each one in turn. For instance, one of the trails will lead them directly into the NASA Space Program. They could spend months searching for a ghost in there, while another one leads them from the bank through Harvard University and directly into the FBI computer. Hopefully they will go straight to that one because both programs are top secret, so trying to get any of these agencies to give up information to the UN will cause all kinds of logistical problems. Hopefully we're covered."

"Tell me what you've found so far."

"Thank God we anticipated the lot and brought in the laser printer, there must be two years worth of work copied out there. I don't know yet, but I sensed we may only have one crack at this one, so I've copied everything I could lay my hands on. I only finished about an hour ago. I have been checking and double checking myself to make up certain that these false trails are not too easy for them to find."

"I thought you said that if an inspector programme spotted our trail it would automatically shut down the system?"

"Correct and that's what happened. The bank's computer stopped operating but I already had the entry code for the UN account by then and so began laying the dummy trails to NASA and FBI. They'll be going be searching to find out who's entered their system and how much information has been stolen and more importantly, where it's gone. Hopefully they will find one or other of the false trails first, that at least gives us a bit of time to cover our tracks."

"So how did you get back into the UN computer?"

"Easy. I originally got in via the Berkley University mainframe, it's a method I use quite often and that's the route I went this time. Before the bank cottons on to which account has been played with I had to get all the information downloaded or later UNSECP is going to find out that somebody was messing around in their account and if that happens today they will change their pass codes, entry systems ...everything. Strike while we have advantage on our side, that's my philosophy."

"Quite right! Have you managed to look at anything or find out exactly what they're up to yet?"

"No. I've been too busy concentrating on getting it into print to look at anything, however, I can tell you though is that the account now has a name. It's called, *United Nations Special Environmental Program.*"

"We knew that though?"

"Yes but what I did find out is that this is basically a supposed Killing Program?"

"Wha? ...That doesn't make any sense at all."

"I know, but there it is. I can't see why such fantastic sums of finance are being provided for controlling numbers of animals, you had to think they would be better off using the funds for saving animals rather than controlling their demise."

"Everything about this doesn't feel right. How much longer are you going to need?"

"I'm just about finished, then I'm going home to have a wash and shave and then go back to the office."

"That reminds me, you've been to see the doctor because you've got a painful back. OK?"

"OK." Although exhausted George seemed totally in his element here as he continued tapping away at the keyboard. He was preparing his system for complete shutdown. The man had done everything he could, this was like the biggest computer game he had ever played in his life ... and seeming to have won the game. Patrick knew they had reached the end of the trail as far they were concerned, the answer had to lie somewhere among the printouts, there was going to be no second crack at this.

"Patrick. I'm not going to leave a calling card just yet so if we find the slightest hint that they are to us, then it would not be wise to give them some extra leverage to find our hacking team. That would eventually lead them straight to us."

"Good thinking George. I think we should get these printouts away from here now, we don't know their strength or power and if this is as big as we think and they manage to trace it back here we don't want anything that will point us out. You store this computer away elsewhere as well as the servers, drives and printer material will also have to be well hidden. I suggest a lock up storage somewhere distant."

"Right I will do that straight after work, I already have a facility as a backup. My thought is for me to get rid of this stuff."

"Why are so nervous? I thought you did everything to stop them finding you."

"I have. But this isn't like a normal hacking job, something about this one scares me shitless. Don't ask me what it is? It's like a thief or rapist just knowing he's been seen. It's only a matter of time before he's caught ...I feel the same way"

"Then go ahead and destroy all the evidence. Get rid of the backup drives, the computer, printer and modem and anything else that could point to the fact you've been here at all."

"What?"

"George, I'll look after the printouts. You've done everything and more, I don't want you involved. Do you understand?"

"But I want to see this thing through to the end."

"You know nothing, you've seen nothing. If there's even a slight hint that we may be caught out, I don't want you involved, these people seemingly play for *very* high stakes. Whatever they're doing it's got massive support and they'll play for keeps. From now on, we have a business to run ... That's all."

"All right, but if you need any help, let me know."

"George don't think I'm trying to be nasty, you've already done everything asked for and more now it's better if I go on alone. I don't want anything leading to you."

George seemed to momentarily slump at his computer, Patrick could see that he had dented the man's pride George had done all the work and now here he was telling him to stop.

"I'm going to the bank now. See you back at the office."

"Yeah right." George didn't even look up, Patrick thought he might see things more clearly once he had had a good clean up. At the door, he turned around towards George.

"Listen, George. You know and I both know the Raymond Chen's of this world? They're here to stop us finding out whatever it is we are not supposed to know, I just don't want you hurt. Thanks a million for what you've done, why don't you simply take the day off and get everything out of the way. I'll tell them you won't be in because the doctor's given you the day off."

"We'll see."

George was extremely weary, Patrick was certain that once he had had a rest he be able to understand. The man had been on an extreme high for several days and now that they had possibly reached the end, he was tired and felt very let down.

"I'm just taking these down to the car."

Patrick lifted two of the many boxes of printouts and carried them to the stairs to his Porsche. Returning to the flat he found George again in a state of excitement.

"Now *we know* they're after us, as I was closing down and checking my false trails for the last time I found that they have already started following one of the trails. I came across it and they have gone for the NASA trail, it won't be too long before they realise I sold them a dummy ...Shit!"

"Well then, get out!"

"I've got to do this check and double check, but now I've got to destroy the ghost at the office, no sense in leaving it in there to be found. You're right. I'll then get rid of everything. I suggest you get those fucking printouts hidden where nobody will find them."

Patrick was worried as he lifted another two boxes, after several trips he had all the information down to his car.

"See you later, George." Having loaded the printouts into the car he drove straight to the bank, his initial thoughts being to deposit the boxes there but then thought better of it. The less people that knew about this, the better. He signed the transfer documents and then phoned his office.

"Anything for me, Miss Han?" She gave him two messages that were of little importance.

"Listen, I'm taking a friend to lunch and won't be back until about three. Take any messages."

He drove to his home in Amersham to find Mrs. Jones busily cleaning the bath.

"I haven't been home for some time, why the devil are you cleaning the bath?"

"It still gets dusty you know? We can't have that now can we?" She looked at him sceptically.

"Mrs. Jones... you see these boxes? I'm putting them in the study and sometime in the near future I'm going to be spreading the papers all around the room and making *a big* mess. I don't want you touching them at all. Do you understand? Leave my study alone for a while."

She pulled a face of disgust and carried on cleaning as if he hadn't said anything at all.

"Mr. Rodgers, I'm employed to keep this place clean my way and if you don't like it..." She let the words hang there.

"Impossible woman!"

Patrick quickly moved the boxes into his study, locked the door and clipped the key onto his key ring. He had a quick cup of tea and then went back to London and into the office.

George hadn't arrived back, he must have decided to take the day off after all, Patrick decided.

"It's nice to have you home early for a change, the weekend is coming up, let's go out and have something to eat and take in a show?"

"Kim. I'm way behind and need real practice time so I want to spend a week alone at my house, so that I can pit my wits against a real chess-playing computer. Do you mind?"

"Of course I mind, at first you ask for a couple of nights off, *now* you want a complete week off. What did you think I would say?"

"I tell you what. Why not come home with me? We can spend a week together there and then move back here."

"No chance. If we go to your house, then how do you expect me to compete with that machine. If I interrupt anything you'll be ramming it down my throat forever, no thank you, you go but don't make a habit of it."

"This is the last week before the competition, I really do need to practice."

"Why don't you pack up your computer and bring it here?"

"Because the last time I moved it, it went out of kilter. I don't want to move it."

"I tell you what Patrick. You spend this week at home. Finish your damned competition and then come back here, but then, you better make up your mind. It's either me or that bloody game. I can face competition from another woman, but I'm getting more than a little fed up with having to play second fiddle to a mere game."

"I promise that this is the last time. It will never happen, believe me."

"Now. If you're going to lock yourself up with a machine for a while, then I want you all to myself for tonight."

"Right, let's go and visit Claude and see what delights he can throw together for us tonight."

They got back to the flat at after midnight.

"Let's have a bath, if you're going away for a while, I can't let you go without giving you a special send off.

"While they were bathing Kim got out and then poured some liquid into the hot water. She stirred the water so that the blue colouring spread throughout.

"Lie back and let that soak into you.

"Slowly and with a satisfied smile etched on her face, she started drying herself. He felt his skin start to tingle like a thousand prickly shocks were suddenly being thrown at him, it was as if the water was gently massaging his pores. The tingling seemed to become more vigorous, or rather, it felt as if it suddenly changed from a gentle massage to somebody scratching his entire body with thorns. He jumped up out of the bath. Kim howled with sheer delight.

"Here, dry yourself quickly" He rubbed hard at his stinging body and it took almost a full ten minutes for the burning sensation to subside slightly. All the while Kim howled at his Ooohh, Aahhh antics.

"Now relax. You're going to enjoy this."

She rubbed a clear liquid all over his body, he knew that he could trust her funny potions not to do irreparable harm. It felt like an ice bath surrounding his body and all over him and from what was a painful experience, now felt every nerve end tingling as she soothed in the clear balsam. Whatever she tipped into the bath had seemingly exposed his body to an awareness of every pore. His whole being had become sensitive, alive and invigorated with whatever it was she had used, he was ready for her now.

"Here. Rub this on me."

Again another differing little bottle of magic potion was produced. Slowly he massaged her body with this golden oil, making sure that he rubbed it everywhere.

"Make love to me now."

He had come to learn that it was something to do with the mixture of the various ancient infusing potions rubbing together that was the secret to Kim's Asian witchcraft. One minute they were making love, the next he didn't know what had happened for his whole world became alive with dragons, smoke, weird creatures and fantastic colours. At college he had once taken a severe drug trip, experiencing strange scenes at the time but, nothing in his life could surpass these moments when Kim applied her magic. He tried to look down at Kim through the enveloping haze and gauge her expression, it was impossible to focus on whether she too was also going through some sort of weird experience as well. The more he moved, the deeper and more vivid the scenes became. He wanted to stop but couldn't, her progress was forcing him onward, he imagined the growing tempo of his body, mind and soul into racing to this oblivion, yet he wanted to continue to explore the hidden crevices this constant interchange promised. He could hear himself but, it sounded far off in the distance, his screaming becoming louder. Somehow Kim seemed to be trying desperately to defend herself against this imaginary monster attacking her small body. She was attempting to tear the skin from his body with her hard nails, he kept the transfer flowing. He was the beast exploring her inner sanctum and needed to burst her open at the seams. He attacked her with his weapon, his body and movement until his own mind finally adrift all bearing the forces to propel them both ever onwards, he lost all sense of rhyme from his soul. Then both moved towards the volcano mantle in unison, the mental orange explosion was the last thing that they both remembered.

When he awoke the next morning he wasn't sure what had happened or in fact whether it really did happen. The last thing he felt was that he had possibly passed out. He wondered whether they had continued on into the night or had simply fallen asleep after the frightening yet explosive experience. Kim on the other hand, looked so peaceful lying naked next to him, he reached out and lovingly stroked her seemingly frail little body gently.

"Wake up, sleepy head."

She rolled over on top of him and began moving slowly, there was a wicked grin on her face. From far below he felt it again, the pain, the glory, the dragons were all beginning to start appearing again to both of them. They made love all day through Saturday, it was the most fantastic yet, Patrick eventually went to his home in Amersham on the Sunday morning.

The Culling

CHAPTER ELEVEN

"Where do I start?"

Patrick looked at the four boxes containing tens of thousand pages of text knowing that he only had six days to complete his task.

"At the beginning I suppose."

He lifted the first box onto his leather inlaid desk and withdrew a large wad of paper with his pen he began marking a large number one at the top and circled the number and started scanning through the first page. By Sunday evening he completed editing the first box's contents. Throughout the day he had carefully laid out two separate piles on the floor next to him. The larger pile having revealed nothing of interest, the much smaller pile showed items that Patrick thought might need further investigation.

Each time he spotted anything; he had underlined it with his thick marker pen, then marked the top of the page. He continued this arduous task until completing each bundle that would then be placed on its appropriate pile. There were only four small piles on his left, the balance on his right were now safely deposited back into boxes. The only time he left the study was at midday when he made himself something to eat.

The telephone rang, it was Kim. "Thought that I had just give you a call. How's it going?"

"Battling. I'm getting better at it though. Wouldn't you like to come across and give me one of your famous massages?"

He heard her giggle loudly.

"My consulting rooms are here. If you want a treatment, you've got to come here for it."

"By the time I'm finished here, I'm going to be a wreck and I'm going to need the best of your consultations."

Again he heard the staccato giggle, they spoke for about ten minutes then he went to the kitchen and made himself a light supper. Having lived on his own for so long he had become an expert tin opener and was able to put together a meal in minutes.

Returning to the study after watching the news, he lifted the second box onto his desk. About two hours later he suddenly stopped his fast scanning and went back a page to retrace the wording. Reading the text much more slowly now, he took in each and every word. The article was a confidential circular letter from UNSECP to heads of various major industrial companies around the world. It was obvious to Patrick, that most of the names being addressed, were the self-same companies that had been sinking enormous funds into UNSECP. He now had definite proof that these companies were somehow linked into the Culling Program being operated by United Nations. The letter explained that certain funds were being directed to UNSEDP for the development of special monitoring equipment for earthquake measurement and control. It was the word 'control' that had Patrick mystified.

"How on earth does one *control* an earthquake?"

He read on, the letter referred to vast sums required to develop the program and that further governmental support and funding would probably need to be forthcoming in due course. He now had two definite links, but still wasn't sure what the ultimate program was to entail. He marked the various lines and put the wad aside, separated from the existing two heaps. He found very little more by the time he decided to go to bed because his eyes felt as if they were being pushed out of their sockets from inside his skull. The last time he had spent so much time reading was when he was still a university student completing his accounting articles and final exams. He took a relaxing shower and then retired for the night.

"Did you find anything?" George had again been waiting in the car park for the arrival of Patrick's Porsche.

"I thought we agreed that you wouldn't become involved."

"I can't help being curious. I've spent several weeks breaking into their system and now I'm not even allowed to know what I've found. It somehow just isn't fair, is it?"

"I suppose it isn't. The only thing of real interest is reference to earthquake control. But we've managed to link the UN to various governments and this program is being carried out via industrial companies with their full knowledge, I presume with their full blessing."

"Nothing further on what their Culling Program consists of?"

"No. But it's early days yet. What about their computer trace?"

"I'll have a look this morning when I send in the inspector program. If they've managed to reach us in such a short amount of time, I'll be very surprised."

The two men walked towards the building, George was looking relaxed and fully recovered from his long spell at the computer. The weekend's break had done him a power of good, Patrick thought. He wondered what part of his private life had helped, if any. Later that morning George entered Patrick's office and smiled.

"The system is clear and nothing to report." He set down a large list of printouts in front of Patrick. The two men discussed normal business for some time before George left.

"Miss Han. Would you kindly send these printouts by special courier to Seoul."

This was a daily routine. Every day, all special documents and balances were sent to the directors in South Korea, this was done simply as a precautionary hard copy backup. Patrick felt a slight sense of relief that the American Bank hadn't been able to trace anything back to the Silver Beam computer. He met Kim at lunchtime and they had a pub lunch, having decided the previous evening to meet up like this every day. She made it clear that she had missed his being around on Sunday by telling him that she had got used to his being there every day.

At home that evening he continued to examine the long lists of text before suddenly finding what he had been searching for. Somebody at UNSECP had been extremely careless, either that, or else the thinking regards their program was so securely hidden, that nobody expected to be found out. Patrick leaned back in his chair.

"For Chrissake, how do they expect to get away with this?"

He took a long deep breath then reread the letter from UNSECP addressed to various heads of governments. The message and aims of UNSECP was quite explicit. His mind read the words carefully, but wouldn't accept their statement. He sat back and closed his eyes tightly.

"This must be some form of hoax, nobody would try this and hope to get away with it."

He could feel his heart pumping at nearly double its normal rate, now it was crystal clear just why they had gone to such extraordinary lengths to cover their tracks. Their plan was diabolical, he checked the printout again and again, each time reading the message out aloud and slowly. He was trying to accept what was written down in one of the opening paragraphs.

Security Private Memo : Highly Confidential Information

Direct Distribution to : Global Affiliates - Heads Only

"As committed participants of the Culling Program, we now need your government to earmark at least two billion dollars each over

the next two years in order to enlarge and expand research and development. As you are aware, we have already attempted several different investigative pilot schemes in the field of purpose having created industrial accidents such as Chernobyl, Servaiso and Bhopal. As well as this, we have now created a deadly chemical compound related to the AIDS virus that can be injected into foodstuffs. However, the main drawback being that both methods mentioned above are uncontrollable to a major degree. In order to cull a minimum of ten million human beings per annum under controlled circumstances and worldwide without arousing suspicion, we are going to have to find more stable method, an alternative solution to the problem.

UNSEDP have now started development of a new program initially instigated by the Russian Federation that simulated high intensity earthquakes made against United States of America.

This new programme is now codenamed "SWOP" (Save World Over Population). SWOP has had its initial feasibility trial run and all reports showed that the results were extremely encouraging and potentially stable and fully controllable.

As expected during that first trial run, although successful in terms of loss of life, remained uncontrolled incorrect targeting and impacting within the wrong country. The development of this program needs to become far more accurate and efficient. New trials begin shortly on a second SWOP feasibility earthquake project that will hopefully introduce far superior targeting methods. As agreed, most of the funding will eventually be regenerated back through those appointed companies (The Affiliates) involved with the manufacturing of components within these experiments."

Memo From : Head of UNSECP

Again Patrick sat back and breathed deeply.

"This is an organised human killing program. Ten million people a year, Hitler and Goebbels struggled to hide their deeds and then only managed six million in six years. How the hell do they expect to get away with it?" Patrick's body was still shaking, he decided not to go any further because he needed time to think and take this in. He moved to the drinks cabinet and poured himself a large whisky downing it one movement and then poured himself another.

"Why the hell did I have to pursue this?" His mind was spinning at a thousand miles an hour. trying to fathom out what he had just read and the consequences it was totally unbelievable, too large for him to comprehend at that moment. Governments, large business and world leaders were all in collusion to rid the planet of ten million people a year. No wonder they wanted it kept quiet he thought, questions came flooding thick and fast into his somewhat confused brain. Who was going to decide just who was going to die? Was the program aimed at only the Third World? How did ordinary men send their fellow humans to the slaughter yard? Were subversive elements going to be targeted? The self-questioning remained endless and he needed to know. If true, this problem was so huge that he needed to talk to somebody about it. But who?

"The only people that I can trust are George and Susan." He looked at his watch. Nine o'clock, he lifted the telephone and called.

"George. Sorry to call you so late, but I've got to talk to somebody or else I'll go mental. Could you come here tonight?" The voice at the other end agreed, Patrick gave necessary directions and George said he would be there within an hour.

"Here read this and then tell me if its my imagination." Patrick watched the man's face carefully and noticed sweat beads start breaking out on his companion's forehead as the full extent of the printout's enormity sank in. The Oriental's eyes, reduced to two thin slits, he put down the sheets of paper and placed his hand on the desk as a support to steady himself.

"I need to sit down."

"Let's go through to the lounge."

They went through and sat facing each other, he could tell that his companion's mind was reeling in desperate disbelief as his had done earlier in the evening. George's slightly yellowed complexion was now dull gray, Patrick couldn't help wondering whether he had gone through the same gamut of emotions and suffered as much mental torment as George was clearly undergoing now. He was still feeling somewhat shaky but could see that his Korean friend was taking it rather more badly than he had.

"Destroy it and forget you ever saw anything, that's my suggestion."

"Do you know what you're saying George?"

"I'm perfectly aware, we don't stand a chance against them. What started out as a hunt to find a massive fraudster, has now become something totally different. This is organised murder on an unprecedented scale... The idea of a madman."

"You mean you could let these bastards go unpunished? Just because they are more powerful than us and are backed by major governments, we let them gaily commit genocide on a scale never known to man. I couldn't live with myself if I walked away from it now. Could you?"

"Happily. These people have taken all sorts of expensive precautions to hide themselves. They are so devious that if you even tried mentioning it to anybody, you would simply be spirited away and never heard of again. It's as simple as that. Believe me, I know."

"I can't walk away, somebody, somewhere, will believe us when we show them this."

"Listen, Patrick. If you show anybody that letter and can't prove to them where it came from, you could at best find yourself in jail.

Don't forget, your government, my government and the most powerful governments in the world are all involved. It's a catch twenty two situation, you don't stand a chance against these people."

"What do you suggest then?"

"On Friday you gave me an instruction to trash everything, it's time for you to bow to your own words. Get rid of everything and then let's forget about the whole damned program." The man was clearly petrified and Patrick at that moment couldn't blame him.

"Want a drink?"

Patrick went to the drinks cabinet and poured himself another whisky, he also mixed a hefty vodka and coke for his companion. George's hand was shaking furiously as Patrick handed the drink to him.

"Don't worry. The same thing happened to me when I first read it. Now look." He held out his hand. It wasn't quite rock steady but it had relaxed. Possibly because he had already had five stiff whiskeys he admitted to himself.

"It will take an hour or so to sink in, then you'll start thinking somewhat differently. We can't let them get away with this, somehow we must attempt to stop them."

"No way! I don't want anything more to do with this, I'm out as of now. Patrick, don't be a fool, give up now otherwise you're dead." George lifted the drink and swallowed it in one go, just as Patrick had done. This time he went across to the cabinet and poured his own drink.

"Tell you what. Let's leave it for a few days before we do anything and then if you're still of the same opinion and I want to go forward, we'll go our separate ways. But don't dismiss it out of hand George because you won't be able to live with yourself if you just walked away."

"Just give me the chance, I'll walk."

"OK, that's got to be your decision but I'll continue reading the printouts and see if I can find anything else. I should be finished by the weekend, if by then, you decide to step out, I'll accept your decision gracefully." The two discussed the program for another hour, then George decided to leave Patrick.

"See you tomorrow."

Patrick watched the taillights disappear down the road and around the corner. There wasn't much traffic at that time of night, but unseen by anybody, another vehicle started up further down the road and roared away towards the corner.

"Silly maniacs." Patrick shut his front door and went back to the lounge to collect the empty glasses. "Mrs. Jones will go mad if I leave them here." In bed, he called Kim because he still felt that he desperately needed to talk to anybody. She had obviously been asleep before she answered the call.

"How's my favourite girl then?"

"Sleepy. How's it going?"

"At last I'm winning. Tonight, I've at last had my first breakthrough."

"Good. You're sounding far more your old self, but remember what I told you. Don't let it become an obsession."

He didn't know how to answer that, somehow he wasn't sure they were discussing the same subject. They spoke for another ten minutes before he hung up. There was no way he was going to be able to go to sleep; his overworked mind was still racing in this particular Grand Prix.

The Culling

CHAPTER TWELVE

As Patrick read through the many printout sheets the story became clearer, he could now picture in his mind what was happening and how UNSECP intended running their 'Culling Program'. Various governments were funding a major environmental scheme to rid the world of at least ten million people per year. He wasn't yet sure whether the main United Nations Committee was fully aware of the program. It seemed that this was a covert plan, devised and operated by several major members in order to regulate certain densely packed populations, while leaving others to freely expand. These members were about to play god with the human race, it seemed that the main cull was initially to be aimed at China, India and Indonesia. With another two million per annum being targeted at Africa, Eastern and Western Europe and lastly, a further million targeted at specific areas involved with terrorism. The main stumbling block facing the program was that the members were finding it difficult to devise a suitable method of killing that was acceptable while remaining untraceable. Patrick felt that they were still seeking to find the perfect but undetectable murder mechanism tool. So far, they had looked at creating wars among ethnic populations, wars across common boundaries, industrial accidents on a major scale and then a killing virus called NX2, which acted very much like the AIDS virus and being injected into the food chain. Now, they were researching natural disasters such as targeted earthquakes and development of hurricanes and tsunamis. The elite members of this club had appointed several major industrial companies within their countries to carry out the research and manufacturing processes for UNSECP. This fantastic dream to curb growth on earth had been set up several years before and they had realised that if their plan became public knowledge, the hue and cry caused worldwide would probably stop their efforts to balance the world's environment. Therefore, they had as few members as possible, all hand picked trustworthy companies, which would handsomely gain from the program, were allowed into the project. To safeguard themselves, government funding was passed through these company's accounts into a special bank account in New York under the UNSEDP heading. This account was quite legitimate as a development program on environmental matters for the United Nations. What was unknown, at the time was that this secondary and secret program had been set up to tackle the problem of overpopulation and how to reduce it. Nothing to date had worked and population explosion was taxing world resources. No matter how governments tried, they were unable to control this high production rate. Industry was being pushed to clean up the earth and yet, the same industrial companies were being forced to expand and come up with new products to satisfy the overpopulated human species. World resources were fast dwindling and the only way governments could find to combat this explosion was to introduce this obscene Culling Program.

Once they had managed to achieve an acceptable method of culling, their plan was to concentrate on poorer nations with rapidly expanding populations. Then later to move into areas like Western Europe and America. Wars created the easiest solution, but were unpredictable in their outcome, as well as having long-term complications. Industrial accidents tried out in Bhopal in India, Servaiso in Italy and Chernobyl in Russia weren't having the desired effect and became counter productive. The NX2 virus was ruled out because of the length of time that food could be stored and the unpredictability of it reaching the intended target. Also, this method was bound to attract unnecessary questions thought Patrick. Their next stage was to introduce a series of natural disasters that would be fast, efficient and non-detectable. This plan to master earthquakes, involved extremely heavy costs. The program intended achieving this chaos by creating a series of specialised earth tremors at exact points around the globe. These in turn would all be directed to a specific location that would weaken earth plates at that point.

With enough concentration, the plates would vibrate from the extreme pressures all meeting up simultaneously below the target area and a simulated earthquake would result possibly equal in size to the largest nuclear blast ever recorded.

One thing that caught Patrick's attention was that they had already managed to affect the first earthquake. The plan was set up and aimed at Northern India, but the earthquake was way off its intended target and took place in Southern Russia. UNSECP understood that much more development had to take place before they were able to control this exercise. They also learned from their first trial, that this was a viable solution, also feasible and that they could carry it through with a modicum of success. However, they needed to concentrate the accuracy of their experiments and the following year had been spent correcting the problem. The site pinpointed this time, according to the documents in Patrick's possession, was to be in lower Northern Iran. Mainly as a trial but also because of that country's refusal to halt their nuclear programme. Huge geological surveys had been taking place, with careful research planned to create massive sea explosions, which would cause lateral frequency earth tremors to reach this specific central point at once. The initial undersea explosions ranged from points in the Indian Ocean to a point near the South Pole and in the Atlantic Ocean. The explosion and ensuing tremors would then balloon outward in a single direction to travel away from the initial impact points just like ripples would flow across a quiet pond, the earth's crust would ripple outward just like the still pond surface. These explosions had to be timed to the last second with the distance of travel calculated exactly, so that the full force of these impacts came together at a specific point simultaneously when the resultant tremors converged and met together at the exact appointed position. If not, then what had happened in their last experiment, would occur again and could affect a position, continents away from their initially intended target.

This next experiment was going to be tried in an area with a smaller and less mountainous population. The reason Iran had been chosen, was that the governments concerned were being shunned by the Islamic Mullahs or leaders but more explicitly, they were backing global terror organisations and had refused to give up their deadly nuclear manufacturing programme hidden in an underground areas such as Datkerah and Traveh. The west needed a valid reason for being allowed into Iran once more, as far as Patrick could ascertain this intended earthquake would then force Iranians to ask for outside help.

The costs to carry out these development experiments was substantial, special explosives, monitoring equipment, backup vessels and specialist geological survey teams had to be covertly paid for. If they could perfect this method, they would be able to create wholesale slaughter in densely populated areas as well and without the world knowing that these natural disasters had been man-made.

These catastrophes would also open up large unpopulated areas which would then allow an individual government to repatriate its people there. This would help to release heavily burdened towns and cities from their overpopulated hardships.

The only unanswered question in Patrick's mind, was whether the main United Nations committee was aware of this diabolical plan within their confines. Somehow he doubted that anybody outside the band of elitist governments and industrial companies knew anything about what was being planned.

He finished reading all the printouts by Thursday evening and carefully placed most of them in their respective boxes while keeping the informative sheets aside. These he placed on the top of the last box and then placed all four under his desk out of sight.

Another thing worrying Patrick was that George Li had not attended work since Wednesday. Twice, he tried contacting him at home without success, his telephone just rang. He hadn't left any messages and nobody at the office had heard from, or seen him since Tuesday.

The Culling

Patrick drove to Wandsworth and easily found the road that George lived in, it was among a long line of semi-detached high-rise houses that had definitely seen better days. He parked his car around the corner before making his way to the address and knocking on the door several times. After ten minutes George's neighbour peered out and told Patrick that George had left on Tuesday evening, when he enquired whether George had left a forwarding address the old lady said that she had seen him and another man leave the building together, all she knew was that he was carrying a suitcase.

Patrick felt the hairs stand up on his neck, the disappearance of his colleague was a little too coincidental for his liking. On Friday night Patrick joined three friends and they went to the chess competition together, he was rusty and didn't do very well, although his team ended the evening as runners up and Patrick collected a trophy. He informed his companions that he no longer had any time to concentrate on chess competitions and therefore, he was resigning from the team. Afterwards he suddenly decided to go straight to Kim's place rather than on Saturday morning as previously arranged, up to that point he hadn't fully realised just how much he missed her companionship until now. Arriving at her house at eleven o'clock and finding the road packed to capacity with vehicles, he drove to the end of the block where he squeezed the Porsche into the tightest of parking spaces on the opposite side of the road, walked slowly towards the house. Before reaching it, he saw her front door suddenly open and light from inside silhouetted a man's frame in the doorway. He stopped dead because he recognised him immediately, the man turned back towards the light. He could see Kim in the hallway directly behind the man who said something before turning and walking towards Patrick.

As the man moved in his direction he wanted to turn and run, but instead he quickly faced towards the river before bending down pretending to tie a shoelace. He needn't have worried because the other man didn't quite reach him but instead got into his vehicle and drove up the road past Patrick. He risked a quick second look at the person in the car, there was no mistaking who it was driving the vehicle, it was Raymond Chen all right.

"What the hell do I do now?"

Was Kim having an affair with the man? Was this a business or social visit? He wasn't certain. He was sure that Raymond didn't know they were living together unless she had told him. His mind spun in its uncertainty, right then he couldn't decide whether to go in and confront her or whether to go home and arrive the following day, pretending to know nothing and wait to see whether she said anything. At the moment his blood was boiling and his brain jumbled picturing Kim treating Raymond in the same manner as she had him, worse still had it been in their communal bed. Shades of Sue having an affair rose from deep within, he felt the hate and jealousy rising once again to mix together with his already boiling blood. Patrick instantly knew that if he entered that house right now, his dormant temper would get the better of him and he would do something stupid, like kill Kim. Reasoning took over before he turned and walked to his car and moved off, driving slowly past the house he looked up and saw that the only light on, the one in their customary bedroom. Around the corner he pushed the pedal hard down to the floor, all the way back to Amersham he tried to vent his fury on the machine and cursed his luck that no police were on duty that evening. He felt like having a good scrap right now, him having been a glorious fighter in his young days needed somehow to vent his spleen on someone just then.

The little red light on his answer-phone was flashing as he entered the door, he pushed the button and Kim's voice was at the other end.

"Patrick, I trust your competition went well, would you please call me when you get in. It doesn't matter what time it is, please call me." His temper had softened somewhat, but he knew that to call now would be courting disaster. At times like this he could demonstrate a razor for a tongue that easily could offend. Going to the drinks cabinet, he poured himself a stiff whisky then sat in his favourite armchair, for a short while he turned up the volume on his stereo to almost full blast. The house almost shaking to the rhythm as the beat of his favourite band played on, so as not to disturb his distant neighbours, he switched across to using the large earphones, placing them on his head and turning off the main speakers. Next to him was a full bottle of whisky, he drank to excess that evening and the bottle was almost empty when he finally retired at three o'clock.

"Why didn't you return my call last night?" This was the first time that he had seen her in a foul mood.

"Well. We were runners up in the competition and everyone stayed on and had several drinks before going home."

"What time did you get home?"

"After midnight."

"That's a lie. I called at midnight, then at one, then at two and still the phone was on the machine." Patrick caught on the spot suddenly realised that he must have had the music on so loud that he hadn't heard the telephone. He decided to tell her what he had been doing. He smiled sheepishly as he spoke.

"I had earphones on and was listening to music, a relaxing way that I often do when I've been under stress. I must have missed your call." Her face pulled back tightly which told him that she thought his excuse was a poor one. He didn't blame her for her the sceptical look.

"Well, the reason I called, was to warn you that you may be receiving a visitor this morning."

"Who?"

"Raymond Chen came here last night. In a strange way your damned chess competition helped us, luckily you weren't around, otherwise we would have some explaining to do."

"What did he want?"

"Apparently one of your staff was contacted by some American bank to inform them that they had traced a virus in their system and when they tried to find it, it then led them back to our computer. He couldn't reach you, so he tried to find George Li but he's been away from the office since last Wednesday. So Chen came here to find out if I would help him have a look at the system. I told him that I wouldn't have any idea where to even start."

"That sounds a little far fetched, he knows something about us and so, what did he say then?"

"Nothing, he left, I think he went to find someone else who could have a look at the system."

"I better go to the office, I'll see you later today." He took her in his arms, the top of her head came up against his chest as she snuggled tightly against him.

"Promise, I was listening to music last night."

"OK. I believe you, thousands wouldn't. Go to the office, if Raymond is there watch what you say and I'll see you later." He drove to the office and found Raymond Chen and two of his staff seated in front of the computer stations.

"Patrick. I'm glad you came in, it seems that we have a problem which we can't seem to find."

"What's the matter?"

We had a tip off by somebody that thinks someone has placed a virus within our system. According to an American bank, their experts followed the virus trail straight to our computer."

What? "Have you put an inspection programme into the system

to see where it is?"

"Yes. But the strange part is it can't find anything. What do you think?"

"I don't know enough about the technical aspects, it could simply be another one of those damned bugs. It seems as if our computer has some kind of inbuilt fault, strange things appear and then disappear without trace. I could suggest treating the same way as before."

"This time I think there must be something there." Last time he had waved the matter aside very quickly. Patrick could see that the man was worried now.

"So what do we do about it?"

"There's not much you or I can do. But, I've called in a computer doctor, if anything is hidden in there, you can be sure he'll find it."

"Who's this expert?"

"He's name is Vladisky Ormon from a company called Heker Jong, they are the bank's accountants and apparently he has just the person we need, a computer whiz." Patrick smiled feebly as he felt the bottom of his world falling out.

"Our paths have crossed so if there's nothing more I can do here, I'm off for the weekend. Good hunting."

"See you on Monday." Raymond turned back to his computer terminal. Patrick hoped George Li had covered their tracks well enough.

"Where the hell are you George?" Patrick didn't want to face Ormon, but somehow knew he had to somehow stop the man's snooping or becoming involved with Silver Beam International.

"Just when things were going so well," he muttered to himself.

The Culling

CHAPTER THIRTEEN

"Steve Hearns here."

"Yes Steve, what can I do for you today?"

"We have a major problem. The bank has just called us and their system has closed itself down. It appears to have found an intruder or a virus but when we checked we couldn't find anything there at all."

"So what are they doing about it?"

"It's impossible for them to operate without their computer, so after doing a full security scan check and finding nothing, have given the all clear to continue to operate as normal."

"Right don't do anything; I'll be on the first flight out, I should be there just after midday your time." Vladisky Ormon replaced the receiver and called his secretary. He gave her quick instructions then left the office bound for Heathrow Airport. He always had a small suitcase packed with a change of clothing and other essentials required for just such a fast departure. The short balding man with heavy eyebrows was a Polish Jew that had been one of the lucky ones during the Second World War. His mother had had the foresight to fear a German invasion of Poland and had walked from their village to Gdansk. There, she managed to bribe a fishing trawler captain to take her as far as Holland and she then walked to France begging as she went, for food for her and the two babies. In France she sold away her last item of value, a large gold Star of David which had five diamonds mounted at the points. The sixth diamond had never been there as far back as her family could remember. The escape had been strenuous and Orman's baby sister had died from exhaustion shortly before them leaving for Britain. The boatman took her to England and left her on the

137

beach, she had one aim in life then and that was to reach the safety of her Cousin Rachael's house in London. Fortunately the boatman had drawn a little map naming all the towns from Dover to London for her. Being early morning she started pushing Orman's beat-up pram towards London and was lucky to be given a lift by a lorry heading in her direction. Armed with only an address she finally reached her goal, she had been a large buxom lady when she left her husband and two boys back in Poland and when she died two days after her arrival she was only skin and bone. Vladisky never forgave the Russians, Germans and Italians for the deaths of his entire family. His aunt Rachael became his mother and only friend, as a small boy he fully understood what had happened and vehemently vowed that he someday would have his revenge on the world. Now he was the principal partner in the firm of Heker Jong Associates, one of the largest management and account practices in Europe. It had large offices worldwide and Ormon had managed to take over some of the largest accounts with his clever manipulation and forceful skill. He hated his fellow man and his initial goal had never left him. The company had several major industrial companies on its books and when the UNSECP plan was devised, he was approached and asked to set up and control the financial systems for the entire project. Now, if somebody had placed a virus into their banking system, it could wreck years of hard work. He was almost at the point of obtaining his life's ambition, the power and means to kill off those people that had taken his family away from him.

"Right let's see what we've got."

After arriving in New York he had gone straight to the bank's computer room where he was now seated in front of one of the many computer terminals. He stretched and cracked his fingers before setting to work on the keyboard in front of him; it didn't take very long to ascertain that there had been something invasive lurking about in the UNSECP account.

"This wasn't a virus in here; someone was having a snoop

around the account."

"How do you know that?" An agitated Steve Hearns and a bank computer manager were seated on either side of him.

"A virus finds somewhere to hide in an account. It waits around sometimes for years and then on a specific command becomes activated. This activation can take many forms, from transferring funds, to wiping out all the data from the computer. If there were a virus here, I would have found it."

"Then how do you know somebody's been looking at the account?"

"Consider the inside of a computer being like a gigantic maze of passageways. Except each passageway has a message controlled by a gate at both ends. Each gate has a sign on it referring to the message inside. Nothing can pass through those gates unless it has the correct password. Then a message goes out from here and into the maze. This way, an instruction redirects itself down various passages until it reaches a final destination. When it gets there, sometimes the gate is open and the message inside is relayed to the screen. Other times the gate is not only closed but locked as well, in order to unlock it, you need a special password. Once you've given the word, it allows you in and then out again. But what most thieves do is take the information then close the gate behind them. What they can't, and don't do is lock the gate behind them again. If it were a virus, then it wouldn't normally leave the passageway and if it did then the Inspector Programme would be able to follow it through the various gates until it was found. Do you understand?"

"Fascinating, but if it's not a virus, then who's been in to look at the account?" The bank official was out of his league in these security matters.

"Hackers probably. Possibly they are looking for a way into the United Nations computer because it is linked to most important computers around the world. These hackers find the security files and sometimes sell the information. What we have to do is check that these hackers haven't transferred some of your bank's funds to their account. If not, then we have to find out what they were looking for."

For several hours the short man searched through, trying to locate the reason for the hackers' entry into the bank's computer system.

"They've taken nothing and they haven't gone on from here, so they've retraced their steps back to where they've come from."

"So what do we do now?"

The relieved bank official leaned back in his chair. They had spent the whole day searching, checking and re-checking the data banks, it was well past closing time and he wanted to get home.

"We go hunting to see where he's gone, but first I must put a special programme into the system, so that the hacker can't get in again."

Ormon began tapping away, and after two hours sat back in his chair. He was absolutely shattered mainly because his own time clock was still tuned to British time and he had gone for forty hours without sleep.

"There. That bastard won't get back in here; your bank is now as safe as houses. I'll need to come back tomorrow and spend some time until I know where the hacker originated from."

"Be my guest. I'll arrange a room for you two to be able to complete you uninterrupted work."

"Steve. Will you drop me off at the hotel? I've still got a lot to do." He worked through the weekend and on until Tuesday when he suddenly came across one of the false trails George Li had put in. Working methodically he slowly followed the programme until he found the trail leading to Yale University.

"These hackers are looking for information. If they're going through university computers then they are using them as a hub to get into governmental projects. Still, let's see what they're searching for. Whoever's on the other end, knows their business and we can't leave anything to chance."

Ormon spent Tuesday searching until he reached the NASA Space Program. He followed the trail into the program for another two days, searching and finding nothing.

"They haven't done anything in here, now I wonder why? Because there is a mountain of information that someone searching for could possibly find, my gut feel is that I think that they have possibly brought us into a dummy trail to confuse matters. It's time to go back and start all over again." By Thursday morning he had found what he was looking for, it was another trail. He followed it until he reached the FBI computer.

"This is more like it, probably the FBI have somehow cottoned onto the UNSECP program, then we could be in real trouble. Let's see what they've found out, so we'll be able to cover our tracks." He entered the FBI computer and searched, for the next two days he went through everything he could find.

"Nothing. I don't think it was them either, as far as I can see, they aren't looking for anything either, it must be that damned hacker laying false trails. He's clever. OK, then back to the beginning again. I'll find this bastard if it's the last thing I do."

Then he eventually found a trail to Silver Beam (London) International and followed it down the line once again.

"Nothing, again a dead end trail. Whoever these hackers are, they don't give away much. Let's start again."

For another two days he searched and found nothing. He had

done everything possible in his power and was certain that he was now wasting his time searching anything further. He had either found somebody technically cleverer than himself; the alternative was there really was nothing in the system to find.

"He's disappeared, I think its Checkmate."

"Is that the end of it now?" Steve had sat and watched his superior meander through the most secretive files on earth with the ease and grace of a ballet dancer.

"Let's have a quick look into UNSECP system and see that everything's in order."

He tapped away for a few minutes.

"Shit! Why didn't I do this in the first place, it's the most obvious, somehow whoever it is, has also gained entry into the programme and had a good rummage through everything." He spent the day following the trail that again led him through Berkeley University to Yale University and back to the dead end trail at the back.

"What they've done is found the account then come into the UNSECP programme route by another route. When they finished looking about, they've then laid off several false trails to disguise themselves. We've been here before so my guess is that the NASA Space Program and the FBI systems were both simply smoke screens to confuse us. That leaves us with just Silver Beam International; I think we have to have a good look at it again." Steve looked thoughtful for a moment then scratched his cheek.

"Why would somebody who's already part of the UNSECP programme go to all this trouble to look at the files."

"What?"

"They're part of the program. It's dealt through by a South Korean Government company."

"That's it. The key is via South Korea, what the hell is the hacker doing? He would have taken the trail back to South Korea if he had taken their name off the UNSECP file. Somebody in their London operation is the hacker. We've got to stop him quickly." Steve picked up the telephone and called a number known only to him.

"Who's the contact at Silver Beam International?" He waited for a few minutes while the person on the other end checked. Then he wrote down the number, again he dialled.

"Let's see if they're at work yet, it may be too early for them. Hello, is this Silver Beam International? Can I talk to a Mr. Raymond Chen please?" Steve listened for a while then was connected to someone else. Again he asked for Raymond Chen, then replaced the receiver.

"Guess what? Mr. Chen is still in London. How convenient for us."

"Get him on the line." Steve called London and was given the man's after hours telephone number. Again he dialled.

"Mr. Chen? This is Steve Hearns in New York, code number AA2211/C. Please check it out and call me back at this number." He replaced the receiver and waited the telephone rang.

"Mr. Chen, I would like you to speak to Mr. Ormon my financial controller." Steve handed the instrument across to Ormon.

"Hello, Mr. Chen, we have a major security breach problem, it would seem to end at your company's London computer terminal. I think you and I have to have a careful look at it and quickly, you already know what's at stake if this information is leaked or corrupted." Ormon waited as the man on the other end asked certain questions.

"What I want you to do, is get your best operators on to the job. Have you got a virus detector or inspector programme?" He waited.

"That's OK. Just get them to send in the inspection programme for the moment, then don't let anybody near the machine until I get there. I'll leave now, expect me tomorrow morning at your offices. Before anybody can change anything we must check out your computer. If the offender is there, I'll find it." Ormon replaced the receiver.

"Steve. Get me to the hotel and then to the airport, we've done everything necessary that we can from here at the moment." He just managed to catch the last flight that day to London. Ormon was worried, if the program was leaked to the outside world his entire life's work would immediately be destroyed. His thinking right then was if he could only reach the person, he would make sure that they died a horrible death. He had initially instigated this Culling Program and so it was all his and he had no intention of letting some hacker interfere with his life plans. Those peasants that had taken away his family were going to be made to suffer and feel what it's like to lose their loved ones, Right now the hacker was in big trouble, he was going to stop them. One more person added to the death program was neither here nor there. Ormon reclined his seat into the bed position, lay back and tried to get to sleep.

CHAPTER FOURTEEN

"What's the matter? All weekend, you've looked like a dog that's lost its favourite bone."

Patrick had spent the rest of his weekend in a state of panic that had quickly begun turning to fury. The thought of Vladisky Ormon poking around his department again was becoming too much for him to bear, they had just returned from a trip to the Malvern Hills, where they had a lunch and a super day out. Their standing ritual of going somewhere different each Sunday, to some beauty spot to have lunch had only been broken once.

"It's Raymond Chen. He's bringing in Ormon to check the computer for viruses and I thinking that we didn't exactly part on the best of terms so this is going to be tricky, the thought of him at Silver Beam is too much for me to bear."

"You're joking of course."

"I wish I was, that little bastard has somehow managed to wheedle his way in and by this afternoon I could be out of a job."

"How come?"

"Part of my contract states that there will be no interference from any source whatsoever and that I'm free to take whatever steps deemed necessary. I've decided that this morning both he and Raymond Chen be evicted from my department. If I don't stand up for myself today, they'll walk right over me."

"Don't you think that's a slight bit rash."

"If it is, then they can go over my head, my feeling is that either the main board supports me, or it fires me. I simply cannot have these two involved after all the work that I have set up." Patrick knew he had to act quickly mainly because he wasn't absolutely

145

certain that George Li had managed to disguise their activities. Somehow this insignificant little man had managed to detect the source of the hacker and now stranded without George, Patrick felt vulnerable and that he had to put a stop to their enquiries. The only course open to him was to try to assert what authority he had left to him.

"The chairman may question your motives." Kim knew that in a South Korean company, what came from the top was always carried out without question. What she didn't know was whether Patrick with his Western background or Raymond, a long serving government employee had the full backing of the board. She understood that he was taking a terrific gamble.

"Kim, I cannot have full authority on one hand and no authority on the other. This time I've got to stand up and make my position clear so if the board overrides my decision this first time, then I'm nothing but a skivvy to the company."

"I suppose you're right but I would suggest that you do it gently and without both guns blazing. Rather you should be calm down, have a look at what they're up to, then order them out and take over yourself. That way Raymond Chen doesn't lose face and as you are fully aware, us Orientals can stand anything but, we cannot take losing face very well. If you force Raymond Chen to leave by causing a scene, or without mutual agreement then you better be very careful. He's a powerful enemy to have against you."

"Raymond, can I see you in my office a minute." Patrick walked into the office and as he passed Raymond and two operators he made his request.

"Sure." The man followed in his footsteps as Patrick held his door open and when Chen had passed through, closed it.

"Please bring me right up to date, have you managed to find any viruses or anything out of the ordinary?"

"Not yet, but we're still looking."

"We? Meaning who exactly?" Chen made a sweeping motion with his arm and then pointed to the female computer operators that he had been sitting next to.

"The three of us as well as a Mr. Ormon from Heker Jong Associates. He told us that he knew you and that he will be in a little later."

"Do you mean you've spent the whole weekend searching through the system and there are no bugs to be found?" He could see that the man was feeling rather sheepish at the moment so Patrick pushed home his attack.

"I know Mr. Vladisky Ormon very well, he is one of the most incompetent person that it has been my misfortune to work with. The fact that he has also revealed a massive chip on his shoulder to me and others also, that he always created problems for others does that not worry you? As well as that, you've found nothing after two days of searching, I think that enough time has been given to find if there was anything affecting our security and nothing has shown up. Where did you get the information that there was some kind of virus entering our system anyway?" Patrick was quite aware that Chen had been tipped off from outside. Chen just didn't have the necessary experience and know how to find something as complicated as this so the warning had to have come directly from Ormon. Possibly that's what the sudden departure to America had been about.

"By the time the American bank came onto us, one of your staff had already told Mr. Kang that he suspected that there was a virus in the system." He looked at Patrick, trying to find a way out of the questioning.

"Who is this person? I want to know why they discuss this department's affairs with outsiders to the department and not approach me. Whoever it is no longer works here as of this

147

minute."

"I think it was Mr. George Li."

Patrick knew immediately that this was a lie because George had already expressed his total dislike for Kang to Patrick. He said that Kang was just a Korean lackey who would tell tales about his own brother to cover his own inability.

"When did he tell him this?"

"Last week, I think."

"Right, I'll have a word with him when he returns to work but until then I would prefer to run my division as I see fit. In the meantime I will keep a clear eye on the whole system and if anything whatsoever appears, I promise you, you'll be the first to know. Can I leave it to you then, to contact Heker Jong and inform them that we do not need their services?"

He knew that by putting it this way he had given Chen the necessary let out.

"Why don't we give them one more chance to have a look for this virus?"

"No. I do not want them or anybody else for that matter, having free license to search through this company's most guarded information, it just would not be right.. If there was anything amiss and it at least could be corroborated then perhaps. But for some pure speculation, no, I'm not going to have total strangers in this section. You've done your work as security and found nothing. Now, I insist that until anything shows up on the system that we be allowed to get on with our work without hindrance. This department reports directly to the chairman on a daily basis, if we are not allowed to carry this through then you can be assured the chairman will be asking some very direct questions. I will have to give direct answers and will not be able to excuse you from stopping our work and I do not want to do that." Patrick knew that he had used a typical chess move. The man opposite had fallen into his own trap and there was nowhere for him to go. He had to capitulate gracefully.

"All right. I'll call Mr. Ormon straight away, but if you even suspect anything, I need to know immediately." He had made his point but could do nothing about it. He rose and left Patrick's office, the two helpers followed him away.

Back in his office, Chen called Ormon and told him what had happened. Vladisky Ormon was furious and did not tolerate being told what or what not to do and immediately insisted on being allowed to come and inspect the system. When told that he wouldn't be allowed to, he furiously told the security man what he thought about him.

Raymond Chen knew full well that Patrick had the full backing of the chairman and if he tried to force any type of confrontation with him, he would end up being the sorry loser. With the barrage of abuse that had poured down the line he then took an instant disliking to the little man at the other end of the line.

"Mr. Ormon. There is no need to get personal, what Mr. Rodgers says regarding his financial division has the full support of the South Korean board of directors. Unless you can prove the Silver Beam connection, I suggest we handle this in different fashion."

Ormon swore, he had some of the world's top governments behind his scheme and didn't need to be told how to conduct himself. If necessary, he would make sure that Patrick was relieved from his post by the senior minister responsible in the South Korean Government. Chen decided not to argue and told the man to use that route; because it was the only way they were going to be able to shift Patrick. Ormon replaced his receiver and immediately sent an email letter to UNSEDP and a copy to his South Korean contact, asking them to get in touch with him. By sending it to the development program with a special coding number, he knew that the head of Culling Program would contact him immediately. He pushed the button on his intercom.

"Get me the file on Patrick Rodgers." A few minutes later, his secretary walked into his office carrying a pink folder, he took it from her and started going through it line by line. Twenty minutes later he scribbled something onto a yellow pad.

"I'll show you Mr. Bloody Rodgers, you can't screw around with me." Again he pushed the button on his intercom.

"Tell the terrible idiots I want to see them here immediately." Ten minutes went by before the men he referred to arrived at his door. Both were over six foot tall with seemingly Herculean physiques.

"You wanted us, Mr. Ormon."

"I wouldn't have called for you if didn't want you, bonehead." He watched the man flinch. The two knew that he could have them sent away forever because they both longed for the day when they would be able to take him apart, piece by slow piece but, for the moment they had to endure his caustic jibes.

"Here. Take this." Ormon handed over the slip of paper to the redhead. Ivan examined the scribbled note his flaming ginger beard bristled as he chewed on his lip while reading it.

"Go there and see what you can find, what I'm looking for is a computer. Make it look like an ordinary burglary. Do what you normally do, mess it up a bit, make them think it was done by some of these filthy black punks." This time it was the turn of the other man to boil because he was black, with a massive scar running from one ear, across his chin and around to the other ear. He knew from experience that the little man was goading him in particular and breathed deeply, but would loved to have taken the man's head between his hands and squashed it like a lemon. Both he and Ivan had discussed how they could tear the limbs off this detestable little coward, if only they could lay their hands on his files and were sure that he didn't have anything to blackmail them with. One day though, they were sure they would get that opportunity and when they did, they both knew they were going to enjoy every moment of his demise.

"Now get out. I don't want to see you two idiots until the job is done." As they turned to the door, each caught the other's eye, they both knew what the other was thinking at that moment. They hadn't risen to his baiting as they normally did, Orman clicked his tongue as he always did when he was in a foul temper. He lifted his receiver and called Silver Beam again, then asked to talk to Miss Lee. Maybe he could get her going.

"Miss Lee, this system your company sold to my client is a load of crap, get your so-called experts in there and try to get it working properly. Why that idiot ordered your system instead of sticking to a reliable British or American system, I'll never know.

Kim infuriated the man even more by not arguing or talking back, she simply took every insult he could hurl at her in her stride. Replacing the receiver, he started thinking about who else he could vent his spleen on.

"Bloody Rodgers." The man had beaten him for the moment and he did not take second place to anybody. Again he lifted the pink file, he had been searching for some dirt, anything with which he could use against Patrick.

"Right. We'll have to make up something to discredit you Mr. Rodgers." Suddenly a cruel smile crossed his thin lips, adjusting his oversized spectacles he then rubbed the thinning patch on his head. "If there isn't a virus there right now, then what's to stop me putting one in another on, that'll get him out of the way very quickly."

He started scribbling notes and putting them into the file. He pressed the intercom button.

"I need an urgent message sent to Steve Hearn in New York." His secretary again entered the office, notebook in hand. "Arriving New York, same flight as my last trip. Collect me at the airport. Arrange use of bank's computer for two hours, look forward to seeing you then. Regards Ormon."

The girl left the office and he immediately collected his overnight bag from the cupboard, before placing the pink file in his briefcase.

"All right. Let's go and crucify that sonofabitch." Vladisky Ormon left the office and headed straight for Heathrow Airport.

At the bank with Steve Hearns he again entered into the Silver Beam computer in London, quickly working through several accounts he found the one he was looking for. He opened the pink folder on the desk and entered instructions to the computer, it didn't take long before he was satisfied with his work. Steve watched in amazement.

"That's brilliant, you've got him over a barrel. Let's see Mr. Rodgers talk his way out of that." Ormon finished his work and shut down the bank's computer.

"I'll teach that bastard." Steve felt the shudder up his spine as he saw the cruel smile cross Orman's face. He made a mental note to never cross the man.

CHAPTER FIFTEEN

"Right then. We'll call this one 'Operation Christian,' the location is in Central Iran. The pinpointed area is Traveh that is in central northern Iran quite close to or near the salt mining areas southwest of Teheran. Last time we missed our target completely and were too far to the north, let's try and get it right this time. We envisage a mortality rate of to be only about between ten and twenty thousand people."

Steve Hearn had just flown in from New York via Denver Colorado, then by helicopter to the base and was now seated at a long table with his advisors. The group all understood what huge ramifications their experiments were going to have on the world. Only one scientist among the group had been there for trials of the first American fission bomb in 1945. He knew what their work entailed and how quickly the second world war with the Japanese Army had been brought to a close with the bombing of Hiroshima. Now he was still one of the old guard that had no qualms about carrying out these latest tests. In his mind, he was a scientist, only working for the good of all mankind and their continued survival. The rest were all of a younger generation with one main purpose in their lives at present and that was to rid the world of unnecessary humans who were fast destroying the planet and its resources. They all agreed that if the population explosion was left unchecked, it would only be a matter of time before the world faced crisis point. Already the ozone layer was being slowly destroyed, and with Third World countries changing from agricultural societies to manufacturing operations, the speed at which the crisis would arrive was alarming. The only country that had curbed growth to date was China with its one child per family policy. Even that, was coming to an end and with the large changes of the communist government the sleeping giant was fast stirring and gaining on the United States of America.

Pressure was such that the world's population would double

every ten years from the turn of the century, as it was, mankind in certain areas were already struggling to feed itself. More food meant more chemicals having to be produced, which in time, would find its way into the ecological system. This would quickly hasten the demise of all natural resources and force the world to strip yet untouched areas in its search for more resources and larger spaces for breeding of animals. Eventually scientists could see the earth becoming one massive desert as the rotation processes became effective. All of this self-inflicted carnage was being forced upon the planet because the only animal remaining unchecked was man. Increasingly poorer nations would be placing pressure on richer nations to supply food and funds, even though their populace would continue to grow. Everybody realised that something had to be done, yet nobody had been prepared to take the lead. When several major environmentalists came with a joint plan to start culling humans, it had been welcomed behind closed doors by several important governments. The only problem was how to go about it without the massive outcry that this would inevitably bring. One of the main leaders showed them a blueprint plan of how this could be done covertly with the knowledge of all governments concerned.

Steve Hearn had been made projects co-coordinator of the program and Vladisky Ormon the financial co-coordinator. The two men worked closely together, whenever Steve needed funds, it was Ormon's duty to approach the parties concerned. The project had taken the environmental blueprint and looked at all aspects of war. First, with links into various countries through the United Nations, they had helped start several conflicts. This was time consuming and the results not always controllable. Next they worked on a series of controlled accidents at major industrial plants. Chernobyl was a large success in terms of clearing major tracts of land. Fatalities though, were not high in the short term and because of natural events and unpredictable spreading, they found that areas were affected that they hadn't wanted touched.

A scientist by the name of David Spielman had started work

monitoring disasters, and claimed that he could copy these natural phenomena. Steve heard of these reports, and decided to visit Spielman at his small laboratory in Israel. He flew to Tel Aviv, then was driven to the town of Beersheba where he met David Spielman for the first time. The small hotel didn't have any properly working air conditioning and Steve was sweating profusely as he was introduced to the short balding man wearing thick bottle end glasses. He was exactly what Steve imagined a genius nuclear scientist would look like from comics that he had read as a youngster. Spielman was a strange looking man, and his shiny head was almost as pointed as an egg pinnacle above the wide eye stare which were enhanced by the thick round glasses.

"I've heard some wonderful reports about your work Dr Spielman, but I must say, we are more than a little sceptical."

"Why, don't you think it's possible to simulate Mother Nature?"

"In a report that I have received, you claim that you're able to make any earthquake happen at a nominated place. That's what we find impossible to believe." The little man's brown tanned skin went red as his jowls filled out. He reminded Steve of a large bullfrog about to blow up.

"So you want proof, then tomorrow you come to my laboratory and I'll show you evidence." They made arrangements to meet outside the hotel at five the next morning. Steve wished that he had stayed at a decent hotel in Tel Aviv with air conditioning and modern facilities. This town wasn't built for tourists and he found he couldn't sleep because of the closeness and high humidity. David Spielman looked as weary as Steve felt when he collected him the next morning.

"I've not had any sleep setting up an experiment for you to see. We head south into the Negev desert where I conduct my trials. Fortunately the government financed some of my ideas; otherwise, I would never have reached this stage. You are not the only one that doesn't believe my theories Mr. Hearn."

For nearly two hours they bumped and pitched along an almost indistinguishable track until they reached a small concrete building, it was miles away from anything. Steve was surprised when they entered the tiny building. Air conditioning cooled the sweltering heat so that as they walked into the little building Steve found himself sucking in breath because of the cold. In the middle were stairs leading down to a basement bunker where David Spielman and two women scientists carried out their controlled experiments.

"This is where my wife, Ilona and my daughter Beth have helped me fulfill my lifetime dream, the only problem is that it would take millions of dollars to carry out a full project of any sizable scale and my government have far more pressing areas to be funded."

"How does your theory work?"

"Oh, it's not just theory Mr. Hearn and I intend to carry out a proper trial for you today. After we've had something to eat and drink, I intend to show you exactly how my so called is put into action, you will find out with your own eyes that it works."

At midday the two men got back into David's vehicle and drove about six hundred yards out into the boiling desert. Steve noticed several bomb craters holes as they drove to a spot where several old trucks and junk had been piled up into a towering heap. Next to that were piled stones and rubble that had been scooped from the earth and loosely stacked up.

"Just for hypothetical reasons, we have to imagine that this debris is a town or city and it is our central target. Do you agree?"

"Yes I suppose so."

"Now walk with me."

Steve calculated that they walked outwards from the piles for about one hundred and fifty yards before David stopped.

"This is where we placed the first detonator, this little capsule contains the radio that'll set it off. You won't even hear it when it goes off."

"How come?"

"Ah, that's my secret for the moment and when somebody pays me to develop this further then, and only then will I release my secret. Come walk with me." They walked in a large arc to several more locations where David then inserted capsules into the waiting canisters. Steve could see as they moved around that the canisters seemed to be at different distances from the central pile of debris. It seemed to him that the positions were randomly picked for the purpose of David's demonstration.

"There, all five are in place now, let's go and have something to drink, it's getting very hot out here." The freezing orange juice straight from the refrigerator almost burnt Steve's throat.

"Now we're all ready for the trial, I suggest we go up top so that you can film it in-situ as it happens. The women both know exactly what to do because we've carried out the experiment so many times that we can almost do it blindfolded." They made their way back into the intolerable heat and walked a short way towards the distant pyramid of junk.

"Here this should be about close enough for you to watch without feeling the tremor. You need to record this and we don't want your camera to seem as if you had the shakes. Do we?" Spielman smiled at his own joke.

They were about two hundred yards from the large pile when David spoke into his hand held radio telling Ilona to start the trial. Steve lifted his camera to his eye and adjusted the lens, determined to capture the experiment in every detail. David gave Steve a running commentary as to what to expect.

"The detonators are being set off at different intervals by radio sound waves. All you might hear is a dull thud as they explode, keep your eye firmly fixed on the pile, don't take your camera away. It may seem as if nothing's happening, but don't take your eye off it."

Steve heard a slight thump somewhere to his left, a few more and then nothing. For about five minutes everything remained still and he was just about to give up, when suddenly the heap just seemed to explode outward and collapse from within as it came tumbling down in a great surge. Fascinated, he watched the debris and junk being smashed to the ground until nothing was left standing in its original position.

"Jesus! What the hell happened there? One minute nothing and the next, well, it just sort of blew up. Did you have some form of explosive inside that stack?"

"Not at all. If you would like to help me rebuild it anywhere around here, I'll carry out the trial again so that you can see there was nothing placed in the middle."

"But how did you achieve that chaos?"

"By lateral frequency tremors from the detonators. Don't ask me to explain any technical details, but at least you now know that my theories work."

For two days Steve helped David rebuild the centre pile twice times, only to see them flattened as if by some magic illusion.

The whole trick was somewhere to be found in the small electronic charge placed around the centre spot. David took exceptional care to place these at differing fixed distances from the debris once it had been piled high. They were not simply placed randomly as Steve had first suspected.

"This is fantastic, it's exactly what we've been searching for, you must come to America and demonstrate it to our scientists."

"No, if you want me to come to America then you will first have to bring your people here to witness my experiments. All this has cost a lot of time and money to perfect, anything else does not count, if you want to take it on board it needs to be funded properly. I insist that I head up any operation to expand any trials, but it will need vast sums of capital, possibly running into billions to fund the program correctly."

"The money is no problem if you're able to guarantee the required results.

"Could you carry out this type of work from one central monitoring point and make that happen anywhere in the world?"

"I don't see any reason why not. All this is a mock-up of the real and larger trials, larger resources would allow us to spread the whole program on a worldwide basis."

"Right answer. I'm going back to America immediately to report my findings and by next week I'll be back here with a team to see what you're achieving here. In the meantime could you put together some form of study and costs so that when they're finished checking, we'll be able to move to the next step as quickly as possible."

David could see that Steve was both excited and still somewhat confused by what he had learned over the last three days. For the first time in all of his trials, he felt that possibly this man confronting him could hold the key to develop his lifetime theories a lot further.

Two weeks later Steve and three scientific accomplices together with Ormon Vladisky arrived in Israel to be shown a further series of trials. The scientists were impressed with the results and confirmed that David Spielman had come up with the solution to their problem if the tests were proved on a much broader scale. Vladisky went through some rough calculations that David Spielman had put together and then when the trials were almost over asked David and Steve to join him.

"These figures are a load of rubbish. You calculate that it will cost roughly a billion dollars to perfect this experiment, being very conservative, my calculations show that it will be between four and six times that amount at least." Steve could see that David was starting his bullfrog trick again and was about to explode.

"Bullshit! I know what the costs will be, I've been through them often enough to work them out in my bloody sleep. If you don't like it then you better pack up now." Steve looked at Vladisky and felt that their answer was about to slip away from them. He had been dealing with these learned men for long enough to know that their pride didn't allow them to be wrong unless proved.

"Wait a minute now David. I think that all that is being said, is that if we are going to do the thing correctly, then we have to spend vast sums on the project rather than skimp." Vladisky had wanted to see how far he could push David and hadn't expected the sudden outburst.

"All I'm saying is that your cost for buildings, ships, computers, back-ups and so on, are way out of line. What I've been doing while you and the others were playing with your toys was to do a cost control exercise. This project done properly, is going to cost at least four billion dollars."

"So, what now?" asked David.

"We approach our principal funders and acquire ten billion dollars just in case the experiment fails and we have to look at alternative schemes."

"What! Failure is impossible, you've seen the evidence for yourself. How can it fail?" Steve could see the David was starting to become het up once again and knew that he had to separate these two because every time they had come into contact the two short men became like terriers fighting over a bone. Ormon enjoyed goading people and David Spielman took the bait almost every time. Much more of this and Steve was worried that David would simply pull out and find someone else to sponsor his project.

"Right, Ormon. We leave today, you let me know when the money's in position and in the meantime I'll negotiate terms with David and the Israeli Government to transfer this project to America."

Later, when David was alone with Steve he said something that convinced the project leader that he had acted just in time.

"Part of my terms will be that that man will never be allowed anywhere near me or the site at any time. I don't like him and he'll cause upheaval and disrupt the project so, if you and your sponsors cannot live with that condition then we don't have a deal."

Steve left Israel with a lot on his plate, he had to sell the scheme to the various governments and Vladisky was not allowed anywhere near the intended project. It wasn't going to be easy.

The Culling

CHAPTER SIXTEEN

"Terry? It's a voice from your past, bet you can't guess who?" Patrick waited as the other voice tried several suggestions on the end of the line.

"Not even warm, it's Patrick Rodgers." His friend laughed and for a while the two brought each other up to date with their lives and what had happened in between their schooldays and the present.

"Can we meet up sometime this afternoon? I'll buy you a beer and give you the story of a lifetime." The voice immediate changed pitch from old friend bantering to the status of editor of the "Daily Informer." His professional curiosity immediately wanted to find out what the basics were, Patrick refused to be drawn, not knowing whether Raymond Chen had the office telephones tapped or not.

"Believe me, I wouldn't have called you unless there was something of substance here. You must remember that at school I would take punishment for my principles, It's punishment time again because this has the same type of feel, kind of earth shattering and bearing a very serious principle at stake right now and trust me, knew you have to be interested."

"All right. I'll see you this afternoon a six at the Lazy Dog in the Strand."

Patrick replaced the receiver and lifted the heavy pile of computer printouts on his desk feeling a slight amount of smugness creeping in. He was about to put paid to that little man from Heker Jong.

"My god! This journalistic life has taken its toll of you old friend, it must be all those newspaper parties that's given you that paunch." The two gave each other a firm embrace. Terry had gone to seed, his blonde hair now receded into a monk's fringe and

Patrick noticed the yellowing nicotine-stained fingers pointing at his stomach had thickened with time. The man had never been tall as such but now, he was almost as wide as he was short and he tended to waddle rather than walk.

"That, my son, cost a lot of money to create, so don't mock it." The two laughed heartily as Patrick ordered the drinks, they moved to a private corner table. Terry was greeted by just about everybody in the room because this was his normal watering hole also the place where he spent most of the time away from his office. For several minutes they discussed their happy schooldays. The two had shared a room for three years and had become very close and good friends, Terry even remembered how upset Patrick always became with his untidy habits and persistent sloppiness. In those days, like a nagging wife, Patrick had always cleaned up behind him, yet although they differed in their personal hygiene, the two had got on extremely well.

"Now, what's this mind-boggling story that's going to make me famous all about? Wait, first let me get the next round in." Patrick watched his friend waddle to the counter. The man's habits hadn't changed in all these years, outwardly he had always been a bit of a mess, but his brain was undimmed and now seemed even sharper than ever. He addressed that brain as the fat man once again settled himself into a comfortable position in the corner to listen to Patrick's story.

"Before I start, everything I tell you now must be treated in confidence and my name kept out of it. Understand?" Terry nodded.

"It all started when we came across huge unexplained amounts of money that appeared in our accounting system. We decided to check it out."

For two hours Patrick told his friend everything that he knew right up to the present. Terry didn't interrupt once and only occasionally scribbled a note into his small pad. When Patrick had finished, he slowly shook his head from side to side.

"Every once in the lifetime of a journalist, a story of such magnitude comes along that is totally unbelievable. It takes a good nose to realise whether to run with it or not. If I didn't know you as well as I do, I would have walked away now thinking you were a total crank."

"Thanks very much."

"I need to see those printouts with my own eyes. Also, I need to talk to this George Li. Do you have any idea where he is hiding out?"

"None whatsoever, and he is the only person with the knowledge to prove everything to you. What he was doing and how he broke the codes is a total mystery to me, I wouldn't even know where to start with computer hacking."

"I'll set my dogs adrift, they will keep trying to find out where he is, we have our ways. Now let's go and collect those documents, they need to be kept in a safe place, believe me when I tell you this." Patrick called Kim and told her that he was going to pick up something in Amersham for an old school friend he had bumped into and he could hear the disbelief in her voice when he told he would be late. She said angrily that she had been stupid to believe that he had finished with this Amersham business. Terry also made a call to someone, but said that because he was a bachelor, he didn't have anyone to worry about. His messy lifestyle could remain in chaos and he liked it that way.

Patrick said they would take his car, and then he would drop Terry back in London on his way back to his girlfriend's house. On the way the men happily recounted major events of their school life.

"Nice. So this is how the other half live." Patrick opened the front door and allowed his guest to walk through ahead of him.

The Culling

"Jesus! I thought my place was a mess." Patrick stood looking at the entrance hall and beyond. His mouth fell open as he gazed at the wreckage that had once been his pride and joy.

"Christ! Bloody vandals, look at what they've done. Don't touch anything." Surprisingly the phone was still intact and Patrick immediately called the police and reported the incident. He moved through to his study and looked under the arch in his desk which had been scarred and the leather inlay torn to shreds. His heart sank.

"Terry!" The friend's face was completely calm and devoid of any emotion. He had been in far worse situations than this and was studying everything with a trained reporter's eye. Terry went back to the telephone and called his office.

"What's the address here?" Patrick told him. After he heard Terry complete the call he shouted to him.

"They've taken the boxes. Everything's gone."

"C'mon let's have a look around. A common thief will not be interested in computer printouts. They will steal televisions, video machines, mobile phones, computers or anything else they can turn into immediate cash." The two went to the lounge and the first thing Patrick noticed was that his chess computer had been taken. Along with it were the television and his stereo set. He looked at the walls, now graffiti sprayed in various colours were slogans like "Scumbag, White Pig, Arsehole" and the likes.

He searched back through his mind to try to find anyone who would be so vindictive or bear some form of grudge against him. The only person that had any noticeable feelings about the Amersham house was Kim. But there is no way that she would have ordered anything like this. Somebody had used the expensive Chinese carpet in the centre of the room as a toilet, his cold passion took fire suddenly.

"Shit! If I could get hold of these morons, I would take them apart and make them eat that." Throughout the house they found the same sort of mess, intruders had left nothing unturned. They had gone into every drawer and cupboard not content with just the stealing goods, they had fouled everywhere with massive amounts of paint from spray cans. There was a shout from downstairs.

"Hello, we're upstairs." Two policemen appeared on the stairway.

"Mr. Rodgers?" Patrick introduced himself and showed the two men around the house. They busily took notes of missing items as they made their way through the place with him. Terry was making his own inspection apart from the men. He had seen similar break-ins before, normally by hard up youngsters in inner city areas.

"Must be kids. Why the hell do they have to make such a mess?"

Must have nothing better to do in life." The younger policeman was examining the graffiti when he answered his own question

"Oh my god. Kim." Patrick called her and gave her the news. She wanted to know if he wanted her to come to the house, he told her to go to bed and he would be home as soon as they had finished. He then called Mrs. Jones and arranged for her to let the fingerprint men into the house next morning. She became highly distraught at receiving this bad news and started crying. When the two policemen had done everything they could, Patrick saw them to the front door.

"Remember. Try to disturb as little as possible tonight in order to let our forensic teams have a good look first. Maybe they can lift some prints on that back window where they broke in. Goodnight, sir."

"Come on. Let's have a drink." Patrick went through to the lounge and looked into the drinks' cabinet.

"You can have whisky or brandy, they've wrecked everything else."

"Whisky please." Patrick upturned then sat in his favourite chair, it had been razor slashed several times with a blade or a knife. Both were weary as they sat facing the massive brown pile in the centre of the expensive carpet.

"This wasn't done by youngsters." Terry had hardly said anything since walking into the smashed house and his pensive expression didn't change as he said the words.

"This was carried out by professionals "

"What makes you say that?"

"Several things, they've tried to make it look like the work of disgruntled teenagers. But they haven't done certain things that youngsters would normally do."

"Such as?"

"Kick in windows, boot or shoe scuff marks to be measured or leave footmarks against cupboards and walls. Professionals carried out this job because there isn't one trace or clue left behind.

"You can't be sure though. Can you?"

"Of course not. But I told you before, a good journalist develops a nose for these things. For instance, there are things left behind which are always taken by youngsters. There are other items taken that would never be touched by any self respecting thief. No, this was a professional job." There was a knock at the front door. It was two photographers from the 'Daily Informer'. Terry instructed them to take pictures of everything, they knew exactly what he wanted, because they had done this type of assignment many times before. Patrick found a torch, he and Terry hunted around the perimeter and the rest of the garden. They found nothing except for a page of computer paper at the side of the house. Both men urgently scoured the contents in the torchlight. It wasn't of any use to them because it didn't have any of the vital details printed on it.

"What do we do now?" Terry simply raised his eyebrows.

"We have no evidence, and there's no way I can print something like this on somebody's say so. We're stuck. It's a pity you didn't call me in earlier, then we could have taken them on. With no proof, you can't just go around accusing governments and the United Nations of setting up a program to supposedly kill millions of people a year. They would have us into court before our feet even touched the ground and they would have every right to sue for damages. Why don't you go home and sleep on it, that little girlfriend that you told me about is probably worried to death by now."

After the cameramen had completed their task and left the premises both men went to the front door. Terry stopped and looked around then moved his chubby arm in a semi-circle.

"This is most likely the start of things to come. If I were you, I would keep one eye always open, you can bet that they aren't finished with you yet." They drove to London and as Terry got out he scribbled something onto his pad, handing Patrick the sheet of paper.

"Here take this, it's my special number. If you hear anything at all, call me at that number, day or night. Just make sure you leave a message where you can be contacted." Kim was sitting in her favourite position, book in hand, she listened silently to Patrick's description of the devastation caused to his home. After several questions she went to the kitchen and brought back a plate of cold meats and salads. When he had finished she took him to the bathroom and drew a hot bath.

This seemed to be her remedy for everything Patrick thought. He watched as she poured some of her magical potions into the water, his body tingled as he dried it. In bed he cuddled up close. Kim could see that Patrick was suffering a mild form of shock, although he would never admit to it. Kim rocked him gently and thought about what she had got herself involved in. This big man was now like a defenceless little child wanting some form of relief to help overcome his shock. She no sooner got out of one messy affair and now it seemed to her as if she was getting herself into a more complicated relationship. She thought that for such a small person, lately she was having to take on the world's disasters and trouble, was it ever going to end? When was it going to be her turn to find contentment?

The following morning Patrick woke up feeling ready to tackle the world for whatever was in that potion must have contained some form of relaxant or sleeping draught, he decided. He didn't remember anything from that moment he was holding her in that close and blissful embrace.

At the office he called Mrs. Jones at his house. She was still very unnerved by what she had found awaiting her. Mrs. Jones asked him when he was coming back to live at the house. He explained that he might not come back since he had instructed the insurance assessor that he didn't want to see the place until it was back in shape.

"Will you see that all the repairs and replacements are made? In fact will you be kind enough to oversee all the insurance matters?"

"Certainly. But wouldn't you prefer to pick the furniture or the paint colours?"

No, Mrs. Jones. I want nothing to do with the house until it's back in some semblance of order, then I may sell it. I know that your taste is impeccable and that everything will be carried out to my satisfaction."

"If you aren't coming back, then I'm going to arrange for my eldest son to stay here so that this doesn't happen again. Do you mind?"

Patrick thought about it for a moment, he didn't want to place the boy at risk from these killers. He decided that they had got what they came for so the house was pretty safe again.

"No problem at all. Also let me know what I owe you for all of this extra work you're going to be doing."

Then he called Sue his ex-wife, to Patrick's utter relief this time she answered, he told her what had happened.

"I'll go straight out and meet the insurance people if you like and make arrangements with them."

"I've told Mrs. Jones to take over and sort out the mess."

"Patrick, I still have a vested interest in that house. I insist that I have some say in the refurnishing and decorating. Don't worry, the old girl and I still get on pretty well together and we'll work out something."

She said that she was not on duty for a few days and would go to the house straight away and also arrange to meet the insurance man.

"Thanks pet. Your power of the purse touches my very soul."

Raymond Chen was making his way towards Patrick's office as he replaced the receiver; he was in no mood for the security man's nonsense today.

The Culling

CHAPTER SEVENTEEN

There were no questions when Spielman got his way and was put in charge of the earthquake and tornado project. He immediately started converting a disused nuclear silo into a central command post. It was a massive undertaking getting everything exactly to his specification. After nearly a year in the making, they started installing the enormous electronic control section that Spielman considered necessary. He acquired seven large research ships which were fully kitted out as floating laboratories and would act as the radio detonating bases. These were carefully controlled by teams of scientists specifically hand picked for their knowledge of nuclear fission explosions. The enormous scientific project was based and controlled from the specially constructed control centre on the Colorado Kansas border. A second station was built high into the Sangre de Christo mountain range to the west of the central base station. Between the two, one at low level and the other at high level, they were able to monitor differences in earth movement and impact forces worldwide. They also locked into several NASA and other satellite watching stations, the explosions around the world were not to be outward impact blasts, but special type direct-travel explosions that would spread outward through the earth's crust by lengthways detonation. A circular ring, many miles from the intended site was pinpointed. As each tremor moved towards this outer ring, a double volley of explosions in exactly the right place was set off simultaneously. Like a funnel, this would help force the large rings of tremors into a straight line course.

Steve looked up at the huge electronic map of the world spread full length across the far wall and saw that the diagrams looked like a series of smaller and larger pears converging on the intended spot. It had been a long time coming, but now, having completed one trial run, he felt he knew the drill and what was expected to happen. After so much time they were at last getting what they wanted. He enjoyed moments like this, everyone beavering away, yet beneath it all, clearly feeling the strain starting to take over and within himself he knew that tension was now building up. The bulbous shapes were where the initial explosion would take place and the smaller area indicated the secondary detonations which forced the tremors towards the target. Where the circular explosions took place, he could see that they would all condense and multiply in veracity, forming thick splines converging on the chosen spot. From the circular points, the map looked for all the world like the centre of a gigantic flower with its deadly petals moving in towards the central core. He knew that this directional forcing of explosions could be heightened or lessened to create the size and type of final impact required. By lessening the explosions on one side and increasing it on the other they could force the final blast to travel in any desired direction. What they still had to get right, was pinpointing and controlling accuracy of the exact regions, because this was still an operational hazard still to be overcome. His excitement grew as he studied the map in front of him, seeing that the outer explosions were dotted around the world from seven points where the ships were already busily taking up their positions.

He laughed loudly as he saw the ironic names given to the initial detonation points given that this operation was called "Christian". Whoever had set this up, had a wicked sense of humour he thought. The sites where all the ships were now to be stationed, had biblical names. Then his eye travelled to the central area called Revelations, the last book in the Christian bible and he found himself giggling loudly.

The group before him now consisted of David Spielman, with two of his assistants and Olaf Gunderson who was head of the seven specialised ships. Also Heidi Zenger, head of the computer operations involved with the mathematical control and Tanaka Ozowa chief geologist of the program. They had all decided the date in June when the next earthquake was going to take place.

The red headed Heidi Zenger pointed to the large map showing everybody where the computer had pinpointed the initial tremors to take place.

"There are two on the fifty degree longitude line, these are called Matthew at the top and Acts at the bottom. There are three to the right of this line, and they are Mark, Luke and John. The two to the left on this line are Romans and Corinthians. That way the disciples are to the right of the intended target. To the left we have types of people from olden times, so there can be no confusion in identification and it's easier to remember them that way."

Steve realised just how much attention to detail had been applied to the this operation.

"Whoever thought up those names has a weird sense of humour."

Heidi looked at him indignantly, letting him know that it was her, before continuing with her brief.

"As you can see, the outer points are at varying distance from the target area. The first one to be set off is Luke in the Pacific Ocean, followed by Roman and then Corinthians." The computers had pinpointed exact timing between explosions and Heidi explained why they had picked the formation to match with flights of satellites.

"The only detection of the explosions are possibly going to be from the various seismic centres around the world. They will find it difficult to pinpoint the difference between natural earth movement and our artificial vibrations though. This is mainly due to the frequency range that we'll be adopting." She looked at the gathering to see if there were any questions before continuing.

"The inner ring for correction and concentration will be located at three thousand miles from the core. This allows us five sea borne stations and only two land-based stations, cutting down any chance of discovery. From here, the tremors will funnel to this point here called Revelations, and "Poof," hopefully we have a earthquake equivalent to eight on the Richter Scale."

"What sort of mortality rate?" Steve knew that the team had picked this spot well, because the population was fairly small and widely scattered over this mountainous region.

"It's difficult to tell. The target is Traveh, it's a religious city and the computer predicts between ten and twenty thousand in the town, but our main concentration is the heavily fortified nuclear reactor. We have such limited details of that area and its population count, that it could end up being half or double that amount."

"Thanks Heidi."

She looked at the others through large owl-rimmed spectacles to see if they all understood, then leaned back in her chair and tossed her long red hair back over the chair with a quick flick of head. Steve couldn't make his mind about her, she never had much to say for herself, yet her work was unquestionably of the highest order.

"Now Olaf. How long can we expect for your ships to be in position?"

The tall Swede got to his feet, Steve loved the singsong lilt in his voice. The only problem with the man was, that Steve had found, that he always had a menacingly serious air about him.

"In two weeks all the ships will be in place, we will need one more week to get everything ready. The computer firing mechanisms will be ready on due date." He sat down and locked his huge hands together in a praying gesture in front of him.

"That only leaves us with Tanaka. You're sure that the different core density en route won't create problems."

David Spielman spoke up for the first time.

"Steve. We have checked and rechecked all the figures. Heidi has put everything in the computer and this time we won't have the same experience as last. We have taken core samples from every point towards the target. There is nothing to worry about, this time we have it exactly right, the main earthquake will be in the designated area of Iran."

"I'm not questioning your ability. I'm just checking myself. This one exercise has cost us over a billion dollars so far and I wouldn't like it to end up wiping out New York because we haven't got it right."

David Spielman was a very sensitive man, he never liked being told that he was wrong.

"I can understand that. The reason for us being so far off-course last time was that we hadn't taken the various core denseness into full consideration. This time we have gone to extreme lengths to make sure that these co-ordinates and earth consistency are correct. That still does not mean that this will be right on the target, but believe me when I predict, we will be very close."

"Right, ladies and gentlemen. We go and next month in June we will see if we've got it right or at least almost close this time. God knows, we've been at it long enough now."

Steve stood up. Everyone at the table started packing up the vast amount of paperwork in front of them. The decision had been made and Steve knew full well that the next few weeks would be tortuous on his nerves. The waiting period before blast off always had him in a frenzy. Only after the result, would he be able to sleep properly once again.

"One last thing before you go. This one has to be good and at least just about correct. We think we've been discovered and are taking steps to rectify the situation, if we don't, we're going to have the world's press sniffing around to find the truth. Time is not really on our side."

Surprise, fear and disbelief crossed their faces

"Please try not to let this affect your project target and keep this buttoned down tightly, if we get found out, the world will be wanting our blood." There was a definite buzz between his colleagues as they started filing out of the room. He indicated for Heidi Zenger to remain behind.

"We have a problem"

The attractive scientist looked surprised.

"What?"

"We must change the entry coding system. Vladisky Ormon has found that some hacker has been looking at your computer data."

"Impossible!" The red-headed Swiss computer expert stood up. Steve knew that she was highly strung and like David Spielman, could not accept that she was wrong.

"They have managed to reach the system via the bank account."

"I told that idiot Ormon not to have the separate bank account name and now look, this stupid mistake has allowed an outsider into the program."

"Be that as it may, he thinks he knows who's responsible and is busily following them. I don't think it's going to be long before whoever hacked into the program is going to be history, but we must take precautions." Heidi sat down again. Steve liked her being cross, it was the first time he had seen any strong emotion shown.

"I insist that we take charge of our own security. If this gets out, it will be the end of the program and only the people in this room know the full extent of the program. Spielman has it so cleverly set up in divisions that not one section knows about the other. An expert computer hacker is the only person who could link all of these cells and realise what the whole program is about."

"I know. Still, leave that end to Ormon and concern yourself with shutting the coding down so tight that nobody can gain entry again." Heidi stood up, stretched and lifted her papers.

"By the time I'm finished this, I'll be the only person in the world that can get into the program." As she left the room Steve examined the large map on the wall next to him. The different coloured pear shapes converging on one central point made a fabulous sight to him. After all their hard work he didn't want everything to be lost and hoped that Vladisky had managed to track down the invader. He felt himself shiver slightly, knowing that if their plans were discovered the sponsors would deny any knowledge of the project. Whoever was tapping into their computer programme had to be stopped, and quickly. His eyes were drawn to the centre point where the petals came together in Iran.

"Bang. You're dead, may Allah bless your soul and take you to his breast. Shortly you bastards will rest in peace."

He collected his papers and left the room. It was going to be a long month with the next exercise, and someone out there steadily hunting them down.

The Culling

CHAPTER EIGHTEEN

As he fastened his tie he looked at himself in the full length mirror to make the final adjustment to the Windsor knot he had just completed. He had always been a snappy dresser and today he wanted to look especially smart. The blue suit offset his gray hair very well. He flicked at some unseen dandruff and went to the front door, three and a half weeks had taken forever to pass, but at last the appointed day had arrived. With a certain amount of pride, the tall figure of Steve Hearn pushed through the door and into the heart of the operation. The various heads of the project were all gathered together in a glass fronted office to his left. For a brief moment his eyes swept across the busy communications centre before him. Looking at the hive of activity he thought that his could be a major operations room at NASA or any of the other main installations throughout the world waiting for a moment of impact, no matter what it was. Directly in front of him was a huge electronic map which was linked to the seven ships through the main computer.

He looked at it and could see the seven pear shaped lines of the trajectory tremors' path mapped out, a gigantic deadly flower with different length petals all in separate colours, converging on a central yellow centre point where the earthquake zone was intended to strike home a deadly message. He knew that the next two days were crucial and that the main impact wouldn't take place until the next evening.

During the nineteen hours, all seven outer detonations would be carried out in sequence. Four hours later the corrective explosions would balance any differences in timing and a further four hour wait until the main tremors met at the epicentre in Central Iran. It meant that everybody would be working solidly for the next thirty hours at least, he simply hoped that each of the project leaders had had a good nights sleep because he knew full well that they were going to need it in order to maintain concentration. He turned left and made his way to the glass office.

"Morning, everybody. Everything still on track?" He knew that all was ready, but there was a sense of expectation and nervousness in the air as individually they greeted him. Everybody had played their part in the three week run-up and now here he was, the conductor ready to lead his scientific orchestra.

"Right. David, what time is the first detonation?"

"Luke will go in about two hours, forty five minutes and four seconds. This will be followed by Romans, approximately eighty five minutes later. Eventually ending with John."

"What time is the last one?"

"The time difference between first and last is approximately nineteen hours thirty two minutes and twenty two seconds according to the schedule.

"Any problems?"

"Not really. If we have any problems it will come from Luke."

"Why?"

"It has the furthest to travel and comes in from the East across vast wastelands of China, and then through mountainous regions of Afghanistan. We've managed to take readings from various places, but have been unable to take enough geological core samples to our satisfaction. Both regions are at war and getting in our exploratory parties was almost impossible however, several local oil research cores were found and we had to base our calculations on these. Whether they will be enough we are not sure, so we've made several strength corrective detonations just in case. I'm sure we've got it about right this time."

"What happens if this one is a problem and arrives late?"

"The only difference that it will make is that the main blast will become slightly unbalanced and force the impact to travel from west to east, a little further than we have anticipated. Once Mark and John close up, the vibrations will stop and hat we will have is, a devastation area running across the country instead of a limited section that we've controlled."

"Let's hope that you've got the calculations right then, if this experiment works out then in the future we go for a limited target with a main city. If this one goes wrong, we will have to continue experimenting until we're sure we can hit an exact target. By the way, are the observation ring teams all in place in Iran?"

"I haven't heard from them in the last three days, communications to the region are almost impossible."

"All we need now, is for them to stuck away somewhere and unable to record the event as it happens. That'll be just great. Tanaka, they're your geologists, where the hell are they?"

The Japanese geologist lowered his eyes and inspected the papers in front of him.

"They are all in their allotted positions already and working on exploration cores for the Iranian Government, you must remember that these are all field men and remain on site, so don't worry, this is not the remotest part of the country but they are being very careful because there are eyes and ears everywhere in Iran so, you can't expect them to report daily."

"For all of our sakes, I hope they're where you say they are." This was your responsibility David to make sure. David Spielman scratched at his thick bushy hair, it was a nervous gesture that became more prevalent as time for detonation arrived, a faint hint of a smile spread across his unshaved face.

"We've done everything possible. I'm sure that the success rate will be within two per cent, but we are aiming for one hundred. Two per cent will place the central point between a hundred to two hundred miles away. That could hit Teheran and instead of twenty thousand fatalities we could end up with more than a million. Therefore, we must be spot on."

"Our orders are not to touch any main cities until we have learned a lot from data on the previous earthquake and how better to control the epicentre. That's one of the reasons for these corrective detonations and if calculations show that the final target is going to be missed once the tremors reach the inner circle, we are able to abort the whole thing by a diversionary blast well before it enters the impact zone." David looked at Steve aghast, he then shook his head vigorously because he had not been told about this measure and most certainly was not in agreement with this action.

"There is no need for this underhanded action, we as your main team should have been informed because those corrective explosions are for us to speed up or slow down the main tremors line of travel by forcing them into a wider or narrower passage and we would need an equivalent detonation to stop them."

"Exactly and that's why Tanaka has permission to stagger the inward tremors so that they criss-cross the main area and move on without causing any damage whatsoever. There would be some structural damage but nothing like the chaos caused if all lateral vibration reached the impact spot simultaneously." Now David was furious. He jumped to his feet and banged his hand down on the table causing several members to jump.

"I'm the leader of this project and nobody will countermand my instructions. We need to see the results, even if it goes off course. I will not have anyone stopping such a vital experiment even if it is not exactly to plan."

"Sit down and stop shouting." Steve knew that he had to more than any time before assert his authority, everyone was keyed up and the slightest incident was going to spark the members at the table like it would in a dry timber forest, in no time he would have a raging fire to contend with if he didn't stop it immediately. The Jewish scientist glared at him.

"Sit down and behave yourself." He used the most menacing voice that he could muster. David slowly sank back into his chair.

"Now David, you are in full control and I agree with argument but our instructions are very precise and we can't buck those. However, if the vibration path goes off course and threatens a major city and we can't correct it in time, we have to abort. If not, the whole project could be closed down by those funding it, none of us want that, its not in our agenda or interests. So God forbid if, something goes wrong we can correct the experiment in time, then the impact goes ahead as planned. Otherwise, it's back to the drawing board and we try again and again until we get it right." The heat had been taking out of the moment and David now understood the sense of Steve's argument even though he was not well pleased at how it had been sprung upon them at final countdown, he started breathing more easily as he began to relax once again.

"Now. Let's have some coffee brought in and get on with the plan in hand." The main computer was linked and set to command the seven on-board computers at the initial detonation sites. It took over all control and monitoring which would be shown on the huge electronic board, while various control members sat at desks receiving individual information to each of their stations which was continually fed into a backup computer to double check that everything was on line. Everybody had left the glass office and were seated in front of glowing consoles. Steve was the last to be seated and pull on his large earphones, hearing questions and directions chattering into his ears. The main voice was that of David Spielman seated to his left, Heidi Zenger finished tapping in instructions and handed over control of the mission to the computer, she had programmed the details that had arrived over the last few months from all over the world into its memory. Now the mainframe computers had full control until the final impact when it would hand itself back to her for the next mission. Timing was key and so sensitive that it needed this powerful machine to keep track of everything by constantly monitoring all the information coming into the centre at once. "The Coordinator" as it was called could react and adjust anything within nanoseconds. Steve watched as she leaned back in her black swivel chair, her long red tresses falling down the back as she relaxed into her watching brief and knowing that her job was now completed until the next time. From the moment he had met the attractive Swiss professor he had tried to get her to have lunch or supper with him but she had remained aloof, she always just seemed to be a very quiet and private person and didn't mix easily with anybody at the centre, always keeping very much to herself. For an hour continual last second instructions, checks and corrective action rattled out across the headphones and then came the words they had all been waiting for.

"Zero minus thirty seconds."

David Spielman counted out the time backwards to a definite clicking sound.

"Zero. That's Luke gone, we are on our way, good luck everybody."

Suddenly his earphones rattled with incoming voices from various controllers in the Pacific based ship reporting that their detonation had gone without a hitch. Steve watched as the red petal of the deadly blossom started recolouring from the outer tip moving very slowly, spreading towards its intended target at the heart of the flower shaped electronic picture. He heard David's voice come through the earphones once everybody had reported.

"Thank you, everybody at station Luke, you've done a superb job and we'll talk to you later. In the meantime have a drink this evening on us."

Steve looked at the egg-headed man and smiled.

"Nice gesture."

"That's one down. Still six to go though." For almost an hour and a half, focus of attention switched to Romans in the Atlantic Ocean. The ship had been moored three hundred miles from the American coast above the equator on the fifty degree line. Again the voices from on board the vessel accelerated in anticipation as detonation time neared and before David again started the final countdown.

"Zero. Romans away, thank you everybody, a job well done." The clatter of voices immediately reported back to base, Steve looked up at the electronic board and saw a red and green shadow start moving towards the yellow centre point. The red on the opposite side of the map was now well away along its track when David's voice interrupted Steve's nervous thoughts.

"Thank you again Romans. That was an excellent send off and well done you guys." Steve heard the jubilant voice mockingly ask whether they could also have a drink. David turned to Steve and smiled for the first time since their argument, his eyes looking like gigantic brown saucers through the magnified lenses.

"Go on and have a big one for us. We still have a long way to go yet." Slowly but surely each successful detonation took place over eighteen hours. Each time it happened everybody in the control room seemed to have their spirits lifted to await the next happening. After Romans, came Mark in the Pacific Ocean, followed by Acts in the Indian Ocean and Matthew in the Arctic Ocean.

Steve watched in anticipation as the five coloured shadows approached the inner circle. For the first time he thought of the consequences that the deadly petals were going to have on the lives of ordinary citizens in the region where they all came together. Before long their lives were going to be shattered beyond belief when the earthquake struck, people were about to have their entire life's work destroyed, loved ones both young and old about to be maimed and killed below tons of rubble. Steve turned his thoughts back to the job in hand so as to blot out any sentimental feelings for the Iranian people that they were about to annihilate.

In short sequence Corinthians in the Atlantic Ocean was detonated, closely followed by John in the Indian Ocean, now all they could do was wait and watch as the coloured petals slowly raced towards their respective outer circumference points. Steve didn't know whether it was an optical illusion, but the Luke and Romans seemed to be lagging well behind the others. He turned and asked David about this.

"Don't worry too much about it, At the moment It looks that way because they're both crossing vast land mass areas and according to the computer they're all dead on schedule to reach the outer perimeter at exactly the same time. Another bit of good planning is that all detonations have been so exact that not one of them was picked up by any of the seismic satellites which were all out of range as they were each detonated in turn. She is so clever is that Heidi, she got it exactly right." As David had predicted, every one of the seven colours reached the outer circle simultaneously without hitch, the corrective detonations took place in sequence and the computer reported that everything was exactly on schedule.

Steve although by now was extremely weary and only had short napping periods watched the final phase as the large circles began to reduce in size and the seven continued inwards towards the yellow inner circle. He glanced over at David who looked like an overgrown child playing with his expensive toy, having been given the all clear and he looked up straight at Steve. For the first time in three weeks he heard the man laugh aloud.

"No aborting now. We're on the final flight path. Next stop, bedlam for Iran." For several hours the seven colours made their way to the epicentre.

"Thirty seconds to go."

Mesmerised, everybody watched as the various rainbow petal colours stretched their deadly tentacles towards each other.

"Five, four, three, two, one, zero." All points all reached the centre impact point simultaneously and they held their breaths waiting for what seemed like an eternity to everyone within the large control centre. Suddenly a huge flashing sign lit up across the board - 'MISSION COMPLETED'.

Everybody in the room jumped up and shouted at once, Steve noted that the only person not celebrating seemed to be Heidi Zenger who instead of celebrating was busily taking back control of her once computer again. He hung back within the whooping and congratulatory crowd and patiently waited until she had finished whatever it was that she was doing before sitting back in her chair, only then did he walk up behind her, leaned forward and kissed her full on the mouth. Naturally she was really taken aback at first, but then to his very pleasant surprise he felt her relax and insert her tongue deep into his mouth.

"Let's go out and celebrate tonight." He saw what he then perceived was a somewhat different look had crossed her eyes, at that moment they were now radiant and dancingly alive, it was as if this whole experience had turned her on and now Steve's kiss had been like a the final light switch being flipped..

"OK. Love to, but only if we go out and somewhere alone, I really don't feel like celebrating with everybody, that's not really my scene, backslapping celebrations bore me."

"Sure. I'll make my excuses and we can do it your way." Steve walked away, suspecting that the ice maiden had eventually melted, but he wasn't quite certain why. Perhaps it was because she had suddenly felt the release of enormous pressure of the last months, on the other hand, it could be that she was pleased with her achievement which allowed her the sudden freedom to bring him into her equation today. He was slightly confused at that moment as he tried to sum up his feelings. They had possibly killed thousands of Iranians, yet at the same time he found himself overjoyed at her reaction.

"What funny things the human emotions are." Steve said as David Spielman tore himself away from the others that had gathered around to congratulate him. He threw his arms around Steve and hugged him tight.

"Told you, I could do it, When and where do we go next?"

"Mazel tov David, believe me, I've always had faith in your experiments. Now let's see what the outcome of this is first, let's just hope that Tanaka's crew have managed to record the event properly and weren't somehow caught up in the main earthquake. Should everything have gone to plan and it's a success, we'll probably go for a limited hit on a city, we'll just have to wait and see what the final results tell us." David returned to the group to proclaim himself, Steve sat down in his chair, it had been a while since he had slept, he made up his mind that he would go to his room and have a catnap before going out to celebrate. He looked towards Heidi's chair, she had already left the control room. For some reason he suddenly had a very hollow feeling within, his immediate thought was that it was the first come down off a high or perhaps physical exhaustion was now beginning to catch up with him. Amid the raucous chattering, cheering and backslapping he made his way out of the control room knowing that he had to be at his peak when he was out with the Swiss professor, he was looking forward to this evening.

CHAPTER NINETEEN

The heat outside the large caravan was touching a forty five as the four Japanese geologists sat at the centre table in their large accommodation caravan, they had arrived two days earlier and started preparing the site in Central Iran near the town of Traveh for geology tests to the area. The men were employed by one of Japan's largest oil companies who weren't in dispute with the Iranian Government although most of the European and American companies were not welcome to carry out any such fact finding tests inside Iran, so Tanaka Ozowa had arranged with his government for a specialised team to be near the final blast area. Their brief was to carry out geology tests, to photograph the entire area and report any unusual occurrences in and around the mountainous and salt pan regions. They weren't informed what was about to take place, but were told that shifting earth plates in the area was cause for alarm by Tanaka who had contacted the team two days previously warning them that the seismic station had picked up a warning of a possible impending earthquake and that they were to find themselves a safe area away from any buildings for the next month. The crew moved their position into a long open valley and re-established their camp in preparation. Tanaka said that the geology department needed as many photographs as possible of the area before and after the event, these pictures were to be air freighted directly to Tokyo University as soon as they could in order to give them a complete insight of what happened during an earthquake. Specially damped cameras that would be able to absorb shock were rushed out to the team to be placed around the area that was going to be affected. The men were excited at the thought that they were about to record an historic event, they prepared themselves for the whatever was to happen, their only link to the outside world was by a high frequency radio which connected them to their office in Teheran.

The camp consisted of three specially constructed long-wheeled caravans, an accommodation module with kitchen and ablution facilities. The second was a laboratory unit fitted out with delicate seismic instruments, core testing equipment and density sampling gauges, which had a second room which doubled up as a canteen, computer and map room. The third and largest unit contained drilling equipment, generator and all the tools required to take core and samples from various sites in order to find out what minerals lay beneath the earth's surface. Because of its design, this self contained unit could survive unaided in these extreme conditions for vast lengths of time before returning to base, all units had air-conditioning, powered from the generator so that the men lived in fairly comfortable conditions while working in these desolate surroundings. Two days earlier when they had received their instructions, they had immediately replenished stocks and replaced water supplies in Teheran before making their way to this site. In their current position on the valley floor among the saltpan area they found that their radio connection with Teheran was almost non-existent, so hadn't reported back for two days, there was nothing unusual with this. The leader of the team, Tommy Tsuji had worked in the Gulf area for so many years that he had even acquired an English name because none of the American expatriate colleagues could pronounce his Japanese name properly. He had used this handle for so long now, that even his Japanese crew called him Tommy.

They arrived after their a short drive from Teheran on main highway before swinging east onto a dusty road which was little more than a trail. Tommy inspected the terrain then parked the caravans away from the village and then went to visit the local Imam to seek permission to scour the area for a suitable location. He spoke both Arabic and Farsi quite fluently and knew that the ritual courtesy was to seek out the local Imam for permission to be in the area, It was the duty of the religious leader to grant his blessing and would be one of the few people in the small village that would understand the documentation granting core sampling. After showing the village leader the necessary permission papers from Teheran, the man couldn't do enough to help him. He pointed out most of the villages in the neighbouring area, most of them being perched on the small hillsides of barren stone, most of the space for agriculture were in the flatlands below the series of small villages dotted around the dry and craggy saltpan areas. Tommy found an ideal spot in a dry wadi, which was a watercourse during the rainy season, it was wide and strewn with rocks, but mostly it was safely tucked away from any overhead danger of boulders cascading down should an earthquake materialise. The crew unhitched the caravans and established their base camp, then Tommy tried to contact Teheran. The high outcrops interfered with his signal, so Tommy drove back to the village and reported their position to a local religious leader, at the same time he also arranged to make a telephone call to his office and after nearly two hours of trying, finally managed to get through on a crackling line to report his position. The office manager told him to expect the company's helicopter to arrive in several days time to do some Arial Photography, Tommy then explained that they wouldn't contact the office unless absolutely necessary. For two days the crew became acquainted with the local area and its inhabitants while they set up the special cameras and collected samples.

Now it was Friday, the Islamic holy day and Tommy knew that if the crew started working they would soon be reported to the village religious leaders and from previous experience didn't want to offend the local population, so the crew stayed in the laboratory and carried out tests on some of the samples that they had collected during the two previous days. He knew that the small villages would be desolate and most of the inhabitants would be at home and not tending their crops on this religious day, the radio crackled several times, an indication that somebody was trying to make contact with them, but it would have to wait until Saturday because he would incur the wroth of the Imam if he tried calling Teheran from the antiquated village telephone. The men were all gathered at the table in their accommodation discussing results of their morning's work when the rumbling started.

Immediately Tommy realised what was happening as he

screamed at the others to get out of the caravan and into the open, but his orders came too late, the unit started rocking violently throwing everyone off balance and onto the floor. Tommy managed to grab hold of the fixed table leg and hang on for dear life as the unit bounced and swayed. His heart raced, they weren't expecting it for several days yet, and how on earth was he expected to photograph events when he couldn't even stand on his own feet. He just hoped that the eight special vibration cameras set up in the area were recording events properly. The crew were petrified and like them, he heard himself screaming out aloud from fear of death in this heaving catastrophe as clothes, plates and a series of flying missiles were literally jumping from their secure positions and raining down upon the helpless men, now all strewn about the floor of the caravan. Tommy saw a falling knife embed itself in one of his colleague's shoulder, another received a nasty crack on the side of his head when a glass bottle hurled down from its position on the overhead shelves. The module felt as though at any minute it was about to break into pieces or turn turtle and the men were truly terrified, then as quickly as it had arrived a loud bang suddenly heralded the end of the heaving and everything was silent except for a faint rumble that was fast disappearing into the distance.

For a moment everybody remained where they were. Tommy was the first to react, realising that this could be that slight pause before a new aftershock arrived he screamed for his companions to vacate the caravans as quickly as possible

"Now, out, out, out, into the open." Two of the men scrambled to their feet, the third that had been struck by the bottle didn't move. Tommy grabbed him and tried to get him to get up before realising that he was unconscious, the other two were battling to open the buckled door which was stuck fast.

"Help me!" The two were so intent on getting out that they didn't take any notice of his plea, panic in them was such that they kept attacking the door, Tommy saw that the knife was still firmly lodged in the one man's shoulder even as he threw himself against the door.

"Stop that immediately!" Tommy screamed, it worked immediately as he had hoped it would, their natural obedience to society overrode their panic and they looked at him in startled surprise not quite sure what to do next.

"Lift him and I'll loosen the door." He stood back and with one sharp hard kick the door bowed then gave way flying open with a resounding crack, he rapidly beckoned to the others to follow him out into the sweltering midday sunshine. What he observed beggared belief for once outside, he just couldn't believe his eyes, their equipment caravan was lying on its side where a large boulder from the overhang had crashed onto it while the laboratory unit seemed to have suffered least. He hated to think of the carnage facing them inside that unit as heavy boulders were still bouncing and falling from the overhanging rock-face and coming to rest several yards away from the bottom of slight incline. Palm trees had lined the wadi, now there was nothing except huge chunks of stone that had cascaded down like some sort of avalanche from above.

"Thank goodness we found this open area." He found himself saying this aloud. The tiny village that had been precariously perched at the end of the wadi no longer existed, it had been flattened. Tommy grabbed the knife and extracted it without his companion even realising it had been there, he was still too deeply in shock for it to register.

Within an hour a helicopter appeared over the wadi, then slowly settled down next to the camp, the pilot refusing to stop the machine in case an aftershock appeared. The manager ran toward the four men who had recovered sufficiently to begin attempts at cleaning up some of the chaos caused to their units. They had used the three four-wheeled drive vehicles to pull the equipment module into an upright position. It would probably take them a full day to assess the damage.

"Quickly, where did you station the cameras." Tommy instructed one of the men and he and the manager drove away and around the area trying to collect the them. When they returned Tommy saw that only two seemed to have been undamaged of the five recovered. In the laboratory they had facilities to develop the film, so he instructed one of his companions to do so, while he and the manager returned to the helicopter to take a flight over the nearby villages. Tommy took a spare camera with him to record the aftermath.

The pilot had already radioed Teheran and reported the earthquake to the authorities there, everywhere was the same, all the villages were almost flattened, the mud-built little houses had fallen like a pack of badly arranged cards on and around the peasant population. Those who had escaped were digging with their bare hands trying in vain to free loved ones caught beneath the rubble. As the helicopter passed over the top of these confused villagers, Tommy watched the people pleading with them to come to their aid. They knew that if they landed they would be overrun with villagers insisting that relatives be flown to hospital, there was nothing they could do for the moment but inspect and report back their findings so that Teheran was aware of the total picture in the area. Being a mainly agricultural area there was no lifting equipment, or heavy digging machinery, the people seemed so helpless in among this disaster. Tommy wished he could help in some way, but this had been an act of God and the population was going to have to come to terms with their grief he thought, as he wondered how many had died that day.

Back at the camp his colleague had finished developing the photographs, the manager said he couldn't wait for them to see all the pictures because he had to get the helicopter back to Teheran and they were running short of fuel. Tommy's colleague hadn't told the manager, but before they had returned, he had printed several sets from the negatives as keepsakes of their escapade in Iran. They spent the rest of the day getting the generator working, without it, life was going to be more unpleasant than it already was.

Several times screaming and threatening villagers approached them for help to evacuate the wounded and dead, but Tommy knew that as soon as they had fixed the generator, he was getting away from the area. He knew that soon the villagers would be seeking food, transport and shelter, and it wouldn't be long before they turned on the foreigners and took away everything, maybe even their lives. As soon as everything was packed and stowed, they broke camp and headed back in the direction of Teheran along the smashed and boulder strewn track. Tommy hoped that he had made the decision in time and that they were going to be able to bypass this chaos and not come across any incensed tribesmen along the way.

The Culling

CHAPTER TWENTY

On the morning following the earthquake a meeting of all heads of department took place at UNSECP headquarters, there had been a series of parties on the base after it had been learnt that "Operation Christian" had been relatively successful. Now the full reality of their trials was spread out on the table in front of them. Newspapers with explicit pictures of trapped and dying people spread across the front pages bringing the true meaning of their experiments to bear, Steve was seated in his usual place at the head of the long table and noticed that the state of euphoria from the previous day had somewhat dampened down, mainly because tiredness had taken over.

"Everything was perfect except for the fatality count. The Iranian government has estimated losses so far to be in excess of thirty thousand people, this is almost double the predicted amount but that really doesn't matter in terms of our objective that we have misjudged this amount this time, we must attempt to narrow our mistake ratio down. Very difficult to do, I agree but as each experiment proceeds we must try to get our figures as close to a hundred percent correct." David Spielman as usual did not accept that there had been any mistakes on their part.

"Our only misjudgement was the intensity of the epicentre and not the number of civilians living in the those areas, I told you that we did not have enough exploratory information. The Iranian figures for people living in the district was about sixty per cent incorrect, if they had regular census like most countries, we would have been able to work accordingly. Instead of allowing Revelations to cover such a wide area, we would have reduced the intensity of the detonations to accommodate a narrower epicentre."

Steve knew that what David had said was correct for he had already received calls of congratulations from the various officials of the governments involved in their program. The only reservation expressed from them was that they were expecting only half the number of fatalities and so slight misgivings were expressed that the trials were not yet conclusive enough and that UNSECP needed to carry on with further experiments until they could prove total success.

"David don't take this as a jibe at what has been achieved, all of us are over the moon at the scientific results, but we still haven't got total control. We have to double our efforts to make absolutely sure that we achieve our goals. Our eventual target is to cull ten million people a year in selected regions and we must be able to forecast our results in advance, we cannot expect to double the amount of fatalities on one side then reduce it in another area.

"Does that make sense?" The man didn't have an immediate or definitive reply.

"Yes, it all makes sense but, we are only able to make it happen and cannot control the end result without the correct data being fed into the system. The fact is we are working a little like a blind man being asked to tell you how many people are on a path ahead, he can but guess, that too makes sense."

"I agree so we are going to have to try again, hopefully we have all gained a lot of experience from this trial."

"Totally impossible without good data and we can but guesstimate population density and the percentage that will be affected. What we can't do, is try to estimate which buildings will topple and which will stand."

"We've got to go on with our experiments until we can find a formula that will bring down the rate of error." Steve was adamant as the rest all shook their heads, they were in agreement that they wouldn't be able to reduce the margin of mistake without clear data figures. Once the earthquake took place they no longer had full control of the situation and anything could happen. Steve looked at Heidi Zenger.

The Culling

"What about "The Co-ordinator," wouldn't it be able to reduce our present margins?"

"Yes. At the moment it is programmed to take all the facts fed in and make a prediction, however if I changed the programme to take all factors into consideration, such as numbers of buildings, how many storeys and other ancillary information, then it would be able to calculate the figures more accurately. You must clearly understand though that this is going to take a lot of ground research for intended targets." Steve looked at the bespectacled professor, and couldn't believe that this was the same lady he had shared the night with. Gone, were the sparkling bright eyes, she had returned into her shell like a tortoise. For months before "Operation Christian" she had appeared exactly as she looked now, reserved and sophisticated. As he looked at her for some consolation, he thought back to the previous evening.

After a two hour deep sleep he had got up and had an ice cold shower to shock himself awake. Invigorated, he carefully chose his clothes and set them out on the bed, for tonight he would dress casually and the barathea blazer with its monogrammed silver buttons would round off the selection nicely. He drove across the large compound of small bungalows and stopped in front of number 1067, he still was unable to believe that it was the same woman that he had spent so much time working with who now opened the door. He had got so used to seeing her wearing a white dust coat that he hadn't pictured her in anything else, tonight she was wearing an off the shoulder blue and green tight dress with small white Far Eastern characters emblazoned down one side. Her owl-rimmed glasses weren't stuck on the end of her nose and the shock of red hair that normally fell down her back was tucked up elegantly with a large black clip holding. Steve suddenly became like a teenager out on his first date as he sucked in a deep breath before greeting her.

"Would you like a drink before we go?" She stood aside and allowed him into her personal domain, all houses at the base were very similar in shape and furnishing but hers definitely had the touch of a woman, it was quite unlike his own working home with the extra touches that she introduced. There were old fashioned Balinese silk drawings carefully framed and dotted about the walls, on the mock mantelpiece he saw a couple of carefully mounted 18th century Scottish flintlocks complete with ram's-horn butt and on another wall she had skilfully placed two samurai swords hanging in front of the black and gold feudal lords intricately woven robes. Steve sat down as she hurriedly moved to the stereo and turned down the volume when asking him what he would like to drink.

"Do you have any Irish whisky?"

"No, but I have Scotch, if that will do?" There was an air of authority about her tonight, Steve was taken in completely as she moved around the room now, this definitely was not the same timid professor that he had spent many months working with.

"You look exceptionally pretty tonight, Heidi."

"Does that mean I don't usually look pretty?" Her directness had always baffled him, he wasn't used to being handled so bluntly, he was used to women using their wiles to soften him up. She didn't, instead she always spoke her mind and he was never quite sure just how to handle her offhand approach. When they finished their drinks they left and Steve had especially arranged for the transport helicopter to take them to Denver. All through dinner that evening she seemed to be free and released as she chatted warmly about her home in Switzerland and her flat in London. Not once did she mention the project or her beloved computer, maybe her introspection was caused by nerves and now that she had accomplished her goal and she had decided to reveal the real Heidi. After dinner the two sat and chatted for a while, before then taking a taxi ride back to the heliport and back to the base. It had been such a relaxing evening that back at her house she even invited him in for coffee, but as he closed the front door she turned and faced him.

"Let's have coffee later. Come with me, tonight is for fun." She took his hand and led him through to her bedroom and as they entered she turned her back towards him.

"Please loosen this." She pointed at a small clasp above the long zip, she felt Steve's slightly trembling hands fumbling at the clasp, when it loosened she felt the zip being pulled it's full length and Steve's arms encircling her before his lips lightly touched and kiss her ear ever so lightly. His breath was warm and sounded slightly laboured, she teasingly moved forward easing out of his arms and walked to her double bed, dimming the bedside light then turned and faced him and slowly but seductively let the Chinese dress fall to the floor around her ankles. Her eyes never moved from his gaze as he watched her reveal herself to him, it had always fascinated her to watch the power she had over men at this moment.

"Well, are you going to stand there all night or are you going to join me?"

He had not realised that she had been wearing nothing whatsoever under her dress, it took him by surprise as she eased herself onto the bed. She knew that he didn't need a second invitation as he quickly stripped to his underpants. Men never seemed to take everything off at first she thought, it was if they were always ashamed that their intended lover would see something imperfect about their manhood in that brief moment. She watched as he sat on the edge of the bed with his back to her and removed the offending disguise, then only did he roll over and as he did so, she jumped off the bed.

"Hang on, I won't be a minute." She entered the bathroom and quickly went to the cupboard and withdrew a bottle of tablets, taking one then quickly using a damp cloth to wipe down her body from head to toe. He was lying on his stomach as she came back to the bed, smiling inwardly to herself she immediately straddled herself across the man's back and started rubbing his shoulders, then steadying herself on her knees she grabbed his right shoulder and pulled at it to indicate for him to turn over. He complied and she let herself down gently feeling his manhood pushing against her, right then she didn't want him inside her but against her as she sank downwards pinning the thing against his stomach moving forward and backwards very gently letting him rub between her legs. As they moved, her eyes never left his face and his closed eyes, the momentum grew and she remained fully in control and revelled in watching this trapped man squirm below her, his hips moved in unison as he tried in vain to manoeuvre himself into her, but she wasn't ready for him, well not yet. Each time his hands moved forward to touch her, she reacted quickly by placing them back onto his chest. She knew exactly what she was doing to him and was thoroughly enjoying watching his actions. Her orgasm started to build slowly and she began moved faster to gain maximum friction against lower female extension that grew as felt and watched the manly figure thrashing below moving increasingly faster, he was also reaching the same point as herself and just as the great surge from him flooded across the front of her body she moved very slightly allowing him to now slip right up inside her. Then with all her energy she moved up very slowly allowing her full weight to drop like a steam hammer onto the upright pinnacle each time. The powerful pelvic muscles helped on each movement upwards, the suction hard and tight at his organ and the pressure downwards forced him deep into her almost pushing her innards into her chest. His painful pleasure seemed to excite her even more as she forced him between continual bouts of pain and pleasure. He wanted her to stop, but at the same time he wanted her to continue. That night they reached the heights of ecstasy together, he exploding as she continually dropped hard onto him, occasional stopping the urgent rise and fall to slowly rotate herself on him like an live insect that had a pin through it. She let out a loud scream and leaned forward and took a mouthful of his flesh in her mouth and sank her teeth deeply, drawing his blood into her mouth. As she subsided she released the bruised and torn skin and moved down his body, not sure whether his trembling was from fear that she was about to do to his manhood or what she had done to his shoulder, or whether he was still in the state of orgasm.

The Culling

Slowly she slipped her mouth over him and sucked the last remnants from him tasting a mixture of herself and his juice intermingled with each other, it had been a long time since she had had a man's delight and tonight she was going to make him suffer his pleasure. As she felt him relax, she bit hard into the head of what to her looked a little like a British policemen's hat. Then as he started to shout she gently licked and sucked again letting him relax, all night she attacked his body and senses in this manner so that when he left in the morning he was covered in bruises and marks. As he got dressed to leave his overwhelming feeling was that he had been chased through a bramble patch but by the same token he had never had an experience like it and the only areas left unmarked were those hidden by his clothes. Heidi watched Steve painfully getting dressed and lay back admiring her handiwork, she also knew from past experience that he would try to be back but for now, she had had her fill and didn't need anything more. He was handsome and nice enough, but he certainly wasn't her type.

Steve still could not believe the change in this shrieking, biting and violent lover he had spent the night with, he looked straight into her eyes to try to get some form of recognition of their escapade. There was nothing, David's voice interrupted his most inner thoughts.

"So what's our next target?" Steve's head snapped back to the present, they were all watching him eagerly.

"It looks like we are going to have to go for a smaller, and more precise target to prove that we've got full control of the program. As the Far East is where the largest overpopulation is, we have decided to go for a target there."

He stood up and pulled down the roller world map built into the ceiling before seating himself once more and picked up a black pencil shaped item and pointed it at the map. A fine red dot appeared on the map which was then moved across until it rested on a point to the north of Manila in the Philippines.

"As before, we have chosen an area where the government is giving the Western powers a spot of bother. The Filipinos want to shut the strategic American bases and possibly let Communism take over that country. they need to rely on outside help and if we get it right, then you'll have proved to our sponsors that the program can now move from experiment stage to full-blown reality. The other reason that this town near Manila was chosen is that it's on the edge of an island complex so if you miss the target then you hit the sea or possibly one of the smaller islands. This time, ladies and gentlemen, it is your biggest test yet."

David could see that the target of Baguio was, unlike the two targets before because it was right at the heart of a small island and not an easy spot in the middle of large land mass. He knew he had to get it exactly right because this was possibly the final test to see if they could miss a large city and hit a smaller town close by. It would be like aiming at a bull's eye, if they hit the outer rings of the target, this test would be deemed a failure.

"How long have we got to prepare?"

Steve stood up and started collecting his papers together.

"Four and a half weeks. Is that enough? Will you be able to get the ships into position by then?"

The others started to move, four and a half weeks was the tightest schedule time to get it right.

"Have to be long enough Steve. It's a hard task but be sure of this, we'll do it."

Everybody in the room knew that the timing wasn't beyond their capabilities, but secretly wished that they had more time to work on the project and iron out are possible gremlins. David looked down at the large file then handed out instructions from it to all seated at the table. This operation had a new name for the earthquake and his mouth curled wickedly at the corners as he read the operation name and although all seven support ships had their names left unchanged, the new project was going to be named "Operation Buddha".

"Well, everyone let's go to it, this is going to be tough assignment but let's show those unseen faces just how accurate we can be."

The Culling

CHAPTER TWENTY ONE

On Friday evening Patrick arrived at Kim's house, he was tired and frustrated, for three weeks the police had contacted him four times and still no result and. the officer that arrived at the office today was also of very little help when he stated that the chances of catching the culprits was almost nil but that they wouldn't give up trying. Mrs. Jones had been on the telephone at least twice every single day with an update report, so far the house had been repainted, windows and furniture replaced, although she was having trouble with items like his chess computer. Every time she asked him to come to the house to inspect what had been done, he immediately found some sort of excuse to remain away by telling her to get on with it and that she was doing a fabulous job. What he didn't tell her was that he had lost all interest in the place and that he was thinking of selling it as soon as it was finished. He somehow got the feeling that the place had been jinxed, that feeling had first developed when he had taken Sue, his new bride back to their marital home and later found out that she was having an affair. Now all he could picture in his mind's eye was the state of the place when he and Terry had left it and now he no longer really cared whether it was made better than before or not.

"Is that you?" Kim's voice came floating down the stairway as he let himself in the front door.

"No. It's your other lover sneaking in for a quick session before that other idiot gets home from work." He heard her infectious giggle and suddenly felt a whole lot better with life especially when she appeared at the top of the stairs having obviously had a shower because her hair was still damp and she was wearing her short silk dressing gown. Kim took on the pose of a seductress as she loosened the cord of her gown and slowly opened it although not revealing all of what lay beneath.

"Hello, my sexy lover, you must be quick otherwise we will be caught out by that other idiot." She enticed with her mock French accent, he raced up the stairs two at a time so that by the time he reached her she had lost her composure and was on her knees screaming with laughter. He easily lifted her and carried her to her favourite couch and set her down it was useless to continue the play acting because Kim was literally doubled up with laughter. He flopped down next to the couch and took her little hand in both of his.

"You, my little flower, can change the most difficult day to the most pleasurable moment in a man's life." Kim's laughter changed to a tender smile and she ran her fingers across his cheek very slowly not having to make any comment, they were both sure of each other. Ever since the event at his house Patrick felt in complete harmony with her it was as if she had resented his past and with the defiling of this one material root to his former life, they had become far more comfortable with each other. Somehow this definite bond had been sealed with his rejection of his previous links and what they had meant to him, she then ran her hand under his chin and he felt a tender surge within himself for the seemingly brittle little elf seated alongside him.

"What do you want for supper?" He buried his head onto her now exposed tiny breasts.

"You!" The momentary tenderness was lost as she again squealed with laughter yet again but undaunted, Patrick lifted her and carried her up the stairs to the bedroom. Their lovemaking was fierce and fiery until they both lay back totally exhausted. Neither said anything for a while, content with everything that had just passed between them then the telephone rang and she answered it. It was one of her friends he thought as she started chatting away in her mother tongue, suddenly the intonation of her voice changed and he looked at her and could see concern written right across her lovely features. For several minutes she questioned the voice at the other end before replacing the receiver and letting out a deep sigh lay back against the headboard.

"Patrick. What is happening to you, have you gone mad?"

"What are you talking about? The only thing I'm mad about is you."

"Did you think you wouldn't be found out?"

"If you had explained what you're on about, then maybe I can answer your questions."

"You know full well what I'm on about, its about your special banking arrangements."

"I still don't know what you're talking about."

"Patrick! Don't play games with me, this is serious. You've been stealing from the company and now you've been found out."

"What?" He sat bolt upright.

"That call was from a friend who told me that Raymond Chen is trying to reach you. He has accused you of embezzling funds from Silver Beam into your own account."

"Then I better go and talk to Mr. Interfering Chen, right now shouldn't I." He moved to get off the bed.

"No wait. I think you owe me an explanation first."

"How am I supposed to have transferred these amounts?"

"Simple, by computer instruction to your bank account, you are in charge of the finances, what could be easier?" Realisation struck forcefully, had Terry not warned him that there was more to come. This was it and somehow either Raymond Chen or more likely Vladisky Ormon had managed to implicate him on an embezzlement charge.

"You know what this is of course, it's a setup."

"What do mean? A setup."

"I've been conned, framed, duped, call it what you like. Somebody has rigged the computer to trap me."

"Why would they want to do that?" He placed his hands on the girl's shoulders.

"Kim, I now realise that thing at my house wasn't caused by hooligans, it was these people. I haven't been entirely honest with you and I think it's time you knew the truth. Do you remember those evenings that I said that I was practising for the chess match?"

"Only too well, did that have anything to do with it?"

He told her everything from beginning to end, she didn't interrupt once but sat cross-legged on the bed listening to his fantastic story. When he finally reached the part where the house had been burgled she simply nodded her head.

"What I don't quite understand is just how this madcap thing is going to be carried out, please explain more clearly how you think it might happen, you cannot simply make an earthquake happen can you?" Kim asked.

"There were several more documents and among them were several white paper copies and explanations of Russian attempts to set off earthquakes in America during the cold war period and although I do not fully understand how they are going to achieve it, I can sort of piece together and work out the theory that that they intend using."

"Well explain your theory then; I really need to understand just how it works in order to believe what sounds like something from some fantasy movie. Questions would be asked, in today's world they couldn't get away with it." Kim said quietly.

"Right here goes, remember this is only my clouded picture of how they intend achieving their diabolical dream."

"Sure, but get on with it." Kim urged.

"Imagine a very calm pool with a large cork at the centre. Got it? Now picture yourself tossing a sizable stone anywhere into that pool. What would happen next?"

"Plop! The calm pool surface is now disturbed?"

"Exactly, there would be ripples spreading away from where your stone entered the water, those ripples would eventually reach the cork and it would move slightly wouldn't it?"

"Of course it would."

"Right, now the same scene, same place, but this time you hurl several stones into the pond at the same time and have managed to space them equally so that each send out ripples that all meet up simultaneously with that same cork. What would happen to the cork then?"

"I don't know, it would probably bob up and down, wouldn't it?"

"Exactly, now picture seven explosions happening around the earth as if they were your stones being tossed into the pool, these explosions would also cause rippling through the earth's mantle and if it could be controlled, so that where all those ripples joined up by coming together at the same time and place, well, that would be the same as happened to the cork, the earth at that point would bob up and down. Now that's my theory."

"Whoa, are you serious?"

"I'm only telling you what I have managed to glean so far, sounds far fetched but Kim just imagine what any country would do in similar circumstances, if a controlled earthquake suddenly brought down the houses of parliament in UK or, congress in session in the

USA or, any third world government at an exact point in time when all members of that government were under one roof. What is a slight movement on a pond would be devastating on a global scale and an entire government killed off in what will then be seen as simply a natural disaster. Nobody will question a natural disaster would they?" Kim did not say anything for several minutes while taking in the enormity of what Patrick had so simply explained.

"If this isn't a figment of your imagination, the world is in big trouble and you can't go back and face Chen."

"And why not?"

"I warned you right at the outset to make sure your back was covered, this man is strictly government and has ways and means to have you locked away for a long time. It would have been easy for him to get someone to order the computer to transfer funds straight to your account."

"No it wouldn't, there are certain checks and balances within our financial system that would have shown up any discrepancies like that immediately. So if he did this within the last two days it would be completely explainable and I wouldn't be prepared to go to the board with my complaint now, would I?"

"This has been going on since you started with the company."

"How do you know that?"

"My friend told me."

"Jesus. There's nobody, not Chen not anyone, except George Li that could possibly have the skills to program the computer to do this wicked act. It has to be that little bastard Vladisky Ormon behind it all, somehow he's managed to gain outside entry and fiddled the accounts."

"If you go back to the office, Chen will have you arrested immediately and you won't get the chance to clear yourself, at this moment all the cards are firmly stacked up against you. The only way to find out the truth is for us to find a good hacker and go into the system. That way you can have the account investigated and if possible, change the evidence against you."

"We'll have to move very quickly though by Monday the whole thing will be difficult to prove." For several minutes they sat facing each other, both brains were racing madly as Kim moved to get up.

"Don't you have any idea where we can find George Li?" Suddenly Patrick had a brainwave, he went to cupboard and searched through the pockets of his suits, he extracted a slip of paper and returned to the telephone. Reading the numbers from the slip of paper, he dialled the numbers.

"Mr. Terry Gould please." The voice on the other end asked him to wait, then his old friend was on the other end of the line.

"Terry. It's Patrick Rodgers, you were quite right, they've moved again but this time they have targeted me and I'm in deep trouble." He told Terry everything that he and Kim had discussed.

"Have you had any luck with George Li yet?"

"No, the man seems to have vanished into thin air, we are certain that if he left the country then he didn't pass through any of the conventional routes because we've had them all checked. That means that he's hiding somewhere in Britain or he's managed to get out without being seen, a third possibility that we must face up to, is that he is being held somewhere against his will." Patrick could feel the invisible net tightening in around them.

"We need a good hacker quickly and need to get into the computer and change whatever he's done to my account."

"Where can I contact you, give me a couple of minutes to find someone who I think can do this type of work. I'll set up a meeting then let you know where to meet me." Reluctantly he gave Terry the telephone number then replaced the receiver and turned to Kim who was busily pulling on a pair of tight blue jeans.

"Maybe we've struck it lucky, Terry's going to try to find a hacker for us."

"I will come with you, I know that I am no hacker but I know the system well enough and could possibly help to find what we are looking for. If Raymond Chen is behind this then I want to get back at him for all the problems he's caused literally thousands of innocent people back in our country."

"I want you kept away from all this."

"No Patrick. You have chosen to tell me everything and now I believe you, I'm still not certain that you've told me all you know, but you're in this over your head. Where I can be of assistance, I want to help. Don't forget, I work with both Raymond Chen and Ormon. Ormon is probably the most detestable European that I've ever met and I could easily believe that he's behind this." The telephone rang. Patrick wasn't sure whether to lift the receiver in case it was someone from the office for Kim. She answered the call and immediately handed him the instrument.

"Hi Terry." His friend said that he had found a hacker in Fulham and gave Patrick the address where to meet him in half an hour.

"Okay, see you there. Oh, by the way, I'm bringing Kim with me, she is a computer expert and may be able to lend a hand."

"It's only fifteen minutes from here, let's have a quick cup of coffee before we go." Kim started walking down to the first floor when the front door buzzer sounded. Patrick tensed as Kim asked who was at the door. It was Raymond Chen. Kim said she would be right down, she quickly told Patrick to stay upstairs.

"Don't come out until he's gone." Patrick stayed behind the bathroom door, leaving it open just enough to be able to hear everything going on. From what little he could understand of the language, he made out that the man insisted coming into the house. For a while the two spoke normally, then Patrick noticed that the pitch of their voices was changing, Chen was becoming angry, his voice changed so did Kim's in response. He heard his name mentioned several times then as quickly as it had flared up, so the argument faded until there was nothing. Patrick moved slowly to the bedroom door to try to listen what was happening. He heard shuffling then the front door closed with a metallic click, slowly he made his way down the stairs until he could see the entire lounge, Kim was lying on the floor. He raced to her and as he lifted her she moaned.

"What happened?"

"That bastard hit me. He said that I contacted you last time and he wanted to know where you could be reached tonight, I kept on insisting that I didn't know and he suddenly hit me." She sat up painfully

"I'll take him apart. Patrick started moving towards the stairs, but she jumped up and lunged at him.

"Don't, Patrick. This is nothing, the main thing is, he hasn't found you. You wouldn't achieve anything by it and he would know about us then." Patrick looked at his watch.

"Christ, we should have been in Fulham five minutes ago." After going to the kitchen and washing her face, Kim went out of the front door first, while she was doing this Patrick called Mrs. Jones and asked if her son was sleeping at the house. When she answered in the affirmative he told her to call him and tell him to be extra careful tonight. Kim walked up the one side of the road and down the other and after making certain that Chen had left the area, she called to Patrick who quickly took her by the hand and ran to his car. He turned the Porsche out of the street and roared away towards Fulham.

The Culling

CHAPTER TWENTY TWO

"I've tried everything I know, but I can't get into that computer programme, whoever set it up, really knew what they were doing. It will take me days or even weeks to get in." They were seated in front of rows of computers set up for customers to practice on, the long shop had one wall filled entirely with software and games, while the other had any number of different sized computers. The shop owner had tried everything he knew to give the correct command to enter Silver Beam's computer system, the entry code had been changed sometime during the day. Patrick watched the little screen, feeling a touch of despair washing through him as he saw his last chance quickly fading.

"We haven't got that amount of time." The hacker looked at him and shrugged his shoulders helplessly.

"Without the code, I would have to spend some time trying various combinations until I came up with something. There is no other way."

Kim had been watching the frustrated hacker battling away and suddenly got the idea to short-circuit the hacker.

"Maybe there is. What if I went to the office and got hold of the new code."

"No. If you go to the office and they found out you were helping me, you could be in danger as well."

"It's the only way, there are only two operators on duty at time of night. If they were told that I had work to do they would have to give me the new code."

"Listen. You've just had a run in with Chen, if you now pitch up at the office to work he's going to think it a bit suspicious. He'll put two and two together and come up with the correct answer." Kim pulled her nose up at Patrick and put out her hand.

"Give me your car keys, I'll be there and back again before you can blink." Terry's uneasiness suddenly manifested itself as he made his thoughts known.

"Going there is bad enough, arriving there in Patrick's car is downright stupid. Now if you're determined to do it, then we all go in my car. That won't be recognised, you go into the building and we'll watch the front of the office area, that way if this character Chen is there, you don't go in. We watch the building until he leaves and only then you can try. I've been at this game a lot longer than you two amateurs, so if we do it, we do it my way. Agreed?" Both readily shook their heads in approval Terry turned to the hacker.

"Billie, you wait here for us, and you better be here when we return." He turned and waddled his way toward the front door of the little computer shop. The two followed in quiet silence, each battling with their own thoughts. They got into Terry's car and drove to Kingston.

"What kind of car does Chen drive?" Terry was cruising towards the car park where he could see two small Japanese vehicles.

"It's not either of those, it's a silver Honda." Patrick remembered seeing the car outside Kim's house when he had nearly blundered in on them. He hoped that Chen was still driving the same car.

"Right Kim. Before you go, is there a back exit, just in case he arrives while you're in the building?"

"Yes, but I think it's locked at night though."

"Here take this and if he should arrive, I'll call you. If it rings, get the hell out by means of the stairway. Don't use the lift, otherwise you'll walk straight into him." He handed her his mobile phone,. he told her he would contact her by means of his car telephone.

Patrick was glad that his friend was with them, he was correct, they were amateurs. Kim asked Patrick for his office keys which were attached to the ring that had his car keys. They watched as she quickly made her way to the front door of the building and disappeared inside. Instead of taking the lift, she decided to walk up the stairs, just in case Chen had arrived with one of the computer operators. On the second floor she quietly made her way to the entrance, as she had thought, there were only two South Korean operators, one lounging back in his chair eyes closed, while the other chatted to him. She pulled herself upright and strode forward into the office greeting them in their mother tongue in a stern manner. Both men, surprised to see their sales director in the office at that time of night, suddenly pretended to have a lot of work to do. She knew that they were nervous and told them she was doing some work at home and needed to print out something quickly. She sat down at one of the spare desks and started working at the keys, one of the men shouted to her that the company entry code had been changed. Without seeming concerned she asked him for the new code, as he read it out she noted it down on a slip of paper. She quickly entered the computer with the new number, then printed out a test programme for herself, when the printout had run, she explained that she was working on a new contract, but Mr. Kang the company's managing director would be upset to find her taking work home because this was against company policy. She told them that if they told anybody that she had been in the building, she would have them both fired for not working while on duty. They knew she could make things difficult for them, both men agreed that her having been there would not go further than them and both breathed a sigh of relief as the diminutive figure strode out of the office.

"Good girl." Patrick wrapped his arms around her and gave her a kiss before opening the back door.

"Piece of cake, there were only two of our nightshift operators on duty." Victoriously she waved the code on the slip of paper at them, she explained all the details as Terry pulled into the road and turned the car towards Fulham.

Billie the hacker put in the number and immediately entered into the Silver Beam computer system, Patrick leaned forward to gain clearer access to the small screen.

"Now let's have a look at my account." He studied it from start to finish.

"Print it out." The hacker pushed a button and the printers spewed forth several

pages of paper.

"Nothing. Now let's go to our banking account file." Patrick couldn't find a thing in his personal file. He quickly pushed several buttons.

"Print that." Again the printer noisily ejected several pages of information.

"Here it is. It's credited my account with over sixty thousand dollars. Now we've got to find where it was taken from." Patrick took over the keyboard, for over an hour he searched various accounts, then he found what he was looking for.

"That's why it didn't show up in our daily figures. There has got to be an accountant's brain behind this, Chen could never have thought of placing the amount under a management fee from head office. Sooner or later it would have come to my attention, but for Chen to find this, he's got to be in league with Ormon." Terry looked at the strip of white paper.

"You're still an embezzler according to this. You've taken a lot of money and had it transferred to your personal banking account. I'm willing to bet that if you check your account, you'll find the money there. So how do you explain that?"

Patrick turned to the hacker.

The Culling

"Do you think you could get into the bank's computer system?"

"No ways. These banks are geared up to stop this type of thing,. you would have to be the best hacker in the world to be able to get in. It's way out of my league." Kim took the keyboard and started tapping away. Patrick watched as she connected the computer in Seoul with the one in London. Once she completed that, she tapped in details and the screen showed Raymond Chen's account. He didn't quite understand what she was looking for. She looked up at him and smiled evilly.

"We may not be able to extract those funds from your account, but what if we transfer large sums into our friend's account and then feed the lion's share into his private banking account in Korea? We transfer smaller amounts to various names around the world the same way that he has done here. That way, it will appear to be a conspiracy or at worst, a payment for services rendered, with him as the principal thief. We could implicate our Polish friend in the conspiracy as well."

"Brilliant." Terry laughed aloud.

"With the computer printouts we could nail the bastards if I published it. Let's call it gutter press journalism." He smiled broadly.

Patrick placed his hands on Kim's shoulders.

"No, you mustn't do that because I'll be implicated no matter how you look at it."

"What we've got to do is stop Chen from being a nuisance, once he finds out we're onto him then Ormon could easily change the accounts again. What we need is a backup safety net. Somehow, if we implicate Chen, Ormon and Heker Jong by creating a dual fraud and leave it like that, then I will possibly be safe from any conviction. They'll only be looking for one transfer, not two, then later we sink the buggers."

Kim started tapping away at the account. She found a special government grant account and transferred two million dollars into Chen's special account number two that she had created. She transferred various amounts to London, Australia, Nigeria, New York and Singapore. The funds were then carefully filtered into various manager's accounts. She left his account with one million dollars and transferred half a million into a special escrow account in Patrick's last firm in the name of Vladisky Ormon. Patrick guided her, making sure that any accountant looking at the figures wouldn't be aware that the amounts were being moved into fraudulent accounts. She then moved half of the amount into a bank account that Heker Jong used. An hour later she had completed the task.

"Right, one down, one to go. How do you propose we set this one up?"

"Billie, have you ever hacked into any large organisation?"

"Yes. I use Cambridge University as my hub. It has links into several large pharmaceutical companies. You can link Silver Beam into one of them." The hacker took over the keyboard and in a few minutes had got into one of Britain's largest firms."

"Right. Kim move funds from that account and place a hundred thousand pounds into Silver Beam." He pointed to an account on the screen, she tapped away then handed the keyboard to Billie. He transferred the amount through the Cambridge computer back to Silver Beam.

"Right. Now put it into that account."

"Done."

"Right that's it. We've managed to get ourselves out of a hole! Terry, Billie, how can I ever thank you enough?" Terry laughed loudly and slapped his friend on the shoulder.

"Don't worry about Billie, the newspaper will take care of him. From my end when the time's right I'll get my reward from being able to publish the full story. Glad we could help in the meantime. C'mon let's go for a drink, there's a pub down the road that is really a restaurant. I know the owner and your thanks, will be to buy us a meal and several drinks. How's that?" Kim and Patrick followed Terry to a little place opposite the old Fulham Gasworks.

"Don't worry about the decor, it tends to be a little risqué, but the food's excellent."

Terry was right, they all ate merrily with several bottles of house wine assisting to remove the earlier cares of the evening. Terry offered Billie a lift back to his shop and Patrick and Kim carefully made their way back to her house, hoping not to be stopped and breathalysed. He didn't say anything to her as his mind searched for any loopholes that they may have left open. These people were vicious and were not going to take this lying down when they found out.

The Culling

CHAPTER TWENTY THREE

"I'll call you from the office." Kim started walking down the stairs to her front door.

"This is crazy, I've got nothing to fear."

"Patrick, we agreed that this would be the best way just in case there was something that we've overlooked." The two had decided that Kim would go to the office and have a quick look at the lie of the land, she would then call Patrick and tell him what to do.

"OK. Try to call as early as possible, I want to get to the bank as soon as possible before coming to the office."

"Love you." Kim was through the door and gone, Patrick walked across to the window and watched her back her car out of the driveway and drive to the corner. He looked across at the river. the early morning sun spread a cosmic gold sheen on its surface. Something was missing, it was one of the few times that the lone oarsman was not practising on the glorious river. He turned on the radio before settling down with the morning paper, having some time to kill before Kim reached the office. After having a slice of toast for breakfast, he had decided to go straight to his bank and return the funds lodged in his account. That way, he figured that before anybody realised it, he would be able to replace the funds in the correct account and then report the incident to the main board. This way he would be able to prove that he was innocent of any fraudulent dealings with company's funds, he would also be able to trap the two that he suspected were carrying out this vicious attack on him, sitting alone, he wished that he had never embarked on this venture in the first place. With hindsight, if he had known what problems it was going to cause he would never have asked George Li to hack into the bank in the first place. His thoughts turned to his affable South Korean friend and colleague and he wondered where he was right at that moment, knowing that the man had been scared out of wits and Patrick simply hoped that he was somewhere safe. Picking up the newspaper and continued trying to concentrate on the news and what was happening in the wide world.

Kim's voice sounded highly distressed when she called.

"Patrick. Raymond Chen has already called in the police, they are here and waiting to arrest you the moment you walk through the door."

"Shit! When did he call them?"

"Apparently he came in yesterday then called someone and told them what was going on. Within half an hour the police were here and Chen showed them everything."

"We'll have to put plan two into operation then."

"Before you do that I suggest that you contact Terry and tell him what's going on."

"Good idea. Call me back in twenty minutes, I don't want to call you just in case someone recognises my voice. That way, they'll know that you're somehow linked to me." Patrick replaced the receiver and then called the private number Terry had given him. The reason for the special number was that Terry was continually on the move and always in contact with his office secretary who would be able to pass on any messages quickly.

"Can I speak to Terry Gould please?" The voice at the other end told him that Terry never arrived at the office before eleven, Patrick explained that it was very important that he speak to him urgently. The person at the other end asked him for his contact number and told they would immediately try to reach Terry. Within ten minutes the telephone rang, it was Terry sounding as if he was still half asleep.

"What's happened?" Patrick explained what Kim had told him.

The Culling

"I'm going to go into the office and show them what Raymond Chen has been doing, before I do I'm off to the bank to return the illegal funds back to the company."

"Just give me a minute to think this one through. I'm not at my best at this time of the morning old son." Patrick listened as Terry replaced the receiver and then he heard a distinct click, which he assumed was Terry's lighter.

"I don't think your idea is a good one."

"Why? I must clear my name."

"Let's look at each step from now until you reach the office, we'll have to insert hypothetical situations and try to imagine what will be said and done."

"All right. First I go to the bank and tell them that I would like to see the balance of my account, then when I see it, I tell the bank that there has been a mistake and that somebody has made an error and transferred the wrong amount to my account. I then ask them to return it to Silver Beam."

"Nothing wrong with that except, what if they unbeknown to you call the company by telephone to verify the amount. The first thing that will happen is that the police will immediately send somebody around to arrest you at the bank, You will be there waiting and they'll do that before they do anything, "

"What if I write a letter instructing them that there's been a mistake?"

"Hypothetically, the company could have already notified the bank. What I suggest, is get yourself straight to a really good lawyer and take him with you to the bank. Before you go, tell him what you've found out and what your intentions are."

"OK. Do you remember John Dunlop? Well, he's my attorney, so I will go straight there first and tell him everything. He'll understand."

"Don't tell him all. Just about what happened on Friday."

"Next thing, once you've done this, then you go straight into hiding again." Patrick couldn't understand why he shouldn't be allowed to go straight to the office to clear his name.

"If you go there, the odds are you're going to be arrested immediately. That leaves Chen free to use the computer and with you stuck inside a jail for maybe twenty four hours gives them time while he and possibly Orman stack up evidence against you. Also, if you get there and tell the police what's happening regarding Chen's account, it will look highly suspicious that you have not yet reported it. On that basis they will still arrest you, because you've said nothing about this anyway, then they will report the matter to the board and In the interim, they will be free to change everything."

"What the hell do I do now?"

"Go to the lawyer then to the bank, get those two chores out of the way first. Then go into hiding for a while, book yourself into a hotel or somewhere safe. Later today we'll get together and draw up a plan of attack on Chen without his knowledge. Once that's done we wait and let them find out about him. That way you'll still be implicated, but there is a fifty-fifty chance you be allowed to explain your story with the voluntary return of the funds, you'll probably have cleared yourself."

"That could take days, weeks even."

"Only idiots rush into situations without thinking out the full ramifications. My warning if you care to use it, if you go rushing in you're placing yourself in a very precarious position."

"You're the chief, I'm the Indian so I'll comply, against my better judgement mind you."

"Good. Now where do you want to meet for lunch?" They made arrangements to meet at a pub two miles from Chiswick.

"By the way Patrick. Do not drive that Porsche today, if the police are onto you, they could also be on the lookout for the car and with licence plate recognition fitted you could be picked up."

"Oh Jesus. This gets worse by the minute."

"For the few of days your whole life is going turned upside down and be hell for you. Just keep your pecker up, now is the time to get your chess head on and think. Just remember you're fighting in the big league now, what the hell did you expect? These people are going to fight you with everything they've got, until you've got hard proof against them, nobody but, nobody's going to believe your whole story."

"You do."

"I'm a newspaper man, also you're a friend in need, and I could never walk away from that. Besides that, I've got to believe you now, because we're getting first reports that there's been a huge earthquake in Iran in an area without fault lines and I can't ignore that."

"What?"

"You heard me, everything you've told me has got to be true because I simply cannot believe in coincidences of this proportion."

"Thanks Terry, see you at one." Patrick was scared, the telephone rang, it was Kim calling from a callbox.

"I couldn't get through, you must have been on the line for half an hour. What did Terry say?" They spoke for a while as he repeated everything that had happened she was considering each step.

"He's right, that's just what Chen wants you to do, you go racing

231

in there, he'll have you removed from the office so that he can build up a case against you and clear himself. I'm glad your friend is on our side, I think with him about, we at least stand a tiny chance to beating these people."

"But what do I do with myself in the meantime?"

"First you take the Porsche and put it out of sight in the garage, then get yourself down to the attorney's office. C'mon Patrick, wake up, get off your butt and stop feeling sorry for yourself, you're going to have to move quickly and in the meantime I'll keep tabs on what's going on at the office and then see you this evening. We mustn't do anything out of the ordinary that will attract attention."

"You're right, I'll see you this evening."

From Victoria bus station Patrick walked the three blocks to the attorney's office, the brass plaque at the black painted door of a Victorian house read John Dunlop and Partners. The receptionist asked him to follow her into a luxuriously furnished office, his old friend sat back in his leather chair and smiled. Patrick noticed that John's dark hair was graying at his temples and that the once superb athlete was just starting to acquire a slight paunch.

"Patrick. This is such a pleasant surprise, fortunately I'm in court later this morning so I was able to make your appointment. What can I do for you?" Patrick found it a bit awkward to start with but as his story moved along, it became easier to get out. Finally he sat back and put both hands behind his head.

"Well that's quite some story, do you know why this man Chen is out to get you?"

"Yes, but that's a completely horrendous other tale, right now I've got to protect myself and that's why I need you to come to the bank with me."

"I'll not be party to anything illegal and what you've done is downright criminal. If you and I weren't old friends, I would throw you out of my office."

"I thought it best to tell you everything, these are not your run-of-the-mill criminals. You know from old that I never lie, this time you're going to have to believe me and in blind faith take my word that this is not a prefabricated story." John stared at him long and hard while making up his mind, he was possibly looking for a flinch that would betray Patrick. There was none and he knew from their schooldays and later business dealings that Patrick wasn't given to making up fantasies of any untruth let alone something of this nature. Then again he was a lawyer and had seen men do the strangest things under stress, in his favour was that Patrick had brought his practice one of his largest accounts and for this he felt he owed his long standing friend a special favour.

"OK, let's see, we're going to have to be quick otherwise you're going to have to wait until I'm finished at court." John called his secretary and dictated a short letter for Patrick, telling his secretary to type it immediately. When she disappeared into her office, he searched a large pile and finally picked out a buff folder tied up with a thin pink band. Within minutes the girl was back with a completed letter and John let Patrick read through it. It contained instructions from him for the bank to return what he considered were illegally placed funds as they were not his, nor had the funds ever been ever been his property.

"Here sign it and let's get down there." At the bank Patrick asked for a statement of his account, the teller disappeared and two minutes later presented it to him. He examined it and sure enough, there was the amount, now converted to English pounds and credited to his account.

"As I thought, this amount here is not supposed to be in my account."

"Whose account should it be in then?" the teller enquired sarcastically. John Dunlop, who was standing beside Patrick immediately intervened.

"Young man, this amount has been transferred to my client's account incorrectly, he has a letter for your manager instructing your bank to return the amount to its rightful owners. Now could you see to it that your manager gets this letter immediately." To make sure, Patrick double checked the name of the manager, John wrote the name and time of delivery on the letter, replaced it into the white envelope before handing it to the surly young man who he made sign for the receipt of the letter.

"Thanks a million John for accompanying me here, it would seem that the bank hasn't yet been contacted by the police or the company."

"I'm glad that I didn't have to rescue you from the long arm of the law. Still, I think you're being silly doing it this way instead of confronting them in proper fashion, if you were any other client, I wouldn't be party to this subterfuge but, you've chosen your path and I must respect your views."

"Believe me, there's more to this than you or I could ever imagine. My life is on the line here and I don't intend giving it up without a hard fight, the law right now is not really on my side yet and that will only hamper me getting this sorted out."

"I understand and for all its peculiarities, I still think the law system in this country works."

"Then why am I being set up and being hounded by the law, when others are setting me up and are the culprits?"

"That's why you're going to have to tackle it head on, anyway, I must be off, otherwise I'm going to be late for court."

"Once again, John, thanks for your help."

"You have my home and private numbers, please call me at any time if you need my services. I've got a feeling that this is just the beginning of a painful road for you." Patrick watched the man walk down the road, before making his way back to the Victoria bus station to meet Terry for lunch. as prearranged They discussed the incidents to date.

"I really do hope that you realise you've got to keep out of sight for a while."

"I feel so bloody helpless."

"Yes, that I understand but, hopefully the company will shortly latch onto our friend Chen and the missing money, alternatively the pharmaceutical firm will quickly pick up and trace their loss, then at least both Chen and Ormon will have some explaining to do."

"Yes, but it still doesn't help me now."

"It would help less if you were stuck away in jail, at least this way, you can keep in contact with the real world." Patrick left Terry at three o'clock and took a bus to Chiswick. The world had suddenly become an extremely hostile place and around each corner he imagined that there would be some further danger lying in wait to trap him. For the very first time in his life he was truly frightened, he reached the safety of Kim's house where he locked the front door and breathed a sigh of relief.

CHAPTER TWENTY FOUR

"Did anything further happen at the office today?' Patrick hardly gave Kim time to get inside the front door before asking the question.

"You can't believe what's gone on, fortunately I've been kept right up to date by one of the computer operators who owes me a big favour. Would you like a drink?" Kim rarely had a drink so soon after arriving from work, her usual custom generally being to have a hot bath before she could relax fully.

"Yes please, so tell me what happened?"

"After I spoke to you this morning the policemen waited around for about half an hour and then when you didn't show up they told Chen that they were going to send someone to your house. They left and I had to go to the financial department to see about the costing for one of my projects. When Chen saw me he called me into your office which he's now using for himself, he was feeling very pleased with himself at the time and bragged to me about how one could never trust a Westerner. While I was there one of your accountants asked to speak to him and being the show-off that he is, told the man to talk in front of me. The bank had called and told us that they had written instructions from you denying any claim to the money in your account and wanted to transfer it back to us. They needed instructions where the money should be sent." She sat down on the couch next to Patrick handing him a large whiskey as she did so.

"What happened then?" Kim let out her staccato giggle.

"You should have seen him, he went all colours of the rainbow and screamed that someone had betrayed him, it was a little scary at the time, he was something like a deranged person, slamming his hand on the desk and shouting."

"And then?"

"When the initial shock had passed he told the accountant to tell the bank that the funds should stay in your account until the matter had been sorted out."

She took a long, noisy suck at a piece of ice from her drink, this habit had always made Patrick cringe, especially when she started to chew the ice.

"The bank said they had clear instructions to return the money and could not hold onto it, they then informed the accountant that they would be returning the funds to the bank account from which it originated. Chen went absolutely mad once again and that's when I left him to rave on." She bit hard into the piece of ice, Patrick felt his skin crawl and his body gave a slight shudder.

"He was fuming when I left him."

"Was that all that happened today?"

"Oh no, he apparently went right around the office accusing all sorts of people of betraying him realising that you must have had some inside information and had been warned. Then he must have sat down and tried to figure it out logically, because he called six operators into the office and started questioning them. The people had all been on duty this weekend. Would you like another?" He handed her his glass.

"Then later he came to my office and accused me of somehow having tipped you off."

"Not very sociable of him, was it?"

"That bastard hit me and now he's threatened me and the other six with our very lives if he found out who let you know."

"So what happens now?"

"Chen is going to recommend to the main board that the company installs a new financial director, I suppose it will be one of his trusted lackeys, but that's not everything that happened."

"What else?"

"I had a call from Seoul today, Chen must have told them that he spoke to me and the others, because they asked me if I knew whether you had been accused of fraudulently siphoning money from the company. When I said that I had heard, they asked me about your involvement with Chen. Do you think that they could have located the missing funds that we placed in his account yet?"

"It's possible, they have excellent accountants in Seoul and if they've stumbled onto the missing money already then our friend Raymond will be in for a rude awakening." Both sat with their own thoughts until Kim got up.

"C'mon let's have a bath then go and have dinner somewhere, I'm not just going to sit here and let this thing get to me."

"Why not rather stay in? It would be far safer."

"You're right and wrong, we'll have to be careful, but if we go to Claude's place, I think we'll be safe. Let's make a final decision in the bath."

"You go ahead, I'll be there in a minute, I must call Terry and let him know what's happened." Kim was stretched out in the bath when he finished talking and he got into the bath, she lay back against him as they tried to let the day's problems of the day soak away. They dried each other then went through to the bedroom and made very tender love. It was as if they were allowing each other to take some form of solace from their respective hardships by letting their feelings flow between them. Two hours later they both secretly escaped from their house which had seemed to imprison them. Like two fugitives, they carefully studied the road outside to make sure nobody was watching before leaving the building. Away from it, both of them felt reasonably safe in the moving car as she drove out of her road with him lying down in the passenger seat, they weren't sure whether they would be coming here for some time to come. Far from being relaxed throughout the evening, both were nervous and locked in pensive thought. Claude remarked that they were not their usual happy selves.

They left the restaurant earlier than usual both deciding that it would be better to have an early night. Their venture out of doors had proved a dismal failure tonight, just as they got into bed a loud buzz sounded. Patrick looked at the bedside clock it was only ten o'clock.

"Who the hell would be calling at this time of night." Fear passed through both of them as they lay listening to the persistent buzzing of the front door. Kim lifted the receiver and asked who it was. She quickly cupped her hand over the mouthpiece and mouthed to Patrick.

"It's Raymond Chen."

"Tell him you're in bed and that you'll talk to him in the morning." She shook her head.

"He'll think it suspicious, I'll try to get rid of him quickly." She told him to hang on and that she would be down in a minute to let him in. She got out of bed and went to the cupboard and slipped into a long yellow dressing gown.

"Stay hidden until I tell you." Patrick walked to the bathroom and quietly closed the door until it was slightly ajar, he stood and listened at the crack, for a while Kim said nothing and allowed Chen to carry on shouting. Suddenly as if her patience had snapped, Patrick heard her start shouting back at Chen. If he dared slap her again this time thought Patrick, he would hang the consequences and wring the man's scrawny neck like a chicken. In preparation he quickly pulled on a pair of trousers and a shirt which were carefully folded in a heap near his feet, being as silent as he could, he slowly drew on his shoes wanting to be ready just in case the man tried anything funny. He tiptoed to the door, listening to the raging argument taking place on the first floor, he could occasionally grasp words here and there, understanding that she was now threatening him with something. He hoped that she hadn't lost her cool altogether and told Chen what they had done, suddenly the shouting stopped and Patrick heard two loud reports which sounded as if they had come from a gun, followed very quickly by fast running footsteps beating a retreat down the stairs and then he heard the front door slam. He raced down the stairs taking two or three at a time, Kim was slumped on the floor, blood pouring from her shoulder all across the yellow silk. He lifted her up gently and Kim smiled weakly at him.

"That's one of them out of the way. If I die, make sure that he's sent back to Korea, they'll know what to do with him." She passed out. Only then Patrick saw a second patch of blood spilling out onto the side of her head. It was low down the back and the red liquid mingled with her black hair, matting it together before falling onto the clean carpet. He laid her down carefully, and immediately went to the phone to call for an ambulance. He told them that there had been a shooting and that he thought Kim would die. When they asked for his name, he gave a fictitious one, somehow his brain remained cool under this enormous pressure, but he knew he needed help. He immediately redialled and asked for Terry, desperately wanting to go across and hold the unconscious body of Kim. When Terry eventually came on the line, Patrick rattled off the facts.

"Get any money you've got and get out of there immediately, leave the front door open so that the ambulance men can get in." This surprised Patrick, how could he leave the place at a time like this? His conscience felt as if it was tearing him apart.

"I can't just leave her lying there like that."

"Patrick listen to me carefully, once they arrive the police will be close behind and if they find you there, you will be arrested for fraud and possibly murder. You've got no choice, get out and do not use your mobile, get to a telephone box and call me. I'll pick you up, do it now!" Patrick replaced the receiver and took a quick look at the form on the carpet. He wanted to pack cushions round her head to stem the bleeding, but something in Terry's voice made him realise he was more future use to her away from the place than staying by her side.

Then and there he made up his mind to find Raymond Chen and kill him, he raced upstairs and found his briefcase knowing it had enough money in to see him through a couple of days. Then he heard the fast revving motor of a vehicle roaring down the short street as he arrived on the first floor.

"Shit, too late." Patrick raced down the stairway to the front door and as he opened it the ambulance pulled up in front of the house, he quickly pointed to the first floor and as the second man passed by, Patrick placed an arresting hand on his arm.

"Save her please, the person that did this is called Raymond Chen and he's South Korean. Remember that name, Raymond Chen." The ambulance man shrugged free of Patrick.

"Tell that to the police, they'll be here in a minute." Patrick turned and made his way across the road and up along the pavement. Curious onlookers were starting to appear and look out of their windows, as he reached the corner a police car drove towards him. It took every bit of will power that he could summon to prevent himself from running as the vehicle passed him speedily making its way towards the house. Patrick walked purposefully with briefcase in hand not wanting to attract any undue attention. Patrick quickly reached the main Chiswick to London road and caught a bus, as he got onto it he could see other police cars appearing from both directions lights flashing and sirens blaring, he automatically presumed that the ambulance man had given them his description. Within minutes a wailing siren of an ambulance came past them heading in the direction of London and he wondered if it was possibly the same one that had been at the house. He alighted at

Hammersmith Underground and went straight to the pay telephones and called Terry to tell him where he was.

"Patrick walk up the road towards the Olympia Exhibition Centre and on the right you'll find a pub two blocks up, I forget what its name is but you can't miss it. Wait in there for me and for god's sake don't wander around. If the police have put out an all points description of you, then you could be a sitting duck where you are. Keep your eyes skinned and if you can change your immediate appearance in any way, then do it now. I'll see you in half an hour."

"What about Kim?"

"Don't worry about that for the moment, I've got one of my best reporters on the matter. Before I reach you, I'll be informed what her condition is.

"Just get yourself away from that station and off the streets to the pub, I'll see you shortly." Patrick took off his anorak and left it over the railing outside the underground station. At the first corner, walking towards Olympia he saw a lone policeman walking towards him. The black uniform was still a fair way off but he did feel panic surging up from deep down inside and wanted to turn and run, but knew that he had nowhere to run to. There was a newsagent on the opposite corner and he quickly crossed to it and bought two magazines and a newspaper. The policeman approached he boldly stood near the lit up news agent shop opened the paper and pretended to be reading. The uniformed man stopped and started talking to the news vendor, Patrick felt slightly rubbery in his legs as he turned away from the two men and walked slowly towards the pub and possible safety. When he felt he had put enough distance between them he folded the paper and quickened his pace, once inside he breathed a huge sigh of relief and ordered a double whisky. He needed the drink.

The Culling

CHAPTER TWENTY FIVE

The barman rang a large brass bell after he had already called time for closing. Patrick began to panic because he had explicit orders to stay put until Terry arrived. The door opened and his friend waddled in, he tried ordering a drink, but the barman was having none of it.

"C'mon, let's go to a place that I know where they'll serve a thirsty man a drink," he said in a loud voice, Patrick gathered up his brief case and followed his friend.

"Relax, act naturally, you've got nothing to fear that way."

"Have you heard any news about Kim? Is she all right?"

"Nothing yet, but don't worry, I've put a bloody good reporter on the job. She'll find out what's going on and let me know."

"Jesus, Terry she means everything to me and walking away from her like that was the hardest thing that I've ever had to do in my life."

"I know, but if you had stayed you would be in some police station now trying very hard to answer some extremely tricky questions. I'll contact a friend of mine and find out the lay of the land as far as you're concerned and Jenny will keep a watching brief over Kim and she has strict orders to stay there until she's relieved and my staff will keep me up to date."

"I want to find Chen, I'm going to kill that sonofabitch."

"Don't you try anything like that. Do you understand me?" They reached Terry's car and drove to the heart of London and a quiet drinking hole that Terry often used for just such an occasion. For a while they sat drinking and discussing what had to be done next.

"Have you got anywhere else you can hole up? You can't go back\to Amersham or Chiswick, they'll be watching out for you." Patrick thought for a while then got up and went to the telephone. He dialled a number and spoke to his only real friend asking whether he could stay for a while and that he would explain later. He returned and said that he had a bed for a few days.

"C'mon, let's get you there, we both need our beauty sleep." They drove across town to Battersea, Terry dropped Patrick outside an old Georgian flat situated right across the road from the large Battersea Park. Patrick watched the tail lights move down the road and turn left at the next corner, he briskly strode along the pavement and past the corner where Terry had just turned. Further along the block he turned to see if anybody was watching him, not seeing anything out of kilter then entered the old red brick building. The front door was open which he thought unusual, because all these old places had a front door security buzzer systems, on the second floor he knocked on the large black door.

"What have you been up to, has that little girlfriend kicked you out?" Patrick walked straight past his ex-wife and into her flat.

"How little you know, she was shot tonight and I still don't know whether she's dead or alive."

"My god, what sort of people are you mixing with these days Patrick?"

"It's a very long story, I 'm in big trouble, I'm so weary and tired, can we please leave it until the morning?"

"Of course we can, I really didn't mean to be flippant and I'm sorry. Can I get you something to eat or drink?"

"Right now I would love a good cup of strong tea." Patrick was shattered as he flopped down into a large chair while Sue disappeared into the kitchen at the back of the house constantly returning to check on him, she had always been the same, her butterfly action flitting in and out of the room preparing something for him. She was tall and very beautiful with model proportions, her long black hair was gathered into a tight bun on top of her head. He had often wondered why she simply didn't let it fall freely, it looked so much nicer that way. By the time she cooked him an omelette he found himself starting to nod off.

"Tired?"

"Bloody exhausted."

"I was going to make you sleep on the couch but what the hell, you were my husband once and you're still my best friend. Come on, you can sleep in my bed, it'll be like old times, sleeping together without making love. We'll see what we can do about getting a fold up bed if you intend staying a little longer."

He didn't argue and followed her to her bedroom.

"Want a shower or anything?" He opened his briefcase and took out a small black bag. It was an airline freebie but it had shaving kit, toothbrush and toiletries. After disappearing, five minutes he reappeared looking slightly better than when he had gone in. Sue was in the double bed and had lifted the duvet on his side, as he started stripping Sue watched her ex-husband carefully. Unlike her, he had put on some weight, but otherwise was as she remembered him.

"Funny, this feels very strange, for years I would get into bed with you just like this and it was a chore. Here you are again and I feel like a totally stranger is about to get into bed with me."

He didn't take off his underpants as he slipped under the duvet. Sue wasn't wearing anything, so her habit of sleeping nude had not changed but being able to stretch out and relax again felt good. He let out a long sigh, sat up wolfed back the omelette and drank the cup of tea that she had made up earlier. Suddenly the events of today caught him by surprise and he could all he could think about the events without having to worry about himself. A lump welled into his throat and he felt a combination of remorse and fury pass through him. Feeling something like a little boy lost, tears suddenly came to his eyes, Sue watched him carefully without and saying anything, could feel the confusion and grief emanating from her ex-husband.

"Would you like to talk about it, or do you want to go to sleep?" He put down the cup and turned towards her and just shook his head. She moved over towards him, knowing that this was not the time to talk because he needed support and comfort at that moment. She turned off the lights.

"Come and let me give you a cuddle." Without resistance he moved to her and took her in his arms, he was like a little baby being comforted by a mother as she moulded her soft body into his. They lay like that with her slight rocking motion sending him into deep sleep. She wondered who or what had done this to him because he had never been a man of extremes, in fact the very opposite, gentle and too predictable for his own good she thought. It had been those traits that had forced her have an affair while they were still married, when she needed excitement, he hadn't been able to give her the type of feeling of excitement she craved. Right at that moment she felt extremely comfortable and fell asleep still holding him tightly.

Sue woke up in the early hours of the morning, she was unsure at first, then realised what had woken her. Her arm had almost gone to sleep with Patrick's weight on it, slowly she extracted her arm then shook it vigorously to get it to respond. The blackness of night was just starting to fade to the arrival of the early morning sun. She rolled over and looked at the clock and realised that there was still more than three hours to go before she had to get up. This morning she was flying to Bahrain and wouldn't be back for three days, at least he could use her flat during this time to sort himself out. Quietly she left the bed and went through to the kitchen to make herself a cup of tea. The first thing she always did in the morning was have a cup of tea and a cigarette before starting her day. She made two cups just in case before sneaking quietly back to the bedroom, as she sipped away she listened to the gentle snoring of the man beside her. She tried to remember when last she had woken having a man in bed with her. She realised it must have been at least two years previously before today, it wasn't because of her looks, she was only twenty nine and considered extremely attractive by most men and even though she had had many lovers after separating from Patrick there hadn't been anyone that she wanted in her bed or could honestly say she would spend the rest of her life with. Her work took her to various places in the world and she enjoyed being an air hostess but still missed having a firm relationship in her life. Patrick had been her first lover and now as she looked at him she wondered if he were still the same sterile lover that she had married or whether his girlfriend had managed to prise him out of his shell. The thought suddenly had appeal to find out whether he had changed in all these years of their being apart. She would never admit it later but whether it was interest, boredom or that little devil on her shoulder she did not know but she finished her cigarette, put it out before sliding down gently so that her head was below the duvet. Slowly she edged up towards him until her body was once moulded with his, she felt Patrick move slightly and cough as he started to wake up and she closed her eyes pretending to be asleep again. She felt him move away and get out of bed and go to the bathroom. He came back into the bedroom and stopped at the window, she moved up the bed slightly to watch him and saw him standing looking out the window overlooking the park.

"Morning, you're up early." He turned and looked at her.

"Sorry, I didn't mean to wake you, this is the best time of day."

"I woke up earlier and made you a cup of tea, I don't know if it's cold, I can make you another if it is." He came back to the bed and climbed in.

"Just like old times, isn't it?"

He lifted the cup and drank the tepid brew, replacing the cup on the bedside table he slid down below the duvet.

"Do you want to tell me what's been going on?"

"Not just at the moment, I'll tell you all about it later, let's go back to sleep."

She cuddled up to him and he didn't resist, at first they just lay there holding each other to draw comfort before she started slowly running her fingers across his broad back, slowly allowing her hand to move lower until she reached the only bit of clothing separating them. She felt his hand start moving as well, it ran the full length of her torso until it reached the lower part of her buttocks, she shuddered very slightly each time the tempting fingers reached the bottom of her spine and move down towards the upper part of her thighs. For some time they continued this way, neither prepared to advance any further than these comforting movements. Her thoughts went back to their married days, never before had he been so tender, it had always been getting into bed followed by sex and then to sleep without any variation. No matter what she had tried, it always ended up the same. Suddenly without warning his hand came up and tilted her head so that she was looking straight into his eyes but all she could see was loneliness and desperation. She felt like a magnet being attracted to this sad man and moved toward him and gently placed her mouth against his. She wasn't sure what was going to happen next, he was either going to respond or more likely was going to chastise her in his usual fashion. He did neither, simply withdrawing his lips, he slid down the bed and softly took one of her breasts in his mouth and started to suck ever so gently at her hardened nipple. Not knowing whether this was his form of wanting to be mothered, she didn't move and enjoyed the moment for all its worth feeling a slight tingling sensation as the soft sucking became more urgent and then he moved slightly to reach the other breast. His tongue worked furiously around the nipple as he intermittently continued to suck and nip at both breasts. She separated from him and turned onto her back to allow him easier access to the front of her body,. knowing that she had to let him do what he wanted because he needed some form of self confidence and if she stopped him now his turmoil would become greater than it was at present. The sensation within her grew as his mouth teased and taunted her desperately wanting him to move down the length of her body, but knew that he must be allowed to go at his own pace. With great difficulty she restrained herself from not reaching down and touching him which was becoming an overwhelming desire. As if he knew her every feeling, his gentle fingers moved down between her legs and teasingly tugged and stroked her pubic hair while his mouth kept their attack going on her twin mounds. Never before had any of her lovers titillated her in this manner, she could feel the build up to orgasm arriving from not far away. Her throat was dry and she sensed that her head was swinging from side to side as she wanted him to stop and make love to her. At the same time she was in ecstasy and didn't want him to stop what he was doing although at the same time somehow realising that the involuntary movement of her hips were to try to get him to react differently, but no matter how hard she tried, he kept the relentless gentle attack going. Without warning the orgasm struck her with such force that she let out a loud scream and only then did he allow his taunting fingers the luxury of pushing themselves against her Venus mound. The explosion within her whole being was something that she had never before experienced and it seemed to go on and on even when the shaking and shuddering had subsided, he again started from the beginning, allowing his mouth to take in the hardened nipples and his gentle fingers to tease at her. Again and again she exploded under his oral assault and in tumultuous intensity that never seemed to end, her whole body remained quivering for several minutes after he finally rolled onto his back and lay there for a while.

"I needed that."

"You needed that?" She reached over and slipped her hand into his briefs and found his penis standing hard and fast to attention.

"No, don't."

"Why not?"

"I needed to give you something, I don't want anything in return."

"Well my boy, you haven't yet given me everything I need and what would you say if I told you I want more than you gave me."

"Then you must take it yourself."

"I will." She tugged at his briefs and felt them give way then pulled him over on top of her, for some time they made extremely slow and gentle love. This definitely wasn't the same man that she had been married to all those years ago, this was the man she wanted now.

"It's a pity times aren't different," she said as she indulged herself in something she had never ever experienced before, this was total love as she had always imagined it should have always been.

CHAPTER TWENTY SIX

Patrick waited until after Sue left for the airport, her work meant that she would be away for three days in the Middle East and again that feeling of abandonment and loneliness crept in and also Patrick had an overwhelming sense of some shame and guilt because he couldn't make up his mind just why he had allowed himself to stupidly make love to Sue that morning. After taking a long hot shower to wake up but also in a strange way try and cleanse these feelings away, he went through to the kitchen and made himself some breakfast. His thoughts kept returning to his oriental partner's little bleeding body at the flat and for the first time since it happened found himself suffering short bouts of absolute remorse. He kept lifting the telephone receiver and replacing it because he knew was still too early to call Terry but he needed to know whether Kim had survived the night as well as the fact that inwardly he knew that the call must be made from a public telephone to avoid detection.

"You bastard Chen!" Patrick suddenly let out his feelings in a loud shout as if all the pent-up emotion suddenly reached breaking point inside his still weary body. That was one of the ways he simply needed to vent his feelings aloud and as he shouted he brought his fist down on the kitchen table with such force, that for a moment he thought he had broken his hand. Leaning forward he placed his head on the table only felt a flood of warm tears, for a while he sat at the table crying softly, allowing this mixed liberating flow of fury, guilt and frustration soak away onto the kitchen table. By the time he had finally disposed of all anger, he made himself a cup of coffee then went through to the small lounge and stood looking down across the busy road to the park. It was turning out to be a beautifully sunny morning and he decided to risk going for a walk to help pass time away until he could call Terry. After an hour strolling through the park he returned and used a public telephone to make the important call to his friend.

253

"Have you found out anything about Kim?"

"Yes. She's in a bad way and in a coma, her wound to the shoulder isn't too bad and that won't take long to heal however, the wound to her head apparently seemed to have only been a superficial wound, but the doctors are very worried that it may have damaged a nerve. They can't seem to find any reason for the coma because there should be nothing really wrong, still she remains unconscious in this coma. They think that it could rectify itself in few hours but could take days or weeks, the specialist are due to see her today, she is having an MRI scan and then they will interpret those scans. It's positive news, we will know more later."

"The main thing is that she's not dead, sis they indicate her chances of a full recovery?"

"They can't say yet except all they told Jenny was that time would tell once they had carried out various tests and at the moment they are letting her body try to recover naturally."

"What about Chen, have they arrested him yet?"

"That's the bad news, there's now a warrant out for your arrest. With all of the incriminating evidence stacked up against you, you've become the prime suspect because they now know that you were living with her. My son, you're in whole lot of trouble until Kim wakes up."

"Don't worry too much about me, her testimony will clear me once she comes out of the coma. We somehow have to nail Chen for this."

"Whoa, slow down and first things first, I've arranged for Jenny to remain at Kim's beside but what worries me most is that Chen is still roaming free. He is fully aware that he's bungled the killing and that when Kim revives, she will be able to have him put away for a long time. He is also part of the conspiracy and these boys are in the big league. My thinking is that he or his associates could arrange for her to have a medical accident. You're safe as long as you stay hidden, but Kim's life is in real danger." Patrick suddenly felt a cold shiver, he had been so involved with thinking about Chen that he had temporarily forgotten about the involvement of the governments. Kim was now in a government institution and there was every chance that Terry could be correct in his assumptions.

"We've got to get her away from that hospital as quickly as possible, I'll go there this morning and find a way to get her out"

"Don't you even dare move from there, I've already made arrangements for her to be transferred to a special sanatorium today. I have a story building here and nobody is going to steal it from me by having Kim killed, that's why Jenny and another colleague are standing constant guard over her at the moment."

"Well, that's a relief, can I at least see her when she's moved?"

"If you so much as move out anywhere, there's every likelihood that you are going to be picked up and then we're all in trouble. Get it through your thick skull old son, you've got to remain undercover and do not do anything stupid like using your mobile or the telephone wherever you are in hiding at the moment."

"I can't just sit here twiddling my fingers all day, I'll go mental."

"True but find yourself something to do until lunchtime, then call me back and hopefully by then, I should have the full story and we can start planning our strategy from there."

"All right, talk to you later." Patrick replaced the receiver and let out a long sigh, at least Kim was still alive he thought. He crossed the road and made his way back to Sue's flat, in the front room he inspected her bookcase in the corner. Searching through a vast array of paperbacks he selected one and returned to start trying to read but found that all concentration was continually being interrupted by thoughts of the last twenty four hours. Finally he went back to the bedroom and lay down, Terry's news about Kim had managed to lift a huge burden from his shoulders but there was nothing he could right now, he shut his eyes and fell into deep sleep.

"Terry, what's happening?" Patrick had slept soundly until one o'clock and then made himself a sandwich and coffee before going to the public phone again and calling Terry.

"They are moving Kim this afternoon and I need you to meet me at nine o'clock."

"Why?" His friend told him that he needed to discuss various aspects and to plan what they were going to do about Chen and Ormon. Patrick said he would call Terry at eight o'clock and tell him where they should meet up, Patrick had purposely given Terry a false address last night when he dropped him off because then, he was not sure why, but from the moment of the shooting he trusted nobody, not even Terry, but now, having rested and in the clear light of day, he felt rather stupid about his extreme distrust of his old friend last night. His suspiciousness of telephone calls made him nervous and with what he had read, Terry's telephone calls could be monitored, so he wasn't prepared to give out his address on the line. When they attacked his house he had agreed with Terry to never divulge anything on the open line that could incriminate either of them. If his own government was involved, then it wouldn't take them long to trace him through one of his friends. He knew that none of them would even think about him staying at Sue's flat because very few people knew that he had even remained friends with her.

"Jenny, let's get over to the hospital. Is everything arranged?" His companion lifted a white dustcoat from the back of her chair and turned to him.

"Boss, you've had some hair-brained schemes to get in a story before, but this one takes the biscuit, you realise that should we get caught out, this newspaper will be flushed down the toilet. You realise that, don't you?"

"This is the big one Jenny, trust me, I feel it in my bone, if anybody gets to her first our whole story goes up in smoke. C'mon let's get going, otherwise we'll miss all the fun. Have you arranged for a photographer?"

"Do pigs fly? Of course I have, he'll be opposite the entrance and record the full thing." The two took the lift to the ground floor and walked through a narrow passageway into a courtyard where they climbed into her car. They drove to the King Edward Memorial Hospital a short distance from Chiswick and parked in a side road so that they could have easy exit and not be picked up by the hospital security cameras nor did they want to get caught up in among the visitors searching for parking spaces when the time came for them to make a quick getaway.

"Well, let's go and kidnap our patient." The girl fell in step with her fast-waddling editor, Jenny had recently returned from a dangerous assignment in Beirut and used to fast moving events and the only difference between her usual mandate and this was that she had always been simply a recording onlooker. This time, she was to be an accomplice in what she knew to be wrong and she wasn't too happy with the situation because this caper made her feel that she was placing her career on the line. Pitted against that was the excitement of capturing a major story that was stopping her from denying her editor the satisfaction of giving this plumb to any other reporter who would be willing to sacrifice his or her principles.

"The ambulance will be here in about four minutes, both porters have their instructions and our two nurses should already be inside by now."

"What if somebody stops them and asks for papers or something?"

"Don't worry, they're both professionals, ex-nurses, they know the drill. They're collecting Kim from the MRI unit for X-rays and various tests when if we are lucky because it's such a large place and I don't think the left hand will know what the right hand's doing. By the time they discover the missing patient and her records, she'll be long gone."

"Let's keep our fingers crossed that it all works out correctly, the only thing I hope is that Kim isn't worse than we have been led to think because then we are in hot water."

"No, I promise that there's very little wrong with her physically, the sanatorium will be able to handle that side without problem, it's her coma that's got them all so worried and hopefully they will be able to bring her around in time to help my friend." They entered the hospital wing where Kim was being kept, a shabbily dressed man sitting at reception got up and followed the two. They moved through the sanitary corridors until they reached the end and walked up a flight of stairs, at the top they found two nurses dressed in operation outfits with elasticised loose caps and untied mouth masks which had been pushed down to their necks while on their feet they both wore material overshoes. Behind them were two burly young men dressed in long green hospital jackets, between them was a hospital trolley.

"Everyone ready?" Nobody said anything, they were all too nervous and simply

nodded their agreement.

"All right, let's get on with it." Terry and Jenny watched as the four made their way along the corridor and swooped into a doorway, the shabbily dressed man made his way to the top of the stairway and expertly pulled two cameras from the small black bag that he was carrying. He quickly lifted the cameras in turn and started adjusting for correct lighting, within minutes the two bogus porters came out of the door and headed towards the lift. The continual clicking from the camera was the only sound that Terry could hear, shortly afterwards the two nurses followed the fleeing trolley down the corridor.

"So far so good, Richard get yourself down the entrance. Pronto. We have got to record everything. I just hope they put Kim in the right ambulance, that's if it's there on time."

"Don't be such a pessimist, c'mon let's get down there and watch the fun." As fast as he possibly could, he followed his young reporter down the stairs but instead of turning right and past reception, they turned left and through a large double swing door. They were just in time to see Kim being loaded into the waiting ambulance, the four people with her had changed their dress somewhere between collecting the patient and getting her into the waiting vehicle. The two men were now wearing ambulance men's uniforms and the two girls were in their normal nurse attire. The shabbily dressed photographer clicked away as the ambulance pulled away from the loading area. It had all gone like clockwork and nobody had even questioned the group.

"Couldn't have been easier, c'mon let's get to the car, Richard you know how to get there, the instruction is to take it easy so that you can be there ahead of them." The photographer finished packing his cameras and disappeared around the corner.

"He must have parked somewhere nearby so that he could get away quickly."

Terry looked at his companion with pride, she had organised a very difficult task with immaculate precision, Terry absentmindedly took a cigarette out of the packet and placed it in his mouth.

"Not here, do you want to draw attention to yourself, you cannot smoke in and around a hospital." He clicked his tongue as he placed it into his jacket pocket, they calmly strolled through reception out to the car where Terry called the office to see if there was anything for him. Jenny drove towards Richmond and the sanatorium while he spoke to the deputy editor and told him that he and Jenny were following up something in Fulham and that he would remain in contact with the office.

After they reached the place and sorted out everything regarding Kim, they started back towards London, a call came through to them on the car phone. It was Terry's deputy editor who told them that a story of a hospital kidnapping had taken place at the King Edward Hospital. Terry said that they weren't far and would get down there immediately to cover the story with Jenny. He told the voice to contact Richard the photographer and make sure he got down there as quickly as possible, he also instructed his deputy to hold the front page. Jenny smiled sweetly at her editor.

"Looks like we've got ourselves a good story. I wonder who would want to kidnap a patient."

They both laughed as she turned right at the traffic lights.

CHAPTER TWENTY SEVEN

"How could you be so stupid?" Vladisky Ormon was on the telephone to Raymond Chen, who had just been informed him of the shooting of Kim, the South Korean was now asking for his help in the matter.

"Are you sure that she's dead?" The man said that he was certain because he couldn't have missed from that close range.

"Stay where you are, I'm going to check out everything then I'll be back to you later. Have you located Patrick Rodgers yet?" Raymond told him that Patrick had gone underground somewhere and that his entire staff and associates were still searching for him.

"Bloody hell, that's not good, can't you people do anything correctly? I think we must meet and I'll get my contacts busy, you stay right there, I'll be back to you shortly." Ormon was furious as he replaced the receiver, thinking that his plan would have got Rodgers out of the way once and for all but now, he was going to have to take care of him personally. He called somebody in one of the ministry departments and asked him to find out everything he could about the girl. Chen had already given him details from her employment record. He cursed Raymond Chen, thinking that the man had gone absolutely mad, for he was a key player for the South Korean contingent and had now placed himself in an awkward position over some petty argument with one of his staff. Didn't he know that the project was far more important than any petty squabble? The person on the end of the line said he would get back as soon as he could, Ormon looked at his watch it was almost eleven o'clock and he wondered why Chen had taken so long to contact him. Within an hour the man that he had contacted called back, he reported that the girl was still alive and had been taken to King Edward Hospital. What was more important was that Patrick Rodgers was being sought in connection with the shooting, Ormon's brain suddenly started spinning like a whirlwind, thanking the man for the information, he replaced the receiver.

"Get me the terrible twins immediately." If Patrick and Kim Lee were connected in some way then she could have been searching for something right under his nose without him knowing it. He hadn't had any reason to suspect a mole working so close to him, no wonder Patrick had managed to evade their trap he thought. Of course she was acting as his eyes and ears in the company and would be listening to things going on in and around the office, the door opened and the two huge men entered.

"What the hell took you so long? When I say immediately, I mean just that." Ivan started to make an excuse but was cut off in mid sentence.

"I'm not interested in your lies, I need you to do a job and it has to be done as quickly as possible." The two men looked at other, they knew from his tone that he was worried and whatever he wanted them to do was going to result in hardship for someone. Ormon scribbled a name and address on a sheet of paper and tore it off his pad.

"Here. This little lady must meet with an accident and it has to be today, the job was bungled and you must finish it quickly, now get out and do it and if you mess it up, God help you both. I don't want any excuses, all I need to know is that it's been carried out, also you know the house in Amersham that you turned over. Did either of you see any photographs of the owner."

"Yes, I did." The black man with the huge scar spoke for the first time.

"What I want you to then is for you to get back there today, I need a photograph of the man on my desk by this afternoon, do you two lunkheads understand me?"

"Do you want us to break into the place in broad daylight, what if we're seen?"

"I couldn't care, before you go to the hospital, go to the house and collect that picture first, bring it back here and then by this afternoon or this evening I want your news that the girl out of the way. Now you thickies get out of my office and don't return until you've carried out the instructions to the letter. Remember what I said if you fail." Both men winced inwardly, the little Hitler always treated them with such contempt and there was nothing they could do about it. He kept himself away from the limelight and expected them to place themselves at risk, if it weren't for his stranglehold on their past, he could and would be their next victim. They left the office and headed towards Amersham.

Mrs. Jones was busy in the bathroom when the front doorbell rang, she sighed and put down the sponge. She opened the door to a large black man in overalls carrying a toolbox, he produced an official looking card.

"Telephone inspection, we have to change the instrument and check the line." She handed back the card and looked carefully at the man.

"I've had no instructions that you were supposed to come and do work here." The man bent and started lifting his box.

"Oh, well, if you don't allow us to do this today then it won't be done for another three or four months, take it or leave it lady, I'm not waiting for you to mess me about."

"No wait. I suppose it'll be all right, it was just that Mr. Rodgers didn't warn me that you were supposed to be here." The black man turned and whistled, another mountain of a man appeared, she noted that In his hand he had a telephone. She allowed them past and they walked into the hall, the black man turned to her again.

"Is this the only instrument in the house?"

"No. There's another upstairs."

"You check this one and I'll do the other." Without waiting, the white man started up the stairs towards the bedroom.

"No wait, you mustn't go up there." The old lady was confused, she couldn't watch both of them at the same time, at the top of the stairs the man turned and called down to her.

"Look, madam, we've got a job of work to do and I must check the extension telephone. If you're worried about it, why not come up and watch over me?" She was desperately trying to find a way out of the problem, because if she went upstairs the man left below would be out of sight and if she stayed down here, the man could be rifling through Mr. Rodgers' valuables. She quickly made up her mind and so followed the white man up to the bedroom, the black man knew exactly where he had seen the photographs in the study even though the house looked completely different from when they had left it in such a mess several weeks before. He slipped into the lounge and quickly searched the large cabinet until he found the photograph albums. Without waiting, he stripped out several photographs of Patrick, then he looked through two more. There was a more recent picture of the man together with a woman, he quickly pulled out two more photographs and replaced the albums in the cabinet, he slipped the pictures into his overall and checked that everything was in order before making his way back to the hall. The telephone started tinkling furiously, lifting the receiver he heard the voice of his companion in the bedroom above.

"Just give me a minute to change the instrument." On the floor above, the white man took a screwdriver from his pocket and pretended to make several adjustments to the wall socket by removing the cover, clicking his tongue several times then replacing it, he turned to the old lady hovering around near the doorway.

"Everything here seems to be in order with this unit now, let's see if my colleague has managed to sort out the problem on the one below." He pushed the button several times again and they heard the downstairs instrument chiming in tune to his gestures.

The black man lifted the receiver and told Ivan that he had completed the task.

"Everything seems to be in order now, let's go downstairs and see if there are any faults down the line still." They found the black man busily packing tools back into the box. He had carefully placed a small listening device in below the mouthpiece of the new instrument that he had replaced, just in case they needed to monitor any calls from the house.

"That's all from my side, you see, one, two, three and you have a new telephone system, it's a good thing you didn't send us away now if you'll just sign here, we'll be on our way." The black man handed her an official looking sheet of paper saying that the work had been completed and the times of arrival and departure. She filled it in and signed it, the two men left the house and Mrs. Jones breathed a huge sigh of relief.

"You can't be sure about workmen today, they'll steal the teeth out of your mouth." She muttered to herself as she shut the front door and walked around the house to make sure that nothing of value had been stolen while she was upstairs. Nothing seemed to be amiss.

"I wonder why Mr. Rodgers didn't notify me of their arrival. I thought I was supposed to be taking care of everything. When he calls, I'm going to give him a piece of my mind." She was still muttering to herself as she made her way to the bathroom.

On their way to the hospital they stopped to change their clothes and transport vehicle. Ivan went to Ormon and delivered the photographs, he looked at them for some time thinking that he had not been aware that Patrick had been married. He checked through the pink file and found that the man had been divorced for several years. He did not give her much credence but he picked out the best picture to circulate it, he simply needed to have this man disposed of before the police managed to locate him, mainly because there may just be some awkward questions asked involving Chen. He wasn't particularly worried, even if the police did reach him first there were ways of silencing him, because if he started shooting off his mouth then it could leave the government having to answer some sticky questions if anybody believed him, it would save him a lot of trouble if they could find him before the police did.

"Take this and if you see this man, I want him followed because I want to know where he's hiding out. Now you two barbarian get out there and make sure my other instruction is seen to, I'll be here until you report back, I want her dead.." Ormon handed Ivan a colour copy of the marriage picture and the large man left the office to join his black companion who was waiting in the car.

"One day will be one day, we'll get our chance to get even with that runt." The black man sneered at Ivan, he knew full well what his associate was thinking and feeling and he wholly agreed with the man's sentiments. It was late afternoon when they left for King Edward Hospital, half an hour later they pulled their car into the parking lot.

"Let's see now." The receptionist at the hospital went through the lists.

"Yes, here we are, she was admitted last night. According to this list, she's in intensive care a private ward on the first floor. Take the lift or stairs and ask the sister on duty and she'll show you where Miss Lee can be found and also tell you if she's allowed to have visitors." The two men made their way to the lift and as the doors opened they were almost bowled over by a trolley with a patient being pushed into the lift. Ivan looked in both directions and saw a shabbily dressed man making his way along the corridor towards a fat man and a woman.

"This way, the ward must be down there where those people are." The fat man and his female companion left and went down the stairway just as they reached the double doors. They found the sister at her desk.

"We've come to see Miss Kim Lee, we're friends of hers, can you tell us where she is?"

"Miss Lee is still in a coma and on our critical list, you won't be able to visit her until she has improved."

"Can we just have a quick look at her?"

"No, I'm afraid you cannot because she is not currently on the ward."

"But, we were told she was here."

"She is, but she's been taken for MRI scans, if you wait she should be coming past soon, then you will see her."

"Thank you. Which building would she be going to?" "It's in this building on the ground floor laboratory, but they won't let you see her while in there. she could be ten minutes or an hour. If you want to wait you'll have to wait in reception." Ivan turned quickly and grabbed his friend's arm and made his way through the doors.

"C'mon let's get to the ground floor this way." The two men walked quickly down the stairs and along the corridor. In the distance ahead they saw the fat man and his pretty companion turn the corner.

"Here's the laboratory." Ivan walked straight in through the door. A young blonde

technician was sitting at a desk filling out a report. She looked up at the two enormous men.

"Can I help you."

"Yes. One of our workmates is supposed to be here for tests. Miss Kim Lee and before we go back to the office we would like to just have a quick look at her."

"Even if she was here you wouldn't be allowed to talk to her, but as you can see, there's nobody here at the moment and according to my schedule I have a young man for a test of a cancerous growth in a few minutes. No Kim Lee I'm afraid."

"Could there be another laboratory that she could have been sent to?"

"No, this is the only MRI laboratory in this part of the hospital." The two men left and started walking towards reception. There was a man sitting there looking along the corridor to the lifts. The fat man and his companion passed them and walked out of the front door. Ivan asked the man if he had seen the trolley. He pointed to the double doors down the short passageway.

"C'mon." They passed through the doors into the ambulance loading bay to find an elderly man sitting on a long wooden bench and asked if he had seen the trolley.

"I've been waiting for over an hour for an ambulance to take me home. They drove off that way with the person on the trolley." He pointed towards the gate at the far end of the grounds, somebody had their lines crossed thought Ivan as he and the black man made their way back to the first floor to question the nurse again. She was totally dismayed and quickly telephoned the laboratory where Kim was supposed to have been taken.

"Something's very wrong." Ivan knew instinctively that the bird had flown, what was the little runt going to say to them now?

CHAPTER TWENTY EIGHT

"You stupid idiots stay there and see what develops and if you spot anything out of the ordinary, let me know immediately." Vladisky Ormon was talking to Ivan who had informed him that the girl had already been moved from the hospital. What he had purposely omitted to tell his boss was that he and the black man must have actually passed her coming out of the lift on a trolley. Earlier in the day Ormon reported back to Chen and explained what his plans were and now the whole Culling Project could be at risk because both Patrick and Kim were still out there somewhere, free to reveal whatever information they had managed to acquire from the computer invasion under Ormon's control. The situation had now moved to a code red situation and become very serious indeed and it was time to call in all the resources at his disposal. Lifting the receiver again he immediately called his contact at the Ministry of Environment and gave him the story, warts and all. The person at the other end of the line promised that he would have the full weight at their command brought to bear on locating the two fugitives. He needed as much information on the two that he could get, Ormon promised to have copies sent around by courier immediately. He pushed a button on his desk and when the girl entered he handed the pink file to her.

"I want full copies made and sent to this address." The entire machinery of government would be working in his favour before the day was out, his henchmen were maintaining a watching brief at the hospital and had been instructed to report anything that would possibly turn up, there wasn't much more he could do at the present. Now it was a matter of time before he had those two informers within his grasp, he knew that if they moved position at all they would be spotted and reported, it was a pity that they seemed to be just one step ahead of him all the time he thought. At the hospital Ivan was busy talking to the duty nurse on the ward, she had already called in the hospital security man, who had in turn called the police. His companion was busily questioning the old man still waiting for his ambulance, there seemed nothing to go on and that the operation in removing Kim Lee from the hospital had been carried out with perfect timing and precision. Both felt helpless, but they had been ordered to stay on and see what transpired, the black man finished his questioning and went to reception, he desperately wanted a cigarette. Large signs were displayed forbidding any smoking so he made his way out the front door to the corner of the building. From this position he watched a procession of vehicles entering the parking area at the side of the building. He lit a cigarette and drew smoke deeply into his starved lungs. Walking across the parking lot towards him, the pretty young blonde and her fat waddling companion attracted his attention. They were in deep conversation as they passed on their way to the front door. He watched them and only when they were some distance away did the penny drop, he was sure that they were the couple who were in the corridor earlier in the day when Kim had been snatched. They must have seen something he thought, as he took a last long draw on the cigarette he started towards the front door to catch up with the pair.

On their way to Kingston, Terry had received a call from Patrick on the car telephone.

"Listen we've managed to get Kim away from the hospital and so she's safely in our custody now."

"I'm going mad just sitting here doing nothing, I really would like to see her."

"All right. I'll meet you where I dropped you last night at exactly nine o'clock this evening. Now don't be silly and wait in the open for me, stay hidden until you see my car, I'll stop at the same place and hoot three times, get to the car as quickly as possible. You'll be safe with me and I'll arrange to get you through the back way at the sanatorium." There was a long pause at the end of the line.

"Are you sure that it'll be safe wondering around a hospital?

What happens if somebody recognises me."

"We've done this sort of thing before as you may have gathered and this particular sanatorium is a special place that we fund for just such an event. Kim is being looked after by some fine specialists, the only thing you have to worry about in the meantime is that you keep yourself out of sight. Don't take any chances, if you're not there when I arrive, I'll drive around the block and repeat the exercise. If you have any suspicions or there's any risk at all, stay hidden."

"Right. Then I'll see you this evening. I don't know if I've said this before, but thanks for your help, I promise you I'll make it up to you when I'm clear of this mess."

"Don't worry about that, I'll see you later." He placed the telephone back in its cradle and turned to Jenny.

"Poor bastard. He's a pawn in a much larger game and if we see the end and get our story, we'll have at least managed to strike back a blow for the little people who are unable to defend themselves against these corporate and governmental giants." Jenny turned into a parking spot, and switched off the motor. She collected up a pad and checked her hair in the mirror.

"Wonder how long it will be before Richard gets here?" Inside the hospital they made their way to the first floor, at the entrance to the ward they were stopped by a uniformed policeman. Terry looked through the window in the door and recognised his old friend Inspector Muldoon talking to a nurse and a large man. He asked the policeman at the door to call the inspector.

"Gould, what are you doing here? Has your paper at last demoted you back to reporter? It's about time." The thin-faced inspector had come out of the ward into the corridor to talk to them. The news media had a love-hate relationship with the police force and like relatives, they used each other when it suited them, yet each of them despised the other's profession.

"Inspector Muldoon, you have a tongue like a viper. If ever you need a job as a reporter, don't be afraid to come and see me first. Now what's up?" The inspector gave Terry a wry smile and Jenny noticed that his pencil-thin moustache was badly trimmed on one side.

"Four people walked in here about an hour and a half ago and cool as you like, snatched a young South Korean girl away under the pretence of needing some tests done to her. We know she was loaded into an ambulance and driven away." Jenny scribbled down notes in her book.

"Did you get any descriptions of the kidnappers?"

"Yes, but as always they tend to be vague and conflicting, our identikit boys are on their way over."

"Any witnesses?"

"Only two of any consequence, firstly the nurse in there and then there's an old man that was seated at the ambulance receiving area. I'm afraid he's a little past it so there's not a lot to go on. That's where you come in, we desperately need to get a lead on her as quickly as possible. For some reason the bigwigs have already started sticking their noses in we've had a quick look at the camera footage and nothing, it's strange that. We'll get a picture across to you in an hour, could you run it in this evening's edition, preferably on the front page."

"Only if I get an exclusive on the story today then you've got front page."

"Okay I hold the story until five o'clock then I must release it to the rest of the media. It will have to go out on television news this evening, what I am prepared to do though, is tell them that your paper gave us a tip-off on the kidnap."

"Done. Now if you'll give Jenny all the details, while I talk to

272

those two, we'll get out of your hair so that you can get on with your job. It won't take us long to finish up here and you make sure that you get the identikit pictures sent across as quickly as possible." They busily collected the facts and then made their way downstairs to their car. As they pulled out of the hospital parking area Terry called his office and started deciphering their notes to the sub editor for the front page story. It would still catch the final edition today as long as they received the pictures in time. At the office the two edited the final wording and Terry called through to Richard to find out whether he had organised the pictures yet. Terry suddenly had a brainwave on their way to the office and managed to get Inspector Muldoon to take his photographer to Kim's flat and get hold of a picture of her. Richard had taken one of the pictures from the flat and was having it duplicated for the story. The identikit arrived at their office with seconds to spare, Terry looked at the four faces and agreed with Jenny that all four were a mile away from the team that they had used. If anyone could identify them from the pictures, it was going to be pure fluke. Terry left the office and drove to Battersea Park where he had dropped Patrick the previous evening. As he neared the flat he stopped and checked in his rear-view mirror, a long way behind he noticed that a car with two occupants had pulled up and double parked. They could be nothing, but Terry decided not to take any chances, he moved off quickly and glanced up again. The vehicle was such a long way off that he wasn't sure if it were moving forward slowly or not to keep pace with him. He turned left and accelerated up the narrow road to the next corner, saw an open parking spot ahead, pulled in and switched off the motor and waited. He heard the squeal of tires before he saw the vehicle shoot past the narrow road up towards the High Street. He quickly started his car and turned around in a hurried three point turn, by the time he reached the corner he saw the following vehicle swing left into the High Street. Back at the door he hooted urgently, Patrick slipped across the road and into the passenger seat.

"Get down and stay down!" Patrick didn't argue and immediately pulled at a lever on the side of his seat which fell back so that he was in a lying position below the window line.

"What is it?"

"I'm being followed and we've only got a minute or so before they realise that I'm on to them. Let's get the hell out of here." As he moved forward he saw the other car coming from the opposite direction and wondered if they had seen him make the pickup. Accelerating to the roundabout he swung sharp left across the Thames and then left again along the Thames Embankment. Twisting and turning through the streets of Chelsea until he was sure that he was no longer being followed.

"Okay, you can sit up now. Paste this on your top lip and put on this baseball cap." Handing Patrick the blue cap inside which he also found a false brown moustache inside. Behind the sun visor he used the mirror to line up the piece of hair on his upper lip. Terry looked at his friend, the transformation was fantastic, he now didn't even look remotely like the man who had entered the car.

"Now let me bring you up to date." As the vehicle moved west toward the sanatorium, Terry explained everything that had gone on during the day. When he arrived at the small hospital he drove straight around the back and stopped behind a large bush.

"Get this on, you'll probably boil in it but it was the only coat I could rustle up in the short time that I had available. It's just in case we bump into someone that remembers your face. From now on, no amount of precaution is going to be too great." He leaned over to the rear seat and then handed Patrick an old greatcoat.

"It's army surplus, but many a winter's night it has kept me warm. So don't knock it for its looks." Patrick noticed that it had dirty stains all down the front and back, but he battled to slip it on inside the cramped confines of the car. It seemed to envelope his frame and he judged that it was three sizes to too large for him.

"Ready? Then let's go and see how that little girlfriend of yours is doing." They made their way through a small rear door and up a narrow stairway to the first floor. The corridors were wide and clinical as they turned left and walked noisily towards a man sitting on a chair outside one of the rooms.

"He's our man just in case, nobody's allowed into that room without his permission." The man got up and from his pocket took a key and unlocked the door.

"In you go, I just want a word here." Terry waited until Patrick had gone into the room and was out of earshot.

"That is Mr. Rodgers, he must only be allowed to visit in my presence or if Jenny brings him in, at no time if he comes alone, do you let him anywhere near that room. If he comes in by himself get help immediately, because he could be here under duress. Tell Charlie as well." Terry found Patrick sitting at Kim's bedside holding her hand and talking to her, not being sure if the frail looking little Korean could hear or understand him, but he spoke to in a soothing manner nevertheless. He spent most of the time apologising to her for not being there when she needed him most and telling her that he loved her so very much. After half an hour, Terry indicated with a nod of his head that it was time for them to go, Patrick kissed her very gently on her lips and imagined that he felt her respond ever so lightly. As they made their way down the flight of back stairs Patrick could no longer hold back his rage.

"That Raymond Chen is going to pay for what he's done to Kim. I'll kill him if ever I get my hands on him." At the bottom of the stairs Terry turned to his friend and put his hands on Patrick's shoulders.

"From tomorrow we at the newspaper are going to concentrate and highlight Mr. Chen. He'll become an embarrassment to his government before long and hopefully be sent back to South Korea."

"You can't do that."

"We have to cut down your odds and until Kim regains consciousness, we don't have a fighting chance. Chen is only the monkey, he's definitely not the organ grinder. With him out of the way, we can then concentrate our efforts on bringing Ormon to heel because I think he's a big player within this whole outfit and we must force him into the open." They left and drove back the same way they had come returning to Battersea.

CHAPTER TWENTY NINE

In Vladisky Ormon's office a post-mortem of the recent events was busily taking place.

"Well, at least you two brick heads have managed to narrow down our field of search." Ivan and the black man were standing in front of Vladisky Ormon's desk and being dressed down like two naughty schoolchildren. The black man explained that having nothing to go on inside the hospital, he had followed Terry to the first floor and watched from a safe distance as the fat man spoke to the police inspector.

"After a few minutes, I saw the shabbily dressed photographer who we had seen when we got out of the lift when first arriving, to me, two and two didn't add up to four, so when the fat man and the girl left the first floor, I told Ivan that I thought that we should follow them. We followed the vehicle at a safe distance until it reached the "Daily Informer offices."

"What then."

"We waited, hoping to follow the fat man or keep an eye on the girl, it depended on who moved first, we may have had to split up."

"We missed the girl somehow but followed the fat man when headed towards the Strand and parked his car there. Ivan stayed behind the wheel and I followed on foot into a pub around the corner. Two hours later he returned to his car, all the time he spoke to a lot of pub regulars but didn't meet anyone of interest that I could see. He obviously drinks there often and Jesus, you think we're big eaters, you should see this guy tuck it away, no wonder he's as fat as a pig."

"Get on with the story," Ormon was becoming impatient.

"Making his way across town he turned left at the roundabout ran alongside Battersea Park, Ivan rounded the same corner and saw that his car had slowed almost to a stop, his car was a good block and a half ahead of us, then suddenly, his car turned into a side street and disappeared from view. Ivan put his foot down to the board until he reached the side street. When we rounded the corner the other vehicle was nowhere to be seen, we raced to the next small crossroads. Nothing, we thought he had probably turned into the High Street somewhere, at the junction we could see a long way down the road to their right, but not so to the left where the road curved, so that's the way we went. At the next traffic lights we could see a long way ahead and knew that we must have missed the fat man somewhere, Ivan swung left again to the roundabout again and that's when we caught sight of him once again.

The bastard must have doubled back on himself and known we were following him, Being a one way he lost us, but I'm sure that the man that got into the car with the fat man is possibly the man you want. I saw photographs of him at the house. It was very quick look as he got into the car, but it's him alright and he's living in the Battersea area somewhere. Now we must just find out where, then we will have him, he will then tell us where the girl can be found.

Ivan thought back to the incident, it wasn't often that he was caught out, as they had turned into the road alongside Battersea Park again the black man pointed straight ahead.

"How the hell did we miss him?" They could see a man getting into the car that they had been seeking, suddenly he disappeared and the car moved towards them very quickly in the opposite direction, as it passed Ivan could see that it was the fat man. The person that had got into the car was not to be seen he was hiding.

"Rodgers, that's who it was."

"Where?" In desperation Ivan searched for a place to turn his vehicle so that he could follow the car moving rapidly away from them at speed.

The Culling

"That's who he's just picked up." The black man looked at him.

"How do you know that?" Ivan reached the corner and swung the car around and straight into the path of the stream of traffic leaving the wildly hooting and braking of oncoming traffic and irate drivers in his wake. At the roundabout he wasn't sure which of the three exits had been taken so he quickly entered the bustling traffic queue and circled right around. The black man spotted the car in the distance crossing the Thames River and shouted instructions to his companion, but by the time they reached the crest of the bridge the car they were chasing was already gone, it could have turned left, right or gone straight ahead. Ivan wondered whether the fat editor had seen them and purposely managed to outwit them, or had just been lucky when he turned into that road. He consoled himself with the thought that they now had a direct lead to Patrick Rodgers.

Ormon remained busy for a while calling anybody and everybody that could possibly help him, he desperately wanted to know who Patrick might know in the area, it was a long shot but he had to be holed up somewhere there. Ormon figured that he must be aware that the police were after him so he wouldn't be openly walking about the streets of London. He couldn't go to his own house, nor could he return to Kim's place, so it had to be with a friend, relative, or somebody that he trusted. His face had been circulated and had even been shown on television, so he wouldn't be hiding somewhere that would jeopardise his freedom. Possibly Gould was moving him to a safe house somewhere, but he had to find out where he had spent the last two nights. He concentrated on an area of three blocks around the Battersea Park.

"We're closing down all your areas of escape, Mr. Rodgers, very soon, you'll make that single slip and then I'll have you." His secretary told him that Raymond Chen was in reception and asked if he wanted to see him. In his usual gloating manner, he wanted to let the South Korean see what advances he had made in tracing the thorn in their side.

"Yes, go on and wheel him in." His smug manner changed as Chen walked through the door and he immediately knew that something was very wrong.

"We've got a major problem here, look at this." He opened a copy of the paper and on the front page was a picture of Kim and alongside it was Chen's picture. Ormon sat down and read through the report, it was exclusive to Terry's newspaper and stated that a reporter had been contacted by the fugitive Patrick Rodgers who claimed that he had been an innocent bystander when his girlfriend had been shot by Raymond Chen in cold blood. The "Daily Informer" also stated that Patrick had accused Raymond of being a hit man for the South Korean Government.

"Shit, that's why he met up with the fat editor, we must get to Rodgers quickly and shut him up."

"What about this? If the police believe this, then things could get very sticky for us."

"Not us you idiot, you have the problem, not us. Don't worry about that newspaper, I have the high-level clout to be able to get it sorted out." Ormon called his contact at the ministry and told him about the twist in events and asked him to get the government to bring pressure upon the police and the paper owners to silence these reports. The horse had bolted and Ormon knew that reporters from across the land would be converging on Chen. If he cracked in any way then they would face a major problem with their project, he had to be removed from the limelight as quickly as possible.

"You must conceal yourself somewhere before the world descends onto your doorstep, go into hiding somewhere, we have a company flat where you can hold up, at least until the heat is off you and we have got Rodgers."

"But they have nothing on me, I'll sue that bloody newspaper for this slander, better still, I'm going to get a hit made out on that bloody reporter."

"No, you won't and don't be so stupid, this isn't South Korea. You have little or no clout here and by the time you've tried to talk your way out of this, they'll have you believing that you're guilty. If Patrick Rodgers has told him about you then he'll probably also have mentioned the Culling Project. This could be the Rodgers's first step to revealing the project to the world, he's possibly found an ally who's working on theoretical hunches without having a shred of evidence but, if the newspaper could drum up enough lateral support to make this credible then both you and the project are in jeopardy. I must find him and stop him immediately, we don't know how much information he has fed to the paper but with him dead, that newspaper hasn't got a story." The South Korean knew that they were on the rack and he especially, could be the weak link in a very powerful chain. He also knew what he would do to a weak link in similar circumstances, he would snap that link so that the problem no longer existed within their ranks. A safe house was the ideal place to dispose of enemies, informers and weakness. He made up his mind, knowing that he had to get away to safety and what he had to do to rescue himself.

"Look, I'm going to my house to collect some things and then I'll call you later to organise moving to the safe house. Okay?" Ormon waved the man away as if he was swatting at an unseen fly.

"I'll hear from you later, on your way out tell my secretary to get in here." Chen left Ormon and made his way across to Silver Beam's offices at the entrance the building he saw the barrage of reporters awaiting his arrival.

"Shit!" For the first time in his life he became aware of what his antagonists must feel like on the run, he immediately swung his vehicle left and carried on past the entrance heading straight for his rented flat, again there were several reporters awaiting his appearance.

"How the hell do they know where I live?" Turning away, he

stopped at the first telephone box he could find and called Kang at the office.

"Get me booked on the first flight to Seoul, I will need some money as well, and I want you to send someone to the embassy with those in the morning. Understand?" Kang agreed. He wanted this man out of his hair as quickly as possible. he was secretly glad that the man had at last been found out and knew that it was only a matter of time before the coward would run from England. He arranged with one of his staff to get the necessary tickets and funds sorted out as quickly as possible. Somehow he was going to make life for the man as difficult as he could in his own little way. He went downstairs to the security man on duty and told him that as far as he knew Mr. Chen wouldn't be in the office today and that he was now at the South Korean Embassy. Twenty minutes later he looked out of his window, only two reporters had remained behind all the rest he suspected would be gathered outside the embassy. He allowed himself a mischievous smile, the man had made life hell for others at home and here, now it was time that he had some of his own medicine.

Raymond Chen was fast becoming an embarrassment to the South Korean Government. Hosts of news reporters and television staff had now invaded their front porch wanting an interview with him about his involvement in the shooting. Now that the news hounds had somebody in their sights, they weren't about to let this foreigner off the hook that easily. All the embassy attaché wanted, was for Chen to be moved out of his building to the airport as quickly as possible. Chen's flight was due to leave at three o'clock but until then, he wasn't about to question the security man's instructions. Chen was still very powerful in their own country and the attaché wasn't going to find himself on the wrong side of the law when his tour of duty was over. At exactly one o'clock Raymond walked out of the front door of the embassy building to face the barrage of photographers. He made up his mind to pretend that he didn't understand English very well as the many cameras clicked away in unison, he tried to force his way through the sea of bodies confronting him. He felt a sudden stinging on his neck and he pushed even harder until he reached the safety of the black car parked against the kerb. He dived into the back seat as a tall embassy man followed him into the car and battled to shut the back door. On their way to the airport Raymond found that he could no longer focus properly and that his head was swimming madly and by the time they had reached the motorway he became violently sick. Sweat poured from his entire body and his head became racked with pain, within a mile of Heathrow, he suddenly flopped loosely against his travelling companion. The man didn't panic as he placed his fingers against Raymond's neck he felt the large swelling of a mosquito bump which was seeping slightly and this security chief was already dead. From the car telephone the embassy man called his office and told them of the situation asking what he should do about it. In front of the embassy most of the reporters had hurriedly dispersed to either get their pictures and stories back to their offices on time or to try and follow the limousine. A tall black man with a camera bag slung across his shoulder was the only one that didn't race away from the building, packing away a long zoom lens and tripod into a special carrying case. Walking away from the building he whistled a Caribbean melody through his strangely twisted mouth, around which ran a hideously large scar.

That night the Daily Informer carried the story of Raymond Chen's murder in full, it also linked his name to a possible computer theft of large sums from a British pharmaceutical company. The whole front page was covered with innuendoes that he was possibly mixed up with a large unknown drug cartel in the guise of an old respectable London law firm and went on to explain his role in Kim's shooting and how, because of the paper's exposure of the man, he had become an embarrassment to the heads of company. It also went on to suggest that his account both in England and South Korea should be inspected by the police. Terry hoped that this would be taken up by some overzealous police chief and link Ormon Vladisky to Chen.

Time was running out for Patrick and Terry just hoped that this insinuating fishing type article would possibly redress the balance or even tilt the scales in their favour. By going to press so quickly with increasing pressure to stop coming from the top and even if they managed to get to Patrick or Kim, this article had now insured that sooner or later Vladisky Ormon would be the one to take a massive fall. He hoped that it was sooner.

CHAPTER THIRTY

"Raymond Chen's dead. I think that somebody within the UNSECP program became nervous with our expose. My personal feeling is that we were getting too close for comfort. With his death the other newspapers will quickly lose interest in the man." Patrick made a call to Terry in the evening from a call box, wanting to know whether he could visit Kim later that night. He was shocked with the news of Chen. Terry told him what had taken place earlier in the day.

"How did he die?"

"Nobody's quite sure yet, we'll have to await the results of a post-mortem. He was holed up in the South Korean Embassy for most of the day and when he left for his escape to South Korea he died in pain on the way to Heathrow Airport, perhaps one of the diplomats there was instructed to put something in his drink or something. Who knows what happened?"

"Surely if the government wanted him out of the way, then they would do it on home ground in South Korea and not here."

"Good point, I never thought of it in that way, Perhaps it's because we could be getting too close to UNSECP killing program and they had decided that he could be a link to their programme. They killed him in such a way to implicate the embassy staff in order to steer onlookers in the wrong direction. This would definitely give credence to my theory that they are trying to shut the door on us by disposing of him in that manner. It's just my idea, nothing else."

"Have you had any joy with George Li yet?"

"No, not yet. If they're prepared to go to these lengths by killing their own, then God knows how little they think of anybody opposing them. That's one of the reasons that I'm being so paranoid that you don't venture out of doors. If you have to, then wear the disguise I gave you for God's sake."

"My reason for calling was to ask if I could visit Kim again tonight."

"Patrick, are you insane or simply being dense? Yesterday I thought that I was being followed. I can't be certain or how they cottoned on to me so quickly, but with my revelation in the paper that you and I had already spoken, these people will now have a possible lead to you through my mistake."

"I realise that, but somehow I think continual visits would help her to regain consciousness."

"Don't talk soppy. I told you that we have very good specialists attending her. Like you, I would love her to come out of the coma. It would make my job a great deal easier. Don't be stupid, if they're on to Jenny Buckley and myself, then taking you to the hospital would be like issuing Kim with an automatic death sentence." Patrick knew that without either of the newspaper people to accompany him, he wouldn't be allowed into visit Kim. He had been looking forward to the visit all day and somehow it had been the only thing that had kept him sane.

"Terry, I feel so helpless just sitting here doing nothing all day."

"Look at it this way, yesterday there were two adversaries looking for you and today there is only one. That's a fifty per cent reduction made overnight, should we give ourselves enough space and time, possibly they will become so desperate to find you and Kim that they will make a mistake. Never forget that you are the main target, without you or Kim being around, I cannot follow them safely because I'm your only real link to the real outside world at the moment and I'm not going to compromise my story, or your lives by taking any chances. I expect these people to make a move on myself or Jenny shortly and then we'll have our direct lead."

"That's putting yourself at risk as well, if they could kill Chen in full view of the world press then what chance do you stand?"

"Not a lot. You must remember that this is a massive conspiracy, not only in this country, but worldwide. Somehow we've got to make the first crack in the dam wall and once we've achieved that, then the floodgates will open and a rush will develop."

"But putting your life on the line that way."

"This is not the first... Did you hear that?"

"What?"

"There was a click on the line. Dammit, I should have thought, somebody was listening in I think. Patrick get out of there now, you could find yourself with visitors very soon."

"Where do I go?"

"Just get out now, call me as soon as you think it's safe." Patrick slammed down the receiver and raced through to the bathroom and collected the greatcoat while replacing the false moustache and checking it in the mirror. He had a clear presence of mind as he charged through to the bedroom and collected various documents like his passport, cheque books and credit cards from his briefcase. A tramp with a briefcase wouldn't look right, he thought. Lastly he collected two remaining bananas and an apple and shoved them deep into the pocket of his heavy overcoat. Patrick raced down the stairs taking two at a time and at the front door stopped. The front door lock still hadn't been repaired and he gently opened it and looked out to see if he could see anything or anybody out of the ordinary moving towards the flat.

"Nothing." His eyes searched through the orange filtered street lighting into the dark crevices of night. No silhouettes showed up in parked cars and he was safe from prying eyes across the road, unless somebody was hidden among the bushes in the park, everything seemed to be normal. Cautiously he moved forward and across the road, half expecting a shot to ring out or somebody to spring from the shadows and grab him. His body was screaming at him to run yet his brain, still in control, kept him moving at a steady walking pace. He could see the park entrance ahead and hoped that the wrought-iron gates weren't bolted closed for the night.

"Slowly now, don't move too quickly, make it look natural." He continued to talk to himself as he moved away from his enclosed den and to the safety of the night. As he reached the unlocked gate two cars from one direction and one from the other came to a screaming halt in front of the building. Bodies poured out of the vehicles, some moving into the building, others waiting outside watching for an attempted escape. Patrick could see that some of them were in uniform and others in plain clothes and he also knew that when they found the empty flat they would scout the entire area. There were too few of them to search the massive park with its many bushes and hiding places and Patrick doubted whether he was important enough to have a full scale search made of the park. He was at least fifty yards from all of this activity, as he entered the park and found himself a reasonable tree to hide behind and to watch the proceedings. From here he had clear sight along the fence for two hundred yards in both directions, so the police couldn't sneak up from behind and surprise him. For a while nothing happened other than several rapid discussions among those waiting in front of the building on their hand held radios, it hadn't take them long to realise that their prey had escaped once again as they now gathered on the pavement for a quick briefing. Patrick wasn't certain that they wouldn't hunt through the area for him, for all they knew he could have left by car and they wouldn't have been any the wiser. Patrick was in two minds, one part of him screamed to put as much distance between himself and the flat, the other half made him settle down in his vantage point and watch to see what happened. He decided that if the men in uniform looked like moving towards the park he would use the cover of darkness to scarper. Looking at the window he wondered idly what Sue was going to say, hoping that they hadn't made too much of a mess of her flat, for half an hour one vehicle remained outside the building while the police inside stayed behind to inspect or search the flat. As the men got ready to leave, a small panel arrived and two workmen in overalls entered the building. Patrick hoped they were there to repair the damage that the police had caused entering the flat. He extracted a banana from the deep pocket of his coat and began eating it, realising that if they were there to repair the lock he wouldn't be able to gain entry again. He knew he would have to stay away from the area and all the attention because they were bound to be keeping an eye on the flat. Keeping out of sight he watched as finally both vehicles moved off and the lone policeman that had been on the beat moved up the block. He had been given a watching brief Patrick thought. The only thing he knew for certain was that he had get away from the area as quickly as possible. The police could be back in force to search the park, he just did not know so stealthily moving swiftly in line with the perimeter fence he found the next set of gates and crossed the road to mingle with the pedestrians.

"Let's go and report in," he said to himself as he moved across the road and towards the river.

"Terry, you were right, I just managed to get out. The police were there within minutes."

"The police? You're sure it was the police?"

"Positive."

"Don't say any more, you remember where we went on the outing and saw that large bunch of bones?" Patrick racked his brains, his friend was giving him a coded message. He tried to interpret the hidden clue, then it suddenly clicked.

"Yes, of course."

"Make your way there and watch out for a friend who'll meet you on the south west corner sometime tonight. It won't be me, but it's somebody we both know and trust."

"How do we make contact?"

"We don't. If the police are tapping my lines they'll know exactly what our next move could be. They could be listening now and if they are and I can prove it, God help them and their masters. Pass any messages through our friend, I'll make arrangements to receive them somehow." The line went dead, Patrick realised that he was back on his own again, he walked across the Albert Bridge, it looked so peaceful now, if only it could reveal all the tragedy it had witnessed over the centuries, he thought. This would simply be another in its long line of memories. He only had a mile to go and it was a beautiful night so he decided to walk rather than risk taking a cab or bus to his destination.

He reached the Natural History Museum in Knightsbridge almost three quarters of an hour after leaving Battersea. Normally a walk such as this would only have taken twenty minutes, but the weight of the coat and his dodging about and getting lost several times in the back streets took longer than expected. His eyes scanned the brightly lit building across the road, he was certain this was where Terry had meant him to go because they had come with the school to this building many years ago and the bones that his friend had referred to was the huge skeleton of a Tyrannosaurus prominently exhibited all the boys remembered that for days afterwards, they had all sung a song called dem Bones, dem bones, dem mighty bones' . How very juvenile and free they were then he thought as he crossed the road and found himself a comfortable step hidden in the shadows to sit on so that he could watch the south east corner where he was to meet an unknown friend. From this position on the top step he could see down the road, for two hours he sat there and watched the spot as people passed by. Only twice did anybody notice the tramp seated in the shadows and hurriedly withdrew before the dirty old man could touch them for some money. Patrick smiled wryly each time, this was almost a perfect disguise, he was in the correct place and dressed in the proper clothes for the occasion.

"If I stay on the run, this is the way I do it, nobody takes any notice of a tramp." From the corner of his eye he noticed the movement of a car moving slowly towards the corner. In the strange orange illumination he immediately recognised the driver quite clearly, it was John Dunlop his old school friend and lawyer.

"At last."

He was about to stand up and cross the road when another movement caught his eye, Patrick hesitated just that moment long enough to curb his enjoyment by rushing to his friend's car. A second car with two men inside stopped a little way up the road. Patrick decided not to take any chances, knowing that if John didn't see him immediately, he wouldn't drive away, but would circle the block or find a parking space. John slowly turned left and his car moved out of sight along the front of the huge building. The following vehicle moved quickly to the traffic lights and turned left. Patrick couldn't be certain, his senses sharpened to a fine hone during the last couple of days, he wanted to check out the situation before placing himself at anyone's mercy. Staying where he was, he waited until he again saw John's car cruising slowly towards the corner once again. The following car turned the corner as before, it was as if the two were attached by some invisible thread and then it stopped. The bright street lights behind the vehicle showed two dark figures silhouetted against the light. Patrick wasn't sure whether it was the same car, he couldn't make up his mind. Maybe his over sensitive imagination was simply looking for trouble that wasn't really there he thought.

"Better to wait and watch than to go racing in blind." He checked himself because he was talking to himself again.

"It must be the stress." John Dunlop turned left once again and as his car moved along the frontage, the stationary vehicle on the corner lurched forward and down to the traffic lights turning left as before. This time Patrick had seen the driver very clearly.

"If you're want to be my killers, then you're in for a large disappointment tonight my friends." He didn't move, but waited for the expected lights to appear from behind the large building. This time the car moved more slowly until it found a parking spot almost opposite Patrick. He watched for the second pair of lights and not to disappoint him, the same vehicle turned the corner and stopped as before. Patrick watched as John got out of his car then walk towards the corner, this was the correct moment when deciding to place himself in full view, he stood directly under a light and awaited his friends' arrival.

For several minutes Patrick didn't dare move, he was watching to see what the others were up to first, at last, one of the shadowy silhouettes left the car and moved towards the same corner while trying to remain hidden under the slim veil of darkness. Patrick watched from below his pulled-down cap as the large black man stealthily moved past him on the opposite side of the road toward the corner. Passing close to John, he made what Patrick thought was a slight gesture with his hand. It happened so quickly that he wasn't sure that he had seen it or not, or whether it was simply the way the light had fallen when the two had crossed. It was probably his extremely fertile imagination working overtime he thought. One thing he knew for sure though, was that John was being tailed by these two and there was no way he could now make contact. His mind was again travelling at high speed, somehow he had to get away and make contact with Terry instead, mainly because these people were onto John so quickly. His eyes searched for any possibility of making contact with John, there wasn't any.

"No way. If I stay here they'll possibly come looking for me sooner or later."

He waited until he saw the black man duck into the cover of a doorway across the road some way down the street, for some minutes nothing happened then there was a flame of a match in the doorway that gave away the man's position, the man was having a cigarette. With his brain screaming utter resistance,

Patrick lifted his body slowly off its concrete seat and he moved carefully onto the pavement using any bit of the surrounding darkness he could find, making absolutely sure that he embraced the walls and the safety of the night shadows he edged slowly away from his position. His top half was hunched like that of an old man and with a pronounced wobble of a drunk he made his way very slowly in the direction of the car with his foe in it. Instead of walking normally, he tried to persuade himself he was doing the correct thing by swaying slightly to pretend to be a drunk tramp if he was noticed. He hoped that if he was seen moving in among the shadowy wall, his disguise would fool any onlookers. Patrick sweated profusely on the outside, but inside he trembled with freezing coldness as he carefully moved towards his ultimate goal. When he reached it, he slipped down a set of stairs leading to a basement flat. Making sure not to move too quickly that would attract any attention he slowly took one step and then stopped to see if anything was happening. Finally his head lined up with the parapet at street level and none of the men out there had made a move. He was now committed to this hiding place and if they had seen him he was in trouble and he knew it. If they suspected that the tramp was their prey, he was cornered with nowhere to run, he sat down on the bottom step and waited in hope that they hadn't seen him make the move from his seating place. At any moment one of them could appear above him and that would be his end.

"Oh God, please help me to escape these killers." For the first time he desperately wanted to visit a toilet.

The Culling

CHAPTER THIRTY ONE

"The man leads a charmed life, he must have suspected that you two idiots were there, you probably bungled it again. Why I put up with your inefficiency I just don't know, must I do everything myself." Vladisky Ormon just couldn't believe that Patrick had once again slipped away from him. He could be anywhere by now, he had applied all the resources available to him and yet still the man had managed to elude their trap. He knew that he had to find a way of capturing him before the next exercise took place. Somehow he had to create a lure to bring this man out of hiding, the only thing that would possibly entice him out into the open was Kim or his ex-wife. For some time he thought about this new plan, this was like a real life chess game, in his own mind he was the white knight and Patrick Rodgers the black pawn trying to escape the inevitable capture. It was now time to bring in other players into the moving game and to this account he would use the two massive rooks now standing in front of his desk. To date, he had managed to place the pawn in check on three separate counts, but it had escaped his trap on each occasion. It was time to go in for the kill, but he needed to move several players into a position where the pawn would try to help them escape. The more Ormon thought about it, the more he liked the idea.

"We can't keep chasing him, it's like trying to follow a moving shadow, we have got to change tack but instead, we've got to bring him to us and the only way we can do that is to put some of his friends under the hammer. If he's as stupid as I think he is, his sense of fair play will bring him out of hiding and we'll finish this fiasco once and for all."

He gave them instructions and sent them away in his usual hostile manner before calling the contact at the ministry where he explained what he had in mind. Then he called Steve Hearn in America to find out how the next stage of their project was proceeding. A sleepy voice greeted him.

"I wish you wouldn't call me so early, it's hell getting back to sleep every time you do this to me. How's it going your end, have you looked after our problem yet?" Ormon explained the situation and how he intended dealing with it. He left out the Chen incident.

"Ormon. I don't want to tell you how to do your job, but if this man is allowed to roam free much longer, God knows what he may be capable of doing. The entire project could be wrecked because you guys in London have screwed up." The little man at the end of the line quickly assured Steve that he had now cut down all avenues of escape and would soon have Patrick Rodgers safely seen to. Again he asked how the project was going.

"That's why I'm so pissed off with your call. We start final countdown later today and it means that none of us will have any sleep for two days right now I need all the sleep I can get, now I'm going back to bed and I'll speak to you in a few days. Just watch this space for results, I hope the same goes for London."

Steve lay back on his pillow his mind drifted over the last few weeks, thinking how they had progressed with what he hoped would be their final experiment. Everything was now in place and the waiting complete, he tried to get to sleep again, but knew the signs very well, his mind was tumbling over various intermittent thoughts disturbing him. The project was going well, but the one thing that worried him was the way that he hadn't managed to break through the defences of Heidi Zenger, her being back to the cold calculating computer expert, yet again. So far he had tried everything he knew to date her again, but she made it quite clear that she wasn't interested in a relationship with anybody. He thought at first that she had some fixation about herself and had had some type of bad experience in her life and didn't trust herself becoming involved with anybody. As time went on he realised that she lived for one thing only and that was for the damned computer. It was as if she were in love with that machine and had simply used his body for the release that the machine could not provide.

"Man, if that's the case, then we have a deranged mind on our staff." Steve got up and went to the bathroom and took a sleeping draught that had been prescribed by his doctor. The mind was the most powerful thing in the universe he thought and Heidi had been disturbing his powers of concentration lately. There was nothing that he could place his finger on, but he couldn't accept that she was rejecting him. He had watched and seen that her cool attitude was aimed at everyone and not just him, which was when he decided that she was only interested in keeping her job intact. Steve dismissed thoughts that she needed anyone except the machine at first, but the more she rejected his continuous advances the more this fantasy became reality. Now he couldn't wait to see what would happen between them if Operation Buddha were a success.

The team were gathered in the fish-bowl like conference room.

"Ladies and gentlemen this is the big test. If we get this one experiment right then it's all systems go for the entire project. David, what time can we expect the first detonation to happen?" The bald headed scientist leaned forward inspecting something on the file before him. He cleared his throat.

"As you all know we will be sticking to the same format as last time with Luke going in roughly three hours time. This will be followed by Romans and so on until we finish with John. The time span will be approximately twenty two hours and sixteen minutes from first to last. We haven't had to move the ships very far for Operation Buddha, but have had to alter their bearings so as to be precise for the various earth core densities involved. If anything, this one should be a lot smoother than Operation Christian because we have far better data at our disposal regarding the earth's core en route to "Mahayana." David had thought this final place of destruction was as aptly named as had been Revelations in Iran. Mahayana, roughly interpreted meant Great Vehicle to the Buddhist faithful. In their ancient form of teaching which was more evolved than any of the other schools of Buddhism. The main theme was to promulgate the ideal of gaining enlightenment and to help other beings to their release from this mortal coil. This earthquake was definitely going to help the people of the Philippines do that, within the next few days too, he thought.

"As before, if there's any sign of trouble Tanaka will stagger the central detonations to abort the impact. Is that clearly understood?" Steve directed his question straight at David Spielman to make sure that he wasn't going to have a repeat outburst as had happened before.

"Don't worry about us, this time will be more perfect than the last, just you wait and see."

"Well there's nothing more I can say except, good luck everybody. Let's have our pre-celebration cup of coffee and get down to the job in hand."

His eyes moved left to Heidi Zenger, hoping to see a slight glimmer of change in her now that the time had arrived. Her composure remained as unaltered as before behind her owl-rimmed spectacles.

"Can I have a minute of your time when the others leave?" She nodded. For the umpteenth time she expected that Steve was going to try to reason with her. She had to give him his due, he was probably the most persistent person she had ever met. He had tried being nice, then sarcastic and had also been downright nasty. This last stage had infuriated her to the point where she almost lost her cool exterior and wanted to kill him. A different place and another time and she would have no compunction in destroying him for what he had said to her. When the others started leaving she mentally prepared herself for his onslaught of disgusting words. They didn't come, the man was strictly a professional organiser now as he finished discussing various refinements and co-ordinates with her, he looked up from his folder and touched her arm gently.

"Have you put in the security systems that you said you were going to?"

"Yes, this system could never be traced, no matter how well trained anybody was. Not even Mr. Ormon could get in and he knows all about the programme."

"Good. I think we may have a large problem in London and before long the shit's going to hit the fan."

"Why, what's happened?" Knowing that she had a few minutes to spare, he opened his file and extracted a copy of a report and the newspaper article and handed them to her. He watched as she read through the London report and then the newspaper cuttings that had been faxed to him.

"You can be sure that this is not the last we'll hear of it. I just want you to be sure that we're locked down tight and fully protected." As she looked up he saw the change, no longer were the eyes dull, there was the same fire in them that he had seen there before. She stood up and collected her papers.

"Don't worry, it's as safe as Fort Knox. I must get started now."

He watched her glide through the door in the glass partitioning, and move towards her beloved computer. He sensed that the woman out there was building up to something and that by tomorrow he was going to be in for a torrid time once again. He was looking forward to the earthquake, because if it was successful, he automatically presumed it wasn't going to be the only mind-shattering thing happening to him.

"All Right!" He moved to his position beside David Spielman who looked far more relaxed than he had been on the last occasion, in fact everybody seemed less tense in the room. The huge board showed its seven pear shapes now targeted on the small Philippine island of Luzon. Steve couldn't wait for Mahayana to be completed by this particular circle of deadly fruit, as his eyes looked down on the back of the redhead frantically giving her beloved machine last minute instructions. For the first time he began to accept that was to her partner for life and he was only its messenger and inflamed amoretto. His longing was broken by David's voice rattling into his earphones making contact with the scientists on board Luke. The familiar staccato instructions started flowing to and from their command centre as Luke prepared to hand over its control to "The Coordinator" Steve looked up again to see Heidi leaning back in her black swivel chair because her role was complete, she had now handed control to her partner and there was nothing further that she could do until it passed back control to her when the Mahayana impact had been completed.

"Zero minus thirty seconds." Steve watched the numbers reducing at the side of the board against Luke. There were seven such counters all registering different times in relation to their countdown procedure.

"Luke's away."

David Spielman turned to Steve and gave him a broad smile. He thanked the crew aboard Luke and the computer switched everything to Romans. They worked right through until John was on its way. Now all they could do was watch and wait until all of the tremors reached the inner circle together and the corrective detonations were made for final run-in to the target. They had to wait several hours for this to happen. Steve stretched himself and went through to the glazed office to have something to drink. It was a rule that nobody could take any form of refreshment or food into the control room for fear of possible spillage onto the consoles. If anybody wanted to have a smoke break they had especially ventilated cubicles for this as well.

"May I join you for coffee?" Heidi watched for Steve to go to the office and then followed him.

"Sure, why not have a pew?"

"I can't stand this waiting, it drives me mad."

"Join the club." He was surprised that after everything he had said to her that she had actually opened the discussion.

"Steve. After we've completed this one, what's next?"

"Well, I'm not at liberty to tell you but it all depends on how successful we are or not, all I can say is that we haven't got anything specific planned yet, it all hangs on today's operation. If we come through, there'll be a meeting of the various backers involved to sort out their priorities and how to move on from here. Why?"

"I badly need a break. I thought that I had go home for a few weeks if all goes well. Do you mind?"

"There's no problem. in fact I've scheduled that all the main scientists have a four week break before proceeding. The people on the ships have been moaning like stuck pigs for weeks now. None of them have seen their families for over three months.

When were you thinking of leaving?"

"Sometime later tomorrow, is that agreeable?" She looked long and hard at him trying to fathom out if her request would be acceptable.

"Done. I can't see any problem."

"Then, will you have dinner with me tonight." For a moment he thought that his hearing had become defective.

"Are you kidding? Only if it's my treat." She smiled, got up made her way back to her black swivel chair. For the first time that day, she chatted in friendly manner to David Spielman and told him that she was taking a holiday. Steve joined in with their conversation, David was slightly upset with Steve for allowing the break, but when reassured that everybody was going to have a break and it wasn't only Heidi taking leave, he relaxed.

"Yes. I suppose we have been driving ourselves a little too hard. I'll probably go home to my kibbutz in Israel for a few weeks. What about you?" Steve thought about the question for some time then made up his mind.

"I'm going to London, there's something that I've got to help with there."

"C'mon it's time to get busy with the post-detonations. We've still got a long way to go before we can relax." David leaned forward and started running through various checks and instructions with his team." The radio detonations had all been handled successfully; one by one they set off from their outposts towards the central hub.

It was the day after Christmas when the alarm went out that something was going wrong with the directional flow of the tracking paths.

"What is happening ? Steve Hearns was told that one of the main tracks moving in from the west had slowed down quite and it appeared to be struggling to get across the Himalayan mountain range in India. This was now forcing everything, including the impact zone to be pulled westward.

"There are several backup solutions, but we must have an answer and fast, we can abort the mission, alternatively go for a secondary target off Thailand, or battle to keep on track and attempt to pull the whole thing west and back into line." David said, he was quite calm.

"What is your personal recommendation then David?" Steve asked.

"Personally I think we should leave it alone to see what happens and where it impacts. The data gained will be invaluable."

"What do you think is causing this to happen?" Heidi butted into the discussion.

"Steve, the computer model show that this is slowdown is being caused by the Himalayan Subduction. We simply did not have enough geological data from that area."

"What the hell is a Subduction?"

"Think of it as though two cars colliding and one starts to sink straight into the sidewalk." David intervened.

"What, how or why didn't we pick that up."

"Because the newest studies based on computer models of the two plates now show that the formation and continued growth of the world's highest mountain range makes the most sense if a dense piece of India is down in the mantle, dragging the rest of the continent down with it. That movement has changed the rock density in the area and there were no data figures available, but at least we now know it's there." Heidi said.

"That's why I suggested letting the impact take its course, that way we will be able to compensate for any deflections in future and these results will invaluable." David offered.

"OK, you guys just make certain no big cities are involved."

They watched the coloured shapes of first phase go off without a hitch except that the central impact point had now been pulled from the intended original Philippines impact target further south and westward towards the western coast of northern Indonesia. Operation Buddha was well on its way as they all prepared for the secondary explosions and the most important corrective stage to take place. The computer worked to perfection and the lines kept moving menacingly toward mainland of Indonesia.

"Where are those petals eventually going to meet up?" Stave asked.

"The secondary detonations have begun to push it down south and pulled it west, its destined to impact somewhere in the Indian Ocean somewhere off the Indonesian coast." David said.

The watched as the revised position kept moving and finally ended in the Indian Ocean.

"The impact took place at about 1am UTC, that's about 8am local time located about 250 km south-southeast of Indonesia off the western coast of northern Sumatra with a magnitude of 9.0 on the Richter scale." Heidi announced.

"Well at least that blast won't kill anybody going off out in the ocean that far away from land, our sponsors won't be too happy with that."

"There could be another problem but let's not hope so." David calmly suggested.

"What could that be? C'mon David I need facts, I must talk to several of these financiers soon and all I can say at the moment is that we failed because India is sinking. Do you think they will understand that?"

"One word Steve, that is Tsunami. A blast that powerful might raise the sea levels high enough so that all coastal land in the area will be affected. We could have a major disaster to contend with, you better warn your financiers beforehand. This could become very ugly, many people may die today, I just do not know, we have to wait and see what the impact damage has now created." Steve immediately got onto the computer and sent off the necessary communiqué to the financial backers and The Affiliation members.

Several hours later the news of the Boxing Day devastation began to pour in on the wires. Steve listened intently to the incoming reports and he could not help smiling because his team had estimated losses of more than four thousand, but as reports flowed in he knew that the figure would likely to be closer to hundreds of thousands and he knew that the contrarily help from UN forces would save many lives that day. Overall the whole exercise was turning out to have been a major success, they had not hit the target perfectly but that tremor had caused the necessary damage expected to start up the Culling Program and it had worked. When he completed his report to the various backers this afternoon, it was all going to be very positive. He couldn't help hoping that Orman's report from London would be just as positive.

The Culling

.

CHAPTER THIRTY TWO

He had driven this route across the compound ten times at least since Operation Christian and Heidi had only allowed him into her bungalow that once and ever since had refused him entry. He now regretted using strong arm tactics on her, because they hadn't helped in the least, she hadn't got where she was by being a pushover thought Steve as he drew his car to a halt. He was slightly early and decided to sit in the car for a few minutes, she was certainly a baffling type of person he reflected, one minute an ice maiden the next a steaming locomotive with fire burning in her eyes. Her red hair indicated a furious temper that she had managed to keep it in check until their last encounter. Heidi had refused him entry to her house and he had become rather vicious with his abusive taunts about her wanting to sleep with her machine as he tried forcing his way into her domain. Suddenly the ice maiden snapped and hit out at him with a vase which was to hand on the telephone table next to her front door.

"Get out you vindictive bastard!" She slammed the door shut and bolted the lock.

"If you ever try that again, I'm calling security and you'll have to find someone else to look after the computer." Steve remembered the look in her eyes at the moment she lifted the vase, they had blazed with fury and knew full well that if he hadn't retreated when he did, he was in no doubt that she would have caused him severe damage. So as not to jeopardize the project he decided to stop pestering her for the moment and see what happened. His manliness had been denied, but all the same he had never come across anybody like her before and still wasn't sure how to handle the matter, all he wanted to do was get together with her, but she was the strangest human he had yet encountered. To add to his confusion here he was being invited back to her house to take her out his brain tingled as he stopped his car and realised that he loved the unpredictability of this hot and cold running monster.

"How did you sleep?"

"Well thank you. You're early bit come in, I won't be a moment." They had both had several hours sleep since the end of the successful mission. Steve still felt slightly sluggish, but the thought of what possibly lay in store had perked him up considerably. Tonight she wore a tight red silk dress and as she turned he could see the fullness of her backside and knew immediately that she again wasn't wearing any under garments under her dress. She probably wore contact lenses on occasions like this and her full length red hair streamed down almost reaching her hips.

"Pour yourself a drink, I'll only be a minute." The vibrant self confidence that had been there last time wasn't clearly visible to Steve as he poured himself a whisky. He felt honoured that she had taken the trouble to get it in especially for him.

"What's been said by the backers?" She shouted through from the bedroom.

"Not a lot, except that they're pleased with our results.

"What happens next?"

"The main parties get together at a meeting early next week and decide a schedule of targets and timings for us."

"Where's the meeting to be held?"

"In London, England, why?"

"No reason. Just making conversation." She appeared at the doorway, Steve shook his head from side to side.

"You look stunning."

"Thank you Mr. Project Director, now, what surprise do you have in store and where are we going to eat."

"I've got a special surprise for you. Remember the other night when I tried so desperately to get you to come for a special meal with me? Well we're going to do that tonight."

A transport helicopter had again been arranged to fly them to Denver and they went to a restaurant where they were shown to a separate cubicle away from the rest of the diners. Steve didn't know when he was going to have the opportunity to be alone with her again and so he had organised this especially to get away from any distractions. Throughout the beginning of the meal she discussed the project and the people orchestrating it, where they were from and who they were. She had seen most of the information on her beloved computer, so Steve was perplexed when she kept switching the subject back to their work. Heidi was like a puppy with a rag, she wouldn't let go of it until she had answers to her many questions. Last time they hadn't even mentioned business and here she was being unpredictable again. No matter how hard he tried to change the subject, it somehow kept reverting to their work. She was on some form of a high, the aloof mantel had been shed but this was different to anything he had experienced from Heidi in the past. Half way through their main course and when he had revealed most of the facts to her satisfaction, she suddenly dropped the subject and started relaxing into the mood of the evening. No matter how long he lived he would never understand the complexity of women, especially this one sitting across the table, he thought. When they finished the pleasant evening, the helicopter ferried them back to the base, Heidi suggested that they have a nightcap at his house, which was another step out of the ordinary. Steve didn't argue as he drove straight to his bungalow.

"Come on, let's see what I have in stock to drink." She was surprised to see very sparsely his house was even though it was similar in size to hers.

"What can I get you?"

"Coffee please." He made coffee and when they finished their drinks she stood up

and stretched.

"It's been a long day. My goodness I didn't realise how tired I am, it's bedtime for me." Steve stood up and kissed her shoulder as his hand moved to her zip but she moved forward away from him.

"No. I want to go home, I'm too tired." Like a bursting boiler, Steve felt pressure building up within. He thought she was again playing with him and decided he hadn't waited all this time for her to walk out on him. He wanted her now, and he wasn't prepared to accept some silly excuse.

"I understand you're tired, but you don't have to go home to sleep, you can do that here."

"Please take me home, Steve." She had put on her reprimanding teacher look as she moved towards the front door.

"Christ Heidi. You can't play silly arse with me like this."

"What do you mean, play with you?"

"Exactly that, you give me the come on, then when I want to continue, you've become a tease. What the hell is going on here?"

"We had sex, it was fun and you were my one night stand. There's nothing more to it than that, the right place, the right time that's all it was, nothing more." Her eyes blazed furiously as she taunted him and she moved to the front door and opened it wide.

"I don't know what gave you the idea that there was going to be any more, I used you as men use women for their own pleasure and you were the only one available at the time and served the purpose. Now please take me home."

"You bitch!" The floodgate burst within Steve. He raced towards her and, unable to control the days of pent up anger, struck her forcibly with his flat palm against her head and she fell to the ground screaming loudly before getting up and swinging her foot in an arc, catching him just left of his groin.

"You keep your bloody hands to yourself, you pervert!" She had become a wild kicking, scratching feline prepared to defend herself from him. The blow to his lower regions had only just missed its target then he saw red, striking out this time with his closed fist and catching her on the cheek just below the left eye. Neighbours lights started to come on, they had all heard the screaming. Windows opened and someone shouted loudly, Heidi dropped to her knees.

"You bastard! If you try and touch me again you'll find yourself in jail, I'm not available to you tonight or ever!" Nobody in the area could help overhearing her as Heidi leaned forward and began to sob bitterly. Suddenly the haze in Steve's head cleared as his neighbour screamed for Steve to leave her alone. He kneeled next to her and begged her forgiveness as he placed his hand around her shoulders.

"Come. I'll take you home."

She got to her feet and moved to his car still sobbing, the neighbours closed their windows and went back to bed when the car drove away.

"I'm so sorry, I don't know what came over me." She dabbed at her cheek and turned to him.

"What you said was quite correct, I'm the one to apologise, it was all my fault." The car stopped outside 1067 and Steve walked her to her door.

"Thanks for a memorable evening, I'm sorry about my temper, I really didn't know what came over me. Friends?" He put out his hand so that he could shake it. Instead she leaned forward and kissed him full on the mouth, neither allowed the kiss to separate as it became more urgent. Her hand flew down and urgently rubbed hard against the front of his trousers feeling the man's penis harden as she applied heavier movements. She felt his hand grab at her breast and squeeze the nipple with all the force it could muster. She let out a short scream from the pain.

"Sorry."

"Come inside, we don't want the neighbours watching our lovemaking, do we?" She slammed the door closed and turned on the table lamp, the man's hands had already loosened her zip and were inside the frail material playing with her breasts. As she turned to face him there was a ripping sound down her back as the material parted. She whipped off the shoulder straps and let the silk dress drop to the floor. She kicked off a shoe so violently that it flew across the room and smashed the glass frame of one of the ancient Balinese pictures. The other shot off and landed against the front door. She moved forward and unzipped his trousers releasing his gorged pole with a slight hop she placed her legs around his hips and moved down so that he could insert it into her. He quickly moved her towards the nearest wall next to the mantelpiece and slammed her against it then started forcing himself harder into her. Her arms flailed in all directions knocking things flying and breaking expensive ornaments as they were whipped from their positions tearing at him. She felt him explode into her and they both relaxed as they slid into a heap on the floor, she rolled him over so that she was on top of him. Slowly she started to move up and down until she could feel him rise fully into her, Steve's eyes were now closed as she hammered down onto his upright manhood and sensing him reaching his peak again by the speeding up of his laboured breathing. As he felt himself starting to blow she screamed his name so loudly that the entire neighbourhood would have heard her, with a start he opened his eyes and momentarily froze solid. A gun was pointed straight between his eyes.

"What the..."

The Culling

"Keep going, it's only a toy but it makes me feel powerful." Steve relaxed and placed his hands on her breasts. The two hammered at each other as she began screaming as she reached her peak, he felt the throbbing rise as release sent shudders between them. Suddenly and without warning Heidi leaned back and cocked the pistol in her hand.

"Die, you pig." Steve didn't even hear the report as he exploded deep into her. Heidi immediately dropped the imitation flintlock which she had had restored as a real gun to simulate its ancient counterparts, then grabbed her dress and ripped it down the sleeve along the side seam, before putting it on and then fell heavily against the lightweight telephone table which crashed and broke about her. Getting up she checked the room once, then ran out of the house screaming as loudly as could.

"Help me somebody!" By now she knew that several neighbours would have heard the earlier commotion and then been aware of the shot coupled with her desperate calls of help. People were already on their way to her house when she came yelling from inside the front door. One man had even had the sense to call the base police before going across to see two neighbours comforting the redhead with bruise and torn and battered clothing. They found the slumped body of Steve Hearn half lying, half sitting against the wall, his now limp dribbling manhood hung outside the undone trousers, on the wall behind him bore the splattered semi-circle of a mixture of blood and human brains. The police had already had a previous complaint recorded of Steve's attempted intrusion, she had seen to it, but had not pressed charges so the matter was dropped. After all this was the Project Director and head of the camp, they checked her story of his battering with the neighbours at her house and then at his. Everything fitted, he had started beating the timid scientist at his house then seemed to continue attacking her inside her own house. Her neighbours confirmed the story that the couple had only been there a few minutes when the shot rang out and she had run out of the house. The police chief recognised that this had been her saving grace and that she had been raped as soon as she walked in the door. Her story checked out completely, she even had his sperm inside her, the marks on her face and bruises on her back proved her story. The project leader had become obsessed with her, antagonised and bullied her, and then raped her tonight, it was as simple as that. They didn't see that anything would be gained by reporting anything different, it was a straight forward open and shut case of self defence. Heidi told them that she was due to fly to England the following day and this had set Steve going, she told them it was urgent asked them whether she should cancel the trip, but after consulting David Spielman who now stood in for Steve, they had decided that stopping her wouldn't achieve anything. Heidi boarded a plane at Denver and returned to Europe a day later than expected.

Meanwhile back in London Ormon had several headaches to contend with, the missing pair Patrick and Kim, the death of the technical director of The Affiliates, Steve Hearn meant yet another gap opening up within days of the death of Raymond Chen, The Affiliates were becoming nervous. The only bright light for the moment was that the massive tsunami hitting Asia had momentarily taken the news investigation away from him and the project. Gaps in their organisation were like holes in a balloon, he had to get them filled quickly.

CHAPTER THIRTY THREE

Sue was totally confused when she returned from her trip to find her front door badly damaged and with a different lock.

"What the hell's going on." She couldn't believe her eyes as she studied the heavy indentations where a forceful hammer had been used to lever and smash through the timber, her first thought was that thieves must have broken in. Helpless to do anything, she knocked on her neighbour's door and was told about the incident over a cup of tea. The old woman gave her a note with a telephone number of the policeman in charge of the case and Sue called him, he arrived within fifteen minutes with the key and informed her that they had had a tip off that Patrick was staying there. After making necessary arrangements to have the door repaired Sue moved through the flat searching to see if anything was missing. She immediately recognised the hand of her ex-husband at work, everything had been rearranged ever so slightly and she suddenly remembered how meticulous he was and how, during their marriage it would always get up her nose. It was the little things that had destroyed their relationship and made her have her first affair with the local builder that had been doing some repair work at their house. He had been the exact opposite to Patrick, rough and uncouth with an unadulterated appetite for sex.

"Perhaps this escapade is what was required to change him." Sue had been constantly thinking back to the morning that she had left for Bahrain and now except for a few papers in her drawing room, nothing seemed to have been disturbed. That evening after returning from a visit to her aging mother, she decided to go to the high street to collect some groceries to replenish her depleted stocks. Walking along to the corner she turned left up to the shopping area where she visited the greengrocer and the local supermarket that were still open. Laden with two carrier bags she slowly started walking back down the side street, suddenly becoming aware of a second set of footsteps almost directly behind her. Sue felt very uncomfortable knowing that she could be mugged here in the fading daylight even if there were other people in attendance. Quickly she hastened her step, but became more alarmed as the footsteps behind simply increased pace, with fear now taking over, her eyes darted left and right searching for some form of refuge or help should the footsteps begin to increase and she found herself being attacked. Reaching the small intersection in the dying light she could see a young man at the end of the block heading in his direction. She was almost running now, her nervousness having built up all sorts of horrid illusions of what could next happen to her, but quickly realised that the footsteps had now disappeared and for the first time she turned to see who had been behind her. In among the approaching shadows of night, the unknown person following her had slipped into obscurity. She could see the full length back to the high street, the road behind her was empty. Whoever it was, must have gone into one of the houses or got into one of the many vehicles parked along the kerb. Sue breathed a sigh of relief walking past the huge ape like man standing at the corner with his back towards her and lit a cigarette. She silently thanked him for being there at the right time, possibly he had scared off her would be attacker by his mere appearance. Inside the flat she unpacked the goods and made herself a cup of tea, her nerves still a little frayed from the experience, the telephone rang making her jump almost causing her to spill her tea. It was the policeman in charge of the case asking her to go to the local police station in the high street to make her report saying he would be there within ten minutes and asked if she would be able to come immediately. It was only at the top of the road about five minutes walk away and she knew that finding a parking spot would be impossible, she then placed a kitchen knife into her bag and set off for the appointment, this time feeling confident that if her unknown follower appeared, she would be able to deal with them.

All the way to the police station her senses were slightly on edge, as she kept imagining that there was somebody on her trail, but every time she turned to look she saw nobody under the orange street lights. After the appointment with the policeman she quickly made her way back towards the safety of her little flat, at the intersection, a dishevelled figure appeared from the shadows right in front of her. Panic set in, but she quickly tightened he grip on the reassuring knife handle in her bag which she had not released while on her walk. The man held out his hand in begging fashion to her.

"Pretend you're giving me some money."

"What?"

"Don't you recognise an old friend down on his luck?" Sue stared at the man in the dim light, all the time holding tightly onto the knife in her bag.

"No. Who are you?" As she said the words she suddenly became aware of the outline of the man's features, she would have never recognised him in the street had he not stopped her.

"Patrick, is that you?"

"Yes but be careful, we're being watched by that man standing behind the car on that next corner, so don't do anything stupid and listen while pretending to find money in your bag." Sue opened her bag and started searching through.

"I tried to talk to you earlier but you made it impossible and then I saw that big fellow, he's one of those trying to catch me. You'll find his partner somewhere in this neibourhood, he's a big black man. I'm sorry about your flat, but they almost caught me that day."

"The police broke into my flat, how did they know you were there?"

"It's a long story. I need a place to stay, have you got any ideas."

"Why not come back to my place tonight?"

"Because it's being watched and I don't want to do anything

stupid." Sue found her purse and opened it, pretending to take out some money for the tramp suddenly seeing the answer to his problem.

"I know what. Here take this key, it's for my friend's flat and she's away in Bangkok for three days. You can use her place for tonight at least." She handed him the key.

"The flat's along this road, third floor, number sixteen, she looks after my plants when I'm away and I look after hers. I'll call you there."

"No don't, your telephone is probably being monitored."

"Patrick we need to talk, so how do you suggest we do that."

"When I call, you get into your car and drive around, give me your car keys as well." She searched her bag, they weren't there.

"I can't, they're at home."

"Okay, when you get home, take the keys and unlock your car, then pretend to have forgotten something and go back to your flat. Call your friend's number and let it ring five times, that will be my signal. Then give me half an hour, I'll be in the car by then. Now go and don't look back."

Patrick sat down in a heap on the pavement as Sue carried onwards towards her flat. He watched as she turned the corner a block away and out of sight, the big man appeared from out of the shadows further down the road and made his way behind Sue to the corner. After he turned the corner, Patrick found number sixteen and quickly had a shower. He had slept rough for two nights and the mixture of warm days and the infernal greatcoat had made him sweat profusely. By now he was aware of the smell of himself which he had already become accustomed to, although he didn't like it. The shower came as welcome relief, then extracted a new shirt and pair of trousers that he had brought from out of one of the plastic bags that he carried with him. He looked in the mirror and decided not to have a shave, the growth of three days had now taken over from the false moustache, he was almost unrecognisable to himself, let alone to others on his trail. As he went to the kitchen to see what was in the fridge to eat, the telephone rang five times then stopped, he found a half a chicken, and quickly tore off the drumstick and then put on the coat and baseball cap. On his way to the park he ate the chicken, it tasted so good, making his way slowly within the safety of the shadows he searched for Sue's little car. He spotted it some fifty yards from the flat entrance, and blessed his luck because it was on his side of the road near the park entrance. The two men were on the near side of the flat facing away from the car as he stealthily used his newly acquired knowledge to make his way to car. He tried the passenger door, it was locked.

"Stupid cow!" He knew that she had probably unlocked the driver's door which meant him having to move into the street and possibly be seen by the men ahead if the driver happened to look into his rear view mirror at the right time. Patrick felt his adrenalin level soar as he watched the busy street with its continuous flow of traffic and trying to calculate the risk involved in slipping past the driver's seat into the back of Sue's two door car. He knew that the moment he was in, he would have to lie down flat and if they saw him enter and he was down low, he didn't stand a chance if they came across to the car. At least here in the open, if they made a move he could escape through the park into the safety of the bushes and trees. Time was running out for him because Sue would shortly be on her way from the flat to the car, just then he really couldn't make up his mind whether to risk it or not for even the slightest movement from behind, could possibly alert the two big men to his entry into the car. He waited, too scared to make a move towards the car, but when the front door to Sue's flat opened, he automatically knew that if he was going to do it, it had to be now because their attention would be momentarily focused on her and not on the car. He dived forward and scrambled full length across the front two seats, like a worm seeking shelter he pulled himself through the opening into the back and onto the floor. He hoped that his body was hidden enough lying cramped into the tiny space behind the front seats. Thinking to himself that if he had been seen, he was now a sitting duck, he gritted his teeth and didn't dare look up as the door was flung open.

"Stay down, the men you pointed out are not far ahead." Patrick breathed a sigh of relief, it seemed as if it could have worked.

"I know and ten to one they'll follow you. Just drive normally as if you are going somewhere definite, try to distinguish something about their car, like one light dimmer than another, that way you'll be able to keep an eye on them. Remember these are probably professionals so don't do anything stupid that'll make them realise you're onto them."

"I hid behind the curtains and didn't turn on the light when I watched them from my window, I saw you and could have kicked myself for not opening the far side door and you didn't move, so at the front door I tried to take it slowly by walking in the opposite direction before crossing the street and coming back. That way I hoped you would realise they were watching me. Did you see?"

"Nope, I jumped straight in as you came out of the door."

"Where do you want me to go?"

"Go towards London central, somewhere to find several sets of traffic lights. If they're far enough behind you, try and time it so that you just manage to beat a red light, but make it look as convincing as you can."

"Why?"

"If they get caught, then drive naturally and try to find a turning to the left unless the next set of lights are in your favour. That way we stand the chance of losing them, then we can find somewhere to go and talk."

"While I'm doing that, tell me what's been happening." Sue's opportunity presented itself as she turned into Victoria Street opposite the Houses of Parliament because a policeman stepped onto the zebra crossing behind her and put up his hand for the following cars that had to stop, she immediately put her foot down and shot forward looking for somewhere to turn left. She could see the vehicles behind beginning to move as she passed through a set of changing traffic lights. Instead of turning left she turned right because of a break in the oncoming traffic. And quickly wound her way towards James Park and across to The Mall where she quickly entered the mass of traffic around Trafalgar Square. The whole time her eyes kept searching for the following car.

"I think I've lost them."

"Let's be sure, find a narrow street somewhere and turn into it, if any cars follow you then we'll know that they've switched there could be a second following vehicle." Sue did as she was told but nothing followed, she breathed a sigh of relief as she saw the sign for an underground parking garage. She swung in and found an empty parking space that she moved into and switched off the engine.

"Good girl, I'm bloody suffering from cramp back here."

"Then get up."

"No not yet, I think I can last out a few minutes more." Patrick eased himself off the back floor, they went to a small back street Italian restaurant then before entering into the place, he removed his coat and cap.

"Did you know that the coat smells?"

"Until I had that shower, I didn't just smell, I stank." Sue stretched across the table and took his hand feeling sorry for her nest friend who obviously had had a very rough time since she left for Bahrain.

"Okay. Now tell me what's been going on and how I can help you, if at all." During dinner he brought her right up to date; at least by telling her everything he now felt had another someone that he knew he could trust and rely on before requesting a few dangerous favours from her. They got back to the parking garage before midnight and steeled their minds to getting back without being seen, Patrick again lowered himself into the gap between the seats again, they had worked out a plan on where and how they would hide messages for each other. This would also be a failsafe method of getting instructions to and from Terry without causing problems to each other. Patrick had read about this method being used by spies and agents and knew that no matter how close anybody was watching her, this method of communication would go undetected unless they were very unlucky.

CHAPTER THIRTY FOUR

It was tremendous to once again be able to relax and even sleep in a proper bed because the last few nights had been absolute purgatory for Patrick sleeping under the bridge next to the Thames River but having to be very aware of his surroundings and at no time had he wanted to fall asleep for fear of being surprised by the unknown assailants. For tonight though it was a long hot shower to waken himself, but if he were to admit the truth, lingered under the hot jet of water purposely because he knew he had to get dressed into the smelly clothes once again. After searching the kitchen and finding three eggs and some slightly stale bread in a cupboard, he fried them up for breakfast. It was nearly nine o'clock and last night Sue had promised to contact Terry to find out whether anything further had developed. Patrick didn't rush his breakfast knowing that he still had several hours to kill before making his way to their appointed post-box. Anyway, he had nowhere to go and was safely under cover for the moment, he thought.

"Where the hell is the man? I've been trying to reach him for two days, he did not turn up for a meeting with John Dunlop as arranged and he hasn't called in. I personally thought that they must have got hold of him." Sue had gone from home in a roundabout way to the Daily Informer offices and awaited the fat man's arrival. He was at his desk when she got there and introduced herself.

"He's as frightened as a rabbit down a hole with a shotgun barrel in the entrance and now he's running scared, trusting nobody, not even me now. Did you know that there were two men following John Dunlop and that's why he didn't show?"

"Like hell there was."

"The same two men who are busily watching my flat every hour of the day were there and the reason he's so sure it's the same men, is because we gave them the slip last night. Whoever they are desperate to trying to find him but the upside is that doesn't seem to be too worried about them because he knows what they look like, it's the ones in the shadows that trouble him and that he's very afraid of, mainly because he becomes uncertain, that scares him."

"What about me, I've been helping him all along."

"Patrick's real fears are that either you or John Dunlop are in league with the man Vladisky."

"For crying out loud, has the man gone totally insane? The pressure's getting to him."

"Then explain how John Dunlop was followed to their meeting place when only you and he were supposed to know about the meeting? Patrick considers that he's had one close call too many and now trusts nobody." Terry cupped his stumpy fingers around his loosely hanging jowl, his brain racing through the series of conversations that they had had. He could see exactly what Sue was driving at, but didn't have a sensible answer for her.

"I can't believe that John Dunlop had anything to do with it, but then again, he could be connected to people high up in the government. Well at least we know another one of the opposition. I need to talk to Patrick."

"Oh no. If you need to reach him, I'm afraid it's got to be via me for the moment. I'll act as a courier for both of you, that's how he wants it and he'll make contact with me, not the other way around because I don't know where he is."

"Does anybody know you've spoken to him?"

"No."

"If whoever's behind this finds out, you'll become the next target."

"I realise the danger and so does Patrick, that's the reason why he won't let me know where he is, it's far safer that way."

"Alright I accept that, now let me tell you what's been happening."

"Can you write it all down because I won't be seeing him at all, I said that I had be a courier."

"Jesus, he must be shit scared if he won't even see you again, anyway there's plenty to be bullish about, a lot of things have happened over the last few days." Sue waited as Terry scribbled on several pages.

"There, that should tell him everything that I know so far. When can I expect answers to some of these questions?"

"I'll be in touch when I get his answer."

"If you see him, tell him that he won't have to be in hiding much longer. Soon this tsunami will be off the front pages and we're almost ready to go public on this one. Also tell him that I'm sorry about the other night, I had nothing to do with the men following John." If he was acting then he was doing a damn fine job of it, thought Sue. Still, her orders were to trust nobody until they knew who their real friends were.

After midday Patrick moved out from his cover at the flat taking the round about route as he headed towards Battersea Park, it was time to collect any messages from Sue at their prearranged post-box. He hoped that everything had gone smoothly when she met Terry and if he was the weak link then this was the day that his life became forfeit if they realised what Sue was doing for him. He was soon to know the worst he thought moving through the large wrought-iron gates at the far end of the park and quickly got himself among the dense rhododendron bushes along the east fence so that he was hidden from both the road behind and from anybody using the park's walkways. Stealthily he moved in and out of the dark green foliage making his way towards the large open area where the tennis courts and children's playing area was situated. Each time he moved position he felt naked without any foliage cover, but pressed on until he reached the last row of trees and bushes before the large open area. He had found that in among some of the heavy bushes there was space enough to climb underneath and into a central cavity, it was like entering a small cave surrounded with dense green overhanging protection. By moving the leaves slightly he could watch the open fields without detection because this particular bush was perched on a high mound running the full length of the playing field. From here he could survey the entire area and its inhabitants without being seen, it was almost one o'clock and time for Sue to take her walk through the park as arranged. He silently thanked himself for picking this spot, the shade afforded by the huge trees above the thick bush meant that he could shed his greatcoat for a short while.

"I must try and find a lightweight coat for the daytime," he thought aloud as he watched for any sign of his ex-wife.

Sue carefully placed the pages that Terry had given her into an envelope and for the hundredth time checked to see what time it was, she felt that it had better be later than earlier when she took her walk into the park, at last the time she had been waiting for arrived, she picked up her towel bag for the tenth time which she had packed earlier. Making her way downstairs, checking again twice to see that the envelope was securely fixed inside the front of her pink shorts. Patrick had been very explicit on how he wanted everything carried out, no taking of any chances and if others, such as the police were watching her as well, she had to act naturally. Trying hard not to act too casually, she walked to zebra crossing and crossed over to the park. For a while she followed a path leading towards the tennis courts and when she reached them she moved in a wide arc around them towards the play area, at the edge she found what she was looking for. Stopping in the shade she spread a towel on the ground and sat down at the foot of one of the large trees. Looking around the open area, she could see a lot of people from the flats enjoying this burst of sunshine. Topless sun worshippers, men in shorts and swimming trunks, it was almost like being at a beach with grass making up the sea. She had specifically made up a small pack of things to eat for herself in the morning, and after reading a book for twenty minutes took the pack from her bag. Carefully unwrapping the contents that she had brought along to nibble at, she placed them alongside her on the ground. As the sun moved westward and the shadowy area reduced, she found herself having to move position to stay in the shade. She carried on reading until two thirty.

From his hideout Patrick watched Sue circle the tennis court slowly and make her way along the edge of the large open area towards the playground. Then he noticed the tall black man moving in the distance near the clubhouse he was good and even if Sue had turned around to look for him she wouldn't have seen him, he was too well hidden from her. This man was an expert, there was no doubting that.

"That's Tweedledum, now where the hell is Tweedledee?" His eyes scanned all the possible hiding places and found nothing. Patrick could see that the black man wasn't dressed for sunbathing and stuck out among this sun-loving crowd but then Patrick saw the white man, he was skirting the line of heavy foliage and what was worse, straight towards his hiding place.

"Oh please God. He can't have seen me." Ivan was moving with purpose as Patrick starting wondering whether to run or not. Having a logical brain, even though it was somewhat weary, Patrick decided that there were too many odds against him running. He would be caught before he had travelled very far so he simply sat tight watching the man moving directly towards his cleverly thought out hiding place.

"Shit, how the hell did they find me?" The big man was now no more than ten yards from him and moving closer with each step, Patrick prepared himself so that as the man reached into the overhanging cover for him, he would propel himself forward and try to throw his assailant off-balance. Surprise would be the only thing on his side for a split second. If it worked then he would make a run for the gate, he estimated that this action if, he managed it would give him at least a fifty yard start. Once across the road and into the high rise development half way down the block he stood a better chance of escaping, on the other hand, the man probably had a gun.

"What the heck, we've all got to go sometime, I'm going to give it my best shot."

Still crouching, he prepared himself to move quickly when he heard the man pushing leaves to the side, Ivan's soft footsteps reached Patrick's hiding place, but didn't stop as expected, instead the man continued past and away from his concealed hiding place. Patrick suddenly realised that the man was so intent on keeping track of Sue who was now making her way around the opposite side of the ground, Patrick released a huge sigh of relief as the man reached a position some twenty yards further along the grassed bank then sat down in the shade of the bordering trees. Patrick was trapped, he couldn't move now even if he wanted to and also knew that if he made any sudden movements the man might detect him and then the game would be up. The hunted man steeled himself to wait as long as it took and also knew that they could be there for some time.

As she had moved around the tree into the shade, Sue had taken the letter from its hiding place and placed it under her towel. Now she lay on her stomach supposedly reading a novel, carefully she placed the letter into the food wrappers and then crumpled it all into a ball. At a little before three o'clock she sat up and carefully folded her towel, placing it in her bag to prepare herself for the next stage. She had seen one of the men move across the far side of the open playground, but nowhere could she see the nig black man. Patrick had said that possibly one would stay behind while the other followed, then with a sudden movement she started off in the direction of the river which was away from her flat. Setting off at a brisk pace she was quickly on the path that weaved through the abundant number of tall rhododendrons. Sue hoped that she had caught the man she had seen off guard with this sudden movement and that he would be racing across the playing field to catch up to her. Looking to her right, her heart almost stopped then and there as she momentarily caught sight of the black man walking in a parallel line to her.

"Keep walking, don't look back, Patrick if you can read my thoughts you'll know they're both here. Be careful." She tried to force the thought patterns out of her head so that it would wing its way to her ex-husband, if ever she wanted telepathy to work it was now, she thought.

Patrick had become decidedly uncomfortable sitting locked in one position and trying not to move at all, his head fixed so that he could keep watch on Sue and the men at the same time. Simultaneously, he had been able to survey the entire area very slowly to see if there were any others that could be taking more than a passing interest in Sue. He had specifically picked this spot because anybody following her and not suitably attired for sun worshipping in the park would look out of kilter, now it was almost time to act. He saw her move quickly away from the tree and out of sight in amongst the bushes. The big man to his right was clearly caught off guard by her move, jumped up and began racing across the open ground. Patrick's gaze immediately searched the far side of the park for the black man noting that he had been better prepared for the move when it did come, more so than his white counterpart had been because he was already moving from beneath the trees towards the bushes following Sue. Patrick understood that surprise was on his side, he gathered up the coat and put it on before moving across the open ground towards where Sue had been lying, as he reached the spot he quickly stooped to collect up some old food wrappers knowing that nobody watching would even give an old tramp picking up papers a second look. He turned right and moved past the tennis court towards the exit, it didn't take long to reach the safety of his temporary accommodation. Inside he drew breath, it was the first time that he had even stopped and considered how Sue was getting on. He would find out later when they met up as arranged.

"So much trouble for one little letter, I just hope you're worth it," he said aloud as he extracted the pile of papers from his pocket. Carefully extracting the envelope from among the food wrappers he opened it while removing his coat that he slung to the floor then sat on the large old sofa to start reading its contents. The opening line made Patrick throw his head back and take in a deep breath.

"George Li is alive, thank God for that."

CHAPTER THIRTY FIVE

"Is Ivan still keeping watch over her?" Vladisky Ormon was busily talking on the phone to the black man, they had been ordered to report in to him twice a day.

"Where did she go from the park?" The man explained that they had followed her when she walked out of the park and stopped at a newsagent before returning to her flat.

"Okay if there's nothing else, we don't have any other leads, you two idiots keep watching her, I've got a suspicion he is in the neighbourhood and will turn up shortly or she'll slip up and lead us to him. For Chrissake don't you and Ivan let me down again or else I'll have your balls for breakfast. Do you understand me?" The man at the other end of the line seethed quietly under the barrage of words.

"There's a definite link between her and the newspaper man, somehow I'm sure that one of them will lead us to Rodgers or the girl, it's only a matter of time now. Now get back to your post and if she as much as coughs, I want to know about it." Taking out a handkerchief and wiping his forehead as he replaced the receiver, before now, he had always managed to control events by being unduly nasty but, this time he was being placed under extreme pressure from his principals to curb his temper. The whole thing was beginning to turn nightmarish for him with Steve being stupid enough to get himself shot, certainly didn't make things any easier for him. He was fully aware that somehow he had to find Patrick Rodgers or Kim Lee within the next twenty four hours because he could already feel the enemy were seeping towards him like a freezing fog and with those two still alive and free somewhere out there, he couldn't stop it from eventually reaching him. Firstly he had thought about kidnapping Sue in the hope of bringing Patrick out into the open, then his contact at the ministry had suggested that it would serve no purpose because with the newspapers hounding them it would probably be far more prudent keeping watch on her movements while government people kept close to the newspaper editor. Earlier this morning the police had reported a meeting had been held between Terry and Sue, that indicated that they could be getting closer to Rodgers. One slip, that's all it was going to take from one of them and the feeling was one of desperation so it wasn't going to be long now. If nothing happened or they didn't slip up tonight his men had orders to bring in both Sue and Terry so he could personally question them. It was only a matter of time before all of these enemies would be out of the way and his life would be normal again.

"Mr. Ormon, I have Miss Heidi Zenger on the line for you. She states she is the computer controller on a project in America but would not give any further details." His secretary's voice pierced into his thought process, he badly wanted to talk to the woman that had made life difficult for the project.

"Miss Zenger, I'm the London control for the UNSECP Program and I need to talk to you urgently."

"Mr. Ormon, I know who you are, if you remember it was me that objected to the computer security system that was installed." He thought back placing the face to the woman who at the beginning of the project had vehemently rejected his security plans.

"Of course and that's one of the things we need to discuss before you disappear again. Could you come to my office this evening so that we can clear up this matter."

"There's nothing to clear up. Didn't Mr. Hearn tell you that I've developed a new overriding security protection system for the project and I'm the only one that can operate it. It's completely failsafe now." This statement took Ormon slightly aback, in none of the reports to him had this even been mentioned. He wondered why.

"No, he said nothing to me and now that he's dead, I'm the most senior person on the project. That's all the more reason that I be brought up to date and I want you in this office as soon as you can get your little butt down here. There are a few things you need to be made aware of. Do I make myself clear?"

"Yes. Give me your address and I'll be there within the hour."

"Eureka, at last we have them, where is this sanatorium?" Vladisky Ormon then received another call from the ministry informer this time to tell him that his men had followed Terry and Jenny to a building in Richmond. One of them followed Terry and his companion and had seen the room that they entered, there was a guard at the door, and the men watched from their car until the two had left. After changing shifts, they collected doctor's coats and returned to the sanatorium to find out who was being so well looked after. They knew that the guard wouldn't allow them into the room so the men, acting like two doctors carefully questioned a young nurse who innocently informed them that the patient was a young Chinese looking girl suffering from bullet wounds and was in a coma. That's all she could tell them, but it was enough.

"Kim Lee. If we get hold of her then it won't take long to wheedle that bastard Rodgers out of his hiding place. The editor will quickly lead us straight to him when she disappears and then we'll have them all trapped in one corner. The girl, the meddling newspaper man and Rodgers, it'll be one magnificent coup for us. There'll be no evidence that the project even existed with them out of the way." Ormon smiled wickedly at the thought of cleaning up their mess so efficiently.

"Don't worry, I'm going to oversee this one myself, we can't afford any mistakes. I wouldn't trust those goons of mine to carry this out by themselves, I'll be there to oversee the operation myself." At the other end of the line, the voice made its position clear to him.

"You realise that the government can't be party to this intended killing. Capturing and handing over to the Americans was fine, but what you're suggesting is out of the question."

"Of course I do, you get your hands dirty by financing the project, but when the shit hits the fan, I'm expected to clean it up. Don't worry my friend; we'll leave everybody in your precious government untouched. In fact no fingers will be pointed; it'll simply look like another series of murders in this metropolis. You just make sure that the newspaper doesn't make a fuss because they'll be baying for somebody's blood when their editor is found. You cover our backs, understand?"

"There's a Heidi Zenger here to see you Mr. Ormon." It was the front door security desk.

"Yes, I'm expecting her. Send her up." He waited for several minutes before he heard the lift stop further down the hall.

"In here!" His office was the only one with lights on, everybody had already left for the day. The redhead appeared slightly apprehensive as she entered his office.

"Mr. Ormon?"

"Yes, come in and sit down, I won't be long." He opened a large dossier and read through one of the files.

"You came highly recommended. It states that you're Swiss but you did you final degree in Paris. Why was that?"

"My parents thought that the French education system would be better than leaving me at college in Genève." Shutting the file he took a long look at the clever scientist. He didn't like highly intellectual people, they lived in a closed world of their own and regarded him with a certain amount of disdain.

"Right, tell me what happened at the base." For several minutes Heidi explained what had taken place. Before ending her story she became distraught and cried when she recalled how she had shot Steve." Ormon didn't have any pity for this snivelling scientist because in his twisted thinking he felt that she probably deserved what she got.

"Now explain your security system to me, from now on you are going to report to me and I want to know exactly what you're doing." Heidi examined the man carefully. Unlike the rest, her Oscar winning performance hadn't bought the expected reaction. This man was so self conceited that any other opinion didn't seem to matter to him.

"Before I do that would you please tell me what's going on, Mr. Hearn said that there was a security leak from here." By here he had meant London but Ormon immediately took the word out of context thinking that she was referring to his office.

"Young lady, the man was an idiot, the security leak came from outside in the form of one Patrick Rodgers who worked for a company called Silver Beam International." Without stopping, he continued to explain what he had found in the American bank and the involvement of Raymond Chen that had got the project into this mess. He finished off by proudly announcing what he intended doing to his antagonists before the night was over.

"Could they really threaten the project?"

"You have been involved in many deaths of unknown people around the world. Tonight you will see the real thing and then our project will be really secure once again. Now explain your security system to me."

"What do you mean the real thing? Heidi wasn't sure if she fully understood what the detestable little man had meant.

"I'm going to get rid of these security invaders tonight and you are coming with us to witness their end."

"No bloody way."

"Listen, you allowed them into the project and now it's only fitting that you be there at the death. Excuse the pun, it's only when they're properly disposed of, that any of can feel safe again. You may not like it, but you're responsible for thousands of deaths and it doesn't affect you because you're distanced from it. Another three won't make any difference to you except you going to be there to see it happen."

"My God has the whole world gone mad, I absolutely refuse to come with you."

"We'll see. Now, how does this security lock work?"

"Nobody, not even me can get into the system from the outside," she lied. There was no way she was going to admit this maniac into her perfectly maintained system. The telephone rang allowing her time to compose herself.

"Forget her for the moment; there's been a sudden change of plan because we've located the Chinese girl. I'll meet you and Ivan at the Albert Bridge in twenty minutes. Find four white doctor type overcoats from one of the shops in the neighbourhood and be there on time. Now get moving." As he replaced the receiver he shook his head from side to side.

"They're such bloody idiots those two, but they serve my purpose well. I have them right in the palm of my hand and they will never cross me, the silly suckers."

"Why?" Vladisky Ormon had never been the shy retiring type as far as his own achievements were concerned.

"I have some dirt on them which I keep stored in my computer but the smart part is that. I've convinced the stupid bastards that if they try anything then a special file would be sent to the police. They are so gullible that they'll do anything for me." Suddenly he realised he had said too much to Heidi. Ormon stood up and opened a drawer and dropped the pink file into it.

"You can explain the system when we get back. C'mon." Heidi stayed seated.

"Mr. Ormon, I'm not coming with you."

"Oh yes you are." Ormon sneered as he opened his jacket wide to reveal a snugly

fitted brown shoulder holster with a gun showing it's deadly black butt extending from the top.

"Listen you bitch, if you're not going to play your part in the project, then you too will end up like those we're going dispose of tonight. So don't play games with me my girl." His eyes had a peculiarly hardened look about them and she knew he meant exactly what he had said and would carry out his threat without reserve. Steadily so as not to convey her fear, she rose from her chair and left the office with Ormon. Her brain was busily filing through all sorts of possibilities of escape, she knew she had to remain calm if she was going to get away from this madman and remain intact. They reached his car parked on the lower basement level.

"Where are we going?"

"First to collect some of my men; then on to a sanatorium where the South Korean girl is being kept."

" South Korean girl? What's her name?"

"Kim Lee, she the one that works for Silver Beam and is somehow involved with Patrick Rodgers when she was shot by Chen. Pity he didn't do the job properly, but now she will be the bait to attract Rodgers out of hiding."

When they reached Albert Bridge they found Ormon's two henchmen waiting for them on the North side of the river.

"Have you two blunderers managed to find those dustcoats yet?"

"It wasn't easy but we managed to persuade a shop owner to serve us at this late hour," laughed Ivan cruelly.

"Follow me and don't get lost." Both vehicles snaked eastwards and through the fast darkening roads towards Richmond. They found the place with ease and Ormon noted that the building looked almost like most of the surrounding houses. He stopped and quickly indicated for the occupants of the following car to get out.

"Go and have a look around. I suggest that you start at the rear and work your way back here and don't muck it up. All I want you idiots to do is observe what entrances there are and whether we can get in and out without being seen.

"Don't you want to know if there are any guards on duty or anything?"

"I know that already you fool. Just have a look around and see the best way to get in and up to the first floor and out again." The two men slipped into the shadows and made their way to the back of the building. There was a small parking area containing three vehicles where they found the back door unlocked that they carefully entered. Ivan moved up the narrow stairway towards the first floor and stopped behind a fire door. Being careful not to be seen, he looked through the Georgian-wired pane in the door and saw a long passageway. All he could see was a chair outside one of the doors which he presumed was used by the guard.

"It's like a damn church it's so quiet," he whispered to his black companion, "I don't think anybody's expecting us."

"Where's the guard?"

"How the hell do I know, we must find out before trying anything, we don't want any surprises." The two discussed the situation in whispered tones. They waited for a few minutes before the sound of footsteps on the lino-covered wooden stairs at the far side of the passage could be heard.

"Get back." A plump man moved into the passage carrying a plastic cup. He settled himself on the chair and sipped at the cup.

"C'mon, let's get back," whispered Ivan. They made their way to the front door and carefully looked inside, lights from inside kept them hidden from view in amongst the shadows as they looked through the windows at ground level. At the reception they could see a woman talking on the telephone, nobody else seemed to be moving inside the building as its occupants prepared to settle down for the night. Back at the car they explained what they had seen in the building.

"Surprise is on our side, it couldn't be better, we'll have to distract the guard though, he could become suspicious if a batch of doctors suddenly appeared, I think our friend here should be able to provide the necessary distraction." He turned towards Heidi with a smug smile. She felt a freezing sensation run the full length of her spine. Not only was she being forced to observe, now he was going to make her an accessory by assisting with their murderous plan. She had to find a way to stop this lunatic she thought quietly, smiling back at him.

All four were at the fire door when Vladisky spoke to Ivan.

"You go with her and if she tries anything, cripple her." He turned and looked at Heidi and shook his head to indicate that the two should get a move on with the job in hand.

"You know what you must do, so get on with it." Ivan held the door open as Heidi moved into the long passageway ahead of him. She could see that the guard was inspecting them as they moved towards him checking the various names on the doors. Heidi reached him first and as she passed she smiled and turned back towards him.

"Excuse me can you tell me which room Mrs. Howe is in?" For a brief second he turned to answer her, taking his eyes away from Ivan who had nearly reached him. That was enough, the big man moved in on the guard like a cat in full flight attacking its prey. His arm locked around the man's neck and his other arm grabbed the man's head snapping it forward with a swift jerk. Heidi heard the sharp dull thud as the guard's neck bones cracked, the whole thing was over so quickly that she didn't even have time to react. Ivan pulled the man from his chair and with his back pushed open the door and dragged the dead guard into the room.

"Get in there." Ormon was already moving toward her as he motioned for her to follow Ivan into Kim's room. Moving as if in a dream she did as she was told as Ivan laid the guard on the floor and immediately went to Kim's bedside.

"Help me get her up." The black man moved in quickly, the two lifted the tiny figure out of the bed. She was very still and almost lifeless between them, Heidi grabbed a blanket and the girl's dressing gown.

"She'll need something warm to be wrapped into."

"Don't worry about those. Where she's going, she won't need anything warm unless she's off to hell."

"You sadistic bastard." Heidi's temper had been held in check but as she watched the frail form of Kim being manhandled towards the door and then this maniac's remark, she suddenly exploded. Ormon didn't even react at her outburst as he moved to open the door.

"C'mon let's get out of here." He looked out into the passageway. Their entry hadn't even been noticed and with Ormon in the lead, the party hastily moved back into the long passage and towards the fire door. At the door he saw that Heidi had not yet appeared from the room.

"Get her to the office, I'm going to see what that other bitch is doing." As he moved forward Heidi walked into the passageway carrying a bundle under her arm.

"I told you to leave those."

"No chance. You can't treat her this way, I'm taking them, try to stop me and I'll scream." Vladisky drew a short breath and reconsidered the position thinking that he would see to her once they were out of harms way.

"All right now get a move on." Heidi got into the back of the car with Kim without consulting Vladisky. She immediately wrapped the blanket around the unconscious figure as the cars moved off into the night and towards London.

"Good thing it's not winter, you had have caught your death of cold if he had his way," she whispered.

CHAPTER THIRTY SIX

"I can't see them anywhere."

Sue had carefully parked her car and the two went through their ritual motion as Patrick clambered into the back once again, his eyes had also searched for the two men but hadn't managed to spot them.

"Perhaps there's a different crew watching us, get us the hell out of here and keep your eyes peeled for anyone following us." At first Sue imagined that she was being followed but the further she moved through the narrow back streets and around London she became quite positive that they were on their own tonight.

"Patrick, there's nobody following us, something has happened, perhaps they've called off watching me for some reason."

"Find a parking garage and as you get inside the entrance. stop to let me out, I'll check to make doubly certain." Sue did as she was requested; Patrick's keen eye first searched the road outside for any possible sign whatsoever of anything or some form of accompanying movement that could reveal that they had been followed. After a short while and when he was quite sure that they were safe, he walked down the vehicles ramps until he found Sue parked on a lower floor.

"You were right, it would seem that there's nobody out there searching for us. I wonder if they've been called off, I still don't trust them, this could simply be a ruse in order to make us drop our guard or, there might simply be something more important happening for them to pull out or, in order for them to leave us alone after all the hounding."

"What now?"

"George Li is back at his house, let's try to contact him first, we have to get moving and get all the evidence we need against the United Nations. If anybody can get into their computer once again, it's got to be George." The two were careful as they left the building through a back entrance and down the road to a pub where Patrick immediately called George.

"Where the hell have you been?"

"Patrick?"

"Yes. What happened to you George?"

"It's a long story, can we meet?" Patrick gave him directions to park at the side of the parking garage. He still didn't trust anybody and wanted to first check out that George wasn't being followed.

"I'll be there in twenty minutes, your reporter friend and I have set up a special communication network so that I can pass messages to him without anybody being able to find out. Do you want me to arrange for him to be there?" Patrick thought about it for some time before answering.

"Okay George, but make sure he arrives twenty minutes after you do. Is that possible?"

"Of course, looking forward to seeing you again."

From an upstairs window of the pub Patrick and Sue had a clear view of the street running full length along the side of the parking garage. Patrick had first checked that the pub had a second entrance through which he and Sue could escape if they felt even slightly threatened. They waited until they saw George pull his car to a halt half way up the block, as planned, he switched off his motor and picked up what looked like a book to start reading. Patrick asked Sue to meet him and walk to the top of the road and around the corner and then wait for two minutes before bringing George back to the pub. That way he would know if anybody was following them once they passed out of sight at the top of the road. If there was anything suspicious Patrick told her he would place one of the large menus in front of the window and she would tell George that the meeting was off until the following morning.

"Understand everything?"

"Yes."

"Take care my girl, oh thanks, please be very careful." Patrick held her close for a brief moment knowing that he was sending her into possible danger and regretting his inability to do anything else. At least if George was not being tailed then his own possibilities would have increased by one hundred per cent. Sue smiled nervously and leaned forward and kissed him of the mouth.

"Be back in five minutes." Patrick watched her reach the car, his eyes were everywhere searching for the slightest betrayal that George had someone else watching his short computer expert companion. The two moved away and reached the corner then disappeared. Nothing moved as his friends had ambled safely slowly towards the pub, only then did Patrick's senses relax slightly, he made his way to the ground floor and sat in a dark corner. The couple entered and climbed stairs as Patrick waited and made certain that he hadn't missed anything. Nobody followed them into the pub and after several minutes rose and moved upstairs to join Sue and George.

Patrick moved up silently behind the little man and surprised him by placing his hands over the man's eyes, Sue watched on as her ex-husband teasingly kept his hands in place until George answered. Sue giggled loudly as she watched the smiling face change to that of a bewilderment.

"Don't worry George, behind this tramp's facade it's really me."

"I wouldn't have recognised you at all, that's some disguise you've created."

"It's authentic alright. I've been sleeping on the streets and even had the smell to go with the disguise." Patrick sat down and looked long and hard at his friend who was smiling broadly in usual oriental fashion so that his narrow slit eyes seemed to disappear into two thin cracks.

"Now George talk to me, what the hell's been going on?"

"It's simple, when Raymond Chen let it be known that he was going to destroy whoever had been playing with the computer, I started running scared and went into hiding with a friend who lives in Salisbury."

"Why the hell didn't you let me or anyone know where you were?"

"Because my friend, I've learnt from bitter experience what these security pigs will do to others to find out what they need to know. The less anybody knew about me, the better for them, because any contact means discovery. When I read about him shooting Kim I nearly went mad and then the later report that Raymond Chen had died of a suspected heart attack when about to leave the country scared me even more." George lifted his glass and took a large drink before continuing.

"I sat around for several days then got a bright idea. I called Mr. Kang and asked if anybody had been searching for me, I knew that he didn't like Chen and in some funny way admired you. He told me the whole story about Kim Lee and Raymond Chen. He suggested that they could have been lovers or she knew something and wouldn't tell Chen, that's why he shot her. Whoever killed Chen has done us all a big favour, Kang also gave me the telephone number of your reporter friend who had been checking in daily with him to see if you or I had contacted the office. At first I was afraid it had something to do with that computer exercise that we carried out, then I called him from a public call box. He told me in a roundabout fashion that you were and Kim Lee were both safe and that he had been to your house. All that work, down the drain for nothing."

"Do you think we can get into the UN computer again?"

"They know we're onto them and probably locked the program down tight, but we can try."

"I've had one or two sessions with your reporter friend. Honestly Patrick the man is so bent on getting a story that he wanted me to start hacking two days ago, at first I denied any knowledge of what he was talking about and refused to say anything until I had met up with you again. I'm scared, for all I knew he could of been one of them. What do you think?"

"To be absolutely honest I'm the worst person to ask because from my reaction earlier you've probably realised that I too, trust nobody. Two guys have been following Sue for two days in the hope that she'll lead them to me, now they're suddenly gone missing, I think something's up."

"So what do we do now?"

"It's almost time for Terry to arrive, are you still able to use your friend's flat?"

"Sure."

"I suggest we don't say anything to Terry today and I'll meet you there later, we see if we can break into the UN again."

"I've got an idea, why don't you stay there instead of sleeping rough. He won't be back for another two weeks or so."

"We'll see. Thanks for the offer though." Sue suddenly pointed to a car that was moving slowly up the road towards George's parked vehicle.

"Terry."

"Right, Sue go and meet him, same procedure. Okay?" She left the pub and moved up the road in full sight of the two men.

George was the first to spot them, he pointed out the car to his companion. Patrick felt the hairs on the nape of his neck stiffen up in response, two men in a car cruised slowly past the pub and then stopped out of sight of Sue and Terry who was now getting out of his car. Patrick grabbed a large menu and immediately placed it in the window as a warning to Sue. They watched as the driver of the following car pulled onto the kerb while his companion casually walked back to the corner where he stood looking into a shop yet keeping an eye on the two who were now halfway along the road.

"Those are real professionals could they be the men that have been watching Sue?" George was the first to say anything.

"No. That's how they've been able to track my movements somebody is following Terry, I knew that they had bugged his telephone and this explains a lot of things, but I wonder if they're here at his invitation." George whistled softly through his teeth.

"I've already had two meetings with him probably know my face, they may put two and two together if they see me and Sue at the same place. I better get away from here now."

"Oh no you don't, you stay here until we see what happens. Sue and Terry had almost reached the corner at the end of the block. The two men started off in the same direction, one on each side of the road but as the two disappeared around the corner the two men quickened their pace to reach the corner. Sue and Terry suddenly reappeared as the two men were reaching the end of the block. The one on their side of the road continued on and around the corner as the other stopped and turned to look into a nearby window. Patrick drew a deep breath.

"Did you see that? They didn't even miss a beat, you're right, these boys are the real McCoy alright."

"What do we do now?"

"Watch." As the fat man reached the car he turned to Sue and shook her hand warmly then climbed back into his car and sped off up the road. The two men had been caught in no-man's-land as they both raced towards their car. Patrick laughed loudly as their car reversed up to the corner then roared away in an attempt to catch up with Terry.

"What's so funny?"

"Don't you see? If Terry had been an informer, they would not have almost broken their necks catching up with him. He probably didn't even know that he was being followed. We'll see what Sue says when she gets back." George simply shook his head in disbelief.

"Do you trust him enough to believe that he's not one of them?"

Patrick whistled softly, he was confused. As the two men descended to the ground floor bar and sat in the corner just as Sue returned and made her way straight upstairs. They waited for a few minutes before again joining her.

"What did he say?"

"It was incredible, he didn't have an inkling that he was being followed until we came back around the corner. I told him that you were wary and needed to check him out first, seeing the white menu in the window he suggested that there was a man looking into a window and acting suspiciously. On the way to his car he told me to stop and shake hands and he would be back in ten minutes if he was able to shake them off his trail. You saw the rest?" Patrick gazed out of the window for some time.

"Let's give Terry the benefit of the doubt, it could be that we caught them off balance, but I don't think so. Still we can't be too careful." The three ran through the plan once again. Within twenty minutes Terry's car moved slowly up the road to the far corner. He turned and moved slowly back to the pub and once again turned before again stopping his vehicle near George's car, Sue went to meet him but instead of Terry getting out of the car, Sue got into it and the vehicle moved away to quickly disappear around the corner. Nothing looked out of place as George and Patrick watched for any movements. They watched everybody within the vicinity of the pub putting each person came under close scrutiny, both Patrick and George were slightly on edge and nervous that Terry could have used the time away to inform somebody of their whereabouts. Five minutes later the two reappeared; walking slowly this time towards the pub and then back to the end of the parking garage.

"Let's get downstairs, this cat and mouse game is becoming ridiculous." Terry and Sue entered the pub and moved up the stairs while Patrick and George once again remained downstairs for about ten minutes before joining them.

"Nice coat and cap, sit down and shut up, I urgently need to talk to you, we've got to be quick."

"Why?"

"Those bastards may backtrack and I don't want them to bump into you. Now I want you to tell this friend of yours to pull his finger out and try to repeat his last performance. We've got them on the run and some proof that this damned culling program exists will certainly clinch it."

"Okay, but we do it my way. George and I will disappear and when we manage to get the proof we'll contact you."

"That's fine with me, but do it. The whole fucking world is after you and these bastards will leave nothing unturned until they find you. It's a race and you're coming last at the moment."

"All right Terry, we'll get started right away." The fat man heaved himself off the chair.

"By the way, I've got someone checking out your friend Ormon, he's a nasty bit of work and he leaves nothing to chance. Unless you can get into the program and tie him into the project somehow he's going to get away Scot-free."

"We know he's involved?"

"Oh I know that, the two goons that have been watching Sue both work for his company. It doesn't take a genius to work out that he's involved, but with his clout that's going to be hard to prove." Terry's mobile phone buzzed.

"Who did it?" He listened.

"Right. Get some of our boys to meet me there as soon as possible, also get as many photographers there at the same time. Don't do anything until I get there." He replaced the phone into his inside pocket then put his hand to his mouth. The rest could see that he was worried about something.

"Bad news I'm afraid, there's been trouble at the sanatorium." Patrick felt the hair on his neck rise again.

"What happened?"

"Your little friend and his goons have kidnapped Kim, fortunately for you we have also been keeping an eye on the two idiots for the last two days to keep your back covered without you knowing. They've taken her to Vladisky's office block, I'm going in with a team of east end thugs and a crew of photographers. This will make a fabulous story and that bastard has made a huge first mistake and will sink faster than the Titanic."

"I'm coming with you!"

"Don't be stupid Patrick if anything goes wrong you'll be exposed with nowhere to go."

"I can leave George can do his thing if anything goes wrong, c'mon let's get that bastard once and for all." Terry didn't move as he weighed up the possibilities.

"Okay, be it on your own head. One promise though, you disappear immediately the fun is over. You mustn't forget that he won't be the only one hunting you, there are others as well as the police and until we have proof positive in our hands, you're still a hunted man."

"Done. now let's get there and try to rescue Kim. This is my day to no longer be a victim, I've been waiting for that little swine to slip up, remember he is mine. George I'll see you later."

"What about me?" Patrick had become so involved that he had momentarily forgotten about Sue, he took her by the hand, leaning forward to kiss her. His lips lingered slightly longer than was necessary for their parting kiss.

"You go home and lock the door, don't let anybody in, do you understand? I'll post a letter as soon as I know what's happening." She understood what he meant, as the two men headed towards the corner Sue found herself quietly saying a pray to the heavens to keep him safe from harm.

"I hope it works out and they get what they need. It's been lovely meeting you Sue, I'm off to see if I can get a computer to talk to another computer."

"Be safe George, you and Terry are the only friends that Patrick can trust." Sue said as she kissed him on the cheek.

CHAPTER THIRTY SEVEN

The two cars entered the building and spiralled their way down into the depths of the multi-storeyed basement, at the lowest level both vehicles drew up opposite a steel door. Everybody had left building by this time of night and the entire parking garage below ground seemed to be devoid of the usual mass of vehicles, right now it was empty and as quiet as a graveyard. The opening of the car doors seemed to reverberate loud echoes throughout the desolate basement. Ormon Vladisky moved to steel door and unlocked it.

"In here." The store room was fairly large and housed innumerable cans of paint, cleaning material as well as various loose ceiling panels and partitions used obviously for maintenance items for the building. Vladisky Ormon turned the light then slammed the door closed after Ivan and the black man had carried Kim into this cold room.

"Set her down." The two men laid her on the freezing concrete floor, Heidi instantly moved forward to Kim carrying two blankets. She had managed to place the gown on the limp figure in the car, now she was going to make some form of wrapping for the unconscious little Chinese looking girl.

"Leave her!"

"No way, you can't just leave her on this freezing floor like this." Heidi continued to battle to get the blankets wrapped around Kim knowing full well that she was overstepping the mark but she had to play for time.

"I said, leave her!" Ormon Vladisky walked towards them and used the sole of his shoe as a lever to push her away from Kim, Heidi fell sideways by being caught momentarily off balance.

"Don't you ever kick me again, next time you touch me will be your last." The outburst only served to make the little man more angry than he already appeared.

"Do you want to join your friend, I can arrange that quite easily." He slowly slipped his hand into the inside of his jacket and removed the 9mm parabellum gun from its holster. Heidi knew she was gambling with high stakes.

"Go on shoot me if you have the nerve, you're a little man with a major chip on your shoulder able to act like a bully, even those two giants are scared of you and why? You threaten their very existence by telling them you've got something that will be sent to the police if they don't obey you. Then you tell me that you've got nothing and it was just a story so they would do your bidding, what were the words you used to me. Oh yes, those numbskulls think I have something over them." She watched his composed features suddenly turn to a mask of hatred as his gun hand raised and pointed threateningly towards her, she hoped he didn't have the courage to use it. For a solitary moment their eyes locked, she willing him to stop, his filled with utter hatred for anyone that dared to contradict him.

"You lying bitch!"

Heidi realised that she was treading dangerous ground which could make thing worse for her but undeterred by his violent threats, she carried on.

"Those men may be afraid of you, I'm not, you've scared them into thinking that you have something on them when you haven't but I don't scare so easily."

"Oh no?" The stillness of the basement shattered as Vladisky aimed the gun at Heidi and pulled the trigger. She felt one side of her body being ripped as the bullet hit her shoulder and flung her sideways onto the hard concrete. Her gamble hadn't worked as she lay looking toward the little man pointing his big gun at her.

"That's for starters, the next is through the head like this." He swung the gun and pointed straight toward the covering figure of Heidi.

"N-noo!" Heidi heard herself screaming at him.

"Shout all you want nobody can hear us in here, I've made dead certain of that."

"Please stop this, let us go."

"So, you admit you're one of them, well this is what happens to your type of people." Heidi saw the flash coupled to the deafening roar of the black menace in his hand. Kim's body jumped as the bullet entered her body.

"No!" Heidi found herself crawling toward the limp female figure.

"That's right, crawl to the cow and die with her, Heidi flopped over the figure trying to protect Kim from this maniac, tensing herself for what she expected shot that was to come. In that fleeting moment she wondered where he was going to aim the bullet, the back of her head or the other shoulder in order to prolong her suffering. She squeezed her eyes tightly waiting for the sound she may never hear if the missile sailed through her head but all she heard was a clatter of something metal hitting the floor.

"What the.." It had come from Vladisky Ormon and followed swiftly by Ivan's voice.

"So, numbskulls are we, you've made you last mistake, you shouldn't have bragged to the girl.

"She's lying, can't you see, I didn't say anything like that and if you don't let go then your files go to the police you idiot." Heidi turned far enough to see that the black man had Vladisky in a vice-like grip from behind. Ivan was standing with his back towards her, she raised her head knowing that this might be her only chance of remaining alive.

"I promise you that what I said was the truth, he's got nothing on you." She could see the two were caught between her story and his but again, she forced home her wafer thin advantage. "He said that if you ever found out that he was lying to you that you would kill him. If you don't believe me then shoot me now, I just don't care any more but I wouldn't tell you lies at this stage, I'm at his mercy but before dying at least you two know the truth." Heidi dropped her head onto Kim's body in an attempt to persuade them that she was telling the truth, for a moment there was nothing then she heard Ivan's voice.

"What do you think?" Vladisky screamed loudly and Heidi instinctively knew that he had just made a very big mistake. "Don't believe that bitch you idiots!"

"That does it. I'm not having you swear at me again," said the black man before Heidi heard Vladisky Ormon's terrifying scream. Carefully she again raised her head, looking up she watched without compassion as the two men like a pair of possessed demons, began their onslaught by punching Vladisky in the face, the back and wherever they could lay their fists at that moment. Each time the little man tried falling to the floor to try and cover himself the black man would lift him up letting Ivan punch him. Heidi listened in horror as the whole time Vladisky screamed consistently like the little piglet that he was. Her head spinning and she felt somewhat woozy probably from loss of blood, she didn't want to watch the scene any longer.

"Stop screaming you fat bastard, nobody can hear you, you told us that yourself didn't you?!" The racket stopped, with all her strength she lifted her head to see why, the black man had one hand clamped tightly over Vladisky's mouth.

"For years we've suffered your taunts and threats, haven't we Ivan? Many times we've discussed what we had love to do to you and now the time has come for you to beg forgiveness from us, all those harsh words?" He clicked his tongue several times

Heidi saw the glint of a blade in Ivan's hand, her eyes moved to Vladisky's terrified pleading and swollen eyes that by then were almost popping out of his skull. Ivan suddenly grabbed the man's right hand whipped it and as Heidi watched through a growing swell of mist, saw Ivan cut the man's small finger from his hand to hold it aloft in some form of victory salute. Although desperate to watch his end, constant misty unconscious clouds drifted in and out of her brain like flocks of birds migrating to and from their nests. Right then she was unable to fight passing out any longer, once again she dropped her head onto Kim's body. Her head throbbed violently and just then she didn't really care what happened to Ormon, her only thought was her own predicament and impending death at the moment.

"I hope somebody finds me before I bleed to death," she whispered to herself as she lost consciousness altogether.

"We want to speak to Mr. Ormon Vladisky, we know he's in the building."

"Who are you," came the reply from the camera lens. Terry flashed an official looking press card at the all Seeing Eye above, this bluff had worked once in the past, he just hoped that the guard wasn't very astute.

"Police, now open up." The door buzzed and Terry and his back-up team entered and walked towards the young on-duty security guard seated in the foyer of the building. He rose from behind his desk console that looked more like a space ship control panel than a building monitor.

"Where is Mr. Vladisky?"

"I'm not quite sure, his vehicle came into the building about ten minutes ago, but he still hasn't taken the lift up to his office yet." Terry was surprised that the young man hadn't asked to see their identification.

"How would you know that?"

"From these, if he had taken the lift from the basement I would've seen him." The security man pointed at the bank of screens. Terry looked at the changing screen from within all elevators and also noticed that each one covered a full length of passageway to each and every floor.

"So then he's still in his car in the basement."

"That's what's strange, there were two cars that entered the building at the same time. None of the occupants have come up into the building yet, I'm here on my own and was getting worried and was just about to radio in to my control when you came along."

"Do that anyway, we may need some help, we're going to the basement to find them." The security man lifted the radio phone connected straight to his head office.

"They went to level four, so they must still be down there," he shouted after them, when they reached the lift, Terry turned to two of the men.

"You go down the stairway in case they're walking up. What we'll do is start in the bottom basement and work our way up the building to the top." After a few minutes everybody had gathered in the basement.

"Nothing on the stairs, that's Vladisky's car over there." The man pointed to the far end of the basement.

"Fan out and shout if you see anything, Harry is there enough light down here to take any photographs?"

"Don't worry boss, the flash will take care of any deficiency."

"Right let's go, be careful, these guys are killers." Two of Terry's so-called friends were carrying sawn-off shotguns as everybody spread out and moved carefully towards the far end of the basement.

"Stranger and stranger. Nothing, I wonder where they've gone." They reached the far end and one of the cars still had its door open and the inside light on.

"Right, let's try the rest of the building." The photographer pointed to the steel door and raised his finger to his lips.

"Look, there's a light on in that room." A thin crack of light could just be seen filtering through below the bottom of the door.

"Be careful." At the door Harry placed his ear against it then turned to Terry and indicated that he could hear movement, Terry motioned to everybody to move back to the cars. He lowered his voice to a whisper.

"You two try to fling the door open and you two keep your guns pointed into the room. Be careful not to fire too early, those things are lethal and there's a wounded girl in there. You could end up hitting her and that's something we don't want, if we catch them unawares the rest of you get in there and close down Ormon and the goons." Everybody got into position then looked at Terry for the signal, he dropped his arm and the first two whipped the door open and stood to one side. The men with the guns moved through quickly into the room followed by others. What confronted the party was totally unexpected, in all his days as a reporter Terry had seen some horrific things, but never as anything as sickening as what confronted him now. Ivan and the black man's faces froze from happy laughing to absolute terror at being caught out.

"Hands in the air," shouted one of the gunmen threateningly, the two sadists were in two minds but quickly realised they were in no position to argue.

"Drop those." Like one, both men dropped their knives with a clatter onto the concrete floor, Harry's continual flashing camera recorded every movement in the room.

The Culling

"Down on your bellies, you fucking bastards!" Both Ivan and the black man dropped without any arguments, they had been caught flatfooted. While two men moved to search the men for arms, Patrick took in the horrific sight before them.

"Oh God!" Still lying between the two prone men was simply a large blob of blood, Terry's immediate reaction was that it could what remained of Kim, then he saw the two female bodies, one draped across the other lying face down on the concrete beyond that bloodied figure. The two goons had skilfully cut off pieces from the figure and laid them carefully in a line, Ormon's bloodied ears, fingers, toes, nose, tongue and private parts all lined up in a neat row on the floor like some sadistic and macabre biology experiment. They had played with him and stripped pieces of flesh bit by bit from the person, just like a cat would do to a rat, the red monstrosity hardly had a square inch of skin left on his body as it tried rising before it wobbled and slowly sank down onto the floor again. Patrick raced in straight to the female two bodies, knowing immediately that Kim was dead by the messy hole between her eyes. He felt the blood drain as he tried to steady himself.

"Jesus why?" Terry was in close attendance and quickly turned the other body over to check if she had suffered the same fate. "She's still alive. one of you get upstairs and get an ambulance here immediately."

One of the others was obviously practised in first aid, instantly tearing strips from Kim's gown, he quickly stuffed them into the wound then tied a tourniquet around the upper arm to try and stem bleeding. Terry grabbed Patrick and turned him away from Kim's lifeless form.

"I'm sorry mate, this is all my fault, let's get out of here, these men will look after this mess. C'mon we've got to get you out of here before the police arrive, you're still a wanted man." Terry turned to one of his men get a reporting crew in here immediately.

"All this carnage and just to help you get your damned story and now look, what have we even achieved? Kim's death." Patrick somehow knew that Terry was right, but at this moment he just didn't care. Kim was dead; the bloodied piece of live meat that had been Ormon Vladisky having caused him so much trouble stood absolutely no chance of survival, some young woman shot and in a serious condition. Patrick instead of feeling triumphant, felt drained and hollow, he hadn't even had his revenge, the goons had taken that from him. What had been gained and was it all for he thought again, as he callously stepped over the writhing body of his hunter without looking back he followed Terry back into the basement. Terry shouted back into the room.

"Get Jenny to stay with the girl and find out what the hell happened." In Terry's car Patrick looked at his fat friend.

"Doesn't anything ever worry you?"

"For years I worked through the salt mines of journalism and now my oldest friend, you have elevated me to a gold mine and glory and remember, I didn't cause all this havoc, all we do is to record it. If people get hurt or killed along the way it's no fault of ours, I always try to distance myself from events around a story. That doesn't mean that I'm not suffering your loss as well. Does all that that make sense to you?"

"I suppose it could but right no, I'm totally both numb inside and out, my partner is dead so I could not care. Where are we going?"

"To George's friend's flat."

"How do you know where it is?"

"You told me when George first went missing, we've also been keeping an eye on it ever since. Don't worry my friend I'm not one of them, me a little stupid maybe for not realising that I was being followed and that my line was tapped when I told John Dunlop to meet you but, I had never set out to knowingly harm you."

"I'm just so tired of running, I just feel like handing myself straight over to the police."

"Hang in for just a couple more days and the nightmare will be over."

"You said that weeks ago, but how the hell do we fight them? Their tentacles stretch everywhere on the planet, their reach into governments is enormous and they don't care for anyone's life and now look, Kim's dead, so who's next?"

"Patrick, give me just three days, that's all I ask." Terry turned into the driveway of the block of flats after circulating the block twice to make sure he wasn't being followed.

"You and George get the printout to straight to me if he manages to break into their system. Okay?"

"See you Terry."

CHAPTER THIRTY EIGHT

"I can't do it, I've tried everything I know they've shut us out completely." George and Patrick had locked themselves in the flat for two days and tried everything they knew to try to get back into the UNSECP program. Nothing worked, George managed to get into the United Nations file, but no way could he find the program he was seeking, it had just vanished.

"Maybe they've closed the program down." George considered his companion's suggestion.

"No, I don't think so. I think they've just got smart and hidden it somewhere so clever that it would take forever to find it, that they were on to us and have all the resources to employ the most brilliant computer minds in the world. I think, no I'm sure that the program is still operational."

"What do we do now?"

"We keep looking, that's what we do, it could take me weeks or even months, but eventually I'll get lucky and I will find a way through."

"Months?"

"I'm sorry Patrick but I've tried all the conventional means and found no computer traces or footprints that could lead us to them. The only option open to me is to look at every thing in among thousands of files on the UN computer and hope that something turns up." Patrick felt the world closing in on him again as he visualised himself remaining in hiding forever. Was he ever going to get out of this mess? He was becoming impatient to bring his running to conclusion.

Later in the day Terry arrived to find out how they were making out.

"They've beaten us." George wasn't as down in the dumps as was Patrick.

"No, they haven't, all they've done is hide themselves away. I'll find them given time."

"Time isn't on our side at the moment," said Patrick. Terry raised himself from his chair.

"You and I will leave George to carry on, there's a young lady in the hospital that is asking to see you."

"What?"

"The girl that was shot be Vladisky wants to see you, she's also extremely adamant that she won't talk to anyone but you."

"Who is she? I don't even know her."

"Her name is Heidi Zenger and she comes from Geneva, that's all the police or Jenny can get out of her. She refuses to talk to anybody, but then told Jenny that she would talk to you, it's obvious she knows just who you are."

"But I can't just stroll into a main London hospital, the police will pick me up before I move thirty yards."

"It's okay, she's in a different private hospital at our expense and with your beard and some respectable clothes we've arranged for you to go in under cover. Nobody will be looking for Patrick Rodgers at her bedside. Trust me, everything will be fine."

"Terry, if anybody says trust me one more time, my natural instinct is to run a hundred miles in the opposite direction."

"Well then, do I tell her you're not going to see her."

"No. I'm coming, only because I think that Kim must have told her something about me before she died. Otherwise how would this total stranger know about my involvement?"

"Let's get a move on then."

Getting in was as simple as Terry had said it would be. Heidi was propped up in bed in a private room, Ormon's bullet had smashed her shoulder bone but that had now been successfully repaired with a really good outcome predicted. She had also lost a lot of blood and Terry's paper had convinced the doctors and Inspector Muldoon to keep her in hospital until she had managed to gain her strength.

"Mr. Rodgers, I'm so glad you've come to visit me, we've got a lot to discuss."

"How do you know who I am."

"It's a long story but sit down and I'll tell you about it." Patrick drew up a chair next to her bed for a while they passed niceties then she said something that caught him totally by surprise.

"I have to tell you something you will not feel comfortable with, you weren't Kim Lee's only lover, I have been her lover since we first met during our university student days in Paris. So if we look at it realistically, we've both lost somebody so very dear to us. Believe me when I say that I tried to save her, but that pig gave me no chance, he simply shot her in cold blood as she lay there." She wiped her nose.

"I'm sorry to be so blunt but, we don't have much time for niceties." Patrick's whole world turned upside down in those ten seconds. He couldn't believe that his friend and lover had also duped him.

"Did she even regain consciousness?"

"No, I'm glad what those two did to Vladisky Ormon, it would have been what I would have loved to have done to him myself, had I been given half the chance."

"She didn't suffer then, I suppose that we must be thankful for some small mercies' . I'm going to miss her terribly."

"Both of us are, the reason for my trip to London was to try and win her back. She would have had to make a choice between us sooner or later because she sent me a photo of you two together at a restaurant and told me that for the very first time in her life she had found a man who she felt completely comfortable with. In fact, that's why I'm in London from America, I had been told that she was missing so, came back to try to reclaim her or at least try to talk her out of her relationship with you. I now realise why I would have lost out to you."

"Why?"

"She loved us both equally of that I'm sure, but, I always felt that she was a little ashamed of our relationship. One other thing I had come to realise, Kim given the choice, admitted that you were the ideal partner and you would be able to give her children and respectability, something I that would have found impossible to achieve because I demanded no compromises within our relationship."

Patrick found himself starting to feel sorry for her in some strange sort of way, even if he wasn't quite sure of the ground he was treading just then.

"That house in Chiswick belongs to me and it was our shared home for several years before I joined the UN project."

"What UN project?"

"The one that cost Kim her life and has been causing you a lot of trouble, I understand, your friends from the newspaper want me to tell them everything that happened, and why I was shot by Vladisky. Your fat friend has tried everything, he's sharp, that one."

"He only wants to help me by publishing the facts and expose

366

the project for what it is."

"Also possibly the story of the decade for himself, tell me how much you really know?"

Patrick told her everything that he knew and even what George was busily attempting to do. When he finished everything, she just stared at him.

"You're a remarkable young man Patrick Rodgers and I applaud you, no wonder Kim felt the way she did for you. There's a lot you don't know but we'll rectify that tomorrow when I get out of this place. I would like to help by letting you into the program, but first there's something you must know."

Patrick wondered how much more she could say that would shock him. She hadn't done a bad job of it so far.

"Kim was deeply involved in the Culling Project through Silver Beam. Her father is also the chairman of the company, bet she never mentioned that to you?"

So many things suddenly snapped into place at once in Patrick's head. What a fool he thought, I must have loved her very much not to be able to recognise the obvious. In a matter of minutes this little redhead had further shattered his illusions of life.

"How deeply was she involved?"

"Because of her father, Kim was the supplier of computer hardware to every aspect of the project, even the computer in your last company and then again to Silver Beam were all installed under her authority. All the companies and governments involved with the project receive computers from South Korea."

"It was my decision to install that computer at my last company."

"You were probably led to believe that, but with people like Vladisky Ormon and Raymond Chen advising them in advance, she knew exactly what sort of package to make up so that you would install their computer." Patrick shook his head, there was this nasty shadow in the background manipulating him again.

"And me, where did I fit into the framework design."

"You became the uncontrollable factor. Kim genuinely fell for you and arranged for you to become involved with Silver Beam. She thought that in time she could turn you to her way of thinking and that's where everything started going wrong."

"Why?"

"You became suspicious and she tried to steer you away from the project. You persisted and Mr. Lee sent in Raymond Chen to take over. He wanted you killed at the beginning but she stood in his way. The project became threatened and orders came from Vladisky Ormon to kill you then she threatened to expose the whole project and Chen exceeded his authority when he shot her. That's when you took flight and articles appeared in the newspapers and pointed the spotlight at Chen, it was only a matter of time before news of the Culling Project was leaked and people started talking. Vladisky Ormon had to stop you and Kim from talking. The rest is history."

"How do you know so much?"

"I'm in control of The Co-ordinator, which is the centralised computer that receives everything regards the Culling Project. I watched the entire story unfold and decided to pull out of the project when Kim was shot."

"Surely you would be killed for even thinking that?"

"Vladisky Ormon guessed and that's why he tried to kill me. But now, after seeing what monster the project had developed, I've decided to get out and come over to your side."

"How?"

"Tomorrow, I'm going to wipe certain personal things from the main computer then you can copy everything you need so that you have the proof for your newspaper friend, and then when you've got everything you need, I'm going to insert an exceptionally vicious virus into the computer and the first time anyone attempts to enter the project all the stored information will become infected and the whole program will be wiped throughout the world. Do you fully understand the implications?"

"Not really."

"Every company linked into The Co-ordinator will have all of its main data wiped out. It will take them years to replace this knowledge and even if they have backup knowledge it will also take time. The whole system will be thrown out of kilter and destroyed."

"Will that include governments as well?"

"Of course." They carried on discussing the ramifications for more than an hour. Patrick felt like a marathon runner reaching the stadium, he was exhausted but at the same time exhilarated to be on his final lap of honour. He hadn't realised it, but he was holding her hand as they shared a common bond of love and loss for Kim. At last he stood to leave.

"Patrick, please don't tell anybody about my involvement in this whole matter."

"I'll respect your wishes."

"Also, can we remain friends after this has all died down?"

"Why not?" He leaned over and kissed her gently on the forehead.

"See you tomorrow." Terry wanted to know what she had said. Patrick kept away from any intricate details and told Terry that she had been a good friend of Kim's and that Kim had given her the password to the UN computer before dying. Rather let the blame go to the grave with Kim than stay alive with Heidi.

"Take me to see Sue, there are some things I've got to sort out."

For several weeks after the story broke the world went mad as Governments were made to account for their involvement and the whole world was incensed at the prospect of this proposed extermination. It hadn't taken long for the United Nations to draw up a new code of conduct and laws to prevent a similar clandestine occurrence happening without the common people's full knowledge. Terry's name became synonymous with every article written and he's name was put forward for a possible knighthood. Patrick and Sue settled all their differences because the experience had changed him beyond belief, the small things that she felt had affected their marriage in the first place was now a thing of the past. After everything died down they decided to move back to the house in Amersham when Sue announced that she had become pregnant and was packing in her job as an air hostess.

"You and Mrs. Jones have done a splendid job, I wouldn't have thought it possible to reconstruct this place after what had been done to it." This was the first time that Patrick had entered the house since going on the run. The place was the same yet very different with brightly coloured wallpaper, new carpets and furniture.

"Welcome home at last Mr. Rodgers."

"Mrs. Jones, how can I ever repay you for your help."

"By keeping the place spotless."

"I'm afraid you're in for a shock, I've changed and don't intend living like that saint used to anymore, anyway there'll soon be a baby here and no way can you keep a place spotless with them. You're going to have to live with that."

"We'll see," she smiled and took him by the arm.

"Come let me show you around your new house to see if you approve."

Memories of that night when he and Terry had found the place destroyed came flooding back as they moved from room to room. He still wasn't sure whether he would enjoy the idea of staying on until they reached the study, it was the only room that looked exactly like it had before the attack even down to the leather-topped desk but the he noticed the beautifully ornate wall cabinet built into the area above where his drinks cabinet stood,

"It looks exactly like it did before, except for that extension over there, what's that for?."

"That was Mrs. Rodgers's doing, she insisted that this room remained unchanged and I have a confession to make to you..

"You make a confession, now that's a first?"

Before the break in, I moved all those boxes into my garage loft. I told you that I wouldn't stand you messing up the house and the papers were strewn all around the study and as you know, I used to work in an office and did the filing, My intention was to help you to get them into some kind of order, luckily they didn't take too long to sort through and are all carefully stacked in date order in numbered boxes in the ceiling. The four boxes you set aside, are in date order in that new cabinet, Mrs. Rodgers said you would appreciate that. My boy helped stack the boxes in the ceiling but if you want them down here again, I'll arrange it for you?"

Patrick felt the blood rising from his toes right through to his brain. The computer files had been here all the time, he exploded at Mrs. Jones.

"You interfering old..." then checked himself in time and burst out laughing. Mrs. Jones stood by quiet mystified.

"Mrs. Jones, leave them where they are, who knows I may have use for them in the future. The two were joined by Sue, Patrick placed his arm on her shoulder.

"Thanks for this. It is exactly what I needed in my study." He tried to tell Sue about the papers in the boxes. She turned and kissed him gently.

"When I found out about them, I had them copied and had Mrs. Jones file the copies. I hope those original papers never have to come out of the loft, maybe you can use them when you write your memoirs."

He smiled and wondered idly whether Heidi had wiped the computer program completely or whether some unknown force would start getting the whole project going again. He hoped not, because he knew exactly who was involved.

"Maybe the loft will be their grave and we leave them to rest in peace forever. Who knows?"

In a large room that looked like a NASA space control centre David Spielman introduced himself to his companions all seated at computers in rows. Once he had covered all preliminary introductions and what their initial programme would entail, he told everybody about the last introduction for the day. It was to introduce the new projects co-ordinator of the entire earthquake program. David moved across the stage and opened the door to his office.

The long legged, smart and beautiful redhead stepped out onto the stage, many already knew who she was and cheered loudly. She waited until the hooting and hollering had died down... "Good morning everyone, my name is Heidi Zenger and we have an ambitious program ahead of us."

FINIS

ABOUT THE AUTHOR

The Culling is his third published work during 2014 and the story is that Western Governments use scientific evidence that within a few years their world faces disaster from uncontrolled population explosion; especially by burgeoning third-world countries probably creating extra desert regions to ruin the industrialised world. No government could openly admit that it intends killing tens of millions of unwanted people worldwide. A number of major international conglomerates collectively called "The Affiliation" are enlisted to conceal this man-made earthquake programme without any awkward questions being raised... It is a survival war!

His first published work was published in 1989 and was a fictional political thriller named African Chess (Now revamped, updated and published in March). African Chess was loosely based on his South African upbringing and the then apartheid system in place before Nelson Mandela's release from prison.

His next major work published by Marshall Cavendish in 1992 was "The Ancestral Trail" and 'split' into two halves of 26 issues each, making a total of 52 issues in total, all contained consecutive page and issue numbers.

The first half, published throughout 1993, takes place within mythological Ancestral Worlds and describes a boy's struggle to restore good to these worlds. After the initial international run which sold over 30 million copies worldwide, the second half of that series was then created and was published in 1994 and taking place in the totally different Cyber Dimension all about the same boy's attempt to find a way back to his own world. (See YouTube Video)

Graves has updated and re-written "The Ancestral Trail" in three major novels and In January 2014, the first section covering a journey through an ancient world within "The Ancestral Trail Trilogy" named "Long Ago & Far Away" in a 450 page novel was published. The second continuing section of the trilogy covers a cyber world will be published by mid-year and the third section of the trilogy, covering our modern day world will be published before the end of 2014. (The YouTube video demonstrates the Ancestral Trilogy Novels)

www.ingramcontent.com/pod-product-compliance
Lightning Source LLC
Chambersburg PA
CBHW060155260626
47160CB00001B/274